The Sac

The
SACRED
SPOILS

WILL
ADAMS

CANELO

First published in the United Kingdom in 2019 by Canelo

This edition published in the United Kingdom in 2020 by

Canelo Digital Publishing Limited
Third Floor, 20 Mortimer Street
London W1T 3JW
United Kingdom

A CIP catalogue record for this book is available from the British Library.

Print ISBN 978 1 78863 775 6
Ebook ISBN 978 1 78863 713 8

Look for more great books at www.canelo.co

Printed and bound in Great Britain by Clays Ltd, Elcograf S.p.A.

For Hugh and Sara

Cast down by his reverse and deliberating what to do, King Alaric was overtaken by an untimely death and departed from human cares. His people mourned for him with the utmost affection. Turning from its course the river Busentus near the city of Consentia, they led a band of captives into the midst of its bed to dig out a place for his grave. In the depths of this pit they buried Alaric, together with many treasures, then turned the waters back into their channel. And that none might ever know the place, they put to death all the diggers.

–Jordanes, *The Origin and Deeds of the Goths*

Prologue

Rome, 24 August CE 410

Quintus Rufius was half asleep when the horn sounded, so that he dreamed it a summons to a great banquet hall whose tables groaned with food. But the only groaning was his comrades as they threw off blankets and wearily sat up. The horn died away. For a moment there was silence. Another false alarm, thank the gods. Rufius closed his eyes and tried to return to his banquet hall and the only food he'd likely see today; but then a man came running screaming down the street outside, and suddenly there were horns blasting on every side, and he knew that it had happened.

The barbarians were at their gates.

The barracks door banged open and Gaius Villius marched in, a flaming torch in his hand to show the grimness of his expression. He marched along the aisle, kicking the feet of anyone still abed, yelling at them to suit up. Rufius's hands shook wildly as he pulled on chest padding and then his suit of rusting chain mail. He'd never fought in earnest before, just with wooden swords – and those had hurt enough to make him weep. The prospect of doing it for real was the stuff of nightmares, not just being wounded or even killed himself, but of having to do it to others, piercing their flesh with his long sword, their blood gushing and entrails spilling. He couldn't imagine hating anyone enough for that. Not even Alaric and his murderous horde.

Villius was still yelling at them. It made it impossible to think, let alone resist. Rufius strapped on his helmet, buckled on his sword then grabbed his shield and ran out with the others. A few people were fleeing from the Salerian Gate. Villius ignored them. He marched them to where the street narrowed then had them form defensive lines across it. Rufius tried to shuffle to the back, but so did everyone else – and they proved better at it than he. So, to his consternation, he found himself at the front.

God, but he needed a piss. Too late now.

The street emptied as fugitives found houses to hide in. An eerie silence fell. The moon hung fat and low above the houses at its far end. And red, too – that particular watery red of a slit wrist in a public baths. Rufius felt a terrible foreboding, as when that fortune teller hadn't even met his eye. She'd known something, he was sure of it. She'd known *this*. What the hell was he even doing here? He was no soldier; he was a farmer. He should be in Sabina helping his family with the harvest. His elder brother had cut off his thumb rather than be conscripted. But not he. He'd told them that his sister had to be revenged. But the shameful truth was that the thought of mutilation had given him nightmares.

He suffered badly from nightmares, did Rufius.

War cries. The pounding of feet. It was happening. It was happening right now. He couldn't believe how quickly they'd got inside the city. They must have been betrayed from within – it was the only explanation. His body stiffened and tingled. Everything grew slow and sharp and bright. Around the turn of the road they charged, yelling and screaming and waving their long swords above their heads, others carrying flaming brands or spears already drawn back to hurl. And the size of them – he couldn't believe how fucking big they were; it was unfair, for they themselves were a ragtag group made up of those too old and too young for proper units, infirm and weak with hunger too. They drew closer, so that he could now see the crazed bloodlust on their faces. Fuck, but they didn't stand a chance. He was going to die, he knew it suddenly. He was going to be run through and left to bleed out upon the cobbles. Barely seventeen, and never once even having lain with a woman in—

A spear hurtled out of the gloom towards his face. He saw it only at the last second. He jerked up his shield and it thumped into it like a blow from a double-handed war axe, knocking him back against the man behind, who cursed and shoved him forward again. The spear's barbed tip had pierced the leather of his oval shield so that its shaft now hung down heavily onto the cobbled ground in front of him. Before he could pluck it free, the Visigoths were on them. One of them stamped hard upon the spear's shaft, dragging down Rufius's shield and exposing him to his sword. He cried out and threw himself to the ground a moment before the blow could cleave off his head. His helmet fell off and bounced away. He lay there in a huddled ball as the barbarians smashed into their feeble line, treading on his face and body. Swords clashed, people shrieked. And then it was over, footsteps charging onwards, the war cries growing fainter, and all he could hear now was the wailing and sobbing of his wounded comrades.

He was still lying there when a hand grabbed him by his short hair and hauled him to his feet. A knife as sharp as a razor but the size of a small sword was pressed against his throat. He was manhandled through a fast-striding line of Visigoth warriors to find himself face-to-face with four high-ranking officers. 'This one seems fearful enough,' his captor told them. 'If his bladder's anything to go by.'

It was only then that Rufius felt the hot wetness on his leg and the piss squelching in his boot. Shame burned his cheeks. The tallest of the four men turned to look at him. He was maybe forty years old, handsome yet battle-scarred, his long, fair, grey-threaded hair combed into ropes that were then tied in an ornate side knot. 'You know who I am, boy?' he asked.

It wasn't his face that told Rufius the answer, though it matched all the descriptions he'd ever heard. It was his bearing and the deference of those around him. All kinds of flatteries came instantly to Rufius's mind. The kind of flatteries that prudent people paid to rulers in order to stay alive. But he couldn't do it. At this moment of great crisis, his cowardice failed him utterly. He lifted his chin instead, and gazed into the monster's eyes. 'You're the man who starved my sister,' he told him.

The knife cut even sharper into his throat. 'He's our king, you little shit. Address him as such.'

But Alaric only waved his hand for his soldier to relax. 'An honest one, at least,' he said. 'Isn't that what we need?' He turned to Rufius again. 'I'm sorry for your sister. But your emperor could have saved her at any moment by honouring his promise to my people. He chose to feed his chickens instead.'

Rufius stared helpless at him. 'What do you want from me?'

'Look around,' said Alaric. 'Your city is already lost. The only question is how many more must die before we leave again. So I want you to take a message to your commander for me.'

'But I don't even know where—'

'Of course you do. Good honest foot soldiers like yourself always know the beds their generals skulk beneath. I want you to tell him how it will be: the places of sanctuary I'm designating, how his soldiers and citizens can keep themselves safe. All I ask is three days and nights unimpeded to take the plunder we're rightly owed and then we'll be on—' A door banged to his left. Two Vandal warriors came out of a tall, thin house, laughing and dragging a half-naked girl by her long black hair. They froze when they saw Alaric standing there. Their faces blanched as he marched across. 'There's to be none of that,' he told them furiously. 'How many times must I give the order?'

'They started it,' muttered one of the Vandals mulishly, still holding the girl by her hair. 'These bastards raped my wife and then they killed her.'

'Yes,' said Alaric. 'And would you not have wanted someone there, to stop them before they did?'

The Vandal lowered his eyes. The girl tore herself free of his weakened grasp and fled back indoors, slamming and bolting the door behind her. Alaric seemed satisfied. He turned on his heel and marched back across. Rufius gazed at him in astonishment. This man bestrode the Western Empire right now. He had more power than almost anyone else alive. And Rufius knew all too well what power was. Power was their feeble-minded emperor choosing to let this great city fall rather than lose face. Power was the plutocrat who sold out his nation in order to add more land to his already vast estates. Power was the senator who spoke movingly of justice, then went home to beat his wife and rape his slave. Power was the ambitious general who threw his soldiers into pointless battles to advance his own career.

Rufius had never protested or even questioned this. It was simply how life was.

'Well,' said Alaric curtly. 'Will you take my message, or not?'

A strange perturbation roiled Rufius's heart. 'Yes, my king,' he said. 'I will.'

Chapter One

Cosenza, Italy

The packing case was too heavy and cumbersome for Carmen Nero to manage by herself, especially with her purse and overnight bag to think of too, so the moment the train rolled into Cosenza station she pulled down the sash window to look for Giulia Surace, who'd sworn she'd be here waiting. And waiting she was, halfway along the platform, scouring carriages as they passed. Carmen yelled out to her and waved. Giulia waved excitedly back and hurried to the nearest door, running alongside it as it slowed, throwing it open and pushing her way past the small crowd of indignant passengers waiting to disembark. 'Where is it?' she asked.

'This way,' Carmen told her.

'*Porca vacca*,' muttered Giulia in awe, when she saw the size of it on the luggage rack.

'What did I tell you?' said Carmen, not without satisfaction.

Giulia gathered herself. 'We need to hurry. It'll only be stopping here a minute.'

The case was the size of a chest of drawers. It weighed as much as one too, though at least it had wheels on its corners, helpful for trundling across platforms, though less so for lugging on and off trains. At Rome's Termini station early that morning, her professor, Matteo Bianchi, that world-renowned authority on Italy in late antiquity, had dropped it on his foot while helping her heave it aboard. 'Tell your friend, never fucking again,' he'd yelped, hopping around the platform clutching his toes. 'And if I don't have everything back on Sunday night – and I mean *everything* – she better find herself a new university.'

'She's not my friend,' Carmen had retorted. 'I barely even know her.'

'Then why spend the fucking weekend with her?'

An excellent question, and one to which Carmen still had no answer.

With no direct trains from Rome to Cosenza, she'd had to change at Napoli Centrale. Unable to move the case by herself, she'd thrown herself on the mercy of two kindly porters, who'd stowed it on this rack for her. She and Giulia now heaved it down together and rolled it to the nearest door, forcing the milling passengers out of their way. A whistle sounded. Doors banged. Giulia hurried ahead to stop the train from leaving. A limber young black man in denim shorts and a tattered orange string vest gallantly offered to lower the case down the steps onto the platform, only to grunt in surprise at the weight of it. But between them they got it down.

'See,' said Giulia. 'I told you it would be fine.'

'Yes,' agreed Carmen, thanking her benefactor and rubbing her sore palms against her jeans. 'Like you said on the phone, it's just a small parcel.'

Giulia didn't even acknowledge the jab. She pointed to the exit. 'We'd better hurry. They're crocodiles here about parking.'

Carmen shouldered her purse and set her overnight bag on the packing case then wheeled them both across the platform, seething both at Giulia's high-handedness and her own feebleness in not calling her out on it. It wasn't as though she hadn't been warned. Their fellow students at Sapienza had nicknamed her *La Greca*, not for her dark looks or her *Magna Graecia* origins, but rather – as she'd belatedly learned – from how wary one should be when she came bearing gifts. Yet when she'd called out of the blue last night, gushing about how gorgeous Cosenza was looking right now, Carmen would have felt churlish to refuse her invitation. Only after she'd accepted had Giulia mentioned anything about a package.

A silver-haired man in a wide-collared check shirt and stained blue jeans was leaning against the bonnet of an ancient sky-blue Fiat pickup, smoking contentedly despite the station porter berating him

7

for parking in the wrong place. His face lit up when he saw them. He tossed away his cigarette and strode across. 'You must be Carmen,' he declared. 'I... I am Vittorio.' His eyes widened when he noticed the packing case. 'Oof, what a beast! I had no idea. You are so kind, to bring it for us. How you must hate us!'

'Not at all,' said Carmen, disarmed by his charm. 'My pleasure.'

He laughed delightedly at her lie. 'I am so glad you have come,' he said, commandeering the case and steering it around the back of his pickup. 'Our poor house used to fizz with Giulia's friends. Now I never see her. And she tells me nothing, nothing, nothing about Rome. So you will have to tell me everything yourself. All the gossip. Boyfriends, girlfriends – who even knows these days? In return, I will show you Cosenza. You will have a wonderful weekend, I promise you! A spectacular weekend! You will talk of it to your grandchildren! Oh, yes. You think I am joking. I assure you I am not.'

He tried by himself to lift the case up onto his flatbed, only to grunt at the weight of it and put a rueful hand on his small of his back. They gathered around it and heaved it up together, on the count of three. The suspension creaked a touch ominously beneath its weight. It wasn't a vehicle to inspire confidence, its bodywork dinged like hammered pewter and its back bumper held on with tape. Inside, it was hot enough to roast lunch. The three of them sat like chickens on a spit along its bench seat, with Giulia in the middle. The torn green plastic upholstery stuck to the undersides of Carmen's legs. Coloured wiring dangled beneath a dashboard of broken dials, and Vittorio had to pump the accelerator with his foot while turning the key to get the engine started. 'Okay!' he said, raising a fist in mock triumph when finally it caught. 'Home, home, home!'

The railway station lay north-east of town. Home lay south-west. The trip between the two was not a pleasant one. Exhaust fumes seeping up through the floor made Carmen a little carsick, while smoke from Vittorio's cigarettes rasped her throat like a fine sandpaper. She tried rolling down her window but the handle spun uselessly. And Cosenza's outskirts proved dismayingly ugly, their streets strewn with black bags leaking rubbish, and lined by shabby apartment blocks with pocked cladding, as if a bored artillery unit had whiled away an afternoon lobbing shells into the town. She sank into gloom. What had she been thinking, coming here with her thesis stalled and still not having learned Italian? She needed to return to Rome and pull herself together. Plenty of others had had it worse, and didn't mope around like this. She might even have said something to that end had Vittorio not turned down a new street at that moment, the name of which sent a thrill straight through her.

It was imagination that had made Carmen a historian. As a girl, all it had ever taken was a fragment of antique text or a glimpse of a museum exhibit for her mind simply to fly away with her, spiriting her across centuries and continents, putting her at the heart of riotous adventures in alien cultures. History had literally enchanted her. But those magical moments had grown rarer in her teens and early twenties. Too much knowledge had a way of suffocating daydreams. Three months in Rome, the world's most beautiful, romantic and historic city, and not once had she been transported or taken by surprise.

Not until now.

For this was Via Popilia, the ancient Roman road that had run south from Capua to the ancient port of Rhegium. It had been along *this* road that the Visigoth king Alaric had marched in triumph after his remarkably bloodless sack of Rome, having plundered it of its fabulous wealth. It had been along this road too that Alaric had retreated a short while later, after his failed effort to reach Sicily. *This* right here was where he'd fallen sick, most likely with malaria. *This* right here was where he'd died, mourned by his brother-in-law Athaulf and his grief-stricken army. And *this* was where his men had diverted an entire river from its course to dig a burial chamber beneath, in which they'd interred him with anything up to a billion dollars' worth of Roman loot before restoring the river to its previous course and putting the slaves they'd used to death, so that no one would ever find it.

Nor had they, despite countless attempts over the centuries since.

That was when Carmen remembered whispers of the family quest that had obsessed the Suraces for three generations or more. And finally she realised why she'd been invited down, and what was likely in the packing case too.

9

The six of them completed their safety stop together then surfaced close to where Arturo was waiting with the boat. Dieter spat out his regulator and whooped exultantly. 'Goddammit, what a dive,' he said. He reached into his pouch for the large earthenware fragment he'd just recovered from the seabed twenty-five metres below. 'It's his, isn't it?' he said. 'It's Alaric's.'

Cesco Rossi swam across to take it carefully in both hands. He turned it around and held it up to the sunlight. It was the top of a broken oil or wine amphora of some kind, pale brown in colour, the rough size and shape of an upturned soup bowl, but with a spouted mouth and a curved handle large enough to fit a fat finger. There were specks of grit beneath the glaze, its broken edges had been worn smooth by time, and there were faint marks on it that might once have been writing but were more likely simply the result of its age. 'It's Roman for sure,' he said, passing it back. 'It could easily be late fourth or early fifth century, but coarse ware like this is notoriously difficult to date. We would really need to see if—'

'Don't be such a professor, Professor,' mocked Dieter. 'It's his. I *know* it is.' He pounded his chest with his fist. 'I know it in here.'

Cesco let it go, and not just because Dieter and his friends were paying handsomely for this dive. He was wiry, tough and fast, and he'd learned the hard way how to look after himself, but all four of these Germans were steroid gym rats with tree trunks for necks and comic-book physiques. His best punch wouldn't even register, and the moment any one of them caught him, they'd crush him like a boa with a piglet. And it wasn't just their builds. Everything about them said 'fuck you', from their shaven scalps to their black Harleys and full-body tattoos that included swastikas and a pair of crossed claw hammers, seemingly gang insignia of some kind. Hence their interest in Alaric, a cult figure among German neo-Nazis, a prototype Aryan warrior king. Dieter even had his name written in large Gothic letters across his back, prompting Cesco to a little rash mischief the night before, ruminating on how Alaric's Romanian birth and nomadic life really made him the world's first Gypsy. Then he'd noticed the lobster sheen of Dieter's skin and the banked furnace behind his eyes, and he'd swiftly switched topic.

Standing up for yourself was one thing. Suicide was another.

He swam to the boat to help the rest of the party up. Anna pulled her goggles down around her throat like a clunky necklace so that her green eyes twinkled in the sunlight. She leaned back in the water and lifted up her feet for him to take off her flippers. She turned around for him to take off her scuba tank, then he put his hand on her buttock to propel her up the steps.

'Hey!' said Dieter.

'Sorry,' said Cesco. 'I was just trying to help.'

'Yes,' said Anna. 'He was just helping.'

He waited until they were all aboard, came up last. He unstrapped his own tank and buoyancy control device, peeled off his booties and wetsuit, took off his diving cap and shook out his ponytail. Dieter and his friends smirked at each other, as they did every time they saw it. As a dark-skinned, bearded, hipster academic with a gold earring and a nose stud, he was pretty much everything they most despised. He fetched his phone from his dive bag, checking messages as he stowed the tanks. Another invitation from Giulia, his third that day and the most pressing yet, this time including directions. Her eagerness puzzled him. They'd had a fun night, sure, talking Visigoths and archaeology into the small hours, all topped off by a boisterous tumble. But he'd not heard a word from her since. Now suddenly she was stuffing his inbox with invitations to join her on some exciting yet unnamed project. But it would take a great deal more than a few mysterious hints and the prospect of another night together to lure him back to Cosenza.

He hauled in the marker buoys, weighed anchor, gave Arturo the thumbs up. They began burbling back towards Scilla. It was a gorgeous afternoon – why hurry? Cesco handed out bottles of beer from the cooler then gathered up the wetsuits. Anna was still in hers, surely aware of how it flattered her curves. She waited until he was standing right in front of her before beginning to peel it from her arms and legs, letting the rubber stretch like liquorice gum, enjoying his admiration.

He took it from her then sluiced it and everything else down with fresh water from the barrel, hung it all up to dry. Then he sat on the stern bench to watch the coast go by.

Anna came to join him, the roll of the boat putting sway into her hips. 'So, Professor,' she said. 'A question, if I may?'

'Cesco, please.'

She sat beside him, their thighs lightly brushing. 'Cesco, then. A triumph, yes?'

'If my customers are happy...'

'Then, like I say, a triumph.' She put a hand on his shoulder and lowered her voice to a whisper, her breath a tickle on his ear. 'But between you and me... That old pot didn't really belong to this king of Dieter's, did it?'

'To Alaric himself, no,' said Cesco. 'To his army...?' He gave a shrug. 'It's the right date and location. We've found distinctly Visigothic artefacts in that spot before. Yes, it's Roman, but then, that's what you'd expect. The Visigoths had been in Italy for many years, living by plunder. So of course their storage jars would have been Roman.'

'But...?'

Cesco grinned. Anna had taken him aside the night before to confide to him that she was actually a high-end escort hired by Dieter for the week; because she'd rather have him know that than have him think her his girlfriend. 'This is Italy,' he said. 'Finding Roman pottery is hardly earth-shattering, is it? Especially here, among all the wrecks left by our monsters.'

She frowned. 'Monsters?'

He pointed north along the mainland coast. 'There was a six-headed sea serpent called Scylla living up where we're headed. That's where our town gets her name. And there was a whirlpool called Charybdis on the Sicily side. It sucked in whole boats and spat out their timbers.'

She laughed and swept back her hair with both hands, making her chest jut. 'And of course it really happened just like that.'

'Myths are pearls. Each one has its own grain of truth. Hundreds of ships really have sunk in these straits over the centuries. Alaric's fleet among them.'

She looked from Calabria out to Sicily and back again. Her scepticism was easy both to see and understand. The Straits of Messina were a lake right now. And not a particularly wide one. A strong swimmer could cross them easily in less than an hour. He'd done so himself at the age of just thirteen, and four times more since moving here last year – out to Sicily in the morning for lunch, then back again in the afternoon. But he'd also witnessed the fierce autumnal storms that could spring up out of nowhere. Heaven help you if you were caught out in one of those. 'We know precious little about Alaric in southern Italy,' he told her. 'Our sources are wretchedly thin. But after sacking Rome, he led his army down here. We *think* he planned to sail to Sicily then on to Carthage, because northern Africa was where all the grain was back then, and he and his men were sick of going hungry. But we *know* he turned back instead. To Cosenza, where he died. We have two main accounts for what happened here. There was a monk called Tyrannius Rufinus living in Sicily at the time, working on biblical translations.' He leaned across her a little way to point out the island's northern tip, his thigh pressing warmly against hers as he did so. She could have given way, but she pressed back just as firmly. 'See that hill right there? We think that's where his monastery was. Every night, he watched from his window as the mainland burned. He wrote fearful letters about what the Goths would do to him when they arrived. But they never did. Our second source is a Spanish priest called Orosius, who heard from some Gothic soldiers how they'd watched helplessly from the shore as their comrades drowned.'

She looked again at the placid, narrow sea. 'Then they must have been the worst sailors ever.'

'Maybe. But Alaric and his men had been plundering Italy for years before they got here. They'd just sacked Rome. Imagine it's you living on this coast. One day you learn that a barbarian horde is on its way. What would you do?'

'I'd get the hell out.'

'Exactly. Anyone with a boat would have sailed across the straits while they still could, so by definition there'd have been no boats left. Building new ones took time and skills the Visigoths didn't have. Winter was coming and they were already low on food.'

'So?'

'A different Goth general called Gainas faced a very similar problem at the Bosphorus. He had his men build rafts instead of boats. Quick to assemble, simple to paddle and safe enough over a short distance, as long as the water's placid. Unfortunately, they become death traps in a storm. Worse, they're easy to harry, too, if your enemy has proper ships. Gainas found that out the hard way. The Romans turned up when he was halfway across and sank the lot of them.'

'You think that happened here?'

'It's certainly possible. The Goths were great at hand-to-hand, but they were useless at any distance. No bows, no javelins, only throwing axes and short spears. A handful of well-crewed ships with skilful archers could have stayed out of range and showered them with—'

'Hey!'

Cesco looked around and up. Dieter and his mates were advancing towards him, dressed again in their dirty jeans and leather jackets. He relaxed his leg and shifted a fraction away from Anna. 'Yes?' he asked, with a pleasant smile. 'How may I help?'

Dieter had his earthenware shard in one hand, his phone in the other. 'This piece of pottery,' he said. 'This piece of pottery I found in the sand below just half an hour back.'

'What about it?'

Dieter now held out his phone. 'How come there's a photograph of it on your fucking website?'

Maximum Security Prison Number 4, near Jerusalem, Israel

It was with some trepidation that Zara Gold got out of the taxi and looked up at the prison's high slab walls. Was Daniel Kaufman playing some kind of practical joke on her? Was it some ham-fisted attempt at intimidation or even retribution for her recent review? Except that he famously had no sense of humour, and surely even his skin wasn't *that* thin. But why else would he have her meet him here, outside one of Israel's highest-security prisons?

He was waiting for her by the booth, wearing his trademark panama hat and rumpled tan suit. He'd been her mentor once. She still looked up to him in many ways. But progress in history and archaeology too often came only funeral by funeral; and if she had to bury him to make it, then so be it. 'Professor,' she said.

'Miss Gold.'

Her toes clenched. The petty denial of her own status was just like him. But her smile didn't falter. 'All this cloak and dagger. Whatever is it for?'

'You'll see.'

The guard in the booth gestured for her ID. Kaufman took it from her then slipped it beneath the security glass himself, as though she were incapable. There was a glitch with the scanner. The guard had to type her details in manually. Kaufman sighed as though it were her fault. Her card was returned, along with a two-page form to sign. She read every word of it, to get her own back. The heavy steel gate opened. Kaufman had broken his leg in a car crash the year before and it had left him with a slightly sliding gait, as though he was trying to get his left shoe on properly; yet he still walked deliberately quickly, to force her to hurry to keep up. Professors both, yet children too.

They were patted down at a second security point, then escorted along a corridor of flickering lights and peeling paint. 'Not even a hint?' she asked.

'If I tell you, it will influence you.' He looked her up and down. 'It's best you see this… *unsullied*.'

They reached more doors then passed out into the huge internal exercise yard. It had cell blocks on three sides and a wall of monstrous grey concrete slabs at its far end, topped by coils of barbed wire, searchlights and guard towers. Kaufman set off briskly towards its far right-hand corner, where a dozen or so young people in loose clothes and wide-brimmed headgear were working with trowels and sieves. And finally she got a glimmer of what was going on.

'They needed new latrines,' said Kaufman. 'They had the prisoners clear the ground.'

'What did they find?'

'You'll see.'

Sunshine reflected in shards from cell-block windows. Faces pressed against the glass. Many of Israel's most dangerous prisoners were housed here, including a good number of Islamist jihadis. She could feel their loathing pouring down upon her, Israeli as she was, female and uncovered. A man shouted out and then suddenly there was yelling on all sides, a cacophony of cups banging against bars. But Kaufman ignored it so she did too.

They reached the far corner. An area the size of a tennis court had been roped off, the top half-metre or so of hard-packed earth removed down to a blackened stratum of charred limestone and plaster. A honeycomb of smaller pits had been dug into this larger one, each a metre square. A young woman in a straw hat, baggy cotton trousers and a long-sleeved shirt was kneeling on a mat beside the closest, cleaning what lay at the bottom with a cloth and a spray bottle of distilled water. She paused at their arrival, brushed her nose wearily with the back of her hand, then moved aside to let them see. Zara gazed down. It was a mosaic in the Byzantine style, made from tesserae of coloured glass. It depicted two vibrantly coloured birds frolicking joyfully against a bright-blue backdrop, the first sipping dew from petals of sunset orange, the second with a stalk of golden grain in its beak. She crouched for a closer look at the stalk. The Byzantines had made tesserae of that particular colour by embedding gold leaf in clear glass. Along with the quality of the workmanship, it made it instantly clear that this was a very expensive commission. Almost perfectly preserved too, and gleaming from its sheen of distilled water.

'My God,' she said.

Kaufman gave a tight smile. 'Wait till you see this next one,' he said.

He was right. It was even more skilfully realised. More telling too. It showed a pair of spiny-backed fish circling the symbols *chi* and *rho* arranged into a cross. Christian, then. A church. An early and important one. Mid to late sixth century, to judge from both the style and its pristine condition, suggesting that it had been destroyed not long after its completion – either during the Persian seizure of Jerusalem in CE 614 or the Islamic conquest some twenty-odd years later.

'The warden is an old friend of mine,' remarked Kaufman. 'At least, my college girlfriend went on to become his wife. He keeps in touch with me, from time to time, to gloat over this fact. So when his prisoners uncovered the mosaic, it was me he called. He thought I would be amused.' The wry smile he gave at this was so out of character that Zara found herself staring. 'I told him that it was of such great historical importance that we needed both to excavate and protect it. He wasn't happy. His job here is to keep some of Israel's most dangerous prisoners locked up, not to curate Byzantine mosaics. But he did allow me two days.'

Zara looked around in amazement. 'All this? In two days?'

'That was a week and a half ago. We kept finding more. As you can see. It is now a major headache for him. This is his exercise yard. While we're here, his prisoners can't be. They house all kinds of fanatics here, the kind who can hardly be trusted to respect the artefacts of other religions. So they haven't been allowed out since we arrived. They're growing restive. My friend fears a riot.'

She nodded distractedly. Prison riots didn't interest her. Mosaics did. She knelt for a closer look. This particular panel was a little worn towards its left edge, presumably where congregants had once walked or gathered. Yet elsewhere it was perfect, protected initially by the carapace of hardened ash from the fire that had destroyed the church above it, then by the sandy soil that had accumulated above it over the centuries and become packed hard. It was a magnificent find, a privilege to see. Yet it still didn't explain her summons. 'Do you know which church?'

He shrugged expressively. The Byzantines had built dozens of churches in and around Jerusalem, to show off their piety and wealth. And their surviving sources were so patchy that some of those churches barely got a mention – while others, presumably, got none at all. 'We have a date range,' he said. 'Let me show you.' He led her to a larger pit, three metres by two. The mosaic beneath was covered by a dust sheet to protect it from the sunlight, so that she could only see its edges. Kaufman squatted down. Then, like a dignitary unveiling a statue, he pulled the sheet aside.

Zara stared at it, puzzled rather than amazed. It had been cleared but not yet cleaned, making it harder to work out. At first sight, it looked almost like a flag: a blue rectangle hemmed by a sandy-brown border. But what flag would have ships sailing across it, or a line of caravans running down its side? Nor did flags typically have cities at each corner, their Greek names written in clumsy block capitals. Not a flag, then, but rather a map. Specifically, a stylised map of the eastern Mediterranean of late antiquity, with Rome at its top left, then passing clockwise through Constantinople, Jerusalem and Carthage. There was more Greek writing around the perimeter too. With no breaks between the words to help her, and aware of Kaufman watching, it took the most intense concentration for her to work out and translate in her mind. But finally she had it.

God save your most pious servant Flavius Justinian lover
of Jesus giver of these tokens of your glory

Flavius Justinian, better known as Justinian I or Justinian the Great, ruler of the Byzantine Empire from CE 527 through to 565. Patron of many of the great buildings of late antiquity, including Constantinople's sumptuous Hagia Sophia and Jerusalem's own famous Nea Ekklesia, short-lived though that had been. And countless other churches too, across the ancient world. She glanced at Kaufman, her eyes watering. 'This is… this is *amazing*.' She looked up at the grey slab prison wall that towered above her, at the cell blocks either side, and realised how precarious it was.

'Quite,' said Kaufman. 'The prison can't be moved. The mosaic can. Not at once, obviously. But eventually. So the warden and I provisionally agreed a plan. To bury this again beneath protective sheeting of some kind while I arranged sponsorship for a new home where it could be properly protected, studied and displayed. Then we'd come back to cut it out and transfer it.'

'This new home,' she said drily. 'It wouldn't be at your university, would it?'

His chin went up. 'Why shouldn't it be?'

'No reason,' she agreed. 'You deserve it.'

He squinted suspiciously at her until he realised that she was sincere. Then he nodded. 'Anyway,' he said, 'as part of this plan we scanned this whole area to measure the floor's dimensions and see how deep it goes, for a better idea of the logistics.'

'And?'

'There are cavities beneath it. Chambers. A whole string of them. They start directly beneath this mosaic here, run nine metres to the prison wall, then another twelve metres out the other side.'

'Catacombs?'

'I expect so. Though we won't know for sure unless we look. Unfortunately, we may not get that opportunity.'

'What are you talking about?'

'To you and me, this is a discovery of immense historical importance. To my friend the warden, it is a tunnel out beneath the wall of his high-security prison.'

'Oh,' said Zara. 'Hell.'

'Quite. Which is why he has arranged for these mosaics to be drilled through first thing tomorrow morning, in order to flood the chambers beneath with cement.'

Chapter Two

I

There was a bridge at the end of Via Popilia that took them across a broad and stately river that ran through the heart of modern Cosenza. It offered Carmen Nero too good an opportunity to resist. 'So I guess this must be the famous Busento,' she said.

The responses of both Suraces were equally telling in their own way. Vittorio put a hand to his stomach, as if suddenly feeling queasy, while Giulia forced a smile that didn't quite make it to her eyes. 'No,' she answered. 'This is actually a river called the Crati.' She pointed a little way upstream, where two tributaries of roughly equal size merged together. 'The one up there on the right, that's the Busento.'

'Ah,' said Carmen. Silence fell. Their route took them back across the divided rivers. Vittorio again placed his hand upon his stomach and Giulia did the same, as if in unconscious sympathy. It gave Carmen a pang to see, for it brought her own father suddenly to her mind. Their relationships could hardly have been more different, yet he'd influenced her choice of studies every bit as much as Vittorio had influenced Giulia's.

In photos, Carmen's mother had been a strikingly pretty young woman, with dimples, sparkling eyes and bobbed fair hair. Landing jobs had been easy for her. Holding them had been the challenge. Waitressing in the executive dining room of one of New York's top auction houses, she'd managed to spill soup into the lap of a young Italian classical art expert in America on a three-year placement. Within one week, she'd moved in with him. Within six, she'd fallen pregnant. They'd become proud parents, from what little Carmen had gleaned. But then the idyll had turned sour. He'd left America the moment his stint had ended, and had never been back since.

He'd not abandoned them altogether. He'd paid enough support that they could live in modest comfort whenever Mom had had one of her sporadic jobs. And he'd sent her a beautifully wrapped birthday present every year with Italian stamps and a Rome postmark. The gifts hadn't been crazily expensive, but they'd always been thoughtful. For years she'd refused to sleep without Larry, her stuffed lion, beside her. And she still prized the set of wooden dolls he'd sent.

For her fourteenth birthday he'd sent her a gorgeous, hand-cut jigsaw puzzle of the Good Shepherd mosaics from the Mausoleum of Galla Placidia in Ravenna, along with a potted history of the woman herself. She'd looked forward with absurd excitement to her fifteenth birthday. But it had passed without anything arriving. Nothing had arrived the following morning either, nor in the days afterwards – on each of which she'd felt a pounding echo of that first hurt. Her sixteenth birthday had come and gone unmarked too. And every birthday since. She'd wondered whether something had happened to him. She'd almost hoped it had. Better that than being forgotten. Yet the support payments had continued uninterrupted. She'd felt both furious and confused. She'd kept returning to her jigsaw puzzle and potted history as though they could somehow explain it – as though they themselves had been pieces in some larger puzzle that she'd needed somehow to solve. She'd become mildly obsessed with Galla Placidia. She'd read obsessively about her – this remarkable yet relatively unheralded woman. She'd daydreamed of making herself into the world authority on her, and of her father attending one of her lectures and timidly asking a question, for which she'd cut him dead. Yet, since arriving in Rome, she hadn't so much as looked his name up in the phone book. She'd learned the hard way since how difficult parenthood could be.

The silence in the van grew uncomfortable. Vittorio reached across his daughter to tap Carmen on her forearm. 'Cosenza old town,' he said, pointing up through the windscreen. 'We'll take you while you're here. Not to be missed. Especially the castle.' He kissed his fingertips. 'You have to see the views.'

'I'd love that,' said Carmen, though his clumsy attempt at distraction only whetted her curiosity further. They drove past a vegetable market, then a line of men filling bottles at a public spring. They crossed the Busento yet again, this time over a humpback bridge low enough for her to see the rounded stones beneath the water. The bulrushes and bamboos that lined its banks swayed gently in the breeze, until the river was swallowed further upstream beneath a lush canopy of trees. 'I'd imagined it as bigger,' she said.

'You should see it in a storm.'

They turned up a hill, long and steep enough to make their engine strain. The road was so badly potholed that it made Carmen's overnight bag bump and jolt on the flatbed like a Mexican bean. Repairs were underway, at least. The left-hand side of the road had been closed off for resurfacing. They reached the top, turned right and crossed yet another bridge, far higher above the river now, a thin grey thread beneath. Her curiosity grew too much for her. She turned to Giulia with an inquisitive smile. But Giulia didn't even wait for her to frame the question. 'Please don't,' she said.

'Don't what?'

'Don't ask. Not yet. I'll tell you everything later. I promise.'

'Then why not now?'

'We gave our word.'

'Who to?'

Giulia glanced at her father. He gripped the steering wheel tight enough to turn his hands pale. 'A friend of mine,' said Giulia. 'An archaeologist. He'll be joining us tonight.'

Vittorio's hands relaxed again on the wheel, so that Carmen couldn't help but wonder whether this was a lie. 'An archaeologist, huh?' she said. 'Will I know him?'

'I doubt it. He's still young. On sabbatical from Oxford right now, to write a book. But from here originally. From Cosenza, I mean. You'll like him, I know you will.' She gave a shiver of fond memory. 'Wait till you see his eyes! The most beautiful blue eyes you'll ever see.'

Carmen laughed. 'And you'll tell the both of us together?'

'I promise.'

She nodded and sat back. It wasn't in her to push harder. Besides, there was finally some countryside worth looking at, woodland and rolling hills topped by small citadels of brightly coloured houses. A large meadow of wispy grasses was dotted with spring flowers in scarlet, yellow and pale blue. A scarecrow in a high-vis jacket swivelled to follow them on the breeze. She was craning her neck to look back at it when Vittorio slowed sharply and then turned off the road, bumping between a pair of peeling white gateposts then back along a farm track through woods that opened up to their right, sloping steeply down to the river. The land between was crammed with neat rows of vines tethered to teepee frames, and young vegetables sprouting from moist hoed soil; with olive groves and citrus orchards jewelled orange and lemon with young fruit, and a pair of polythene greenhouses through whose translucent fronts she could see long tables crowded with greens. They jolted onwards. The river bent towards them in a small oxbow, making the embankment beneath too steep to farm. She craned to look down it even so, for it offered her best view yet of the—

A flash of yellow to their left. A roar of engine. She looked around in shock that turned to horror as a heavy truck came hurtling out of the trees to smash into their side with such brute force that it sent the old Fiat pickup tumbling off the track and rolling down the steep embankment to the river.

II

Cesco Rossi looked in bemusement at Dieter and his three friends. 'A photograph? On my website? How could there be? You only just found it.'

'That's what I'm saying,' said Dieter.

'There must be some mistake,' said Cesco. 'Let me have a look.' He took Dieter's phone and the amphora handle to check against each other. He frowned briefly, then his expression cleared. 'I remember that piece,' he said. 'It was one of the very first we found here. It looks a bit like this one, yes, but actually the colouring's completely different.'

'It's the same fucking piece,' said Dieter. 'It's broken in exactly the same way.'

'That happens more often than you'd think, with jars from the same batch. They have structural weaknesses in the same places, you see.'

'Bullshit,' said Dieter. 'It's the same fucking jar.'

'What's going on?' asked Arturo, from the helm.

Dieter turned to address him directly. 'Your professor friend here is running a scam,' he said. 'There is no Alaric shipwreck. He planted those pieces himself so that he could charge mugs like us absurd sums to go dive a patch of sand.'

'That's a lie,' said Cesco furiously. 'I can prove it too. I still have that piece in my lock-up. I'll bring it to your villa tonight.'

Dieter snorted. 'Sure you will.'

'I give you my word. Or you can come with me, if you prefer?'

Dieter nodded. 'We'll go there from the dock.'

'After I stow my gear.'

'Screw your gear. We go straight there. You show us that piece. Then you can stow what the hell you like.'

'Fine,' said Cesco. 'But I'll expect an apology. In fact...'

'What?'

He glanced right. They were heading north alongside Scilla's main beach, with its pebbly grey sand and perfect grids of coloured umbrellas, while sunlight flashed like semaphore from the windows of cars on the twisting hillside roads behind. Directly ahead, the great turret of rock on which Scilla's famous castle was built thrust vertically up out of the sea. The town's harbour lay on its other side, barely five minutes away. 'I've got more photos of that piece on my laptop,' he said. 'Better ones, from other angles. You'll see for yourself they're different.'

'Go on, then,' said Dieter. 'Show me.'

Cesco nodded and got to his feet. The Germans parted grudgingly to let him through, bumping him with their chests as he went. He knelt by his bag, zipped his phone away in a pouch. It was a rare luxury, this bag, not just waterproof but buoyant too. He'd bought it last year to take on long swims, packing himself a picnic lunch and a book, then striking out for Sicily or wherever the mood took him.

Another glance towards the shore, at the teenage boys splashing noisily in the shallows, showing off for the girls in their florescent bikinis; and, just ahead, the low waves breaking white around the rocky foot of the castle promontory. He stood and shouldered his bag, pulled tight its straps. He turned to nod at Dieter and his friends, gave Anna a wink, then stepped up onto the rail and dived headlong into the sea.

III

Zara Gold looked in horror at Professor Kaufman. 'Flood the chambers with cement? But he can't! It's not possible. Not until we've had a look.'

'That's what I've been telling him,' said Kaufman. 'He will not listen. Literally. He's not even come in to work today. He refuses to take my calls. He's terrified of a mass escape through a tunnel he'd been told of but hadn't yet dealt with.'

'Dear lord,' she said. 'What do we do?'

'We go over his head.'

Zara closed her eyes. Finally, she understood why Kaufman had called. The prison service was part of the Interior Ministry. For several years she'd gone out with the current minister's youngest son; they'd even been engaged for a while. But it hadn't ended well. 'I haven't seen any of the Bernsteins for almost two years,' she said.

'But you were close, yes? With Avram, not just his son. You can get us in the door. If we can just talk to him...'

'He'll take the warden's side, I assure you. He doesn't give a shit for history.'

'For this he will.'

'Why?'

'Look at the map again. Not as a map but as a journey. One that starts here in Jerusalem.'

She looked back down, unsure what he was getting at. Then she noticed the caravan making its way down the mosaic's right-hand border. Yet it was headed towards Jerusalem, not away. The only means of transport away from Jerusalem was a ship with swollen sails set for Rome. From there, a second ship sailed south from Rome to Carthage, from which a third headed north-east to Constantinople, only for the caravan to take her back south again, to journey's start. Jerusalem. Rome. Carthage. Constantinople. And finally Jerusalem again. All served in a thick Justinian sauce. She turned to Kaufman in disbelief. 'You can't be serious,' she said.

'Why not?'

'Because that story in Procopius is bullshit, that's why not. It's propaganda. *Obvious* propaganda, at that.'

'Are you *sure*? One hundred per cent sure? So sure you don't even feel the need to check?'

Zara hesitated. An hour ago she'd have staked her reputation on it. Not any more.

'That's what I thought,' said Kaufman. 'So let's go see the minister.'

Chapter Three

I

Carmen threw up her arms as the truck struck, but the impact still whiplashed her head against her window, shattering the glass into opaque white hailstones that cascaded all around her even as the Fiat pickup tumbled down the embankment, her companions spinning around her like clothes in a dryer as she alone remained strapped into her seat, lost in the shock and noise of it, the crunch and thump and screech of metal on rock, the screams of mortal terror. Finally, the gradient eased. The pickup tipped up once more, almost regaining its wheels, then fell back on its side and came rocking to a rest.

Carmen lay there a few seconds, too dazed to think. A stone, dislodged by their descent, came bounding down the embankment after them to ding into their roof. It made her aware of the precariousness of the situation. That truck had come out of nowhere. Its driver must have lost control on the road and come plunging through the trees. But what if it hadn't stopped completely? What if it was right now starting to trundle down the slope after them? Panic slapped her to her senses. She looked around. Giulia was lying beside her, with Vittorio on top, groaning, his hand pressed to his cheek, blood squeezing out between his fingers even so. The air smelled pungently of fuel, her leg felt wet. She tried again to release her seat belt, but the buckle was still jammed. She twisted around and wriggled free. She hauled herself up by the steering wheel. The windscreen had come loose at the top, and had turned a murky, underwater green. She stamped it with her foot until it fell away, then scrambled out on hands and knees over shards of broken glass.

To her relief, the truck had stopped where it had struck them. And there was a black SUV parked beside it. Some Good Samaritan come to help. Vittorio crawled out of the empty windscreen then promptly collapsed onto his back, like an exhausted shipwreck victim reaching shore. Blood flowed from his cheek but he ignored it and gestured instead towards his daughter. Carmen crawled back in for her. She grabbed her beneath her armpits and dragged her out, then arranged her in the recovery position and put fingers to her throat to check for a pulse before nodding reassurance at Vittorio.

There came a scuffing noise of boots on stone. She looked up. Her Good Samaritans were coming down to help, the sun directly behind them turning them into black silhouettes. Then her eyes adjusted and she saw that their blackness wasn't due to the sun so much as to the balaclavas and gloves all three were wearing. And, with a sense of disbelief stronger even than her fear, she realised that she'd somehow fallen into the middle of someone else's nightmare.

II

Cesco looked back at the dive boat as he resurfaced. It was swinging around in a tight turn, throwing up a curtain of white spray. He couldn't expect Arturo to help him in any way. He was a business associate rather than a friend, and one to whom he owed a lot of money. But nor would he risk his hull over someone else's feud, so Cesco sprinted the first thirty metres to the relative sanctuary of the shallows, where jagged, protruding rocks forced Arturo to slow right down despite the furious urging of Dieter and his friends.

Cesco reached the promontory. He scrambled up its base to reach the tunnel road that girdled it, then sprinted past a family of family of four in matching flag of St George swimwear and cream of tomato soup sunburns, before racing down into the harbour car park even as the dive boat reappeared, carving a great white scar in the sapphire sea as it roared around the long curved arm of the harbour wall, making the neat rows of pleasure craft bob on their moorings like geriatrics at a fitness class.

Arturo cut his engines as he neared shore. The four Germans leaped down into the shallows. Cesco's fisherman friends Battista and Tomas were winching their boat up the slipway. They appraised the situation instantly and raised their nets as the Germans reached them. He could hear yelling as they struggled to get free, and felt a little ill at the thought that his two friends would soon learn the truth about him, and curse themselves for having aided his escape.

He reached his van, thrust his key into its ignition. The crotchety old engine responded badly to his haste. He gave it a moment then tried again. It stuttered into life. He released the handbrake and began pulling away. Dieter sprinted towards him. Cesco locked his door a microsecond before he could open it. He stood there on the other side of the glass, his face red with berserker rage, veins throbbing and eyes bulging. He punched the window, leaving smears of knuckle blood on it as Cesco accelerated away. He pounded on his side panels and grabbed at his rear doors. Then he bellowed in frustrated fury and ran for his bike.

A pair of dustbin men were blocking the castle road, stuffing card-board packaging into the maw of their truck like parents trying to feed a screeching toddler. With no option, Cesco turned the other way. The cobbled alley of Chianalea was so narrow that his van barely fit, and so busy that he had virtually to keep his hand upon the horn to toot people from his path, winning hard glares from the old women in widow black, the chatting shopkeepers and the tourist couples checking out the blackboard menus. Three of the bikers quickly caught him, but the lane was too narrow for them to pass. It would soon open up ahead, however, and leave him at their mercy. He put his foot down to encourage them to accelerate after him. Then he slammed on his brakes. The bikers tried to stop too, but the first of them crashed into his rear and skittled over his two mates.

Dieter appeared a moment later on his black Harley. He weaved between his fallen comrades then came charging. Cesco muttered a curse as the road opened up and Dieter roared alongside. He turned the wheel and slammed him into the wall. Sparks flew; there was a hideous shriek of metal. Dieter and his bike went skittering. Then he was around a corner and away.

Cesco had planned for contingencies like this. His next identity was all ready to go, hidden in an air duct in his apartment, along with a small amount of cash and certain useful tools. He raced there now, only to find Arturo already parked outside, yelling at his phone. Too late. Word was already out. The mates he'd touched for loans, the bored housewives who'd sponsored his research, the kind couples who'd puzzled about the missing trinkets after having him for dinner – all would soon be converging on his apartment, and no doubt so would his landlady too, armed with a spare key and a demand for her back rent.

Scilla was over for him. The question was where next. He raced along the coast road, thinking as he went. If any of those Germans were badly injured or, God forbid, even dead, the police would come down hard. No hotels, then, or anywhere that would want ID. He had a bedroll and a sleeping bag in the back of his van, but the police were going through one of their periodic campaigns of harassing anyone living rough. His best hope would have been to throw himself on the mercy of a friend – if he hadn't just burned through every last one of them.

Except no. He still had one. Giulia Surace, she who'd sent him three invitations that same morning. Almost as though it was meant to be. The only problem was that she lived just outside Cosenza.

After all these years, it would mean finally going home.

On his return to Italy from England a little over a decade ago, Cesco had settled in Milan, both because he'd been in the mood for city life, and because it had been about as far from his home city as Italy allowed. When he'd made that city too hot for himself, he'd moved to Turin instead, still distant from Cosenza, but also from the Milanese police and the others he'd needed to avoid. Every move since had been made on the same basis, with the perverse consequence that each one had brought him that little bit closer to Cosenza. From Venice to Florence and thence to Rome. From there to Bari, Naples and finally here. He'd been aware that this was happening, and yet he'd let it, because there was a part of him that had wanted it that way.

It was nearly fifteen years since he'd fled Italy for England. Fifteen long years during which even to see Cosenza on the news or on a road sign had been enough to make him ill. Cesco was not a superstitious man, but he was Calabrian, with a Calabrian sense of destiny. Of fatalism too. Circles of life, the primacy of family, the necessity of revenge. So he'd always known deep down that one day he'd return.

He just hadn't expected that today would be it.

III

Central Jerusalem was closing for *Shabbat* as Zara and Kaufman arrived. Shops were pulling down shutters, small businesses emptying of their devout, hurrying to make it home before sunset. Kaufman grew excited as they reached Talbiya. He'd always had a weakness for power. And the man they were about to see had almost as much of it as anyone in the country except the prime minister himself, who he was anyway hotly tipped to replace in the coming elections.

They turned off Pinsker up Yehuda Alkalai. Zara had only been here a few times because she and Isaac had broken up shortly after Avram had been appointed interior minister. His gates were closed, but there were lights on inside the house and she caught a glimpse of his Mercedes SUV. This street was strictly no parking; too many powerful people lived on it. But they found a blue zone further on, at which Kaufman paid by card. There was an awkwardness about him as they walked back. A need to clear the air. 'Those things I wrote,' he murmured.

'It's okay,' she said reflexively. Then she realised that it wasn't. 'Why?'

'Your review, of course.'

'I only said what I thought.'

'Why do you think it hurt so much?'

She looked at him in surprise. Academic life involved the endless exchange of hostile fire, and Kaufman had always seemed as happy taking it as dishing it out. But his latest book had been bombarded from all sides, so perhaps he'd looked to her as his last hope. Or perhaps her own success had simply got under his skin. Whatever the truth, there was no excuse for the bile he'd posted on academic

31

message boards – intended as anonymous, but inevitably traced back – accusing her of plagiarism, promiscuity and – most hurtful of all – betrayal of her family and childhood friends.

Zara had been raised on a religious *moshav* in northern Israel – a community of like-minded families who'd all followed a very particular strain of Conservative Judaism, hostile to outsiders and intolerant of errant views. Her faith had been as true to her as the sea and the rocks and the sun on her face on a summer afternoon. As a brilliant young student, she'd become familiar with all the lines of attack from rival branches of Judaism and other religions too, the better to glory in their defeat. Not that she'd ever shown it publicly. Politeness to strangers had been central to their identity. Only amongst themselves had they revealed their true contempt.

At eighteen, she'd deferred her military service to study history and archaeology in Jerusalem. Questions had been raised about the historicity of the Torah: she'd felt it her duty to demonstrate its truth. Her parents had tried to dissuade her, but she'd been adamant. Her faith was true. What did it have to fear from study? So it had proved for eighteen months. Her intellectual defences had held up well. Until, one day, Professor Kaufman himself had brought them crashing down with the vilest and most underhand of tricks.

He'd asked her for her help.

At that time, he was running an annual excavation of a cemetery near ancient Beit Shemesh. His latest season had yielded finds of wood, cloth and other organic matter whose radiocarbon dating made no sense. He'd found this puzzling enough to ask her – knowing her reputation as an accomplished and scrupulous mathematician – to check his results. She'd quickly found an error with the calibration, saving him considerable embarrassment. It had made her wonder about the reliability of other radiocarbon results – results that supposedly undermined the historicity of the Torah. Envisioning herself as Joshua outside Jericho, bringing the whole sceptical enterprise down with her trumpets, she'd taught herself dating techniques from first principles and had then immersed herself in the raw data. To her horror, however, the walls of Jericho had survived unscathed. It was her own trumpets that had broken.

It had been brutal for Zara, discovering that everything she'd been taught had been a lie. Her next return home had degenerated into argument and furious recrimination, prompting a rupture so brutal and bitter that she'd never even spoken to her parents since – for all that, in moments of weakness, she found her heart almost breaking out of her yearning for reconciliation. As for the immediate aftermath, she'd fallen into disarray until, at a university do, she'd met a young law student called Isaac Bernstein. Handsome, funny, brash, ambitious and atheistic, he'd shown her how to retain the secular virtues of Conservative Judaism without believing a word of scripture.

They'd gone out for eight years, moving from Jerusalem into a Tel Aviv apartment together, he practising law while she'd served her time in the army then studied for her doctorate. Everyone had taken their eventual marriage for granted. In the meantime, the Bernsteins had offered her a replacement family. They'd lunched together at least once a week, and had taken holidays in their Corfu villa. She'd campaigned for Avram, written articles and speeches. In return, he'd invited her into his inner circle, sharing Knesset gossip and discussing strategies to build his party into an electoral force and so make himself prime minister. At first, she'd had to bite her lip at his conceit. But her laughter had soon stopped.

During the last campaign, however, Zara's relationship with Isaac had started to go bad. Something in him had changed. He'd always been outspoken when out stumping for his father, but now he lost his former twinkle. His mild dislike for Arabs, pacifists and liberals had turned into a mania. He'd scoured the internet for new stories to be outraged by. He'd come to believe the kind of crazy conspiracy theories that he'd once invented and spread for political advantage, then had grown angry at her mockery. He'd lost his charm and sense of humour. He'd put on weight and started to go bald. He'd get drunk in public and make mortifying scenes, then either snivel with self-pity afterwards, or make threats.

Then, one night, he'd punched her.

She should have ended it there and then, but he'd apologised so abjectly that she'd given him a second chance. He'd gone into treatment for alcoholism. Things had modestly improved. Then she'd come

33

home one afternoon to find him yelling drunken abuse at a hooker, dressed only in a hijab, he had doubled over the kitchen table. Their split had gone badly. Zara wasn't one to discuss her private life. Isaac and his mother, by contrast, both were. They'd badmouthed her at every opportunity, had lobbied her university to get her fired. That had been too much. She'd visited Avram at the Interior Ministry to play for him a selection of Isaac's drunken voicemails, half maudlin apologies for his behaviour, half furious harangues, including one that airily pointed out that the last person to cross the Bernsteins had been a journalist by the name of Paul Shapiro, and look what had happened to him.

Avram had blanched on hearing this. He'd sworn blind that neither he nor any of his family had had anything to do with Shapiro's death. Zara had believed him. Avram was no killer, and Isaac was a braggart drunk. Besides, Shapiro had skidded in the rain into the back of the van ahead, then had been crushed to death by a container lorry riding up over him. Surely that would have been impossible to arrange. But the recording could still have badly damaged Avram's ambitions, so he'd vowed that the badmouthing would stop at once, that she'd never have to hear from or see any of Bernsteins ever again.

Nor had she. Not until now.

Standing outside his gate, she took a moment to straighten her clothes and to glance at Kaufman to make sure he too was ready. Then she breathed in deep and rang the bell.

Chapter Four

I

The three men arrived at the foot of the embankment in a cascade of stones and loose earth. All three were armed, Carmen now saw, one with a shotgun, the other two with pistols. They walked with remarkable calm, as if out on a Sunday stroll. The balaclavas hid their faces, but not their builds or postures. The first looked to be early twenties, dressed in white trainers, slimline jeans and a plain black T-shirt. The other two were middle aged, dressed in boots, baggy dark trousers and jackets of worn black leather.

The larger of these crouched beside Vittorio. Vittorio gave a moan when he saw him, a mix of recognition and dread. He raised a hand and made to speak, but his throat was so clogged with blood and saliva that he coughed out gluey red spatters instead that the man in the balaclava irritably brushed off his trousers. Then he pressed the muzzle of his shotgun against Vittorio's cheek and looked up and around at the elder of his companions, like a gladiator for a thumb.

This second man walked over to the pickup. A hand to his chin, he studied the kicked-out windscreen and the trail of dust and blood that Carmen had left while dragging Giulia to safety. He turned to his colleague and tapped his ear to indicate that the shotgun was too noisy. Then he looked away again. The other man set down the shotgun to pop the clasp on a sheath strapped to his leg. He drew out a hunting knife with a long serrated blade then held it up so that the afternoon sunlight glinted off it. Vittorio moaned again, his face a deathly grey. The man knelt astride him, pinning his shoulders beneath his knees. He clamped a gloved hand over his mouth then muttered something that might have been a prayer or even an apology before plunging the knife deep into Vittorio's throat, directly beneath his ear. He held it there a moment then brought his free hand down to shield himself from the spray as he sawed across his windpipe and carotid. Then he wiped his blade on Vittorio's shirt and stood and walked calmly over to Giulia, thankfully still unconscious. He glanced at his companion for confirmation before slitting her throat as well. Then he came across to Carmen and knelt upon her shoulders too.

She wanted to fight, she wanted to be defiant, but somehow she was unable. Her violent trembling suddenly stopped. She could see his eyes through the holes in his balaclava, dull like a backward pupil, darkly bloodshot and wrinkled with the mild distaste of a man about to plunge a blocked loo. His mouth was open, breathing hard from his exertion, his tongue coated with a pale yellow fur and his teeth spaced, grey and wonky, like headstones in an abandoned cemetery. She felt, simultaneously, both total dread and immense calm as he placed his hand over her mouth and—

'*Attenti*,' said the other older man, evidently the boss. He came and squatted down beside her. '*Tu chi sei?*' he asked. Who are you?

Relief made Carmen sob. But the stress was too much for her rickety Italian. 'I'm sorry,' she said. 'I don't...'

The man grunted. '*Inglesi?*'

'America,' she said.

'Passport?'

She looked around for her purse. It was still lying inside the Fiat's cab. She nodded towards it. The youngster went to fetch it for him. He opened it up, took out her phone and then her passport, checking her photo, visa and entry stamp. Then he nodded at Vittorio and Giulia. 'How you know these people?' he asked. There was a disconcerting gentleness to his voice, and something off about his accent, too, though she was far too stressed to work out what.

'I'm at university with Giulia,' she said. 'Sapienza. In Rome.'

'You are here why?'

'She invited me. There was a parcel she needed bringing.'

'A parcel?'

Carmen looked around. The packing case had spilled from the back of the pickup and had tumbled all the way to the river's edge. 'There,' she said.

'What is it? Why she want it?'

'I don't know. She never said. I swear.'

The man fell silent. He gazed at her. She gazed back. If eyes were windows to the soul, then this man at least had one. Where his partner seemed dully indifferent to his butchery, this man was haunted by it, like an aid worker overwhelmed by a famine or some other natural disaster. Yet the only natural disaster here was him. She met his gaze with as much candour as she could muster, letting him see inside her. Finally he nodded. 'You will be quiet for me one minute, yes?' he asked.

'Yes.'

He gestured for the youngster to cover her with his pistol then walked off a little way with his colleague with the cemetery teeth. Their lack of hurry bewildered her. But then, she realised, it wasn't as if they could be seen. The steepness of the embankment at this point and the thickness of the surrounding woods put a screen completely around them. Fifty yards either side, where the gradient lessened and the landscape opened up, they'd be in sight of the road and other houses too. An ambush, then. One designed to look like an accident, in the hope they'd break their necks in the tumble. Unfortunately for them, she'd survived, kicking the windscreen out from within then dragging Giulia to safety, leaving a trail of blood and dirt all too easy for the police to read. So they'd given up on their initial plan and simply slit their throats instead. Now she herself was the only problem left for them to solve.

The discussion grew animated. Famine Eyes held up her passport. Cemetery Teeth scowled and waved his bloodstained knife. She watched transfixed, unable to make sense of it, but knowing that her life depended on the outcome. The debate ended. The two men walked back over. The verdict was in. Cemetery Teeth gave a set of car keys to the youngster who set off back up the slope. Famine Eyes squatted back down beside her. 'Please forgive us for all this unhappiness,' he began, with his incongruous courtesy. 'But my... my *companion* here is worried – *understandably* worried, I think you will agree – that if we let you live you will tell of this unpleasant business to our good friends in blue uniforms.' She could smell dust on him, and sweat, and a lemony shampoo. She'd never been so terrified of anyone or anything in her life. 'I say to him, we are men of honour, not of evil. This girl is not our enemy, our faces are hidden from her, she knows none of us. What is it that she has seen to cause us grief? He says, why take the chance? Two dead people, three dead people, for us the rope is just as long. And he has a point, I think you will agree.'

'I won't say a word. Ever.' Hope made her realise how badly she wanted to live. 'I swear it. On my life. My mother's life.'

He nodded slowly. 'So you would like, then, for us to let you live?'

'Yes. Please.'

'Even though to let you live is for us a great big risk?'

'Yes.'

'You will be in our debt, you realise? Big in our debt?'

'Yes.'

'Good,' he said. 'Now look at your friends. Please.' He gestured towards them without looking their way himself, as though squeamish of the handiwork he himself had ordered. She turned to look at them: their contorted postures and ugly stillness; the plastic pallor of their skin; the glossy red wetness of the blood on their clothes congealing dark around their wounds; the flies as green as emeralds already settling upon them. She closed her eyes in cold horror then looked back up at him. He said: 'Your friends owed my employers a very great debt. Money, yes, but not just money. Respect too. They gave their word to pay it all back. They never did. They never even tried. They thought they could make do with promises instead. So... now you know what happens to people who do not honour their debts to my employers. Debts such as the one that you agree you now owe me. Do you understand what I am saying?'

'Yes. I... Yes.'

'Good. Then let me tell you how you will honour this particular debt.' He reached out and touched with his gloved fingertip the gash

38

on the side of her head where she'd banged against the window. He didn't press hard, but it was so sore that she winced all the same. 'When our good friends in blue uniforms come to talk to you, you will tell them this: you will tell them that you were on your way home from the station when something bad happened, but you have no idea what. You banged your head so hard that you...' He paused, frowning, searching for the right phrase.

'Lost consciousness?' she suggested.

'Yes. Just so. You lost consciousness. When you woke again, it was to find your friends already dead and no one else here. You never saw me, or my companions, or our vehicles. You never saw anything at all. Do you understand?'

'Yes.'

'And you'll do it?'

'Yes.'

'Now listen closely, because this is very important. You will think, when we are gone, that you can be clever, that you can tell the truth of it to our good friends in blue uniforms in the most strict of confidence. But there is no such thing as the most strict of confidence with our good friends in blue uniforms. Please believe me on this. Their salaries are for shit. The only way they make enough to live any kind of life is by taking envelope money from me and my friends. You know what I mean, envelope money?'

'Yes.'

'Good. So I tell you this as a friend. Whatever you say to them, we will find out. Maybe not at once, but within an hour or two. A day at the most. They will sell your life to us for a hundred euros, and think they have made themselves a most excellent bargain. And do not listen to their promises to keep you safe. To put yourself under their protection only means that we will know exactly where to find you, and when you will be most vulnerable. My employers will have you killed then for sure. Then they will have me killed too. For I will be the one who chose to let you live. To talk, therefore, is to kill me as well as yourself.'

'You have my word. I'll never tell anyone anything.'

'Good.' He glanced around. The youth was dancing back down the bank, a roll of black tape in one hand, a sponge bag in the other. He held the latter out to his boss, who stood to take it. He still had her passport, which he now tucked away in his pocket. 'In case you decide to go back to America,' he said by way of explanation, 'and think you can talk to our good friends in blue uniforms there.'

'I gave you my word,' she said.

'Yes,' he said, unzipping the sponge bag and taking out a syringe and a small brown flask. 'And now I have your passport too.'

II

Cesco stopped at a petrol station outside Gioia Tauro with a car wash and a small auto parts store. He parked and turned on his phone. His various inboxes were filled with fury and accusations of betrayal, with threats and demands for repayment. He listened to or read a little of each, as a kind of penance, before deleting them all, saving only the message from Giulia with directions to her house. That done, he removed his SIM card so that no one could trace him through it.

Any search would be for a dirty plain white van. Ideally, he'd trade it or at least respray it, but he didn't have time, so he ran it through the car wash instead then went into the auto-parts store from which he bought a pair of adhesive A.C. Milan banners for his side panels, Italian and European flags for his rear doors, snowflakes for his windscreen and a dancing Hawaiian girl for his dashboard. Pleased with the results, he decided to give himself a makeover too. At a discount store up the road, he bought new clothes and toiletries, along with scissors and an electric razor. He took them into the toilets to change, then studied himself in the cracked and tinted mirror above the sink.

Cesco didn't like to think of himself as a conman or a thief. Not at heart. He saw himself, rather, as someone making the best of the hard hand life had dealt him. Denied the use of his own name and *codice fiscale*, he'd had to adopt false ones instead. That in turn had limited him to jobs that avoided scrutiny. He'd cooked and waited tables. He'd picked fruit and vegetables. Mostly, however, he'd tended bar. He enjoyed it and had the aptitude, good-looking as he was, well presented, cheerful, with an excellent memory for faces, a gift for languages and a sympathetic ear. Yet, as a once-precocious child, it had stung his pride that this was all he'd ever be.

Cesco had always had a gift for spinning bullshit on the hoof. At school, he'd used it to entertain. Back in Italy, he'd used it to sprinkle himself with the stardust his real life had lacked. In Milan, he'd pretended to be an up-and-coming actor. In Turin, an abstract painter. All it took was bravado, a website and a certain skill with social media. He wasn't quite sure why, but playing such roles gave him a brashness he lacked as his own true self – a brashness that, to his glad surprise, appealed to a certain class of married women. Was he to blame for adding spice to their lives, or for accepting their little loans and gifts? And, when they thoughtlessly forgot to reward him in this way, was it really so wrong of him to correct their oversight directly from their purses? He'd had his setbacks, of course, including arrests for theft and burglary. He'd also been set on a few times by furious husbands and their friends, but he'd usually been able to give as good as he got.

In Rome, he'd reinvented himself as an aspiring photographer. He'd always enjoyed taking pictures, and he had a flair for catching striking-looking people in dramatic settings. He'd set up a website showcasing his best shots and then contacted the leading agencies. He'd only done it for cover, so he'd been gleeful when he'd actually made some sales. His sunset at the Spanish Steps had become a popular postcard; a young couple he'd captured kissing against a huge wave breaking on the Camogli coast now adorned the jacket of a romantic thriller. A couple of regulars at the bar where he'd worked had asked him to do their wedding. His digital hadn't been up to it, so he'd nicked a proper camera and gone to work. Word of mouth had won him ever more commissions. Soon he'd been earning more from photography than from serving bar, for half the effort. Yet, perversely, he'd come to hate it, for it had exposed too much of his own true self. So one morning, without a word, he'd got on the train and left.

In your mid-twenties, being a struggling artist was romantic. Approaching your thirties, it was pathetic. When he'd eventually reached Naples, therefore, he'd presented himself as a doctoral student writing a thesis on the city's Duchy period. He had a perverse ability to soak up knowledge like a sponge when he needed it for a scam. Working in a bar by Porto Nolana one night, a party of drunken Romanians had tried to chat up a pair of exasperated young French-women. Intervening in such situations had been part of his job, so he'd engaged the Romanians himself. They were doctors, it had transpired, as well as amateur historians, organising a touring holiday that broadly followed Alaric's own route. Raised in Cosenza as he'd been, Cesco knew Alaric well. The spirit of mischief had duly taken him, and so he'd spun them a yarn about how he and some historian friends had dived the Messina Straits a couple of years before, where they'd found traces of a Visigothic ship. The Romanians had been so excited by this that they'd offered him absurd sums to show them where. There was a dump outside the city he knew of, where the Romans had ditched their old pots. He'd gone there that night to fill several plastic bags with broken earthenware from approximately the right era. Then he'd driven down to Scilla to seed a plausible section of seabed with the shards.

The expedition had gone swimmingly. He'd relished his return to Calabria too, the cadence of conversation and the familiar slang, the mountains and the sea and the particular scents and flavours of its food. So when Naples had grown too hot for him a couple of months later, he'd reinvented himself as Cesco Rossi PhD, in Scilla to write a book on the history of the Messina Straits, paying his way with bar work supplemented by shipwreck dives that he advertised on travel websites. He'd also changed his look dramatically, lest his recent Neapolitan friends come looking. That was where his beard and ponytail had come from, the various pieces of metal in his face. But they'd served their purpose now. He therefore pocketed the studs and earring, took out his new razor and scissors. But hair, while easy to cut off, was a bugger to grow back. So he settled for trimming his beard down to a goatee and combing out his ponytail with his fingers. Then he climbed back in his van and headed north.

Road signs counted down the kilometres to Cosenza. His back began to ache with stress. He left the A2 south of the city, cut across country. Dusk settled over the landscape. He turned on his headlights. A high bridge took him across a thin thread of river. He checked Giulia's directions then slowed to second gear, peering into the darkness for the concealed entrance to their farmhouse drive. A BMW came racing up behind him, flashing its beams in irritation at his dawdle. He retorted with a middle finger only for the white gateposts marking the entrance to the Suraces' drive suddenly to appear on his left. He braked so sharply that the BMW almost rear-ended him, before swinging out around him in a furious screech of horn.

The drive was a cratered moonscape. He wended a careful path around the worst of the potholes. He could see glitter ahead, as though a casket of diamonds and rubies had been scattered across the track. He drew closer and realised it was in fact shards of broken glass. And the edge of the track had been chomped away as if by some kind of landslide. He felt uneasy suddenly. He got out to look. A pickup truck lay on its side at the foot of the embankment, three ghostly shapes arrayed beside it. His heart seemed to stop beating. He'd feared that returning here would mean grief. But he hadn't expected it to happen quite this quickly.

He took out his phone and his SIM card too. But calling the emergency services would give them his number, helping them to trace him if any of those bikers were badly hurt. Even if they weren't, it would be reckless to get involved without first finding out what had happened. The embankment was so steep that it forced him ever faster, trusting to the skill of his quick feet. An overnight bag lay on its side halfway down. The ghostly shapes turned into bodies. Giulia was closest to him, her throat a dark red mess, blood pooled around her head like a grotesque halo. A silver-haired man, presumably her father, lay nearby, his neck hacked almost clean through, a pair of coins placed over his eyes.

Cesco stood there numbly. Such coins were an old Mafia calling card, code for an unpaid debt or other betrayal. He had a sudden panic this was somehow to do with him – that Giulia had discovered his true identity and blabbed of it to the wrong person. Or even that her invitation had been bait. He looked around in alarm, but there was no one in sight. He needed to get away all the same. That much was clear. Get away then find a phone box from which to call it in anonymously.

He was about to climb back up the slope when the third body twitched. He told himself it was only the breeze upon their sleeve. Except there was no breeze. Reluctantly, he went across. A fair-haired woman in her mid to late twenties was lying on her side, her wrists and ankles bound, her face as grey as bone, save for the strip of black tape over her mouth and the dried blood on her temple and below her nose, from which tiny flecks and bubbles blew at every exhalation. He picked up a corner of the tape then ripped it off, leaving her skin reddened like drunken lipstick. The pain of it woke her from her stupor. She rolled onto her back, eyes open in narrow slits. 'Who are you?' she murmured, in English.

'A friend,' he told her.

'Are they gone?'

'They're gone,' he assured her. 'You're safe.'

'Don't leave me,' she said.

'No,' he said.

Her eyelids fluttered and then closed. She seemed to let go of something as she relaxed back into sleep. Her breathing came easier; a little colour returned to her cheeks. She looked childlike and horribly vulnerable at the heart of all this horror. He looked back up to his van. This was the 'Ndrangheta. The fucking 'Ndrangheta. He couldn't get involved. He just couldn't. He needed to find a public phone box and call it in from there.

Don't leave me, she'd said.

Memory reached up out of his deep past like a hand out of the night. He swore loudly. Then he took his phone from his pocket, reinserted his SIM card and made the call.

III

The Bernsteins had a video-entry system at their gate. It was Avram's wife Rivkah herself who answered it. She was, as ever, immaculately made up, but she'd aged visibly since Zara had seen her last. Her lips went thin and bitter when she saw who it was. 'You have a nerve,' she said.

'Thank you,' said Zara sweetly. 'That means a lot, coming from you.'

Hatred burned like coals in her eyes. 'Isaac's not here,' she said. 'He's in America, getting treatment for what you did for him.'

'We're not here for Isaac. We're here for Avram.'

'We have synagogue.'

'Please. This is important. It could help his career.'

Rivkah glared at her several seconds, then the screen went dark, leaving Zara uncertain whether they'd been dismissed. She turned to ask Kaufman his opinion when the gates began to open and then the great man himself appeared at the front door, wearing a sharp black suit and a *yarmulke*. He was a year and a day younger than his wife, but his fitness regime, dyed hair and occasional nip and tuck made him look a full decade younger. 'This is *Shabbat*,' he said as they approached.

'We know, Minister,' said Zara, opting for formality. 'And we're deeply sorry to disturb you. But this can't wait.'

He gazed appraisingly at her. She gazed back. In the end he gave a smile so small it might have only been her imagination. 'My office, then,' he said, opening the door wide. He led them along a gloomy passage to a warmly lit, wood-panelled room, its bookshelves stuffed with impressively academic works in less impressively pristine condition. A large Israeli flag hung in a glass frame on the wall behind Avram's oak desk, along with photographs of him standing beside the American president, the German chancellor and other world leaders. He sat at his desk and waved vaguely at chairs set against the wall. 'This is about that damned mosaic, I take it.'

'You know of it?' asked Zara, moving a chair then sitting down.

'Cohen found out you'd been to his prison. He put two and two together. Though I don't understand the fuss.' He turned to Kaufman. 'He told me you'd agreed a deal.'

'It's not the mosaic, Minister,' replied Zara. 'It's what's beneath.'

'The catacombs, yes. They are to be sealed. Do I seriously need to explain why? Or have we grown so sentimental over a few old bones that we'll put our children's lives at risk?'

'With respect, Minister,' said Kaufman. 'It might be more than a few—'

'No.'

'But we—'

'No. Is there anything else? Or may I now go to service?'

Kaufman turned helplessly to Zara. Zara silenced him with a look. For a man so drawn to power, Kaufman lacked the first idea of how and why it was exercised. *Of course* the minister and his warden wanted the chambers sealed. Not *despite* the chance of finding something important, as Kaufman seemed to think, but *because* of it. Should a full excavation be required, it would cause ructions at the prison, maybe even lead to it being temporarily closed. That would mean finding new places for its inmates, setting off a cascade of transfers across an already overburdened system with massively constrained budgets. It was a headache the minister didn't need – especially with the cure so close to hand, in the form of a digger and a cement truck. Yet that didn't make their case hopeless. It simply meant they had to find the right approach. 'This is your opportunity, Minister,' she said. 'The one you've been waiting for.'

That smile again, amused by her brazenness. 'Go on,' he said.

Zara took out her phone, brought up her photograph of the map mosaic, held it out. Avram could be touchy about the limits of his knowledge, so she said: 'The inscription will be impossible for you to read on this small screen, so please allow me to translate. It says: "God save your most pious servant Flavius Justinian, lover of Jesus, giver of this token of your glory."'

'And that should mean something to me?'

'Flavius Justinian is Justinian the Great, the Byzantine emperor who as you know built countless great churches across the ancient world. Including, it would seem, this one.'

'And my opportunity?'

'Justinian's great ambition was to restore the Roman Empire to its former glory, ruled not from Rome or Ravenna but from

46

Constantinople. He had a problem, however. The Vandals had seized Carthage and were throwing their weight around. So Justinian sent his top general Belisarius to put them in their place. Belisarius destroyed their fleet, seized numerous captives and brought vast quantities of booty back to Constantinople, which was then paraded through the streets. Justinian's court historian Procopius describes it in his *History of the Wars*.'

Avram checked his watch. 'My wife and I really need to leave in the next five minutes,' he said. 'It doesn't look good for a man in my position, being late.'

'As Procopius describes it, an unnamed Jew warned the emperor that certain treasures on parade were cursed to bring about the downfall of whichever city held them, as they'd already brought down Rome and Carthage before them. Justinian was so spooked by this that he ordered them returned to their original home.'

'And?' asked Avram, despite himself. 'Where was that?'

'Here, Minister. Jerusalem. Specifically, to a house of God in the vicinity. Because these treasures were sacred treasures. More precisely, they were *the* sacred treasures. The ones the Romans pillaged from the Second Temple during their sack of Jerusalem. The table of shewbread, the silver trumpets.' She pointed to the wall behind him. 'And that.'

Avram stared at Zara, then turned slowly in his chair to look at the flag of Israel hanging on his wall and the seven-branched candelabra depicted at its heart, most potent symbol of their nation. He turned back to her with an incredulous expression. 'Are you telling me I might have the fucking Menorah buried beneath my prison?'

'Yes, Minister. That's *exactly* what I'm telling you.'

Chapter Five

A hilltop villa near Cosenza

I

Magistrate Baldassare Mancuso was scrawling notes on the margins of a report when word arrived that his old law college friend had arrived with his daughter. He hurried to the front door to greet them, only to discover that their car was still being searched outside the main gates. He could hardly complain. He'd instituted the security protocols himself in response to the many death threats he'd received. Besides, he'd been at his desk since six that morning, so it was good to have a moment or two outside, with these delicious twilight scents filling his nostrils. His predecessor at this villa had planted exotic aromatics everywhere. Baldassare had little else good to say about the man, but he was grateful for that.

The gates squeaked open. They needed a good oiling. A sleek silver Mercedes drove through, wending its way up the spotlit drive to stop outside the front door. Mario and his teenage daughter got out, each looking a little unnerved, perhaps by the thoroughness of the search they'd just experienced, or by the helicopter on its pad, or by the bodyguards currently flanking Baldassare, sub-machine guns held at the ready – though he himself barely even noticed them any more.

He put on his most cheerful smile to set them at their ease as he hurried down the steps. He hugged Mario welcome, then shook the hand of his daughter Bea in both of his. He hadn't seen her for twelve whole years, he told her. She'd been in a pushchair back then. A beautiful child she'd been, though not half so beautiful as now. She blushed and twisted gravel with her foot, trying her best not to smile because of the silver braces in her teeth. It tugged his heart to see it, but he hid it with boisterousness as he led them inside and through to the kitchen. He offered drinks rather apologetically. The villa was not set up for entertaining. They made do with mineral water poured over ice and squeezed lemon, then settled companionably around the kitchen table. He raised an eyebrow at Mario, inviting him to explain. But there was no explanation, it turned out. He and his daughter had simply been on their way down from Verona to Sicily to meet up with his wife and spend a few days with her family. He'd seen his old friend on the news last night, and mentioned it to Bea, along with the fact they'd be driving by his door. And she'd pleaded with him to drop in, because Baldassare surely knew better than anyone that Italy's anti-Mafia magistrates were the nation's new rock stars.

Baldassare roared with laughter. He was short and fat and no one's idea of male beauty, so the idea of himself as a rock star was immensely amusing. But the way Bea blushed made him think it might even be the truth. 'I'm so glad you did,' he told them both, with a sincerity that surprised him. 'Truly. I see so few friendly faces these days. But, as I said on the phone, I don't have long. You wouldn't believe how much work I still have to do. Besides, Alessandra and Bettina will be calling shortly.'

'Are they not here?'

Baldassare shook his head. 'We decided it was prudent for them to stay away until this dreadful business is over. So these nightly calls are our only chance to talk. They keep me sane. I'm sure you understand.'

'Of course, of course,' said Mario. 'No need to explain. I knew when I called you'd be crazy busy. Sunday, isn't it? The big announcement. Or might it be postponed again?'

'I wish,' said Baldassare. 'But no. We're out of time.' Almost one year before, an operation he'd personally directed had resulted in the seizure of a vast consignment of cocaine outside the container terminal of Gioia Tauro, as well as the arrests of the notorious Critelli brothers, their top lieutenants and dozens of foot soldiers in the Cosenza Mafia. He'd been working on the prosecution case ever since. 'It's lay charges or let them walk.'

'And? No hint for an old friend?'

He spread his hands. 'What makes you think I've even decided yet?'

Mario laughed and turned to Bea. 'He was like this at college too. Always looking absurdly deeply into problems. Examining them from every possible angle. I said back then that he'd end up a judge. Didn't I tell you that, Baldo?'

'Yes. Yes, you did.'

'But a hero too. That I never saw.'

A weight pressed suddenly upon his shoulders. Admiration was a terrible burden. 'I'm no hero,' he said flatly. He was about to add more to this, to explain the twists and turns of life that had brought him to this spot. But he feared if once he started, he might never stop. So he drained his drink instead and checked his watch.

'We should be getting on,' said Mario, taking the hint. 'We still have a long drive ahead. I only wanted to see you and wish you well. But we'll be coming back this way in ten days' time. My wife will be with us then. I know she'd love to see you again. Of all our college friends, you were the only one she ever truly cared for. Perhaps we could meet up then, with the big day past? Go to a nice restaurant together, drink a bit too much red wine. Like the old days.'

Baldassare smiled but shook his head. 'I don't really go out any more.'

'Come on, old friend. You mustn't let yourself become a hermit.'

'It's not that,' he said. 'It's that, whenever I'm at a restaurant, I put everyone else there at risk. The staff, the other customers, my bodyguards, the people I'm eating with. It rather takes away the fun.'

Mario blinked. 'Oh,' he said. 'How stupid of me.'

'Not at all. It was a kind thought. But it's how my life is now.'

A few moments of awkward silence followed. Mario pushed himself to his feet. 'Well, then. You must give my love to Alessandra and Bettina. It must be so hard for you, not having them around.'

'Yes,' said Baldassare. 'But this is a war we're fighting. And war means sacrifice.' He hesitated, wondering whether to go on. But he'd promised himself he would, and the opening was too good to miss. 'For me, that means long hours and no more nights out. For my wife and daughter, it means hiding themselves abroad. But we never forget that others contribute too. Taxpayers like your good self, for example. It's astonishing how much investigations like these cost. The suspects we have in prison awaiting charges. The others we are watching. A hundred police officers, lawyers and others conducting interviews, searching properties, tracking funds, preparing evidence. If it goes to trial, it will be *by far* the largest in Calabrian history. We're looking at having to build a special courtroom for it. All put together, it is *insanely* expensive. But such is the price we pay for civilisation and the rule of law. And so a bargain for us taxpayers in the long run, wouldn't you say? Old friend.'

Mario blanched. As a lawyer himself, he knew the investigative powers of an anti-Mafia magistrate like Baldassare. And, too late, he realised that no one would be allowed inside this villa at so sensitive a moment without a thorough vetting. Because in Italy, anyone at all could be Mafia – even an old law college friend dropping by with his charming teenage daughter. 'I don't follow,' he said weakly. 'What are you…?'

'I'm saying you're absolutely right. It's a terrible thing for a man to be deprived of his family for long stretches of time. Too often, we don't realise our blessings until it's too late.' He walked them both back to the front door. He put a hand on Bea's shoulder then clasped Mario's hand warmly between his to bid him farewell, meeting his gaze for long enough to assure him he still had time to settle his taxes properly, if he so chose. Then he waved them off down the drive. He watched until the gates had closed once more behind them, sealing him safely back in his cocoon. He checked his watch again. Five more minutes.

The sacrifices one made.

He breathed in deeply of the fragrant dusk to fortify himself. Then, with a heavy heart, he headed back inside.

II

The first ambulance arrived ten minutes after Cesco's call, parking tight behind his van to leave space for those that followed. He waved the paramedics down the slope. It was dark enough by now for them to need electric lamps. A sturdy, middle-aged woman of obvious competence knelt beside the fair-haired woman and checked her vitals while Cesco described how he'd found her and what he'd done.

A second ambulance arrived, then the police cars, parking in a line all the way back to the road. Ghostly figures in forensic whites shooed him further and further back as they sealed off the scene with tape, set up lamps, scoured the ground for evidence. No one seemed interested in him, so he made his way back up the slope, only to discover that his van was trapped between the ambulance behind and a taped off section of track where the police were collecting shards of broken glass.

The media now arrived, setting up their lighting and cameras. That was the last thing he needed, so he climbed into his van and sat there in the darkness. He turned his phone back on to check his most recent messages. He took down his Scilla website, mothballed his social media accounts and generally wiped his existence from the internet, save only for a handful of references to his life at Oxford University that he'd seeded here and there over the preceding months. A rap came on his passenger-side window. He looked up to see an *ispettore* of the *Polizia di Stato* standing there. Cesco leaned over to roll his window down. 'Yes?' he asked.

'Are you the guy who found this?' asked the *ispettore*.

'That's me,' said Cesco. He got out and went around. Experience had taught him that police were highly sensitive to evasiveness but easily lulled by eagerness. 'Those poor bastards,' he said. 'Murdered in cold blood like that. You see it on the news, but it's not the same, is it? Not when you know them.'

'You knew them?'

'The dead woman, yes. Giulia Surace. She lived here with her father Vittorio.' The *ispettore* took out a notebook and pencil to jot this down. 'I expect that was him down there with her,' continued Cesco, when he looked back up. 'Though I can't say for sure, I never met the man. The second woman I have no idea about at all. Except that she spoke English.'

'You talked with her?'

'A few words only. They'd taped her mouth and her nose was blocked with blood. She was struggling to breathe, so I ripped the tape off. I hope that's okay.'

'Of course.'

'It woke her. She asked me if they were gone. I told her yes. She asked me to stay. I assured her that I would. She went back to sleep again. That's when I called you guys. Oh, and she had tape around her wrists and ankles too, so I took that off too, to make her comfortable. Then I came up here, so as not to get in your way. That's all.'

The *ispettore* nodded. 'And why are you here at all?'

'Giulia invited me. For the weekend. I have her messages on my phone, if you'd like to see? Or I can forward them, if you give me a number.'

'And your name is?'

'Antonio Rossi. At your service, sir.' He took out and handed him his ID. 'I'm an archaeologist by trade. On sabbatical from Oxford to write a book. A history of shipping in the Messina Straits. It sounds dull, I know, but actually it's fascinating. The way Calabria and Sicily have—'

'And you live where?'

'Wherever my research takes me. Recently, that's been in and around Reggio di Calabria.'

'That's where you came from today?'

'No. I was in Gioia Tauro.' He took out his wallet to show his receipts for petrol and clothes, their time and date stamps.

'And how did you know Ms Surace?'

'We dived together last year.' This was true enough. She'd tagged along on one of his Alaric trips. 'We hit it off. You know how it is. We spent the night together and promised to stay in touch. But we never did. Not until her invitation.'

'Any reason someone might want to hurt her or her father?'

'We didn't really talk about ourselves. Though…'

'Yes?'

'Those coins over his eyes. That's 'Ndrangheta, isn't it? An unpaid debt? Because she was broke, I know that much. On our night together, not only did I pay for everything, she tried to tap me for a loan too.' He gave a dry smile. 'Tapping up an academic on sabbatical is true desperation.'

The *ispettore* smiled politely as he jotted it down. 'Anything else?'

Cesco feigned a frown then shook his head. 'Give me your number,' he suggested. 'I'll contact you if I remember anything of interest. I'll forward copies of those texts and receipts too, if that would help?'

The *ispettore* handed him a card. Cesco put it in his wallet. 'You have cards too,' observed the *ispettore*. 'Perhaps I might take one.'

'Of course,' said Cesco.

The *ispettore* glanced at it. 'This says Francesco Rossi PhD. Didn't you tell me Antonio?'

'Yes. Yes I did.' He got his identity card back out to show him. 'Antonio Vincenzo Francesco Rossi. But my grandfather was Antonio and my father was Vincenzo, so I was left with Francesco. Cesco, actually. Except in official situations, that is, such as when I'm talking to the police.' The *ispettore* stared at him for several moments, his antenna finally on alert. Cesco cursed himself inside, not least because he knew his fingerprints would still be on file with the Italian police from his old arrests. But he found a bland smile even so, and put his wallet away. 'Look, officer, between you and me, this was 'Ndrangheta, wasn't it?'

'We don't know that yet. Not for sure.'

'But that's how it appears, right? Only, is there any way you can keep me out of this? Call me a coward if you like, but the thought of those monsters knowing my name...' But the *ispettore* had stopped listening. He was gazing instead at the young American woman who'd just arrived on top of the embankment on a stretcher, the female paramedic walking alongside her. She looked to be awake again, if groggy. The *ispettore* excused himself and went across. He said something to her. She shook her head. He turned to Cesco. 'You speak English, yes?' he called out. Cesco nodded and went across, silently bemoaning his bad luck. They climbed into the ambulance together, sat on a bench seat as the woman was strapped in and the paramedic swabbed blood from her face.

'Doesn't she belong in hospital?' asked Cesco.

'Early leads are valuable leads,' replied the *ispettore* piously. He turned to her. 'This gentleman is Cesco Rossi,' he said in Italian. 'The one who called us in.'

Cesco translated for her. There was no hint of recognition in her eyes, but she found a fragile smile. 'Thank you so much.'

'My pleasure,' he assured her. 'And you're okay with answering questions, are you? Only I can have them take you straight to hospital if you—'

'I'm fine,' she said. 'I just wish I knew anything that could help.'

'Tell us what you can.'

She nodded. 'My name is Carmen Nero. I'm American. From Massachusetts. I'm in Rome for my PhD. It's on a woman called Galla Placidia.' She spoke in considerate short sentences, allowing Cesco to translate and the *ispettore* to make his notes. 'Giulia called me last night. Giulia Surace. She asked me down for the weekend. I came by train. She and her father Vittorio met me at the station. We were on our way back to their house when... I don't know. Something must have happened.' She touched her temple. 'But honestly I don't remember anything more. Not until I woke just a few minutes ago.'

The *ispettore* jotted it all down. 'Any idea why the Suraces might have been attacked?' he asked. 'Or by whom?'

'I can't imagine. But then I hardly knew them.'

'So why invite you?'

'I don't have many friends here in Italy,' she said. 'I think Giulia was being nice. Oh, and she wanted a piece of equipment brought down for the weekend.'

'Equipment?' asked the *ispettore*.

'She never told me what it was. But it was in a big black packing case. It must be at the foot of the slope somewhere.'

'I saw it,' said Cesco. 'It was right by the river. There was an overnight bag too, halfway down the slope. Black with yellow stripes.'

'That's mine,' said Carmen.

'We'll get it for you,' promised the *ispettore*. 'And you have no idea why they wanted this equipment?'

Carmen again touched fingers to her forehead. 'Giulia wouldn't say. Apparently some big-shot Oxford archaeologist was coming to

55

join us. She wanted to tell us both together.' She frowned at Cesco. 'Is that you? The big-shot Oxford archaeologist?'

'Hardly a big-shot. And I'm on sabbatical right now. But otherwise...'

'Well, she was going to tell us both together. But of course...' She gestured at the catastrophe that had overtaken them, then closed her eyes once more, rested her head. Cesco gazed curiously at her. If there was one field in which he truly was an expert, it was bullshit. Carmen had just lied, at least once and probably twice. The first was certain: if she'd been unconscious throughout, why ask him earlier if 'they' had gone? And her denial of knowing what was in the packing case had hardly been convincing. But greater than his curiosity was his desire to get away, so it was to his immense relief that the *ispettore* snapped closed his notebook and nodded to the paramedic that it was time to take her patient off to hospital.

III

The astonishment on Avram Bernstein's face turned almost instantly to scepticism. 'I thought the Menorah was in Rome. In the Vatican cellars.'

'No, Minister,' said Zara.

'But I distinctly remember a fuss the last time the prime minister went over.'

'Yes, Minister. Because it sometimes serves Israel's interests to be angry with the Italians or the Catholics. At such moments, if we have no other justification, we demand the return of the Menorah. They don't have it, and haven't for many hundreds of years. We know this for a fact. They know that we know. But making them deny it anyway still puts them on defence.'

Avram grunted in amusement. He loved that side of politics. 'Okay,' he said. 'But it *was* in Rome, yes? It's on that damned arch. So how the hell did it get to Carthage, to be pillaged?'

Zara gave herself a moment, for it was a complicated story. That the temple had been looted and its sacred spoils taken to Rome after the sack of Jerusalem was indisputable, memorialised as it had been on the Arch of Titus. It was almost as certain that they'd been kept for the next three hundred years or so in the Temple of Peace commissioned by Vespasian to showcase Roman triumphs, thanks to the witness accounts of people who'd seen them there, including two different rabbis. Rome itself had languished, however, too far from the heart of its own empire to make an efficient capital. That empire had also gradually divided in two, the eastern part administered from Constantinople, the western part from Milan and then Ravenna. But the Visigoths, Alans, Vandals and other tribes to the north of their borders were placed under increasing pressure from invaders of their own, a terrifying new tribe known as the Huns. They'd fled across the Rhine and the Danube into Roman territory. The Romans had dealt with this influx pragmatically at first, allowing them to settle so long as they fought alongside their own armies. But it had proved hard to assimilate their huge numbers, so they'd come into conflict too – notably with the Visigoths and their king Alaric, who'd fought bravely for them for a while but who then wanted a homeland of their own in return. They'd invaded Italy to put pressure on the emperor, before losing patience and sacking Rome in CE 410, destroying forever that city's aura of invincibility.

But Zara leaped straight over all this intervening history to land in the 430s instead. 'There was a Vandal general called Geiseric,' she said. 'He made his way from Spain to North Africa, where he seized Carthage and modern Tunisia. It was a major setback for the Romans, for Carthage provided Rome with much of its bread. The emperor was forced to strike a deal under which Geiseric's son went to live at his court. He got engaged to his daughter while he was there, but she then married someone else instead. Geiseric was furious. He sailed to Italy and plundered Rome of everything he could get his hands on, including our sacred treasures, taking them back to Carthage with him.'

'From where Justinian seized them back again,' said Avram, finishing the timeline for her, 'only to get spooked by this wandering Jew into sending them on down here.'

'That's what the mosaic implies, yes.'

He squinted at her. 'And you think it's for real?'

'I think it would be unforgivable not to check. I mean, can you imagine what a hero that person would be, the one who recovers the Menorah? Our new David Ben-Gurion, the nation at his feet.'

Avram smiled. He was no fool, yet nor was he immune to daydreams. 'Tomorrow, then,' he said.

Chapter Six

I

Ricardo Savanelli was enjoying the evening *passeggiata*, pushing his wife's wheelchair along Corso Mazzini. Enjoying, to be specific, the chance to study all these people with whom they shared Cosenza. Stately men with Vandyke beards strolling with their hands behind their backs. Doting mothers being stopped every few moments for a cluck. Dog owners feigning deep interest in shop windows while their best friends did their business on the cobbles. Elegant fops with cashmere scarves thrown nonchalantly over their shoulders. Pretty girls with show-pony hair and high-heeled trots.

They were almost at the town hall when Ricardo's editor called. It was a bittersweet conversation. His semi-retirement had left him at a loose end, so that the summons in itself was welcome. Yet the double murder and the seeming return of the local 'Ndrangheta would have broken his heart if he'd still had one to break. His wife folded her arms when he told her, but she knew what his work meant to him, so he wheeled her back to the car to drive her home, then headed off alone.

The murders had happened barely fifteen minutes away. He tuned to local radio. The on-scene reporter knew nothing, covering ignorance with blather. He fought a yawn. He was tired all the damned time these days, though he almost lived in bed. He reached for one of the energy drinks in the glove compartment to guzzle it as he drove, though his bladder would pay for it later.

There were vehicles parked all the way out onto the road. He pulled up behind a TV van. The slope was such that he ratcheted his handbrake as tight as it would go then left it in first gear too.

He pocketed his notepad, pencil, camera and phone, then set off. An ambulance passed by, no siren on but its blue lights flashing. He bowed his head respectfully, just in case, then muttered an oath at the 'Ndrangheta and spat at the ground. A white van emerged from the drive as he reached it, the young goateed man at the wheel shielding his face from the TV cameras as an *ispettore* gave a preliminary briefing to the media. He could tell from the tone that it was designed to placate rather than inform so he walked on by.

Everyone knew his face. It gave him licence. A grizzled sergeant held his gaze for a full second, and thus the deal was done. For the usual small fee, he'd get copies of preliminary reports and photographs. But he wanted something more.

Giuseppe Macron, the town's chief coroner, was supervising the loading of a pair of body bags into the back of another ambulance. He raised an eyebrow. Macron nodded and turned his back. Ricardo made the sign of the cross then unzipped the bag just enough to see the face within. A silver-haired man, familiar in that way people are when you've shared a town your whole life. He crossed himself again before unzipping the second bag. This one was a punch to his gut. A young woman who'd waited tables at his favourite cafe the past two summers. Her prettiness and boundless good cheer had led him to drink far more coffee than was good for him, and to concoct pathetic fantasies about her finding herself in trouble and turning to the grizzled hack for help.

But not like this. Never like this.

Fifty years ago, Ricardo had been a warrior. He'd sincerely believed he could make a difference. But the Mafia ground one down. Cynicism was the only way to stay sane. Yet looking down at that poor girl, cheated of her life like this, a pulse of that youthful wrath beat again inside him. He felt the need not just to report but to make a difference. And he wouldn't do that here, on ground trodden bare by others.

He drove on up the road until he came to the next building, a shabby apartment block with parking to its rear. It was hard to see through the frosted-glass front door, but he could hear TVs going inside. He pressed various buzzers until he was finally let in by a fat middle-aged man in a tracksuit so tight that he looked to have been inflated inside it with a foot pump. He tried to turn his TV off with his remote but the battery was failing so he had to do it by hand. His kitchen bin was overflowing with crushed pizza boxes, his sink with dirty plates. He offered Ricardo water then took the last beer for himself, pouring it into a clouded glass. 'So,' he said, sitting at the rickety kitchen table. 'Someone got Vittorio at last, huh?'

'You knew him?'

The man nodded, closed his eyes and pinched his nose, embarrassed by the story he was about to tell. 'I came here two years back. A single screw-up these days, it's like thirty years of marriage mean nothing. Anyway. The doorbell goes. It's Vittorio, with a bottle of wine, welcoming me to the neighbourhood. We shared his bottle then one of mine. We commiserated about our marriages. His had gone wrong too. His wife had lost faith in him. That's how he put it. He had a dream, and she'd lost faith in it. I asked him what dream. He told me he was about to find the lost tomb of Alaric the Great and the billion euros worth of treasure inside. And he was *this* close. He couldn't tell me the details, obviously, but he and his daughter had it for sure now. Only he needed to buy the land, and he didn't quite have enough.'

Ricardo fought down a smile. 'How much?'

The man flushed. 'You never met the guy. He seemed so certain. And he showed me all the artefacts he'd found. His house is a fucking shrine.'

'A shrine?'

'Okay, fine, he has a room in it like a museum. Though I swear it was religious with him. Apparently some fortune teller had promised his great-great-grandfather or something that a Surace would one day find Alaric, so his family had been looking ever since, and finally they had it. I asked him how he could be sure. He made me vow silence on my children. Then he showed me this money belt he wore beneath his shirt, in which he kept his special treasures.'

'Special treasures?'

'A gold coin dating to the right era. A pair of Visigothic brooches. A signet ring. Things like that. All found on this one small plot of land he wanted to buy. So, we made a deal. A thousand euros for a quarter share. We even signed a contract. Then the guy upstairs saw Vittorio leaving here one day, came down to warn me. Apparently, Vittorio had tapped him up two years before, as he'd tapped up pretty much everyone round here. They all of them had contracts and part shares. And those coins and brooches he'd apparently just found – the bastard had been showing them off for years.'

Ricardo grunted. Pull a trick like that on the 'Ndrangheta, you might as well climb into your own coffin and wait for them to hammer down the lid. 'Did you challenge him?' he asked.

'Of course. I demanded he give me his gold coin. But the guy was impossible. He'd show you something new and turn your head again. And your grip on it would loosen a little more.' He shook his head sadly. 'I'll never see my money again, will I?'

'Think of it as a life lesson.'

'Look at me. Don't you think I've had enough life lessons?'

'Can I quote you on this? You'll be in the paper. Maybe even a photograph.'

'No photograph. And no mention of the money. I'm behind on my payments, you see. My wife would fillet me.'

Ricardo nodded and closed his notebook. 'Your upstairs neighbour. The one who warned you. Which apartment?'

'Nine.'

He thanked him and went up. There was no one home. His knee was playing up badly by now, so he went to the car to wait. For years there'd been rumours about jewellery and other valuables going missing from the coroner's office under Giuseppe Macron's watch. He scrolled through his contacts for his number then placed the call, catching him as he was locking up after logging the bodies in, off home before his dinner got cold.

'I need a favour,' said Ricardo.

'Go on.'

'I've spoken to three different sets of the Suraces' neighbours now,' he told him. 'All three tell me the same thing. That Vittorio always wore a money belt.'

There was a pause. 'A money belt. Is that right?'

'That's what all three tell me. They've given me a list of its contents too, including a gold coin, a pair of Gothic brooches and a signet ring. So now I'm wondering, what if this is connected to the murders somehow? What if they're even the motive? I mean, think about it. If any of those or the other pieces they told me about are missing, then whoever has them must be the murderer, right? What do you think?'

More silence at the other end. Ricardo could almost hear the anger. 'Let me go see,' Macron said finally. 'I'll call you back.'

'A call would be great,' said Ricardo, opening his car door, the better to flex his knee. 'But a photograph would be better.'

II

They broke out the beers, the shots, the pills, the lines of coke. They closed the shutters, turned down the lights and pushed the furniture back against the walls before blasting out a series of their favourite tunes to sing along to, leaping around the room yelling violence against the Jews and all the other scum while doing stiff-armed salutes. None of it made Dieter feel any better. No matter how many stiff-armed salutes they did, nothing ever seemed to change. Besides, dancing with other men was what faggots did, and the only woman here was strapped to a chair in the corner of the room with its mascara running, snot coming out of its nose and tape over its mouth. And every time he caught its eye it reminded him of how on the boat it had pressed its leg against the leg of Cesco Fucking Rossi PhD and the rage would flare again like oil squirted on a bonfire. He strode across to the music system and turned it off. They all stopped dancing and started looking foolish instead. Oddo was about to say something but then he saw his face and shut up. 'Do something useful,' he snarled. 'Find that fucker for me.'

'We looked,' said Knöchel. 'He's nowhere.'

'He drove me into a wall,' said Dieter. 'He fucked my fucking Harley.'

'It'll be repaired by tomorrow lunch,' said Oddo. 'We can pick it up—'

'I don't care. I don't fucking care. No one does that to the Hammerskins. No one.'

'Yes, boss.'

They broke out their laptops and their phones to pursue their futile search. Knöchel put on the TV for the local news, in case the afternoon's events had been picked up. Then Dieter himself went over to Anna, strapped wrist and ankle to a high-backed dining-room chair. 'One last chance,' he said. 'Where the fuck is he? I know you fucking know. Don't you dare tell me again that you don't. Don't you fucking dare.' But it only turned its head away from him and sobbed like a two-year-old. Fuck, it was ugly when it cried. He couldn't believe he'd put his prick in it. Rage built in him like a pyre. It blazed so fiercely that, if once he gave himself up to it, Anna would be dead before he stopped. And landing himself with a body here would be madness. Disposal was hard enough back home.

People tended to judge Dieter by his tattoos and biker gear. He liked it that way. It made them underestimate him. But he was a man of intelligence as well as violence. He'd taken the Stuttgart Hammerskins from a whites-only social club to the top player in the city's underworld. Their primary source of income was cocaine imported from Colombia and Brazil via the container terminal of Gioia Tauro just a short drive north of here. It had been easy money until their 'Ndrangheta suppliers had been taken down in a huge bust a year back. They'd been scrambling ever since, but now they needed a proper replacement. That was why he'd come here with his crew, to put new arrangements in place. The Alaric shipwreck nearby had been a happy coincidence, giving them a convenient excuse for the trip and a way to kill time between meetings. But now those meetings would have to wait. Because reputation came first. If people thought they could fuck with him and live, he was done. Yet how the hell was he to get even with Rossi if he couldn't even find him?

'Shit,' muttered Knöchel.

Dieter glanced around. The news was on TV, some prick in uniform wailing about a father and daughter who'd just been offed in the town of Cosenza. 'So the swarthies are topping each other,' he scowled. 'Why should we care?'

'No,' said Knöchel. He picked up the remote, rewound the TV a minute, then set it playing. 'Watch,' he said. 'Watch in the background.'

Curious, Dieter wandered over. An ambulance bumped by, siren off but its blue lights flashing. Then a white van with a Hawaiian dancing girl on its dashboard and an A.C. Milan banner on its side, its driver hiding his face from the cameras. Only it jolted over a pothole at that moment, briefly jarring away his forearm. Knöchel froze the picture. They gathered close to look. Dieter stared at the screen in disbelief. The bastard had trimmed his beard and freed his ponytail. But there was no doubt, no doubt at all.

It was Cesco Fucking Rossi PhD.

III

Cesco headed away from Cosenza as fast as his old van and the country lanes would allow. He didn't remember these roads at all, and quickly got hopelessly lost – until to his relief he came to a junction with a sign directing him down to the Tyrrhenian coast. The road was new. It wended around craggy mountainsides and crossed deep canyons on tall thin bridges with views down to Paola's saw-toothed coastline and twinkling lights. Ideally, he'd have put more distance between himself and Cosenza, but the day's exertions finally caught up with him, and it was a struggle to keep his eyes open even long enough to find a spot to park for the night, in a small cul-de-sac away from street lighting and with a water fountain nearby.

He was too hungry to crash, however, so he took his laptop to a pizzeria for a *funghi* and a beer, using their Wi-Fi to scour the web for news. To his immense relief, he found not a word about any incidents in Scilla or any mention of his own name. He ordered another bottle of beer to celebrate, took it back to the van. He laid out his bedroll and sleeping bag, made a pillow of his towel. It was still early, but he was drained and there was nothing to stay up for, so he undressed and climbed in. Footsteps passed outside; a woman urged her dog to do its business against his wheel. He waited until she had passed then turned onto his side. Thoughts from the day kept jabbing at him, of Dieter and his mates, of Giulia and her father lying there with their throats slit beside the pretty American woman with the short fair hair. He kept them at bay with happier fantasies, threading his way between hapless defenders before bending the ball around the keeper to score the winner for—

Don't leave me, she'd said. *Don't leave me.*

He sat up abruptly in the back of the van, covered in sweat, his heart hammering. He buried his face in his hands.

What on earth had he been thinking, going back to Cosenza?

What on earth had he been thinking?

IV

Baldassare Mancuso was still at his desk when Cosenza's chief of police rang to inform him of the murders. It was ostensibly a courtesy call, because they didn't yet fall under Baldassare's jurisdiction, despite their strong whiff of 'Ndrangheta. But the real reason, he knew, was to gloat a little. Having an anti-Mafia team on his doorstep and looking into his city was both an inconvenience and a reproach, and this was his opportunity to point out that getting rid of such people was easier said than done. He tried to return to work after the call, but his concentration was gone. He kept getting up to walk around the room, possessed of a troubling excitement. He knew better than anyone that the Cosenza Mafia were still active, even with the Critelli brothers and their top brass in custody.

It was the nature of the beast.

Italy's other leading Mafias – Sicily's Cosa Nostra, Naples' Camorra and the Pugliese Sacra Corona Unita – were organised rather like large corporations with multiple divisions, each of which recruited ambitious youngsters to fight their way up the ranks. But Calabria's 'Ndrangheta was more like a loose collection of family firms. These were individually known as 'ndrines, and were run by men who groomed their sons almost from the cradle to follow in their footsteps.

Turning such people *pentiti* was therefore far harder, for it meant they had to inform on and betray their families, not just their colleagues and rivals.

The structure had another strength too. Calabria had seen mass emigration over the past century and a half, so that – for example – the Critelli brothers and their top brass had numerous cousins and other kin spread all across Europe, South America and Australasia, making their drug smuggling and other such international ventures into family affairs, and thus far harder to penetrate.

Yet penetrate it Baldassare had.

It had started, as so often, with a lucky break. A Cosenza lowlife called Pietro Schillaci had been caught with a handgun during a routine traffic stop. When the gun had been tied to a gang killing, Baldassare had gone to interview him. He had a knack for getting such men to like and even trust him. So it had been with Schillaci. The Critelli brothers must have learned how close he was to turning on them, for he'd been ambushed in the jail one day, stabbed fifteen times with a sharpened toothbrush. Baldassare himself had announced Schillaci's death in a furious address from the hospital steps. He'd vowed darkly to find the people behind the hit, and make them pay. In truth, Schillaci had survived. They'd smuggled him into this very villa, itself the proceeds of a previous campaign against this same Cosenza 'ndrine, and he'd told Baldassare everything he'd known.

A period of intensive surveillance had followed. They'd come to know the Critelli brothers and their Cosenza 'ndrine in all its malignant detail – the beatings, the murders, the protection, the corrupt contracts, the police backhanders. Wherever there was money to be made, there they found the Critellis at work. But nothing made money like drugs. A tapped phone call hinted at a vast consignment of cocaine about to arrive at Gioia Tauro, source of eighty per cent of Europe's supply. Five metric tons of it, with a street value of half a billion euros. They couldn't risk letting it out of the container terminal so they'd swooped in the following morning, while also raiding dozens of homes and businesses around Cosenza and arresting over a hundred suspects, many still in their pyjamas.

Baldassare had hoped these raids would net him the smoking gun he lacked. It had not. The Critellis were too smart, their network of cut-outs and offshore companies too opaque. For the past year he'd been striving to put together a case against them that a jury would understand. But he wasn't certain that he'd yet succeeded, and now he was out of time. This Sunday would be his last day. The press conference for his announcement had already been arranged. And his choice was simple. One option was to prosecute the Critelli brothers and the rest for conspiracy to commit organised crime. But that would be a gamble, one that could easily result in acquittals for them all, which would be a catastrophe. The more cautious option would be to drop the conspiracy charges against the brothers and their top brass, and bring separate charges only against those foot soldiers where his evidence was watertight. But that would be seen, quite rightly, as a wretched failure.

An email notification interrupted his meditation. The first police reports on tonight's murders had arrived. His eyes were weary of his screen so he sent them to his printer, then he poured himself a stiff brandy and settled down to read.

Chapter Seven

I

It was one of those dreams that Carmen knew to be a dream, yet which was somehow convincing all the same. She was at the pulpit of a huge church of velvety darkness and fluttery candlelight, while the hushed congregation waited expectantly for her to pay tribute to the people in the caskets on either side, whose names and identities she couldn't for the life of her recall. She sensed, moreover, that men of ill intent were watching her from the shadows, and her discomfort grew so acute that she forced herself to open her eyes.

She was lying on her back in a hospital bed in a private room with the early morning sunlight reflecting off the slatted blinds to paint watery yellow stripes upon her ceiling. Her mouth was dry, her temple throbbed and she had such a strong sense that someone else really was in the room that she lifted her head to look. An elderly black man in a charcoal suit beneath a loose white medical coat smiled benignly at her from the foot of her bed. He had lively grey hair, rounded shoulders and a faint tremor in his left hand, in which he was holding a clipboard. 'How are you feeling?' he asked.

'Good. I mean… Good.'

'Do you remember what happened? Why you are here?'

She closed her eyes to think. The train journey, Giulia, Vittorio, a truck in the trees, men in balaclavas swearing her to silence, the shame of lying to the police and that Oxford archaeologist. Arriving by ambulance, an impatient young doctor shining his torch into her eyes. A CAT scan revealing nothing to alarm, yet being woken twice by nurses in the small hours even so, lest she'd slipped into a coma. Yet all so fragmented and uncertain that any part of it might be imagined. 'I think so, yes.'

He nodded. 'We found ketamine in your blood.' He came around the bed to touch a sticking plaster on the inside of her left elbow, which – now that she was aware of it – began to throb. 'They must have injected you with it.'

'Ketamine?'

'An anaesthetic. It can play havoc with the memory.'

'Oh,' she said. She was too tired to care. 'But it'll wear off, right?'

'Yes.'

'Good. Then…?'

'Then?'

'What now?'

He smiled with great gentleness. 'You took a severe blow to the head. From what you told my colleagues last night, you were unconscious even before the ketamine.' His expression didn't alter, yet somehow she sensed scepticism, though no reproach. 'There is no great sign of trauma or swelling. But brains are unpredictable. It is our protocol here to keep someone in your situation under observation for twenty-four hours from the time the injury was sustained. Until this evening, then, assuming no adverse reaction. Six o'clock, say.'

'And… what about money?'

'Do you not have insurance?'

'Yes.'

'Well then.' He smiled reassuringly. 'Try to rest. I'll be back later.'

She waited until he was gone, then peeled back the sticking plaster to inspect the tiny red scab beneath, surrounded by a *café au lait* bruise. Her overnight bag and her purse were both on the floor against the wall. She sat up, only to feel so woozy that she lay straight back down again. She gave herself a minute then tried again, taking it more slowly. Better. She fetched over both her bags to check them. Her passport was gone, of course, but everything else was there. She tried to turn on her phone, but its battery was flat, so she plugged it in to recharge then flopped exhausted back into bed, and let herself doze.

When she woke again, she felt much stronger. She unlocked her phone with her thumb then checked, with a certain trepidation, for messages. She was both relieved and a tiny bit dismayed to discover that there weren't any. It was the middle of the night back home, of course. Besides, how would anyone know of her condition until she told them? An update, then. She needed to couch it perfectly, however, or her mother would freak out and insist on catching the next plane over – the very last thing Carmen wanted. So she took a selfie with a thumbs up then set about composing an upbeat new post for her Facebook page.

II

The van's antique suspension groaned and creaked as Cesco sat up, cold, stiff and drained from yesterday's craziness. He yawned expansively then slung his towel over his shoulder and made his way to the water fountain, where he brushed his teeth and spat white foam down at the drain, soaped and dried his face and chest and beneath his arms. A net curtain twitched in an upstairs window. An elderly woman stared disapprovingly down. He winked at her and felt cheered.

He dressed then headed into town. A kiosk owner was folding newspapers into racks. The local daily had gone big on the Surace murders. He bought a copy, still warm from its bundle, and walked on. A large woman in a red apron was setting out tables and chairs on the pavement. Her shutters were still half closed, but he gave her his warmest smile and she made him coffee, muttering and shaking her head at him the whole time. He drank it at the counter, checking each of the stories for his name, relieved to find only a couple of references to a family friend who'd come across the tragedy and called the emergency services.

There was, however, plenty of speculation about who to blame, and their motive for the murders. Vittorio Surace had got in too deep with the Cosenza 'Ndrangheta, it appeared, for which recklessness he and his daughter had both paid. What startled Cesco was why. There was a photograph on an inside page of various artefacts, supposedly from Alaric's tomb, that Vittorio had discovered near the Busento. That was why they'd needed the packing case they'd had Carmen bring down from Sapienza University. It had contained a ground-penetrating radar, as it turned out, with which to survey the plot in question before they started digging. That surely explained why Giulia had invited him too, for she'd believed him to be an experienced field archaeologist who'd used such equipment before.

He drummed his fingers on the countertop. According to the story, the Suraces had taken the location of Alaric's tomb with them to their graves. Which put Carmen Nero's lies from last night in a very different light. She'd known what was in the packing case, he was sure of it. The only question was whether she'd known where they'd planned to look. His heart began to pump a little faster. What if Alaric's tomb really was out there somewhere, waiting to be discovered? What if the person best placed to find it was lying in Cosenza Hospital, shaken by yesterday's traumas and in dire need of a friend – preferably one with excellent English who she was already disposed to trust?

If Cesco couldn't take advantage of this, he needed to find himself a new line of work. He drained his coffee, folded his paper beneath his arm and hurried to his van.

III

Carmen dozed off again after posting her Facebook update, then woke to the abrupt entry of a formidable tall young man in dark shirt and suit, wearing mirror sunglasses and an earpiece, a holster strapped to his belt. Without a word, he checked the cupboard and bathroom and beneath her bed. He closed her blinds then returned to the door to beckon someone out of view. A second man now came in. He could hardly have looked more different. Short, portly, bearded, rumpled, in his mid fifties, with that kind of grey tiredness that comes from weeks without proper sleep. He gestured at a chair, asking permission to set it by her bed. She was too bewildered to do anything but nod. Relief washed over him as he stretched out his legs in front of him. 'My name is Mancuso,' he said, extending the penultimate vowel in that lovely Italian way. 'Baldassare Mancuso.'

Carmen nodded. She recognised the name. 'The Mafia man.'

His smile made him look ten years younger. 'The *anti*-Mafia man, if you please.'

'Of course. Sorry. I didn't mean to—'

'Forgive me. I only tease.'

'Oh,' she said. 'But why are you here? Was yesterday... *Mafia?*'

'That is what I hope to establish.'

'And you think I can help? I only wish. But I know nothing, I'm afraid.' She touched her temple. 'I hit my head, you see. I was out the whole time.'

'Yes. So I understand from what you told my friend the *ispettore*. I read his notes last night.' He leaned forward with his hands on his knees, as if uncertain how to proceed. Then he glanced around at the door, at his two men on guard outside, and seemed to find his way. 'I live in a villa a short drive outside Cosenza. A very nice villa, at the top of a hill. I hardly ever leave it any more. Too much work to do. And also because, whenever I do go out, I put so many people at risk. Myself, of course. I am nothing like so brave as the stories would have you believe. But also everyone I pass on the street, and those I go to see. People like you. Most of all, though, I worry for my bodyguards. The handsome young man who checked your room just now is called Manfredo. He is twenty-five years old. His daughter celebrated her first birthday last month. And now his wife is expecting again. Yet he *volunteered* to be my bodyguard. He volunteered, despite the danger, because he believes my work – *our* work, I should say – is helping to make our country better. That's quite something, don't you think?'

'Yes. Yes, it is.'

'So you can see why I think I owe him and his comrades a responsibility not to leave my villa without good cause. Yet here I am anyway, even though you remember nothing, even though the murders of your friend and her father are not my case. I am here because of the various statements and reports I received about what happened last night. I read them again and again. Then I lay awake all night brooding on them. Which is crazy! I have insane amounts of work to do, and no time in which to do it! I can't afford to lie awake! But I couldn't get it out of my head. There is something about it all that I don't understand, you see. And I badly, *badly* need to understand it.'

'And?' asked Carmen. 'What is it?'

He gave her an apologetic smile. 'I need to understand why those bastards let you live.'

Chapter Eight

I

Zara was first to arrive at the prison that morning. She checked in with security, who she persuaded with some effort to allow her to wander around the side of the prison, between its huge exterior slab wall and the perimeter wire fence. The sun climbed higher. She stood in the wall's shrinking shade and stared out over the plateau. It had a real shimmer to it today, hot sandy wastes beneath a sky of perfect blue. The terrain here was high, exposed, dry and windswept, so that soil had never settled, leaving it almost completely barren save for the very hardiest of plants. Only the fact that it was made of dolomitic limestone, from which Jerusalem's entire Old City had been built, had ever given it any real value. Yet people had been spilling blood over it for millennia, rival dogmas clashing like sharpened blades.

And no one could deny there was a beauty to its starkness.

She checked her watch again. The others were running late. Getting anything moving on *Shabbat* was always hard, and particularly in times of tension. Religious observance was a kind of patriotism, a flag to wave. She did not attend synagogue any more herself, except when courtesy demanded. It felt too much like a lie. Yet childhood habits died hard, and working on *Shabbat* still felt transgressive. Particularly their work today. For every activity specifically prohibited by the Torah had something or other to do with the tabernacle, even though no part of the tabernacle had existed in many, many centuries.

Yet maybe that was about to change.

The thought made her shiver, despite the heat of the day. She crouched to place her palm upon bare rock. If the Menorah truly were somewhere beneath… She felt apprehension as much as excitement. She heard the scratch of footsteps behind her, looked around to see Kaufman, hands clasped behind his back like a kindly schoolteacher. 'A penny for them,' he said.

'Earth, earth, earth,' she told him.

His eyebrows shot up in surprise then stayed there in thought. To live and work in Jerusalem was to suffer daily reminders of the perplexing core of Jewish faith. Their first temple laid low by the Babylonians, their second by the Romans. How could this have happened to God's chosen people? How could His sacred treasures have been looted and lost? For many centuries Jewish theologians had wrestled with this conundrum, devising ingenious explanations that typically ascribed it to God's inscrutable plan – one that would culminate in His triumphant return at the end of days. One of these, the *Apocalypse of Baruch*, explained away the loss of the temple treasures by claiming that they'd never left Israel at all, but had instead been buried by an angel in the desert outside Jerusalem, and that their recovery would signal not just the restoration of Jerusalem but the start of the Apocalypse. *Earth, earth, earth*, it went. *Hear the word of Almighty God. Receive these things which I commit to you, and guard them until the Last Times.*

Kaufman nodded soberly. 'I thought you no longer believed in all that.'

'I don't,' she admitted. 'But think how many others do. And how far they'll go to make it happen.'

II

Carmen's heart thumped like a beaten rug at Baldassare's question. 'Why is it a mystery that they let me live?' she asked. 'Surely they'd have needed a reason to kill me, not the other way around.'

'No,' said Baldassare. 'Forgive me, but no.'

'Then how come I'm still here?'

'Exactly,' he said.

They gazed at each other for several seconds. There was no mean-
ness in Baldassare's expression, but no softness either. Yet Carmen had
too much at stake to yield. 'You'll need to explain,' she said.

He nodded. 'I have dealt with the Calabrian Mafia for many, many
years,' he told her. 'My first big case as a lawyer, I worked on the team
that prosecuted a man who set off a car bomb in a crowded market to
protest the arrest of one of his bosses. Nineteen people dead, including
five children. You should have seen him in the interviews. It was his
job, he didn't care one jot. If anything, he was proud of what he'd done
– a soldier who'd successfully performed a hard duty. Later on, another
group of them slaughtered fifteen members of a single family gathered
in a Cosenza restaurant for a funeral lunch, including a four-year-old
boy who somehow survived the first fusillade and took refuge behind
a counter. They dragged him out by his ankle and shot him through
the head.'

Carmen felt sick. 'Why are you telling me this?'

'Because these are the same men who let you live last night. The
same kind of men, I should say. And such men don't let anyone live.
Not if they might talk.'

'How could I talk? I told you, I was unconscious the whole time.'

'Yes. But how could they know that? How could they know *for
sure*? Unconsciousness is the easiest thing in the world to feign. And if
you were so obviously unconscious why bother with ketamine? The
injection might even wake you. Also, they taped your wrists, ankles
and mouth, so why not your eyes too, to make sure you couldn't see?
Another thing. I can understand people driving around with adhesive
tape in their car. But what kind of person drives around with ketamine
and a syringe?'

'I thought you said they were Mafia.'

'Yes. And it would make sense if they'd taken a hostage. But they
took no one hostage, as I understand. They killed your two friends
but let you live. And I want to know why. Though I must confess I
do have one idea.'

'Which is?' she asked, her voice betraying her with its croak.

'I think they let you live because you are young and pretty and –
most importantly of all – American. We have a history here in Italy

77

of young, pretty American women involved in murder investigations. Everything goes crazy. On TV, it is non-stop. News crews fly in from around the world. Our leaders grow embarrassed over the lack of progress. They demand results, no matter the cost. We duly flood the area with officers, we arrest everyone we see, we search every building within twenty kilometres. So, then, if I am an 'Ndrangheta killer, I am going to think *very* carefully before killing a young and pretty American woman.'

'Well, then. There's your answer.'

'Yes. Except now a different puzzle. If you were unconscious the whole time, how would they know you were American?'

'Maybe Giulia said something. Maybe they looked in my purse. My passport was in there.'

'It *was* in there?' he frowned. 'Are you saying it's gone?'

'No. That wasn't what I meant at all.'

'Then you have it still?'

Carmen's face burned. 'I don't know. I haven't checked yet.'

Baldassare frowned. 'You were the victim of a terrible assault and you haven't even checked your purse?'

'I only just woke. It hadn't occurred to me.'

'Yet your phone is on the charger.'

'I had to check for messages. I thought people might be worried.'

'Ah. Of course.' His chair creaked as he sat back. 'Then perhaps you should check now.'

'For my passport?'

'Just to be sure.'

'Of course.' She reached for her purse and went through the charade for him, feigning relief over her plastic and cash, horror at her missing passport.

'You're quite sure you brought it down with you?' he asked.

'I take it everywhere.'

'Could it have fallen out?'

'I keep it zipped.'

He leaned forward, resting his weight once more upon his knees. 'So they take your passport from your purse, yet leave your cash and

78

credit cards. How very odd. Can you think why they might have done that?'

'No.'

'Here's a thought. Do you think maybe it was because they didn't want you leaving the country for a while?'

She swallowed. 'Why would they want that?'

'So that you couldn't go somewhere you felt safe, to tell us what you knew.'

'Except that I know nothing.'

'Yes. Of course. I keep forgetting. You were unconscious the whole time.' But then he looked at her lying there and sighed. 'You must think me a terrible bully, after what you have been through, to press you like this. But I have good reasons, I assure you. Reasons you would understand and sympathise with, if I could share.' He fell silent again. 'What if I were to speak to your consulate, to arrange for you to fly back anyway? Would you tell us then?'

'Tell you what?' she said desperately. 'I don't know a thing.'

He nodded sadly. 'Let me tell you a story. One story, and then I go. It is about that restaurant massacre I mentioned. It was of a family called the Carbones, headed by a man called Federico who once owned the villa I now use for my headquarters. We took it as the proceeds of crime, you see, because he was a Mafia boss himself, the right-hand man of a charmer called Luca Critelli, who used to run the 'Ndrangheta here, until his own sons had him gunned down for holding them back. Anyway, this man Federico Carbone. He inducted his own two sons into the 'ndrine when they were just fourteen, but when it came to his grandchildren he finally baulked. His eldest were twins, you see. Giovanni and Claudia, the apples of his eyes. And the violence of the Critelli brothers came to sicken him, so that he couldn't bear the thought of his grandson Giovanni being inducted too, making vows to such men. He made contact with me, therefore, and promised to turn *pentiti* in exchange for immunity. I agreed. He was as good as his word. His information enabled us to arrest the brothers and their top lieutenants. We still needed his testimony to convict them all, however, but the day before the trial opened, he put a shotgun in his mouth and pulled the trigger.'

'What? Why?'

'The trial broke down. We had to let the Critellis go. After the funeral, Federico's immediate family went together to that Cosenza restaurant I mentioned. That's where the gunmen got them. They killed them all, including the four-year old. The only bodies we never found were those of the twins. That was how we learned. People working for the Critelli brothers had taken them hostage a couple of weeks or so before. They'd made a deal with Federico to let them go if he killed himself before testifying. So that's what he did. Then they murdered his whole family anyway.'

Carmen felt sick. 'The twins too?'

Baldassare nodded. 'We arrested a man down in Reggio the following year, for something else. Sometimes, truly wicked men get the urge to clear their consciences. It's astonishing to watch. So it was with him. He told us about his involvement in numerous murders, including the twins. He owned a boat, you see. He was paid to sail it up to Paola one night, where three men were waiting. They had two bodies in the boot of their car. A boy and a girl. They carried them aboard, along with old engine blocks and lengths of chain to dump at sea. They sailed them out then came back empty.'

'Why are you telling me this?'

'Because I need you to understand something. You cannot – *you absolutely cannot* – trust such men. They have no honour, no kindness, no mercy. They promised Federico that they'd let his family live if he killed himself. Yet they murdered them all anyway. Because that is who they are. They will say *anything* to get you to do what they want. They will weep and plead and swear on their mothers' lives. And good people like yourself will believe them, because you want to. But, the moment it suits them, they will betray their vows without a qualm, and mock you for having believed them too. So whatever they promise you, I swear...' He stopped unexpectedly, he stared down at the floor. Half a minute passed. To Carmen's astonishment, his shoulders began to hump. She reached out to touch him only to stop shy. He shielded his eyes with his hand, took out a tissue to dab them dry. 'My job,' he said, as he put it away again. 'The things I see. The things I do. It takes a toll.'

'I understand,' she said. 'And if there was anything…'

He nodded several times. She could see the weakness pass, a new hardness take its place. 'Do you mean that?' he asked. 'Because there *are* things you can do.'

'Oh,' she said. 'Like what?'

'My colleagues in the police are still collecting evidence, as you can imagine. They will need to take your fingerprints, in order to exclude them. Your DNA too. And another statement, with an official translator this time.'

'Another statement? But I know nothing.'

'Even so. Just in case. Also, we've found reconstructions to be surprisingly helpful. We can find another blue Fiat pickup to drive you through Cosenza at the same time of day, to see if it jogs memories.'

She frowned at him. 'You want to make it look like I'm cooperating. Even though it's dangerous for me. *Because* it's dangerous.'

'I'm trying to solve a murder,' he replied. 'The murder of your friend and her father. Don't you want that too?' He pushed himself to his feet. 'You'll never be safe while these men are free. Nor at peace.' He took out his wallet then set a business card on her bedside table. 'You're a good person. I can tell. Too good to keep your silence. The time will come when you need to talk. Don't go to the police when that happens. It pains me to say this, but they're too badly infiltrated. What they learn, the 'Ndrangheta will soon learn too. No. When the time comes, *this* is the number to call.'

III

Cesco was a naturally quick learner when it came to his scams. A year and a half pretending to be an assistant professor on sabbatical had given him enough knowledge about Alaric and the Visigoths to fool almost anyone he met. But Carmen Nero wasn't almost anyone. She was a doctoral student writing a thesis on Galla Placidia, the Roman empress taken hostage by Alaric while she'd still been a teenage girl, before going on to marry his brother-in-law Athaulf and later becoming Rome's de facto regent. He'd never bluff her for long without a serious refresher. His first act on returning to Cosenza, therefore, was to find himself a cafe with Wi-Fi where he speed-read papers on Galla Placidia herself, on Alaric's other contemporaries, on fourth-century Roman coinage, on ground-penetrating radar, fibulae and Gothic burial practices. He grew so absorbed that he lost track of time until a waiter came to stand beside his table, tapping his foot. Cesco looked up. The cafe that had been empty on his arrival was now so full for lunch that it was either order something more or leave. He settled up then squatted on the pavement outside to use their Wi-Fi for one final task, searching for and reserving a suitable apartment.

There was a greengrocer next to the cafe. He bought four oranges and a bunch of grapes then set off. The hospital was undergoing a major refurbishment, its buildings all sheathed in scaffolding and green safety netting. A statue of Padre Pio was draped with votive rosaries, and candles and flowers lay around its base. Cesco looked them over. A cheerful bouquet of tulips would have been perfect, had they not already started to wilt, so he took the half-dozen red roses instead, despite their romantic overtones, then refreshed them by flicking them with crushed diamonds of water from a nearby fountain.

There were signposts on every corner. Unfortunately, thanks to the building work, they kept sending him the wrong way. But finally he found reception. He let it slip, while asking for Carmen's room, that he was one who'd found her and the Suraces the night before. A small crowd quickly gathered. He told them the story with a self-deprecating humility designed to win admiration as well as directions. A charming young nurse volunteered to take him to the second floor, then point him onwards. He gave her a red rose from his bouquet in thanks; her blush put a spring into his step. Then he passed a man with a ravaged face clutching a young boy against his side, and suddenly he felt like shit.

Two burly men pushed through the swing doors ahead, either side of a short, bearded and familiar-looking man struggling to keep up with them, giving him the hurried splayed stride of a man walking barefoot across hot sand. He looked instantly familiar yet still it took Cesco a moment to realise who he was. The moment it came to him, his heart went into overdrive. He stepped back against the wall and dropped his eyes, blanking his expression until they'd passed. Even so, he sensed the bearded man turning to stare at him, as if somehow half recognising him too. But he didn't stop, and soon enough their footsteps faded, and the relief of it made Cesco sag against the wall. He gave himself another minute before heading to the loos to splash water on his face. Then he put himself back into character and went in search of Carmen.

Chapter Nine

It was only a few minutes after Baldassare had left that Carmen received a second visitor. Her saviour from last night peered through the glass panel in her door, and then knocked. She beckoned him in, glad of a friendly face. He came to her bedside to present her with two paper bags of fruit and a small bouquet of red roses. 'How beautiful,' she said, holding them to her nose to breathe in their scent. 'You're so kind.'

'I couldn't have you leave Calabria thinking us all barbarians.'

'I'd never think that. But thank you anyway.' She looked around for somewhere to set everything, before clearing space on her bedside table to lay the roses flat, along with the two bags, which contained respectively four plump oranges and a bunch of grapes that hadn't yet decided whether to grow up green or purple. 'I'm so glad you came. I never thanked you properly last night. You saved my life. Maybe literally.'

'I made a phone call, that's all. How could I do less?' He noticed Baldassare's card. 'So it *was* him,' he murmured. 'Mr Mafia himself.'

'Don't let him hear you call him that. Mr *anti*-Mafia, if you please.'

'What did he want?'

'Oh, this and that. Another statement, for one thing, only with a proper translator.'

'Hey!' protested Cesco.

'Forgive me,' she smiled. 'I should have said an *official* translator.'

'That's more like it.' He settled himself into Baldassare's chair and gazed at her with an unsettling directness. It had been so dark last night, and she so groggy, that she hadn't really taken notice of his looks. Now that she did, she found herself liking what she saw, in particular the startling blue eyes that Giulia had told her of, accentuated as they were by his Mediterranean complexion and long black hair. Indeed, so blue were his eyes that she found she couldn't quite look directly into them. 'I can't believe how much better you look,' he said. 'Last night, you were grey like an English winter. And how I hate an English winter!'

'I'm sorry to have put you through it, then.'

'Oh,' he grinned. 'But that's the thing about England, though, isn't it? The sun always comes out again, and then it's the only place in the world you want to be.' He gazed at her a moment longer, until it became almost intrusive, then suddenly reached for one of the bags of fruit he'd brought. He rummaged through it for an orange, dug his thumb so deep into its navel that juices squirted over his trousers. 'You must tell me the moment you feel tired,' he said, brushing the juice away. 'I know what visitors are like. They never take the hint.'

'Not at all. I like company.'

'And in case I forget to ask later. Is there anything you need? Anything at all? You were poor Giulia's friend, after all. That makes you my responsibility.'

'I'm fine, honestly.'

'You English. Always so polite. Nothing to cause trouble.'

'I'm American,' she told him. 'Causing trouble is what we do best.'

He laughed and peeled off a chunk of skin and pith that he tossed at the bin, only to miss by a wide margin. 'How about money? I hate to be so blunt, but if those monsters stole your purse or—'

'They didn't.'

'A translator, then?'

'My doctor speaks excellent English. And he seems really kind.'

'But this is unacceptable! You have to let me do something. My mother drummed into me this terrible sense of duty, you see. I shall never forgive her for it.'

'You rescued me last night. Isn't that enough?'

'On the contrary, it's the entire problem. Such a mistake to help people, don't you think? They come to matter to you. It's so unfair. It should be the other way around. But it never is. We'll say goodbye and you'll never give me another thought, while I'll be thinking fondly of you for years.' He tore off the last chunk of peel then ripped the

85

orange in two and offered her half. 'Besides, I was hoping that you and I might be able to...' But then he looked at her again, lying there with her head bandaged, and he stopped himself.

'You and I might be able to what?' she asked.

His eyes slid sideways. He crossed one leg over the other and twisted his foot in circles. He was so easy to read, she vowed she'd get him to the poker table. 'Forget it,' he said. 'I shouldn't have brought it up.'

'Brought up what?'

'Seriously. It can wait.'

'I'm fine, honestly. Tell me. Please.'

'Okay,' he sighed. 'But promise to stop me if it gets too much. I mean it. You must promise.' He waited until she nodded, then delved into his bag for a local newspaper already folded to an inside page. 'As I said, I feel a responsibility to you, as Giulia's friend. But I feel another responsibility too, as an archaeologist.' He set the paper on her lap then directed her attention to a colour photograph showing various artefacts on a white background: a gold coin, a signet ring, a pair of brooches and a decorative silver dolphin with its tail torn off, as though it had been wrested from a larger piece. He touched the coin first. 'A Honorius solidus,' he said. 'Minted from 402 to 406 to commemorate victory in the Battle of Verona. That gives us the right date, yes? Now look at the dolphin. Does it not remind you of the gifts Constantine gave to the Basilica of St John? And these two fibulae. I'm no expert on Visigothic jewellery, but they most certainly loved their eagles; and when did the Romans ever use throwing axes?'

'They didn't,' murmured Carmen, but distractedly.

He glanced shrewdly at her. 'What is it?'

She didn't answer, just stared uncertainly at the remaining artefact, an oval semi-precious sealstone ring, dark blue with green and grey flecks, about the size of her thumbnail. It had a device inscribed in it, and faint traces of letters around its edge, but all too badly abraded to make out. Except that it was familiar somehow. 'These were all Vittorio's?' she asked.

Cesco nodded. 'From his money belt.'

'Oh,' she said.

'Oh?'

'When we were driving back from the station, he kept touching his stomach whenever we crossed a bridge. I thought maybe he had an ulcer. But I'll bet he was just checking his belt. You know, like when you see a sign warning of pickpockets, and you instinctively pat your pocket.'

Cesco nodded. 'I don't know if Giulia told you, but I was raised around here. You know how crazes sweep a place? Well, every so often, Cosenza would get swept by Alaric fever. When the river ran low, and the frenzy was on us, the whole city would turn out with spades and metal detectors. No one ever found anything, of course. Except Vittorio, it seems. But that never stopped us.' He gestured at the window. 'The sun is out, it's the weekend. An article in the local paper has a photograph of several valuable artefacts that might easily once have belonged to Alaric and his men, suggesting that his tomb with all its fabled treasure is on the verge of being found. Believe me, this place is about go mad. And what if someone gets lucky? Think of it. All those priceless artefacts looted to be sold off on the black market or even melted down. All that precious knowledge lost forever. It would be the greatest tragedy of modern archaeology. I *can't* let that happen. I… I just *can't*.'

'But… what can you do?'

His look of determination faded. He looked self-conscious suddenly. Aware of his own smallness and absurdity. 'I don't know yet. Except I thought, you being a historian of the era, and me an archaeologist… And both of us knowing Giulia. I thought maybe we could put our heads together…' He looked at her again, lying there in bed, and shook his head. 'Forgive me. I wasn't thinking.'

'No,' she said. 'You're right. You're absolutely right. We need to do this. One hundred per cent. But how?'

He shrugged. 'I did have one thought. Though I'm not sure how much use it will be. Everyone else will be searching for the tomb, right? But people have been searching for the tomb for hundreds of years, and no one has found it yet. So I say let's not do that. Let's use our advantages instead. We know history, we know archaeology.

Most of all, we knew Giulia. She and her father had obviously found something exciting. That's why they called us in. Maybe it was Alaric's tomb, maybe not. But *that's* what we should look for: for whatever the Suraces thought they'd found. If it turns out to be nothing, fine, we can put the whole business behind us. But if it really is Alaric...'

She looked at him doubtfully. 'Sure. But how?'

He sat forward, enthusiasm giving his skin an attractive flush. 'Well, for one thing, you know that packing case Giulia had you bring down? Apparently it contained a ground-penetrating radar. No doubt that's why she invited me along, because those machines are a nightmare to work with if you haven't used them before, which I have. But the point is that that particular model isn't designed to work in water, or even in badly waterlogged places. So why borrow it for the Busento?'

'Maybe it was all the university had. Maybe Giulia didn't know any better.'

'Sapienza will have all sorts. And Giulia was smarter than that.'

Carmen nodded. 'So you're suggesting that whatever they found wasn't directly beneath the river?'

'Exactly.'

'And I was supposed to take it back with me to Rome on Sunday night,' said Carmen, getting into the spirit herself. 'And Vittorio talked of taking me on all kinds of outings while I was here. They must have had a very specific area in mind to be able to promise that on top of everything else.'

'You see!' he beamed. 'A small site far enough from the river to be dry. Already we're making progress. Anything else?'

'There is one thing,' she said hesitantly. It had actually been bothering her for a while. 'Giulia had exams coming up. She'd been studying really hard, but enjoying it too. You know how invigorating revision can be, when it's going well? Anyway, I bumped into her at the library last Sunday. She made a joke about how she'd be virtually living there for the next six weeks. Only when she called me on Thursday night to invite me down, she was already here herself.'

'Something happened, then,' nodded Cesco. 'Sometime between last Sunday and Thursday, something happened that was intriguing enough to bring her down here, despite her exams. Then she realised she needed the GPR, so she called you to have you bring it down.'

'I think so, yes,' agreed Carmen.

Cesco grinned. She grinned too, she couldn't help herself. His excitement was infectious. But then he grew serious again, he checked his watch. 'Look,' he said, 'I've got to go right now, to check out an apartment. I thought if I was to do this properly, I should establish a base here for the next few days. And the place I slept last night, you wouldn't believe how squalid it was. So uncomfortable, and not even its own bathroom!' He raised an eyebrow. 'How about you? Will you be staying here?'

'No, actually,' she said. 'They kick me out at six.'

'Oh,' he said. His ankle began turning its awkward circles again. She vowed to invest in a pack of cards. 'Look,' he said, 'forgive me if this is out of order, but the apartment I'm off to see, it has two bedrooms.'

'Are you suggesting that we share?'

'Forgive me,' he said hurriedly, looking ashamed. 'A stupid idea.'

'No, not at all. If I can't trust the man who just saved my life, who can I trust? Do you have details?'

He took his laptop from his bag. 'See for yourself. Only five-star reviews, Wi-Fi, even a balcony overlooking the Busento. You'll probably think me a fool, but it seemed like an omen.'

She glanced through the pictures. It was everything he said, and nicely furnished, light and spacious too. 'It looks perfect.'

'Then...?'

'Yes. Let's do it.'

'Fantastic. Then how about I go grab it before it goes? Then I can swing by later to pick you up. Six o'clock you said, yes?'

'Yes,' she said. 'Six o'clock.'

'Great,' he grinned. 'I'll see you then.'

She watched him walk to the door and out. Only when he was gone did she realise how cheerful she was suddenly feeling, how inappropriate it was to feel this spirit of adventure. Yet she couldn't altogether shake it. Nor, after the bleak long months she'd just passed, did she much want to. She took another look at the newspaper he'd left her, specifically at the photograph of Vittorio's five artefacts. Again it was the signet ring that caught her eye. She'd seen one just like it before, she was sure of it. But where? For the life of her, it wouldn't come. She took out her laptop from her overnight bag to check the newspaper's website. They had, as she'd hoped, a better version of the picture. She studied it a while without success. But it was important, she knew it in her gut; so she copied and posted it, together with a link to the story, to a late antiquity discussion group she belonged to, asking her fellow members for their help.

Chapter Ten

I

The apartment's owner lived abroad, but their downstairs neighbour kept two spare sets of keys. Cesco handed over cash for the next four days then let himself in. He put his gear in the single bedroom, leaving Carmen the double en suite. Now he needed supplies. There was a cluster of shops and a cafe downstairs, but it was also market day along the river embankment, so he spent a pleasurable forty minutes wandering among the stalls of gaudy shoes and stretchy bright clothes, haggling cheerfully with smallholders touting their own fresh produce, with fishmongers displaying their morning's catch on trays that glittered with salt and ice.

Back in the apartment, he took a deckchair out onto a large balcony ringed by terracotta tubs. As the listing had promised, it looked right over the Busento, barely a stone's throw from where it joined the Crati. A series of weirs had been built to regulate the river's flow through the city, and there was one directly beneath, the roiled water at the foot of which had taken captive several plastic water bottles and chunks of white styrofoam, which now bobbed like exhausted salmon gathering themselves for their next leap. There he continued his refresher course, skimming papers on the early Church, the settlement patterns of barbarian tribes and the Roman emperors of late antiquity. In case Carmen asked him about his time at Oxford University, he investigated their postgraduate courses and found one led by a gorgeous, dark-eyed professor called Karen Porter, who'd recently written a book and fronted a TV series on the famous Sicilian city of Syracuse. He downloaded and played the first episode in the background as he read more papers, turning it up loud when his neighbours got into an argument and then again when a local politician drove by below, campaigning from the back of a pickup with loudspeakers strapped to its roof. He'd only just driven off when there came a loud rumble from across the river and Cesco glanced up to see a line of four black Harleys cruising along the far bank. He fell instantly to all fours and scrambled back inside. The bikes turned up a side street and disappeared. Dieter and his mates. But what the hell were they doing here? Had they tracked him somehow?

He searched again for his name online, but still found nothing. Then he realised. Any man nuts enough to have Alaric's name tattooed across their back was sure to be drawn to news that his tomb was about to be discovered. Even so, he'd need to be careful whenever he went out. His van had already had its makeover; he himself had not. It was time for his hair and beard to go.

He took his scissors and electric razor into the bathroom then set to work.

II

The prison dig creaked slowly into life. A pair of police vans arrived, disgorging a dozen uniformed officers with riot gear who for some bizarre reason set up crash barriers around the proposed drill site, then stood there diligently guarding them, despite the heat. A ministry lawyer came next, driving a blue BMW. She was short and stout and furious, as if she'd been dragged here from her daughter's wedding. She presented Kaufman and Zara with non-disclosure agreements to sign, in which they gave up rights to everything connected with the excavation and any discoveries they might make, threatening punishments for breach so absurdly over the top that Zara bridled as she read. 'And if I say no?' she asked.

'I'm sure you have other places you could be. I know I do.'

Their mechanical digger finally arrived from Tel Aviv, on the back of a flatbed truck. It was a push-me-pull-you kind of device, its opposing arms fitted with a scoop and a jackhammer. They directed the operator to where they wanted him to drill, which was the furthest point from the prison wall that had a cavity beneath. Then they retreated into the shade and covered their ears as the jackhammer turned the bedrock into rubble that was then cleared with the scoop.

The noise was dreadful. The air filled with dust that clotted thickly in Zara's mouth. She went to ask the operator how much longer it would take to make the breach. He shrugged and suggested at least two more hours. She retreated to her car, put the air con on and checked messages on her phone. To her mild surprise, they included dozens of notifications from a late antiquity discussion board that she helped moderate, and which rarely received that many in a month.

She went to see what had caused the fuss and found a link to a story about Visigothic artefacts in a Cosenza newspaper that had been posted by an American doctoral student called Carmen Nero, asking for help identifying a certain signet ring. And an identification was exactly what she'd got, linking it to a sealstone ring held by a Viennese museum, which bore around its perimeter the inscription:

ALARICVS REIKS GOTHORVM

Alaric, king of the Goths.

She got out of her car and went in search of Kaufman. He was lying stretched out on the front seats of the university van he'd brought, loaded with the various pieces of equipment they'd likely be needing later on. He woke groggily to her rap upon his window and removed his panama hat from over his face. 'What is it?' he asked.

She gave him her phone to look at as she explained the background. His eyebrow arched like a fishing rod at its first nibble. 'Cosenza, you say?'

'Not just that. On the bank of the Busento.'

He gave a grunt. 'You wait two millennia for one lead...'

She looked across at the dig site. 'What do you think? Should we say something?'

'To whom? And whatever for? We'll find it or we won't. This doesn't change that.' He gestured vaguely at the jackhammer, still thundering away. 'And we'll have our answer soon enough.'

Chapter Eleven

I

The afternoon raced by for Carmen, so busy was she. It took a good half-hour on the phone to convince her mother she was fine and talk her out of flying over. She spoke to a woman at her insurance company to get her claim underway. She kept returning to the late antiquity message board, where crowdsourcing had already solved the mystery of the signet ring for her, and was now working on the other artefacts. She emailed Professor Matteo Bianchi at Sapienza University to let him know what had happened and promising to do what she could to get him his ground-penetrating radar back. Friends began to call. Some she answered. Others she sent to voicemail. One of those was Charlie. It was a good five minutes before she could bring herself to listen to his message. He expressed his concern and best wishes in exactly the right way, and offered any help he could provide should she need it.

It made her feel quite ill.

Last night's *ispettore* arrived to take her second statement, accompanied by a young woman with excellent English, except with a Calabrian accent so thick that Carmen kept having to ask her to repeat herself while staring rudely at her lips. They took fingerprints and a DNA swab while they were there, then the *ispettore* asked her about her plans and traded phone numbers. Her kindly doctor arrived shortly afterwards. He checked for signs of concussion then declared her fit to leave. She was surprised to find it was half past five already. She dressed and packed and took her red roses down with her to reception, where she signed some forms and gave her contact details, and they took

94

a copy of her credit card in lieu of her passport. Then she sat on a bench and waited for Cesco to arrive. But when he did, he was so transformed that Carmen didn't even spot him until he waved and walked across. 'Your hair!' she exclaimed. 'Your beautiful hair!'

He scowled and ran a hand over his shaven scalp. 'You're not going to believe this,' he said darkly. 'After I left you this morning, I got this itching in my hair and beard. You know what it turned out to be? Lice! *Lice!* That damned pit I stayed in last night.' He gave a violent shudder. 'I have a phobia about those damned things. Ever since school. So off it had to come.'

'Oh,' she said. It was absurd to be unnerved by a haircut. And yet she was. The laid-back academic of earlier today was gone. In his place, a Cesco altogether tougher and more dangerous. She'd have thought a lot longer before agreeing to share an apartment with him if he'd looked like this. But he picked up her overnight bag before she could think of anything to say, and led the way outside. She took out her phone as she followed, ostensibly to check for messages, but in truth to snap his photograph instead, then another when they reached his van, making sure to get his licence plate. She looked up to see him grinning, fully aware of what she was up to. 'Quite right,' he said. 'I could be anyone.'

She nodded at the A.C. Milan sticker on the side of his van. 'Is that your team?'

He shook his head. 'I bought it second hand.' But then he smiled. 'Though maybe we should make them our team.'

'How do you figure that?'

'They're known as the red-and-blacks, from their club colours. *Il Rosso Neri.* We're the Rossi Nero. The reds-and-black.'

'So close.'

They climbed in. He set off for the exit then waited for a gap in traffic before pulling out. He proved an unexpectedly cautious driver, constantly looking around and checking his mirrors, almost as though he was worried about being seen. 'You still have family here?' she asked.

His expression flickered briefly. 'No.'

'Friends?'

'We left when I was fourteen. You know what it's like at that age. I was heartbroken. My life was finished. My girlfriend and I hugged for ages. I made tearful promises that I'd never forget her, that I'd be back to see her as soon as I could get away. I meant it too. Then I started at my new school and never thought of her again.'

'You beast. Where did you go?'

He slid her an amused look. 'My father worked in insurance. He got promoted to head office in Milan. So that's where I went to school. Then I read archaeology at Bologna and went to Oxford for my doctorate.'

'Why Oxford?'

'Because it's the best. And because it looks so beautiful in the photographs. They don't tell you about the fucking rain until it's too late.'

She laughed. 'How did you find it?'

'Oxford? Or the doctorate?'

'Either. No. The doctorate.'

'You're doing one yourself, aren't you?' he replied. 'Then you know.'

'I'm sure everyone's is different.'

'I'm sure they're not. Mine wasn't, for one. Mine was exactly how everyone warned me it would be. On my own, suddenly, while all my old friends moved on. Earning obscene salaries, getting promoted, marrying, starting families. You think, before it starts, that this won't matter. That the life of the mind will be its own reward. Then you realise you were wrong. So there I was. Working in a restaurant to make a little cash while living in a damp bedsit with not enough money for heating or good food, struggling for four years on a thesis I'd already lost faith in, which no one would ever read. It was lonely and frightening and dispiriting, and frankly it was shit.'

'Yes,' she said. And she felt a great weight falling from her, because she'd never admitted this truth so bluntly before – not even to herself.

He smiled again, more brightly than before. 'But the good news is, I got through it. As you will too. And it was worth it in the end.

For me, at least. And always remember that the people ahead of you in the line have been through the exact same thing themselves. You can trust them.'

She gave a little snort. 'I wish!'

'Aha!' he said. 'So *that's* it.'

'That's what?' she asked irritably.

'All day, I've been wondering. A beautiful bright young doctoral student like you, coming to Italy without first getting to grips with our language. This makes no sense to me, not unless you left America in a great hurry for some reason. Your supervisor, yes? What was it? Was he already married?'

'Fuck you,' she said.

He laughed heartily. 'God, we men are such pigs.'

'Yes, you are.' She took a long breath. 'But it wasn't like that.'

'Sure, it wasn't. It never is.'

'It really wasn't. Charlie wasn't my supervisor. Not officially, at least. He was just one of my predecessors in the programme, and very knowledgeable in my area. And he wasn't married either. In fact, we were considering it ourselves. It was… I got pregnant, you see. But then I… I had a miscarriage.'

Silence fell in the van. Cesco looked anguished. 'Shit, Carmen. I'm so sorry.'

'It's okay. It happens. But Charlie and I, we had very different reactions. I was… I was *broken*. He… he tried his best to be sympathetic but the truth is he was relieved. I could see it in his face. So I couldn't be with him any more. I couldn't be in America. It hurt too much. All that fucking sympathy.' She took a deep breath to calm herself, then found a smile. 'So yes, Sapienza let me come here ahead of schedule. And yes, I thought I'd be able to learn Italian once I got here. But I've failed miserably. It takes much more effort than you realise, especially when your heart's not in it. It's not been in anything, to be honest. But please let's not talk about all that, eh? It's too bleak. Tell me something else about yourself. Something cheerful. Like yours, for example.'

He frowned at her. 'My what?'

'Your supervisor. The one you could trust. The one who supported you so well.'

'Oh, yes,' he said. They came to a junction. He leaned forward in his seat to look all around him before indicating right and turning down a side street. 'Forgive me,' he said, gesturing at the road. 'Everything's changed so much since I was a boy. Mind you, I was only fourteen at the time, so not that much of a driver. It's really weird revisiting childhood haunts, don't you find? Everything's so much smaller.'

'You were telling me about your supervisor,' she said.

'Yes.' He stopped at another junction, then indicated and turned left. 'Her name was Karen Porter.'

'Karen Porter?' She looked at him in surprise. 'But she's fabulous. I loved her book on Syracuse.'

He smiled again. 'I'm glad to hear that. I helped her with it.'

'You didn't? That's brilliant!'

'The TV series more than the book, to be fair. I have family over there, you see. And of course I speak the language. Not Italian. Karen speaks that perfectly, unlike some.'

'Oi!'

'I mean the language of how to get shit done in Sicily. I went on a couple of trips with her, introduced her to certain people. The kind you need for a project to run smoothly.'

'You don't mean...?'

He laughed. 'No, no, no. Not Mafia. But Sicilian politics and bureaucracy is very intricate, very personal. The right connection beats a thousand forms.'

'What's she like?'

'Enthusiastic. Knowledgeable. Gorgeous. Just exactly as she appears on TV. Except for the snoring. I never expected that.' He made a gesture to indicate drinking. 'Particularly after she's had a few.'

Carmen squinted at him. 'You and she...?'

'No, no, no. Strictly between you and me, I think you're more her type than I am. We had neighbouring rooms, that's all. And thin walls.'

'Karen Porter!' she sighed. 'You're so lucky. I'd love to meet her.'

'Then I'll arrange it, no problem. But let's find Alaric first, eh? Trust me, if we do that, it will be Karen begging for the introduction.'

The breach was made late afternoon. Zara and Kaufman were both standing by the pit to witness the moment the weakened bedrock finally ceded to the relentless pounding of the jackhammer. The ground shuddered at the impact and a cloud of dust erupted from the hole, sending them into a scurried retreat. Then she, Kaufman and the ministry lawyer all drew closer again to look.

The hole went straight down for a good three metres before opening up into a velvety blackness that somehow suggested a large space. Zara found a stone to drop down, then waited for its clatter. It took a moment longer than she expected. She grinned up at Kaufman, who grinned back at her. For archaeologists like them, nothing quite matched a virgin site.

They fed down an extensible ladder to make sure it was long enough. It was, but only just. They worked its feet until it was solidly bedded, then the lawyer called a halt until Avram Bernstein arrived. It was late enough now that he took the decision to wait until *Shabbat* was over. It grew cool. Darkness fell with its usual rapidity. The first few stars appeared. Avram duly arrived in the back of a black limousine, attended by a humourless bodyguard and a willowy young redhead dressed in photographer chic with three camera bags on her shoulders.

Kaufman issued them all with safety helmets, torches, goggles, masks and gloves, while saving the rock hammers, trowels and find-bags for Zara and himself. Then he exercised his right, as site discoverer, to lead the expedition down. The hole swallowed him like a python with a kid goat. It was tight enough that for a moment it looked as though he might get stuck. But then he was through and into the open space beneath. He stepped off the ladder and vanished, save for the flutter of his torch.

Zara pushed forward to be next. The ladder creaked as she stepped upon it. Then the python took her into its belly too. The strata changed from honeycomb to slate, marking her passage from Palaeocene to Late Cretaceous. Then suddenly it opened up and she was in a long, narrow, high-ceilinged aisle between walls of square-mouthed apertures, like drawers in a city morgue – which was effectively what it was. She looked down. Around the jackhammer rubble lay a macabre carpet of skulls and bones and other human remains, hauled from the various loculi by robbers many centuries before, the better to strip them of their jewellery and other grave goods. At once, any hope of a major find died.

'We still need to make sure,' said Kaufman.

'Of course,' she said.

The others now arrived one by one, gathering on the rubble mound like shipwreck survivors on a rock. Avram came last, trying his best to look dignified while his camerawoman filmed his descent for posterity. But he couldn't hide his disgust and disappointment when he saw the bones – the empty eye sockets and the clumps of black hair still stuck to wizened scalps. 'After all that,' he said.

'We still need to make sure,' repeated Kaufman.

They'd arrived, exactly as intended, at the far end of the chain of chambers as they led away from the prison. The walls around them still bore chisel marks where new loculi had been planned but not yet cut. Kaufman led them in the other direction, treading delicately between the bones. There was a slow creaking noise above their heads, like a giant turning over in his bed. Flakes of stone fell in a gentle cascade and motes swirled in their torchlight, making Zara wonder what cracks and fissures might have been weakened or even opened by the jackhammer.

'Is it safe?' asked Avram warily.

Zara hesitated. But if they left now they might never get another chance. She turned to Avram with a confidence she didn't altogether feel. 'New sites are always full of strange noises,' she told him. 'It'll be fine.'

They pressed on, reaching a short arched passage low enough to make her stoop. A second chamber was set at an angle to the first, like two carriages of a train going around a bend. And this one was clearly first class. It wasn't cut in columns but rather in small alcoves, like private chapels in a cathedral, and its walls were sculpted with tableaux rich in Christian symbolism: fish and birds, fruit and flowers, angels and saintly looking men. There were fewer bones, too, owing to the fewer burials, and all covered by a grey dusting that puzzled Zara until she saw a massive cave-in ahead that had deposited a great mound of rubble across their path. They came to a halt, looked upwards at the cause: the flat grey base of one of the prison wall's vast concrete slabs, whose immense weight had evidently triggered this collapse many years before, covering the chamber in its fallout dust.

'My prison!' muttered Avram.

The way ahead looked so precarious that Kaufman came to a stop. But Zara wasn't having that. She edged past him then clambered up the rubble mound. The walls and ceiling creaked again, more loudly than before. A cascade of dust and small limestone fragments pattered like hailstones. She shook her helmet and brushed it off her neck and shoulders then shone her torch beyond. The passage continued another four metres or so before ending in a wall, and it was all buried beneath the same high mound of rubble. Kaufman arrived beside her. He gave a shrug and gestured to turn back. But Zara ignored him and crawled on.

'What are you doing?' he asked. 'There's nothing there.'

'Does that look like nine metres to you?'

'Nine metres?'

'You told me yesterday that there was a chamber directly beneath the map mosaic. And also that it was nine metres from the wall.'

'Oh,' he said.

'What's going on?' asked Avram.

'There may be another chamber, Minister,' said Kaufman slowly. 'A hidden one.'

Silence fell. Zara crawled onwards over the top of the fallen rubble. The roof creaked yet again and sprinkled her with dust. A lump of sandstone landed by her hand and threw up more. She tried not to think of the immense weight of the concrete slab above her head, the fractures it had put in the bedrock, the damage their jackhammer had done. But she kept thinking it anyway. *If it came down now. If it came down on top of her...* Her heart began to beat ever faster. Her breathing came quick and loud. In the constricted space, it echoed back at her, a vicious cycle that made her feel ever more vulnerable. But she pressed on all the same and finally reached the end wall. She placed her palm flat upon it then rapped it with a knuckle. It looked and felt like bedrock. She struck it with her rock hammer to listen to the sound it made. She struck it elsewhere then turned the hammer around in her hand and smashed the wall so hard with it that it spit back chips. She kept hitting it until a clump of stone the size of her fist fell away, revealing a glimpse of a different wall behind, the join of a pair of crumbling brown bricks held together by grey mortar. Her head swam a little. She became possessed of a dreadful urgency. Kaufman and the others were shouting questions at her but she ignored them, hammering at the wall until she'd exposed four complete bricks, each the size of a small loaf. With the point of her hammer, she scraped away the powdery mortar, then worked one of the bricks back and forth until she'd pulled it free.

She reached her torch into the gap to see what lay beyond. There was another wall perhaps two or three metres away, carved into fantastic designs with a skill that far surpassed anything she'd seen elsewhere. She turned on her phone's video camera then reached that through too, twisting it this way and that to capture every nook and cranny. Scuffling behind. Kaufman and then Avram arrived alongside her. She pulled her phone back out, held it so that they could watch its screen together, then started playing the footage she'd just taken. There was a blur of light and dark as she fed her phone through the hole. Then suddenly the space opened up. There was a mosaic in the dusty floor, an eight-pointed golden star against a backdrop of royal blue. Then she turned the camera to the left-hand wall, to reveal a pair of niches, each containing a silver trumpet.

'Dear God,' murmured Kaufman.

The ceiling next, domed and vaulted. Then the floor again. Now finally to her right. And there it was, standing by itself in a large oyster-shell alcove: a seven-branched candelabra that, even in her camera's modest torchlight, and despite its thick covering of dust, shone with the unmistakeable gleam of gold.

Chapter Twelve

I

There was a church next to their apartment, and evening service had just begun, so that all the nearest parking spots were taken. But they found one on a nearby side street, then walked back together. Cesco had already taken the single bedroom, Carmen noted appreciatively, leaving her the en suite. To her absurd excitement, it had a bath in it. Her room in Rome had a shared bathroom with only a feeble shower, so it had been months since she'd enjoyed a proper bath. She excused herself and ran one now, logging her phone on to the apartment's Wi-Fi, then lying there in blissful warmth.

The church's organ seemed to be positioned right against the wall. Whenever it played, it sent little shivers through the bath, like a broken jacuzzi. She logged on to the late antiquity message board. There were no further breakthroughs, but one of the other members had asked anxiously how she was bearing up after her ordeal. She replied with a cheerful update, hinting at her and Cesco's self-appointed mission, illustrating it with her snatched photo of him and another of the Busento from her balcony that she took from the apartment's online listing.

It was dark out by the time she dressed and went through. Cesco was sitting in an armchair, illuminated only by the soft glow of his laptop screen. She turned on the main lights then dimmed them back down a little. The main room was just as the photographs had shown, with distinct areas for cooking, eating, working and entertaining. 'Mission command, huh?' she said.

'They'll have a plaque up outside one day,' he said. 'Cesco and Carmen, discoverers of Alaric's lost tomb.'

'Who gave you top billing?'

He grinned up at her, his blue eyes twinkling. 'Fair enough. Priority to whoever makes the greatest contribution. Agreed?'

'And who decides that?'

'You're not saying you don't trust me, are you?'

She laughed and slipped through the glass doors onto a balcony ringed with tubs of bright spring flowers. She leaned on the rail and gazed down at the Busento, running darkly beneath, except for a strip of luminescent foam churned up by the weir – and she experienced one of those inexplicable moments of pure happiness that seemingly come out of nowhere. She went back in. Her red roses were in a vase of bubbled green glass. She breathed their fragrance in once more, then stole a glance at Cesco. Since arriving in Rome, she'd been hit on by Italians of every sort, whose attentions had filled her only with such dreadful fatigue that she'd begun to fear she'd never again feel that sweet thrill. She wandered over to him, leaning her leg against the coarse fabric of his armchair. He had Google Maps up on his screen, a satellite view of the thin blue thread of the Busento river as it wound its way through Cosenza, before turning into a wider green swathe as it was swallowed beneath a canopy of trees.

'Do you truly believe Alaric's out there?' she asked. 'I mean truly?'

'I know what you mean,' he said, glancing up at her. 'A lost tomb filled with plundered treasure. It sounds too like folklore to be true, yes? Especially that bit about hiding it beneath a river. I mean, do you know how difficult that would be? You can't divert a river without massive hydraulic works. Even if they could somehow have hidden those while they were being built – which they couldn't – they'd unquestionably have left traces in the ground. Everyone within fifty kilometres would have had at least some idea of where the tomb was.'

'But...?'

'Alaric was the Visigoths' great king, and he died. That much is undisputed. Cremation went out of fashion with their conversion to Christianity, so he'd have had to be buried somewhere. Germanic tribes often buried people beside rivers. Migrants often chose places reminiscent of their childhoods. Alaric was brought up on the Danube, so a river would have made perfect sense for him. They couldn't afford to leave behind a guard to protect it – not forever, anyway. But as long as they restored the river to its previous course, then it would have been well protected against most tomb robbers. Particularly as people wouldn't have known *precisely* where it was – not after the Visigoths had put to death all the slaves they'd forced to dig it out. Anyone who'd wanted to get at the tomb would have had to divert the river again to find it, which would have meant recruiting a slave army of their own. So yes, the basic story makes perfect sense to me. As for how much treasure they'd have buried him with, I suspect a very great deal indeed.'

'Why so?'

'Rome had been plundering gold from across its empire for eight hundred years. The city was filled with great buildings, each containing priceless treasures. Take the Basilica of St John as just one example. Constantine gave it a canopy made from a ton of hammered silver; a vault of solid gold, decorated with life-sized figures of Christ and his angels; fabulous jewels and crowns, golden goblets and fine chains. And those famous dolphins, of course, seventy of them, each made of gold and larger than the one from Vittorio's money belt. And that was just one part of the wealth of just one church. Then there were the private houses, the public buildings, the treasury. The Visigoths spent three full days taking their pick of it. Can you imagine how many carts it would have taken just to carry away all that booty?'

'A logistical nightmare.'

'Exactly! Exactly! Not only would it have slowed them dreadfully, it would have attracted every bandit for a hundred kilometres. Sure, it would have been worth it if they could have made good on their original plan of crossing the Mediterranean to seize Carthage for their new home. But they came to grief on the Messina Straits and were forced into retreat. Winter was now coming. They needed food, not golden angels or canopies of hammered silver. Sure, theoretically they could have traded it. But everyone who heard that the Visigoths were coming would have taken their winter stores straight to the nearest walled town, leaving them helpless. Sieges, yes – they were okay at those. But storming a city was beyond them, unless they got help from within – as happened when they took Rome. So, then, by the time Alaric died, I'll bet you anything that the Visigoths would have come to see all that plunder as a curse as much as a blessing. Besides, extravagant displays of generosity were how new Gothic kings established their authority. And Athaulf was famously open-handed anyway. Didn't he give Galla Placidia some crazy gift on their wedding day?'

'Fifty basins of gold coins,' said Carmen. 'Fifty basins of precious jewels.'

'There you go. So put it all together and yes, I can easily believe that Alaric truly was buried beneath the Busento, and with a great deal more treasure than the savvy historians would have us think.'

'And not discovered yet?'

He shook his head. 'If he had been, we'd know about it. His tomb would have been looted, sure, but surely someone would still have found the shell.'

'So where is it, then?'

He grinned at her. 'And have you nick my place on the plaque? What kind of fool do you take me for?' He set his laptop on the coffee table then pushed himself to his feet and padded over to the kitchen, where he held up a bottle of red for her approval before popping it. 'Didn't Giulia or Vittorio give you any kind of clue?'

She wandered over to join him. 'Like I said, they were waiting for you. At least...'

'At least?' he asked, pouring them a glass each.

She took her wine from him and held it to her nose. It was dark and rich and had that slight grittiness to it that always seemed to end, for her, in a thumping hangover. 'I asked Giulia what was going on. She said they couldn't tell me yet, because they'd given someone their word. I asked her who. She glanced at her father. He got all tense. Then she said you and he relaxed again.'

Cesco frowned. 'What are you suggesting? Are you suggesting it was actually someone else they promised?'

'I guess. But I don't know who. And I could have imagined it anyway.'

'I doubt that. You strike me as pretty perceptive.'

'And you strike me as pretty smooth.'

He laughed easily. 'See. I told you that you were pretty perceptive.' He put on a red-and-white apron hanging from a hook. It was far too small for him and made him look absurd, but he didn't seem to care. He crouched to look through the selection of saucepans. 'Are you hungry?' he asked.

'I could eat a horse.'

'Then off to France with you. In this house, we eat pasta. Specifically, tonight, my grandmother's scoglio. Assuming you like seafood, that is?'

'I love it. How can I help?'

'Take a chair. Drink your wine. Enchant me with your conversation.'

'Please. I'd like to do something.'

'Absolutely not.' He opened the refrigerator and took out a red onion, a garlic bulb, a red chilli and pearly white bags of scallops, clams, mussels and prawns. 'In all my time in Oxford, I learned only one thing of indisputable value. Never, ever let the English near the pasta.'

Carmen laughed. 'I already told you. I'm American.'

'As if there's any difference when it comes to pasta. You want mashed potato, mash some fucking potato. Leave my spaghetti alone. Though if you must help, these clams and mussels need scrubbing. Not even the English can screw that up.' He nodded at his laptop on the coffee table. 'Better yet: take a look at that.'

She wandered over, revived the screen. Google Maps was still up, showing a satellite view of the Busento surrounded by patches of woodland, clusters of housing, an occasional farmhouse and barn. But mostly it was fields and meadowland. 'What am I looking for?' she asked.

'Imagine you're Athaulf,' he said. 'Your brother-in-law the great king has just died. You've decided to bury him beneath the river so that the locals won't nick all his gold once you're gone. How do you go about finding the right spot? In practical terms, I mean.'

'Oh,' she said. She gave it thought. 'I'd choose somewhere secluded, I suppose, to make it hard for people to see what I was up to. Somewhere forested, if possible. And, if I'm diverting a river, then I'd guess on a plain of some kind.'

'Exactly.' He lit a gas burner beneath a pan then cut off and tossed in an obscene slab of butter. He crushed the garlic bulb into it then chopped up the pulp and added it too, then stirred in half a jar of tomatoes. His hands blurred like a restaurant chef when he sliced the onion and the red chilli, whose fierceness he tested by dabbing a fingertip into its juice then touching it to his tongue. 'The Busento runs mostly between steep hills. It's nearly impossible to divert it in such places. But there are several stretches where the terrain levels out. Surely you'd choose one of those.' He binned half his chilli then swept the rest of the ingredients into the saucepan with the back of his knife. He added a splash of white wine and a sprinkling of sea salt, then stirred it with a wooden spoon. 'Now we also know that the Suraces wanted to survey somewhere relatively dry. How can we reconcile this with him being beneath a river?'

'Rivers change their course all the time,' said Carmen. 'Particularly on plains.'

'Exactly.' He rinsed his hands, wiped them dry on his apron. He filled a large saucepan with water, salted it then set it on a back burner. He ripped open the bags of clams and mussels, tipped them into a colander to rinse and scrub. 'The original course silts up. There's an earthquake or a landside. A bad freeze is followed by a sudden thaw. Farmers dig new channels to irrigate their land. It's sixteen hundred years since Alaric died. The Busento will have moved all over the place since then.'

'That's what you're looking for? Its old course?'

He nodded. 'The resolution on those satellite photos is for shit, but the idea still holds. So I thought maybe we could walk it in the morning? Look for traces of the old bed – or anything else that might have got the Suraces excited, for that matter.' He raised an eyebrow. 'Unless you have a better idea?'

'No,' she said. 'That sounds great. Let's do it.'

'Excellent,' he said. 'Then how about you come help me with these mussels? They're not going to scrub themselves.'

II

There was a moment of extraordinary jubilation at the discovery of the Menorah. But it didn't last. Not for Zara, at least. One look at Avram and Kaufman told her that greed and ambition had already gone to work on them, that she'd have to be the adult here. 'We need to leave,' she told them.

Avram stared at her as though she was crazy. 'Leave?'

'To put together a proper excavation plan.'

'This place holds some of Israel's most dangerous prisoners,' he said tersely. 'It's outer wall is sitting above an escape tunnel that runs through weakened bedrock that for all we know might collapse at any moment, thanks to the jackhammer. So fuck your proper excavation. We're grabbing these pieces and taking them with us.'

'You can't.'

'Watch me.' He shuffled around in the constricted space to put his feet against the ancient wall. Then he stamped hard enough that an already loosened brick fell free and thudded to the floor behind. He stamped again and down went another.

'Stop!' cried Zara, appalled, grabbing him by his arm. It violated every protocol, but she could see no alternative. She turned around herself and fed her feet through the small gap, slithering into the chamber, feeling for its floor. Then she took her torch and shone it around. And there it was, right in front of her. A touch smaller than she'd expected, yet her heart thrilled even so. She reached out slowly for it, almost fearful of the contact. She took its stem in her right hand, one of the branches in her left. She bent her knees and braced her back then made to tip it towards her. But she relaxed again almost at once. She let it go and turned to Avram and Kaufman with a rueful shake of her head.

Avram frowned. 'What's wrong? Too heavy?'

'No,' she said. 'Not heavy enough.'

'What are you talking about?'

'It's not gold. It's gilt.'

'Gilt? Are you saying it's fake?'

Zara hesitated. Gilding didn't by itself prove it fake. The Jews had been masters of the craft. Indeed, according to the Torah, several tabernacle vessels had been carved from acacia wood and then gilded. But the Torah was unequivocal about the Menorah. It had been made of pure gold. If this truly was it, then the temple priests had cheated. Announcing this find would make the Jews the butt of a million tedious jokes. But there was a more likely explanation – not least because the ancient Jews had typically gilded with gold leaf, which tended to wear through or peel off over time. The finish of this Menorah was too good for that, suggesting that it had instead been mercury-gilded – a technique in which a base object, typically of silver, had been coated with an amalgam of mercury and gold then heated in an oven until all the mercury had evaporated and only the gold remained. The fumes given off during this process had been so toxic that it had made it one of the most deadly of all professions, with life expectancy in the low thirties. But it had undeniably produced a richer and more durable finish. And it had been a Roman rather than a Jewish craft.

'Why would Justinian build a whole church for a fake Menorah?' demanded Avram, once she'd explained this. 'And what about that chain of custody shit you gave me last night? Jerusalem to Rome. Carthage to Constantinople. All of that.'

Zara nodded. Excellent questions both. 'The chain of custody was only to explain how the temple treasures *might* have ended up here,' she said. 'But the temple treasures had been gone nearly five hundred years by then. Anything could have happened to them along the way. As for Justinian, historians have long been sceptical of Procopius's story. What kind of emperor would discard one of the world's great treasures just because of some vague warning from a mystic Jew? So we've tended to dismiss his account. Except that makes no sense either. Procopius wasn't writing about ancient history. He was recording a victory parade that had recently taken place. To claim that these treasures had been part of it, when he and everyone else knew they hadn't, would have made him look ridiculous and brought the rest of his works into disrepute. And why bother, only to invent a second lie to excuse their absence? So there must be some other explanation. Maybe this is it. Justinian was highly sophisticated. He'd have known it for a fake the moment he picked it up. Which made it a potential humiliation, because he'd just paraded it through his streets as the real thing. So what was he to do?'

Avram nodded. 'Invent a mystic Jew. Get it out of the city fast.'

'Justinian was building churches all over the place anyway. What could be easier than to send this to one of them for safekeeping, and claim piety points for himself in the process?'

'So who faked it? The Carthaginians?'

'Maybe. But look at what we've got. A gilt candelabra and a pair of silver trumpets. Fine artefacts, but hardly unique. So why would Justinian have mistaken them for temple treasures unless that's what the Carthaginians themselves had believed them to be? And why would they have believed that unless that's what Geiseric had pillaged from Rome?'

'Then...?'

'There's a weird anomaly in Procopius. He actually refers to two different sets of temple treasures: the one that Justinian paraded through Constantinople, and a separate set that had left Rome decades earlier.'

'Two sets? And people still take him seriously?'

Zara nodded. Avram's reaction was obvious, understandable and wrong. Such anomalies were actually reassuring to historians, for they suggested Procopius had faithfully recorded what he'd heard, even though it had made no sense. Because sometimes the explanation could take a millennium or more to emerge. 'Geiseric wasn't the first barbarian to sack Rome,' she told him. 'The Visigoths got there first. They're the ones who apparently had this other set. Which is obvious when you think about it. The Menorah was one of Rome's most famous treasures. Everyone knew it was made from solid gold and kept in the Temple of Peace. If you were a Visigoth, where would you go first? Sure, the temple guardians would have tried to hide it, but a sword to their throats would soon have got them talking. But once the Visigoths were gone again, those same guardians would have had some explaining to do. Not to mention a pressing need to replace their primary source of income.'

'Income?'

'Sacred relics were big business. Pilgrims flocked to Rome from all across the ancient world to have the locals fleece them. Animal bones sold as martyr relics; bits of wood from the True Cross. Private viewings of Old Testament treasures such as the Menorah would have been major money-spinners. So what were they to do? Well, the guardians at the Temple of Peace knew better than anyone exactly what it looked like. There was even a helpful picture of it on the Arch of Titus. So it would have been easy for them to commission a replica, except that – thanks to the Visigoths – there was no gold to be had anywhere in the city. So they made it out of silver instead, then mercury-gilded it and put it back on display as the real thing, which is where Geiseric and his Vandals found it forty-five years later. Hey presto. Two sets of temple treasures.'

'Is there evidence for this?' frowned Avram. 'Or is it guesswork?'

'It's guesswork,' admitted Zara. 'But for sure it happened with other pieces. We know the emperor Valentinian replaced one looted treasure, Pope Celestine another. And we can find out easily enough. If this is the original, the gilding will have come from the Negev or somewhere else hereabouts. If it's Roman, it will have come from one of their mines, probably in Spain or Wales. Professor Kaufman can run the tests.'

'Professor?'

'Of course, Minister.'

'How long?'

'I could have results for you in a matter of days.'

Avram fell silent, his brow furrowed. 'A few days?' he asked finally. 'Surely a piece this important merits exceptional measures. A double-checking of your initial findings, at the very least. And by an independent, overseas lab, lest we're accused of getting up to tricks.'

'I'm not sure I—'

'What the minister is asking, Professor,' said Zara drily, 'is whether you can delay any announcement until after the election. That way he can leak rumours of an astonishing find to boost his campaign, while deferring the disappointing truth until it no longer matters.'

'Oh,' said Kaufman. 'Well, yes, Minister, you're exactly right about the need for corroboration from an international—'

'This is absurd,' burst out Zara. 'You don't need a spectrometer to tell you it's gilt. All you need to do is pick it up.'

'You work for a public university,' said Avram. 'You'd be wise to remember that.'

'And you'd be wise to remember that I have voicemails,' retorted Zara, before she could stop herself. But she regretted it as soon as the words were out, so she held up her hand in apology. 'It's for your own good too. Honestly, if you try to get too clever with this, it could easily backfire horribly.'

'How so?'

'Because, Minister,' she said, 'there's a chance – a very outside chance, but still – that the true Menorah is on the verge of being discovered for real.'

Chapter Thirteen

I

They gorged themselves on scoglio and then on the raspberry cheese-cake Cesco had bought in the local market. They rinsed their plates then loaded them into the dishwasher. Carmen went to sit on the sofa, where she played distractedly with his laptop. He emptied the dregs of red into their glasses then brought them over and sat beside her. She set the laptop across both their legs to give him a better view. Already she'd grown accustomed to his new shaven-headed look. In truth, and to her surprise, she'd come to like it. A hint of danger might be intimidating in a stranger, but it was reassuring in a friend.

Their thighs kept touching by accident. Each time, one or other of them would shift away again. Yet then they'd touch once more. And even when they weren't quite touching, she found herself absurdly aware of him, his warmth and physicality and nearness. She had to force herself to concentrate on the screen. There was something surreal about these landscapes viewed from above. Impressionistic. Orchards and groves stippled like Seurat. Ploughed fields with that characteristic Van Gogh swirl. Footpaths and animal tracks cut scars in the meadows, fields and scrub. Elsewhere, peculiar shadows might have been anything from clouds to chemical spills, mounds to dips.

She zoomed in on the Suraces' farmhouse. It gave her a twinge to see it from above, with its sunken roof and the sky-blue pickup parked outside, the tattered polythene greenhouses slinking like grey caterpillars down towards the river. There the neat rows of vines, the budding olives and citrus trees. There the oxbow in the river and the embankment down which they'd tumbled, though the satellite image gave little sense of its steepness. And there the gap between the trees out of which the truck had come. She stiffened slightly at the memory of the impact. Cesco must have sensed her bracing, for he put a hand on her shoulder. She started at the contact, and he raised his palm in apology, even though it hadn't been that kind of start.

He knocked back his wine, got to his feet. 'Limoncello?' he asked.

'Love one,' she said. She watched him pad to the kitchen, his leanness and grace of movement. Then she shook her head at herself and frowned hard at the screen. She zoomed out again to follow the Busento downstream. There was the high bridge they'd crossed. There the roadworks hill with the sharp turn at its foot over the little humpback into Cosenza. The road grew wider now, easier to follow. She dragged her way through screen after screen until she arrived at the junction with the Crati a short distance from where she sat. That must be the church next door, which made that terracotta roof their own, and those spots of colour the tubs of bright spring flowers on their balcony.

Cesco returned with the shot glasses. He sat back down beside her and glanced at the screen. 'Want me to go outside and wave?' he asked.

'You're fine right where you are,' she assured him. But her mind was elsewhere. Bright spring flowers. Bright *spring* flowers. She sensed he was about to say something flippant so she held up a finger to ask for silence. She'd seen something important, she was sure of it. Seen it and missed it. But what? Screen by screen, she retraced her way along the river, over the humpback bridge then up the hill. And there it was. The roadworks. A rush of pure knowledge, headier than any drug, thrilled straight through her. 'You know that thing we were speculating about?' she said, zooming in. 'The thing that brought Giulia down here, despite her exams. I think this must be it.'

Cesco frowned in puzzlement. 'You think they dug up something under the road?'

'No. Not that.' Google Maps provided only limited data on their photographs. Google Earth, she knew, offered far more. She opened it now, zoomed in on the same terrain. 'You're an archaeologist. You'll know far better than me how brilliant aerial photography is at finding sites, right? But it's expensive too. Way too expensive for the Suraces. So what would you have done, if you were them?'

Cesco let out a breath. 'Google Earth,' he said.

'Google Earth,' agreed Carmen. 'The resolution isn't great, but it's better than nothing. Old footpaths, animal tracks, collapsed walls, burial mounds, you can see them all. And new features get exposed by every snow and flood, by every plough and harvest. The trouble is, Google don't release new photographs very often. In places like this, maybe once every five years.'

'The roadworks,' murmured Cesco.

'Exactly,' said Carmen. 'They wouldn't be shown here *unless these photographs were absolutely brand new*. And here's the thing – you can have Google send you an alert whenever they publish new photographs of a particular area.'

'And?' he asked. 'When?'

She pointed to the date at the bottom of the screen. 'Last Tuesday,' she said.

II

Avram Bernstein climbed the ladder out of the catacombs then strode over to his car. Vanna, his photographer, made to climb in the back with him but he wagged a finger at her and pointed her up front. She scowled at him. Sleep with a woman once, they thought they had rights. He buzzed up the partition and took out his phone to search for the story in the Calabrian newspaper that Zara had told him of, proclaiming Alaric's tomb on the verge of discovery. He found it quickly enough, then corroborated the rest of her account too. Not that he'd doubted her. Honesty was at once Zara's finest virtue and greatest flaw.

And you'd be wise to remember that I have voicemails.

He brooded the whole drive home. To make a find like this so soon before the most important election of his lifetime, yet not to be able to use it... For a man of his skills and ambition, it was unthinkable. There *had* to be a way. The only question was how. His most obvious routes were blocked. If he announced the discovery, or let it leak, Zara would go public with her debunking. And he couldn't retaliate without risking her release of his idiot son's voicemails, even though she'd vowed to take them to her grave.

Rivkah greeted his return with a warm smile and an iced whisky. He beckoned her to join him in his office, which he had swept daily for listening devices. Even so, he had her sit beside him on the sofa, the better to confer in low voices.

Friends, enemies and savvy political reporters alike all agreed that Avram was a driven man, and that what drove him was his fierce will to power. They were right about the first part, wrong about the second. The fierce will to power was Rivkah's, not his own. The youngest daughter of a nationalist politician who'd fallen just short of top office, she'd set out to go one better. Not being a natural herself, she'd cast around for a man to do it for her. Avram had been her choice. As for him, his own hunger had always been very different. He never talked about it any more, for it was shameful in a man his age, but what he'd always craved was *glory* – that transcendent moment in which a man became a legend. As a teenager, he'd dreamed of Olympic triumph, but no amount of training had been able to transmute his particular base metal into gold. Then it had come time to serve. For Avram, only Israel's elite commando unit the Sayeret Matkal would do. His timing had been ideal. A group of Palestinian terrorists had hijacked an Air France flight out of Tel Aviv, diverting it to Uganda's Entebbe Airport. The Gentiles had been released, the Jews retained. A daring hostage rescue had been carried out, one of the great triumphs of Israeli military history. It should have been his moment, except that he'd been benched at the last moment for showing excessive zeal. *Excessive zeal!* He'd had to cheer the returning heroes instead, his heart roiled by such envy and bitterness that he'd had to leave the army shortly afterwards. At a loose end, he'd hung around the fringes of far-right groups. That was where Rivkah had spotted him, and groomed him, and married him. She'd pushed him into politics and had guided him ever since. She was, by far, his most trusted adviser.

He told her of his evening: the necropolis and the bricked-up chamber; the thrill of finding the trumpets and the Menorah, only for Zara to dash his hopes by proving it a replica. By the time he was finished, he'd been sipping melted ice for ten minutes. Rivkah took his glass through to the kitchen and returned with it refreshed. 'Tell me about it,' she said.

'I just did,' he said.

'No,' she said. 'Tell me about *it*.'

He nodded. His mouth watered at the memory. Seeing it for the first time, believing it the real thing. The gold of it, the way it gleamed. 'It was like the face of God,' he said.

'Let Israel know that feeling,' she said. 'They'll acclaim you their new David.'

'Then tear me limb from limb when they learn the truth.'

'How will they find out? When you're prime minister, you'll put it behind glass so that no one can ever touch it again.'

'They'll find out because Zara will tell them. And I can't stop her or she'll release those damned voicemails.'

'She gave us her word she wouldn't.'

'I know. But there it is. We can't risk it.'

'What about that man we used before?'

'What man?'

'That man from that company you used. What was their name again? Gordian Sword?'

He squinted at her. 'Zara is family.'

'Zara *was* family. Then she turned our son into an alcoholic and ran away when he needed her most.'

He gave her the long gaze, hoping to shame her into backing down. But it was he who looked away. 'There is one possibility,' he sighed. 'I was mulling it over on the drive home. Just a thought experiment, you understand.' He explained what Zara had told him about Alaric's tomb, how it too might be rediscovered, what might be inside. The implications for their government and their nation if it was, and how they might be able to use it to their advantage, one way or the other.

Rivkah's eyes glinted with a febrile joy when he was done. 'It's perfect,' she said. 'Make the call.'

There was such frank admiration in Cesco's gaze that it left Carmen momentarily undone. She felt fourteen again, sitting on a swing chair on the porch of a friend's house with her first crush, a lanky, cocky athlete called Jason Foster, who'd worn the coolest beard she'd ever seen, as though he'd dipped his chin into a saucer of black ink. She felt so agitated suddenly that she set the laptop aside and jumped to her feet and went over to the kitchen area as though there was something there she wanted, even though there wasn't. But she grabbed the limoncello bottle as cover and brought it over to splash into both their glasses for a toast. 'To our partnership,' she said. 'To the Rossi Nero.'

He laughed and clinked her glass with his. 'To the Rossi Nero.'

The alcohol burned pleasurably in her throat and chest as she knocked it back. Doing her doctorate, she'd forgotten what a joy it was to work on a shared project alongside someone you valued and liked and wanted to do well for, and who valued and liked and wanted to do well for you in return. In truth, she couldn't remember the last time she'd liked someone this much. Their eyes met again, and this time she didn't look away, but rather met and held his gaze, allowing him see into her even as she saw into him, letting it go on and on, far longer than was prudent, savouring every delicious moment of it, as though a compact of some kind was being forged right there and then between them, as though futures were being settled. It was Cesco who finally broke the connection, looking away in mild confusion. He covered for it by picking up the laptop again, turning his attention back to it. 'There's something we're still missing,' he said.

She sat beside him. 'Yes?'

'Tell me if this is how you see it: Google publishes new photographs. They alert Giulia or her father, who study them and perhaps compare them to the previous versions. They spot something that gets them excited. Giulia catches the first train down, despite her exams. Agreed?'

'Yes? Why?'

'Because, if they needed the GPR, why not bring it with her? Why wait three days and then call you?'

'Oh,' said Carmen. She thought for several seconds, then saw a possible explanation. 'Giulia's professor is Matteo Bianchi. You know him, I assume?'

'I know of him, sure. But we've never met.'

'He brought the GPR to the station for me. He was in a filthy mood. He gave me a message to pass on to Giulia. That he wanted *all* his equipment back by Sunday night, or else.'

'I don't...'

'Not just the GPR. *All* of it.'

'Oh,' he said. 'You think she borrowed something else?'

'It would explain it, wouldn't it? She rushed down with this other piece of equipment, only to realise later that she needed the GPR as well, which is why she called me.'

'Do you know him well enough to ask?'

She nodded and fetched her phone. She sat back down beside Cesco then put it on loudspeaker so that he could listen in. Bianchi answered almost instantly, but distractedly, surrounded by the shrieks of raucous children. 'It's me, Professor. Carmen Nero.'

'Ah! Yes.' Instantly, his tone became sombre. A door was closed; silence fell. 'What a terrible, terrible thing! Poor Giulia, I can't believe it! So sweet, so young. Are you okay yourself?'

'I'm fine,' she assured him. 'But look: I want to do what I can while I'm still down here. Only you asked me to tell Giulia that you wanted *all* your equipment back. So I was wondering, did she borrow something else?'

'Our new drone,' he told her. 'We only bought it last month. Its camera has a special infrared filter that we need for our Lake Albano survey.'

'Your drone,' she said. 'Okay. I'll see what I can find out.'

'Thank you. And take care of yourself.'

'You too.'

'His drone?' frowned Cesco once she'd hung up.

'For taking better photographs,' she explained.

'Thanks,' said Cesco drily. 'What I mean is, why would the Suraces need better photographs? If we're right, they'd already found the site

120

in question. So why not just go over there with a metal detector and a spade?'

Carmen frowned at him. 'You're missing the point, aren't you?'

'Am I? Explain.'

'Giulia brought down a camera drone. It can surely only have been to photograph this new site, yes? So all we have to do is get hold of it and the pictures on it will tell us *exactly* where to look.'

Chapter Fourteen

I

Cesco jumped to his feet and began pacing around the sofa, too excited to stay still. 'Good Christ!' he said. 'You've cracked it. You've found us Alaric.'

'Hardly,' smiled Carmen. 'I may have helped us find whatever the Suraces were on to. But that could be anything. And we still need to get hold of the drone, which means calling the police.' She rummaged through her purse for the *ispettore*'s card then held it out to him.

Cesco took it uncertainly. 'You want me to call him? Now?'

'You know what my Italian's like.'

He checked his watch. 'It's a bit late, don't you think?' he said. 'He's sure to realise something's up. Maybe he'll even study the photos for himself. Call me selfish if you like, but we've earned this. *You've* earned this. Our plaque is going to have your name in pride of place, not that of some damned *ispettore*.'

'Then...?'

'I'll call him first thing in the morning. It won't seem so odd then.'

'Okay,' she said. 'Tomorrow, then.'

He checked his watch again, hid a yawn behind his hand. 'Speaking of which,' he said. 'It's been one hell of a day. I barely slept last night. You don't mind if I crash, do you?'

'Of course not. And thank you so much for dinner. It was delicious.'

'A pleasure. Good night, then.'

He brushed his teeth, retired to his room. Then he turned off his light, sat on his bed and listened. To his frustration, Carmen didn't follow his lead but stayed up to watch a movie on her laptop. In the darkness, he wrestled with his conscience. Was he supposed to let this opportunity slip just because he happened to like her and feel a certain responsibility towards her? Longing gazes were all very well, but they had no future together. She'd drop him in a heartbeat when she found out the truth about him, which she was sure to do soon enough.

It was almost midnight before she finally turned in. He gave it another half-hour then pulled on his darkest clothes and crept silently through to the kitchen. He assembled a makeshift toolkit, including a torch, a knife, a hammer and a screwdriver. Then he slipped out of the apartment and down to his van. Traffic was light, though twice he saw police cars. The murders had stirred the city up. A cyclist wobbled drunkenly up a steep hill. A dog barked from behind a wall, setting off a chorus. He dawdled past the Suraces' place. No lights on, nor any other sign of life. There was a farm track a little way beyond their drive. He bumped down it until he was out of sight of the road, then got out.

The moon was fat and bright. It helped him hike across the fields and through an orchard. The light breeze made the trees whisper. There was a flap of wings, a hoot of owl. Somehow it all sounded like reproach. But he made a stone of his heart and ignored it. This was who he was. To deny it would be to make a mockery of his life. He neared the house, crouched to watch. Ribbons of florescent yellow police tape rippled and fluttered in the breeze. Five minutes passed. He went in. The front door was sealed with tape and bore a printed notice in a plastic sleeve that this was a crime scene and not to be disturbed. The ground-floor windows were locked and sealed, but one on the first floor was fractionally ajar. He looked for a ladder, but found instead a lean-to against the side of the house with a pile of logs beneath a tarpaulin, and a cellar hatch. It was padlocked but the wood was so rotten that he simply wrenched it out. The hinges squeaked as he lifted it by its handle. He spat on them and went again. The space beneath was black as ink, and smelled pungently of damp. He shone down his torch to get a sense of the drop then lowered himself into it. Creatures scratched and scurried. Cobwebs caught in his face. He turned his torch on again. The space was small and low, with logs against one wall, an empty wine rack and stained cardboard boxes filled with old linen. A flight of worn brick steps led up into the house. The connecting door was closed but unlocked. He slipped through. He used his torch sparingly as he went from room to room. He found nothing. He went upstairs. A passing car swept yellow light against the wall. There were three bedrooms: Vittorio's, Giulia's and a spare, its bed made up and with a bowl of flowers and a jug of water on the table, ready for Carmen's arrival. He checked beneath each of the beds, in the hanging cupboards and the chests of drawers. Still nothing.

The passage ended in what presumably had once been a fourth bedroom, but which had been converted into the museum room mentioned in the local paper. He closed the blinds before using his torch. There was a pair of exhibit cases in the middle, while the left-hand wall had been given over to photographs, maps and ancient texts. But it was the right-hand wall that drew him. All the Google Earth satellite photos of the area had been printed out, cropped and assembled like a gigantic jigsaw that ran from one end to the other, a complete overview of the Busento valley from its source a couple of kilometres west of here to its confluence with the Crati in Cosenza. Dozens of coloured pins were stuck into it, each linked by a cotton thread to a photograph of some piece of pottery, coin or other artefact, along with a short note about its discovery, an attributed date and its presumed Visigothic connection. The pick of these were on display in the exhibit cases. Others were in the drawers beneath. But there was nothing to compare to the objects in Vittorio's money belt.

The built-in wardrobe had no fitted locks on it, but steel brackets had been screwed into either door then secured by a chain and padlock. The chain was loose enough that he could pull the doors open a little way and shine his torch inside. He saw a metal detector, a pickaxe, a shovel and other heavy tools. And there was a black plastic case on the top shelf, with stickers proclaiming it the property of the Department of Archaeology at the University of Sapienza.

The drone. At last.

To force the lock would make his presence here obvious. He searched for a key instead. When that failed, he studied the brackets of the padlock latch. They'd both been painted over at some point. He scraped the paint away with the tip of his screwdriver, then undid the screws one by one. They were so stiff that his palm quickly grew red and sore. He was still working on them when he heard a noise outside. He turned off his torch and went to the window. A dark SUV was freewheeling down the drive, its headlights and engine off, moonlight reflecting in a yellow band from its windscreen. It jolted over a pothole and its suspension squeaked. Then it rolled to a stop outside the front door. Its doors opened and three men got out, wearing black gloves and balaclavas. They popped the boot and took out a pair of five-litre plastic containers each before vanishing from view. A moment later, he heard a splintering noise and then they were inside.

The 'Ndrangheta. It had to be. Almost certainly the same men who'd slit the throats of Giulia and her father. If they found him here, he could expect exactly the same treatment. Terrified, he looked around for somewhere to hide. But there was nowhere. He tiptoed back to the spare bedroom. He could hear voices below, but not what they were saying. A stair creaked. He closed the door and turned on his torch, smothering its bulb with his left hand, allowing himself only a peachy glow from between his fingers. The bedroom was awkwardly shaped, with a protruding chimney breast and a pair of slit windows on either side. The dressing table and the bed were both too high to hide beneath. The duvet was too thin. His only chance was the fitted wardrobe. He slid open its left-hand door. A few old shirts and jackets were hanging from its rack. There were winter boots on the floor and suitcases on the upper shelf. He grabbed the largest of them then climbed in, slid closed the door, huddled down behind it.

Half a minute passed. The bedroom door opened. He heard a glugging sound. The cupboard door abruptly opened. A pungent liquid was splashed all over the clothes hanging on the rack so that it dripped down onto his scalp and nape. It stank like kerosene. Footsteps hurried off. Silence fell. He could hear a pounding noise, only to realise it was just his heart. There was a shout. An engine started then quickly faded. He gave it another minute, then set aside the suitcase and emerged warily from the wardrobe. Puddles of kerosene on the floor soaked through his shoes to chill his soles. He reached the door, looked out. The first three bars of the famous old hit 'Ancora tu' played on a mobile phone. Then they played again, followed by a popping noise and a whoomp, as though the central heating was coming on.

Except there was no central heating.

That was when an orange fireball exploded up the stairs.

II

It seemed to Zara that she'd only just laid her head upon her pillow when her phone began to ring. She'd been up late with Kaufman devising a plan to secure the prison mosaics and the chambers beneath, while still satisfying Avram and the governor too, so she assumed she'd simply overslept. But then she noticed the pitch blackness outside and checked her bedside clock and realised it was still the small hours. Her phone rang again. She grabbed it if only to shut it up. 'Do you know what fucking time it is?' she shouted.

'And to think you always boasted of being an early riser,' said Avram.

'Minister?' She sat up. 'Has something happened?'

'Not exactly. But we need to talk. I'm on my way over. I'll be with you in ten minutes.' Then he hung up.

She pushed herself up onto an elbow, scowled herself awake. Her eyes were so gluey she had to squint at the bathroom mirror. She was still dressing when her buzzer sounded, so she grabbed one of Isaac's old jerseys that hung down to her knees and went to let him in.

'Apologies,' he said, in the manner of important people who don't mean it.

'Forget it.' She hid her yawn behind her hand. 'Coffee?'

'Do you have any of that apple juice you used to bring us?'

'Of course, Minister.'

'And stop calling me Minister. We used to be friends, you and I. You were the only one who ever dared mock me to my face. I used to hate it. Now I miss it.'

'I miss it too,' she admitted, pouring juice into a pair of tall glasses.

'Then let's start again. At least when it's just the two of us. Okay?'

'Okay, Avram. I'd like that.'

'Good. Good.' He sat at her table and rolled his glass back and forth between his palms. 'Now, then,' he said. 'I have a request to make.'

'A request?'

He nodded briskly. 'What I am about to propose is *highly* confidential. Whether you agree to it or not, I need your word that you won't repeat it. If you do, the prime minister and I will both flatly deny it.'

She raised her eyebrows. 'The prime minister?'

'Yes. Well?'

'Fine. You have my word.'

'Thank you. Then I can tell you that, after my return home last night, I made some phone calls, including to the prime minister. I told him of the replica Menorah we'd discovered beneath the prison, and also that there was an outside possibility that the real thing might be discovered in southern Italy. His ears pricked up at that. He is of the view, as I am, that we need to monitor developments there very closely. If nothing is found, as seems most likely, then so be it. But if this tomb *is* discovered, and the temple treasures *are* inside, we must be ready to act fast. Because there's one other thing on which we also agree. Those treasures are *our* treasures. They were stolen from us by the Romans. A long time ago, yes, but still. They belong to the Jewish people here in Israel, not for the Italians to put on display in some provincial museum. That would be an intolerable insult to our nation and our faith. You would agree with that, I trust?'

She eyed him cautiously. 'What exactly are you suggesting?'

'Nothing dramatic,' Avram assured her. 'It's a question of setting the frame, that's all. Imagine what will happen if the Italians announce that Alaric's tomb has been discovered. Public opinion in Italy and around the world will quickly settle on the idea that it and its contents – whatever they might be – are an internal matter for the Italians to deal with. Now consider a different scenario, in which news breaks that the Menorah and other temple treasures have been discovered. The exact same public will see the exact same story very differently.

They'll think it right and fitting that we Israelis have, at the very least, a seat at the table. And framing is exceedingly hard to shift once it's been established. People hate to change their minds. So it would be *greatly* in our interest for it to be the latter rather than the former.'

'Then yes,' said Zara. 'I agree absolutely.'

'Excellent. Excellent. Which brings me to my request. We will, of course, monitor events there closely through the normal channels. But the prime minister and I both agree that we also need someone on the ground. Ideally, someone not formally associated with our government, to avoid any risk of embarrassment. Someone we can trust absolutely, and who has the right contacts and historical knowledge. Someone already aware of what's going on, and what's at stake, so that we don't have to widen any further the circle of knowledge.'

Zara frowned at him, not quite sure she was following him correctly. 'You want me to go to Italy?'

'Who better?' He took a fat white envelope from his jacket pocket and set it on the table, its flap springing open far enough for her to see the wad of high-denomination euro banknotes inside. 'You're a well-established archaeologist and an expert in late antiquity, so you have a legitimate interest in Alaric. You speak passable Italian, as I recall. You're even friends with this American woman Carmen Nero, which gives you a route to the heart of things.'

'We're not friends. She's a member of a discussion group I help moderate, that's all.'

'That will be good enough for this, I assure you.'

'Good enough for what?'

'Go to Cosenza. Send her a message through your group or bump into her on the street. I'm sure I can leave the detail up to you. You probably wouldn't fly over just for this, so I'd suggest telling her that you were in Italy already. At a conference, maybe, or a friend's wedding. You saw the story about Alaric and had to check it out for yourself. You're a highly respected figure in her world; she'll believe whatever you say. Then use her to find out what's going on. Get as close to the search as you can without drawing undue attention to yourself. Let us know if anything turns up. That's all. It will almost certainly blow over in a day or two, and you can return home. But it would be unforgivable for us not to take such modest steps as these, in case it doesn't.'

She stared at him, unnerved, though not quite sure why. 'Let you know how, exactly?'

'You can't be seen to be there on our behalf. For all our sakes, this has to appear a purely private trip. But obviously we'll need to be kept abreast too, in case we need to respond, so we'll be sending over one of our best men to act as liaison. His name is Dov. He has great cover and plenty of experience. He'll be completely invisible, except to you. He'll take care of all the communications side of things, without exposing you to the slightest risk. And he'll be on hand should you need any other kind of support.'

'What is he? Mossad?'

'I can't tell you that, I'm afraid. You don't have clearance. But he'll make contact with you when you arrive in Cosenza tonight.'

'*Tonight?*'

'Of course. Why else do you think I'd disturb you at this obscene hour? Sunday flights are thin, but there are still seats available on one to Rome early this afternoon, with a connection down to Lamezia Terme. That's a ninety-minute drive from Cosenza, so you'll need to hire a car. And book a hotel room, of course. I'd do it for you, except for the paper trail.' He gestured at the envelope. 'But that will cover it easily, along with any other expenses you might incur.'

'And my classes? My tutorials?'

'I'm sure your university has dealt with unexpected absences before. Or do none of you ever fall ill?'

'And if I won't go?'

Avram gave her a disappointed look. 'Your nation is asking you for your help, Zara,' he said. 'Are you really going to tell her no?'

III

Cesco slammed shut the bedroom door a fraction of a moment before the fireball reached him. He counted to five then opened it again, hoping the first eruption would have died down enough for him to make it to the museum room and the drone. Not a chance. Clouds of acrid smoke came billowing in, scorching tears from his eyes and sending him into a coughing fit. The puddles on the bedroom floor ignited in flaming pools. He put up his forearms to protect his face, but his shirt had been spattered with the kerosene and now caught fire so that he had to strip it off and throw it away as he stumbled blindly for the left-hand slit window. He tried to open it but it had been painted shut years before. He smashed the glass with his elbow. Fresh air rushed in, adding oxygen to the mix. A great ball of flame billowed past him and took off into the night sky like a hot air balloon. He began clearing the frame of shards, thinking he might squeeze through. But he knew in his heart that the slit would still be too narrow for him, that he'd get caught between its glassy teeth then held there captive for the flames. He checked the second window, but it was, if anything, even narrower. The blaze was growing ever fiercer. The smoke was blinding. He couldn't stop hacking and coughing. He could feel it poisoning his system too, clouding up his head.

He ducked down to where the air was clearer to help himself think. There was a vase of flowers and a jug of water on the bedside table. He tipped them both over the duvet then wrapped it around himself like a protective cloak. He crawled across the floor to the door, opened it once more. It was an inferno outside, the floor and walls on fire, spewing out clouds of thick black smoke. There was no way down the stairs. He tried to recall which of the other bedrooms offered the best hope of escape. He rose to a crouch, still huddled beneath the duvet, then stumbled across the passage to Giulia's room, feeling blindly for her door, barging it with his shoulder then falling on through, his eyes now almost completely useless, coughing incessantly, a thickening fog inside his head, weights in all his limbs. Half of him just wanted to lie down, but the other half kept fighting. He forced his left eye open to a squint, glimpsed the window. That was what he needed. A window. He staggered towards it, still clutching the duvet tight. He crashed into it. It didn't yield. He stepped back and butted the pane with his head. The glass shattered and fell out. Instantly, flames grew wild around him, like jailers rushing to prevent an escape. He twisted around and hurled himself out. The remaining shards of glass snagged the duvet's cotton cover and held it back. He hung on to it for a moment, but then his own weight and momentum ripped it from his grasp. He hit the ground hard, turning his ankle as he fell, spilling onto his arm and shoulder, giving his head a crack. He lay there dazed for several seconds, until roused by his own fierce coughing. He felt the scorch of flame still on his skin and scrambled away on hands and knees. His eyes cleared. The house was going up like a funeral pyre. Someone was certain to see it soon. They'd see it and alert the emergency services. He needed to get out of here right now.

He pushed himself to his feet, hobbled gingerly across the fields. His shoes were wet with water and kerosene, making them squelch with every step. He reached his van, drove up to the road. He turned away from Cosenza to avoid the fire engines and the police. It began to grow light away to the east. Traffic picked up too. He felt absurdly conspicuous without a shirt. But somehow he made it safely home. He parked directly outside, hurried upstairs and let himself in, leaning against the apartment door in relief.

The 'Ndrangheta. The fucking 'Ndrangheta.

Screw Alaric. He was out of here.

He washed his face and hands, put on clean clothes, packed, went through to the kitchen. He found a sheet of paper and wrote Carmen a short note, inventing a Sicilian great-aunt who'd just suffered a terrible stroke and wasn't expected to see out the day. The apartment was paid for until Wednesday, he assured her; he'd get back in touch as soon as he heard more. He left his keys on the table, shouldered his bag and went to the front door.

Then he stopped.

A note wasn't enough. Cesco Rossi PhD would never leave Carmen without saying goodbye, however early it might be. He put his ear to her door. He could hear her soft, slow breathing. He knocked then went on in. He stood by her bedside and looked down. She was lying on her back with her face turned to the side, protecting her bandaged temple. 'Hey,' he said. She didn't stir. The little light that made it through the curtains gave her face the same grey pallor as when he'd first seen her, lying unconscious at the foot of the embankment. The way she'd opened her eyes when he'd ripped the tape off her mouth.

'*Are they gone?*' she'd asked.

'*They're gone,*' he'd assured her. '*You're safe now.*'

Cesco hadn't chosen his life. It had been forced on him by circumstance. He hadn't complained about this, but rather had adapted himself to it. Yet there were times when the cost of being an outlaw became clear. When you always had to be ready to leave at a moment's notice, you never let yourself make any true friends; and you most certainly never risked falling in love. Otherwise, the pain of leaving became too much. He didn't know why those men tonight had burned down the farmhouse. But it was clear that the threat they posed hadn't died with the Suraces. To leave Carmen oblivious, with no one to look out for her... He couldn't. He just couldn't.

Yet nor could he tell her the truth.

He went back out, quietly closed her bedroom door. He tore his note into tiny pieces that he tossed into the bin. He returned to his bedroom, unpacked his bag and climbed into his bed. Then he closed his eyes and covered his face with his hands, not entirely sure what was happening to him.

Chapter Fifteen

I

Carmen woke to a faint yet distinctive whiff of heating oil. It concerned her enough to rouse her from her bed. She checked the passage and outside her window, but saw nothing to alarm her. She left the window open to air, then washed, dressed and went through to the kitchen, only to find the same smell there too. She checked the landing and went out onto the balcony, but still there was nothing, so she brewed a pot of coffee then lost herself on the internet for a while, before paying a visit to the website of the local newspaper to see if there'd been any further developments.

The breaking story on its home page stunned her. The Suraces' farmhouse was a smouldering husk. She stared at it in dismay. She'd managed somehow to blank Cemetery Teeth and Famine Eyes from her mind. Now they returned with a vengeance. Unnerved, she went to bolt closed the front door and was about to go wake Cesco when she remembered how tired he'd been last night and how early it still was. Yet she needed to tell him.

With eggs and porcini mushrooms from the fridge, she whipped up an omelette that she put on a tray along with a buttered roll and a cup of coffee. He groaned at her knock. She took it as an invitation to go in. His room had the same smell as hers, only stronger.

'Something terrible has happened,' she told him, setting the tray down on his lap.

He looked gloomily down at the omelette. 'I did warn you to stay out of the kitchen.'

'I'm serious,' she said, drawing his curtains and raising his sash window. 'There's been a fire. At the Suraces' place.'

He gazed at her blankly, as though he wasn't sure he'd heard correctly. 'A fire? How bad?'

'As bad as it gets. Their house is completely gutted.'

'But...' He looked bewildered. 'Was it arson?'

'They're not saying. But it has to be, right? And by those same bastards, too. The ones who murdered Vittorio and Giulia.'

'But... *why?*'

'How the hell would I know?'

He noted the strain in her voice and nodded soberly. 'Give me ten minutes. I'll come through.'

She returned to the kitchen, feeling better. But then she realised what a setback the fire represented for their search. It was certain to have destroyed the drone and with it any chance of finding what it was the Suraces had photographed. But maybe there was another way. Giulia and Vittorio had spotted something on Google's latest set of satellite photos, after all. Maybe she could too.

She brought them up on her laptop and set to work.

II

One of these days. One of these fucking days.

Knöchel was in a filthy mood. They'd moved to Cosenza at such short notice that the best accommodation available had been a three-bedroom place on Cosenza's northern fringe, which of course meant sharing a room with Oddo and his toxic farting. As if that wasn't bad enough, Dieter had rousted them all first thing just to waste yet more hours driving around this shithole looking for a white van with an A.C. Milan sticker and a hula girl, even though it was almost certainly halfway across the country by now. And no doubt Dieter was happily tucked up in bed again, laughing himself sick at them for being mugs. That fucker was getting too big for his boots, that was the truth of it. One of these days he'd push him too far. One of these fucking days.

Except Knöchel had been saying one of these days for three years now, and Dieter was still boss.

He came to a junction. These streets all looked the same. He turned right. It led him down to a river embankment. Because of course it fucking did. The damned place seemed to be made of nothing else. He revved his engine as he went. If he couldn't sleep, why the fuck should anyone else? A bridge ahead. He recognised it from last night. He swore and pulled a U-turn. That was when he saw it, parked in plain view outside an apartment building, a white van with an adhesive A.C. Milan banner on its side. He drove right by it to make sure and, yes, there was the girl on its dashboard.

It was almost in disbelief that he used his Bluetooth headset to call Dieter. 'Hey, boss,' he said. 'I've found him.'

III

It was twenty minutes before Cesco had finished his breakfast in bed, showered, shaved and dressed. He carried his tray through to the kitchen where he found Carmen waiting impatiently with her jacket already on and an enigmatic smile on her lips. 'What's up?' he asked.

She slung her purse over her shoulder. 'Road trip,' she said.

'Where to?'

'You'll see.'

'Come on, Carmen. Share.'

Her eyes twinkled. 'It's a surprise. Humour me. But I'll tell you this much. I think I've solved the problem you raised last night, about why Giulia brought down the drone rather than just going to visit the place they'd found with a metal detector and a spade.'

'And?'

'You'll have to come with me to find out, won't you?'

'Okay,' he said. He set down the tray, pocketed his keys. Only on their way downstairs did he remember that he'd left the van in a different spot from last night. Thankfully, Carmen didn't seem to notice. 'Well?' he asked. 'Which way?'

'Towards the Suraces' house.'

Cesco frowned. He'd passed several cars last night driving away from the fire. Any one of them might have reported a shirtless man in

135

a white van with A.C. Milan banners on its sides. 'It's a crime scene,' he said. 'We'll just be a nuisance.'

'Not *to* it. *Towards* it.'

He belted himself in, pulled away. A few hardy Alaric hunters were already out, snorkelling the Busento's shallows on hands and knees, scouring its banks with metal detectors. Otherwise it was quiet. They went over the humpback bridge, climbed the roadworks hill then crossed back over the high bridge before turning left up Via Virgilio. Cesco drove on until the Surace farmhouse was barely a kilometre away. He glanced at Carmen. She gestured him onwards. He couldn't risk it. He turned up a short track and stopped in front of a tall metal gate with 'Keep Out' warnings and a pair of CCTV cameras on its posts. 'Come on, Carmen,' he said. 'Enough mystery.'

'It's only a tiny bit further.'

'Just tell me, okay.'

She squinted at him. 'Why? What's going on?'

'How do you mean?'

'I mean you went out last night, didn't you? After I went to bed. Why?'

He put on his best baffled face. 'Went out? What are you talking about?'

'I'm talking about the fact your van was parked in a different spot this morning. So you must have taken it out again after I went to bed. Where? Why?'

'Fine,' sighed Cesco. 'You got me. I lied yesterday about not knowing anyone here any more. There's this one girl I kept in touch with. We had coffee yesterday morning, before I came to the hospital. But she's married, so she made me swear I—'

'Did you come into my room last night? While I was asleep?'

'*What?* Why would you even—'

'My room stank this morning. But not as strongly as yours. It stank of...' She looked at him in sudden horror. 'The Suraces' house,' she said. 'It was *you*.'

'This is nuts, Carmen. Why on earth would I—'

'For the drone, of course. To steal the photos for yourself then burn the house down so I'd never know.'

136

His whole life, Cesco's quick tongue had saved him in situations like this. All he'd ever had to do was open his mouth and somehow the lies would come tumbling out, even when he'd had no idea in advance what he was going to say. But now, to his dismay, his mouth simply hung there. Carmen took his silence for confession. She found the *ispettore*'s card in her purse then unlocked her phone with her thumb. His heart sank. He couldn't let her make the call. The police would find out who he really was and then everything would come out. He reached across and wrested the phone from her. She looked at him in sudden fear. She released her seat belt, grabbed her purse and climbed out.

Her phone was warm in his hand. So warm it was almost hot. He stared at it in puzzlement. It was warm even though it had been on standby and in her bag this whole time. And it had a thumbprint lock too. Just like that, he saw it all, including why those men had felt the need to torch the Suraces' farmhouse last night, and what it meant for them both right now too. He looked away to his left. Sunlight glinted off the windscreen of a black SUV as it hurtled down the next track along. He felt helpless. Overwhelmed. So much to explain, so little time. He tried to grab Carmen by her wrist to drag her back in but she yelped and jumped backwards out of his reach.

The SUV was almost at the road. He needed to get out of here. He pulled closed her door then tossed her phone down on her empty seat. She threw him a look of such utter revulsion that he knew their friendship was forever finished. It felt like a knife being slid between his ribs. He reversed out onto the road. Then, in a screech of rubber, he thrust the van into gear and sped off back towards Cosenza.

Chapter Sixteen

I

In nine hours and twenty-seven minutes, Baldassare was due to stand at a podium in Cosenza City Hall to announce to a room full of reporters and the wider world whether he would be bringing charges against the Critelli brothers and their top brass, or letting them all go instead and charging only a handful of their foot soldiers.

All night – all month – he'd been wrestling with this problem. Yet still he hadn't come to a decision. Worse, rather than giving it his best effort now – as any normal person would be doing – he found himself standing in the corner of his office instead, glued to the local news on an old portable TV, as it reported on the blaze that had gutted the Suraces' farmhouse.

There'd been no official confirmation yet, but surely it was arson. More precisely, surely it was the handiwork of the same 'Ndrangheta cell that had murdered the Suraces two days before. Yet none of the people they had under surveillance had gone anywhere near the Suraces' house last night – nor had there been any hint of such an operation in the communications they were tapping. So who exactly were these people? What did this sudden spike in their activity mean? Specifically, what did it mean *for him*?

As well as working on the case against the Critelli brothers and their 'ndrine, Baldassare had completed another project over these past few weeks – developing a plan called Operation Trinity under the wide authority granted him by the *Direzioni Investigativa Antimafia*. It was ready to go, and had been for a week. All he had to do now was press send on his laptop or his phone and a cascade of orders would go out to the regional chiefs of the *Carabinieri*, the *Polizia di Stato*, the *Guardia di Finanza* and the *Corpo Forestale di Stato*, triggering the mass arrests of dozens more 'Ndrangheta suspects in order to search their properties and seize their records. A dozen times a day over the past week, Baldassare had built himself up to topple this first domino. But he'd always lost his nerve. The stakes were too high. The price of failure too steep.

Baldassare had been raised a Catholic. As a boy, he'd been beguiled by the theatrics of its services. All that incense, all those chants and rituals. All those imposing buildings with their glorious art. It had been inconceivable to him that so many people could have put so much effort into something that simply wasn't true. Yet his job had steadily flayed him of his faith. The horrors that he'd seen. In its place, he'd come to believe in diligence, solid information and hard work. But diligence, solid information and hard work had now failed him too, and he was out of time.

He turned off the TV and went to sit at his desk. He touched for luck the silver frame of the photograph of his wife and daughter he kept on it. He bowed his head, clasped his hands and closed his eyes. Then, for the first time in twenty years, he prayed.

II

The instant Cesco reversed back out into the road, Carmen's alarm turned to anger. He'd taken her phone with him so that she couldn't call the police, but another car was approaching fast so she ran out onto the road to wave it down. It screeched to a halt beside her. She stooped at its window, trying to formulate in her mind the Italian she'd need to explain herself. The driver buzzed down his window and smiled reassuringly at her, exposing his teeth as he did so – his cemetery teeth. Carmen froze in shock a millisecond then glanced across at his passenger. It was Famine Eyes. She recognised them both with absolute certainty even though neither were wearing balaclavas today. And any doubt she might have had would have been dispelled by the sawn-off shotgun that Famine Eyes was holding across his lap.

The rear door opened. A young man got out. Maybe the one from before, she couldn't tell. He had a pistol in his waistband and a hunting knife in his hand. The SUV sped off again, leaving her alone with him. She looked around for help but there was no one. She retreated back up the farm track. His knife glinted in the sunlight. She couldn't tear her eyes from it. Her legs turned to water. She reached the gate and waved frantically at the CCTV cameras. The young man only grinned. The gateposts and wall were topped by broken glass, the gate itself by strands of barbed wire. It had hinges at one end. She used them as a crude ladder to reach the top. She laid her purse over the wire to vault it. Her sleeve snagged on a barb and the tug of it unbalanced her so that she landed badly, sprawling on her hands and knees.

She got to her feet and looked around. She was at the bottom corner of a large meadow dotted by wild flowers of blue and red and yellow, enclosed by the wall behind and thick hawthorn hedges, sloping upwards to a whitewashed farmhouse. She set off running towards it. Behind her, the young man used his leather jacket to protect himself from the barbed wire, his knife clamped in his teeth like a Hollywood pirate. He jumped down then came after her, briskly but without urgency, content to let her set the pace. Almost as though he were herding her. Then, to her horror, she realised that that was exactly what he was doing. And where she was too. It had just looked so different in the satellite photos. And finally she understood. Everything that she'd believed was going on, and everything that the Suraces before her had believed, it had all of it been wrong.

III

Cesco watched his rear-view mirror in dismay as Carmen ran out into the road to wave down the black SUV. He saw it stop and its back door open. He was so transfixed by it that he almost drove off the road into a motorcyclist parked on the verge. He put up his hand to apologise only to see that it was Knöchel, one of Dieter's crew. And talking urgently into his helmet microphone too.

But he had no time to process what it meant.

Carmen's phone was still on his passenger seat. It was bugged. It had to be. It was the only way everything made sense. Those men had unlocked it with her thumb while she'd been unconscious, installing some malicious app on it so that they could monitor her and the investigation both, even when it was ostensibly turned off. And maybe they were monitoring it still. He grabbed it up. 'Let her go,' he shouted. 'Let her go or I tell the police everything.'

The mocking laughter shocked him. He hadn't expected it to be two-way. 'Everything!' said a man. 'You know shit.'

'You were at the Suraces' place last night,' said Cesco. 'Three of you, wearing balaclavas, each carrying a pair of kerosene containers. I was there too. I took your licence plate. I'll give it to the police if—'

'Do that and she dies.'

'Then let her go. Let her go and I forget everything. You have my word.'

'And you have mine. Keep quiet until midnight and she can live.'

Engine noise behind. He checked his mirrors. The SUV was behind him and closing fast. He cursed himself for losing focus and tossed Carmen's phone out of the window into a hedge so that they couldn't use it to track him. He stamped down his foot but the SUV was too fast. It quickly caught up. He swerved across the road to block it from drawing alongside. There was a sharp right turn ahead, over the high bridge. He let the SUV draw level on his left side. Its window was down and the passenger reached out a sawn-off shotgun. Cesco turned his back even as he fired. His window shattered. His left arm and shoulder blazed with pain. He wrenched the wheel around even so. With a screech of tortured rubber, he swung out onto the bridge, banging sideways into a buttress. The SUV carried on down the other road for a short distance before it could brake and reverse back up. Cesco sped across the bridge. Ahead of him, Dieter and his other two mates appeared on their Harleys. That bastard Knöchel must have summoned them. They fanned out in a bold but dumb attempt to block him. He drove straight at them and they scattered like skittles. He swung down the roadworks hill towards Cosenza. The SUV reappeared behind him. Again the road was too narrow for them to pull alongside. He reached the foot of the hill and tried to swing the van around, but his old tyres had no more grip left to give and he screeched straight across the junction, riding up a grass bank that flipped the van over onto its side then took it skittering along a rutted track. He flung up his arms to protect his face as he hit the perimeter wall of an apartment block. He spun another turn or two before coming to a halt. His windscreen fell away like a theatre curtain. He was facing back the way he'd come even as the black SUV arrived up the track and pulled sedately to a stop just a few feet away.

The passenger door opened and a middle-aged man climbed out, his face largely concealed by the combination of his mirror sunglasses, his tugged-down baseball cap and the turned-up collar of his black leather jacket. Then he advanced with chilling composure, his sawn-off shotgun held down against his leg as Cesco sat there, dazed and helpless, still strapped into his seat.

Chapter Seventeen

I

It was, perversely, Dieter himself who saved Cesco. Specifically, the rich sputter of his Harley as he pulled up alongside the SUV, flanked by his three mates. The man with the shotgun frowned at them, puzzled rather than alarmed by their arrival. But even that short delay gave time for balcony doors to open and residents to step out, drawn by the noise of the crash. The sheer number of onlookers seemed to decide him. He turned back to Cesco. 'Midnight,' he said. Then, with the shotgun still pressed against his leg, he climbed back into the SUV which promptly reversed out onto the road then sped off up the hill.

Cesco had no time to celebrate. Dieter was after a reckoning of his own, and was indifferent to witnesses. Cesco released himself from his seat belt and scrambled out through the empty windscreen. His van was lying across the full width of the track, blocking the bikes from passing. He clambered over it to put it between him and them. His left arm and shoulder were throbbing violently. His sleeve was wet with blood. He stumbled onwards along the track to an iron footbridge across a mountain stream that fed into the Busento a hundred yards or so to his left.

A glance behind. Knöchel was chasing him on foot while Dieter and the others roared away on their bikes to cut him off from the other end. He briefly contemplated trying to take Knöchel on, but the man was way too big for him, even without his injuries. He reached a footpath. It took him down to the Busento. Dieter and his mates were racing along its far bank towards the next bridge up. He unbuttoned his shirt and pulled it down over his shoulder to check the damage, but there was too much blood for him to see the—

Footsteps sprinting behind. He turned to see Knöchel almost upon him. He lunged for Cesco, but Cesco ducked and twisted and somehow got away. Knöchel had given his all to catch him and now staggered to a halt, hands upon his knees. But he was still blocking Cesco's retreat, while Dieter, Rudolph and Oddo had by now crossed to his side of the Busento and were roaring back towards him. He fled into the grounds of a council building. It was closed for the weekend but had a small recycling area on one side. He jumped up onto a bin, hauled himself over the brick wall behind. He fought through a hedge, crossed a road, ran up a flight of steps. A pair of women stepped back to let him pass. He yelled at them to call the police. He emerged onto another road as a blue Fiat trundled by, a scaffolding pole strapped to its roof like a jousting knight. Two of the bikers appeared to his right. Cesco fled the other way along a derelict alley of bricked-up doorways and boarded windows. Rusted bars protruded from where balconies had once been, and purple wisteria draped tumbledown walls like wanton vines.

He emerged into Cosenza's old town, a labyrinth of cobbled alleys flanked by buildings tall enough to make the neck ache, and narrow enough that you could shake hands across the balconies. A nightmarish game of fox and hounds now took place, in which he used the numerous short flights of steps to gain respite, while Dieter, Oddo and Rudolph used their numbers like a net. He dodged by a cement mixer and a wine barrel, ducked beneath a washing line strung with rugs for sale. His lungs were aching, his legs sacks of rice. He stumbled into a moped and sent it clattering.

He staggered down more steps out onto the Piazza Duomo. Dieter appeared to his left, Oddo and Rudolph to his right. He turned down a slick cobbled ramp into an archaeological park protected by a patchwork of triangular glass panes set at odd angles to one another, to offer tourists good views of the Roman ruins beneath. He ran by a pair of elderly tourists studying a street map, grabbed a railing and swung around to stop himself tumbling down a flight of metal steps. Behind him, Oddo wasn't so fortunate. In swerving to avoid the two tourists, he went rattling down the steps before crashing into the viewing platform at their foot. Right behind him, Rudolph also went skittering; while Dieter hit a metal railing so hard that his back wheel kicked up like a bucking horse and sent him flying over its handlebars. He put his arms up to protect his head but the pane shattered when he hit it and he tumbled in a shower of broken glass down into the ruins beneath, while his helmet pinballed across the other panes before rolling back down again for Cesco to trap beneath his foot like a cocky midfielder.

The Harley was somehow still running. Its guard was buckled but its front wheel looked fine. He picked it up, straddled it, gave it revs. Dieter glared pure hatred up at him from the ruins below. The woman tourist was crying in pain and clutching her elbow. Sirens were closing fast. Cesco strapped on the helmet then nodded down at Dieter and set off along a narrow alley even as police lights lit the piazza behind him blue.

II

The sound of sirens above got Dieter pushing himself to his feet, shards of broken glass spilling from him and crunching beneath his feet. But the moment he put weight upon his left leg, he felt his knee go pop and a spike of pain shot up from it as though someone had swung at it with the pointed end of a pickaxe. He gave a cry and fell back down.

Shouting above. A scuffling noise. Rudolph was trying to make a break for it across the glass roof. But he was collared a moment later by two burly cops. Dieter swore and dragged himself along the concrete floor to the exit, but the fucking door was locked. Ancient stones were scattered across the floor. He picked one up and smashed the handle until the lock gave. He hobbled out and off, clutching his knee. A man shouted to alert the police to his escape. Thankfully, he was still in the old town with its labyrinth of alleys. He put his hand against the wall to hold himself up, then turned this way and that to shake pursuit. An old hag came out onto her porch to check on the commotion. She saw him and immediately took out her mobile. He punched her hard and her head smacked against the frame of her door. She fell onto her back. Blood poured from her nose and mouth and from a gash on her temple. He staggered on, taking out his own phone to call Knöchel. He answered on the second ring. 'Where the fuck are you?' he demanded.

'On my way. Why?'

'It's gone to shit. Everything's gone to shit. The police are every-where.'

'Hell.'

'You need to dump your bike right now. They'll be looking for it. Go jack a car or a van. Come pick me up.' He sent him his coordinates as he limped into an alley. He pulled out a large green wheelie bin overflowing with black refuse bags then sank down behind it, his back to the wall, his leg stretched out in front of him. Now the pain started in earnest. It was all he could do not to cry out. Sirens screeched by. Footsteps pounded cobbles. His left knee was swelling visibly. Gingerly, he peeled down his jeans to look. It was the size of a fucking football already, and turning storm-cloud colours. He was about to call Knöchel again to tell him to get a move on when suddenly the man himself pulled up across the mouth of the alley in a battered blue minivan.

Dieter struggled to his feet and hobbled across. He banged his knee on the frame as he climbed into the back. He howled in agony, he couldn't help himself. 'Shit,' said Knöchel, turning a touch pale when he saw the damage. 'You've done your ACL for sure. I'll get you to a doctor.'

'Fuck that. We clear the house then you drive me home.'

'But—'

'*Home, fuck it.*' That woman he'd punched, who could say how badly hurt she was. No way was he doing time for some old hag like that. Their clinic back in Stuttgart had doctors who not only knew better than to blab, they'd give him an alibi too. He stretched out along the back seats still clutching his knee, trying vainly to find an angle for it that didn't hurt so much. They set off. The road was cobbled and uneven. He bellowed in pain at every jolt. But when Knöchel slowed down in response he yelled at him to keep going. They reached their rented house. Knöchel parked outside and ran on in. He grabbed all their belongings, tossed them in the back of the van. He went back in to wipe the place of fingerprints before reappearing with a blister pack of ibuprofen, a bag of ice cubes for Dieter's knee and a towel to wrap around it. Then he got behind the wheel again and set off north.

The painkillers took a while to work. Even then they only made space in Dieter's head for a different kind of pain to make itself felt. Twice now he'd been humiliated by that shit Cesco Rossi. It couldn't stand. *It couldn't stand.* He punched the roof of the minivan. He'd thought he'd hated the bastard before, but that was nothing compared to the black rage that now boiled inside him like a cauldron of tar. He closed his eyes and brought that little fucker's face to his mind's eye, that cocky little nod he'd given before setting off on his bike. He clenched his fist and kissed it and made a solemn vow. He'd get himself out of this shithole country one way or another. He'd fix his knee. Then, when he was ready, he'd come back for Cesco Rossi. He'd come back and visit such pain on him that he'd have him begging for the knife.

III

The black SUV stayed carefully beneath the speed limit as it wound up the hill roads to Moccono. In the passenger seat, Tomas Gentile switched between the various channels used by Cosenza law enforcement. It seemed as though their good friends in blue uniforms were unaware of their own earlier escapades. Indeed, they had their hands full chasing a pack of bikers through the city's old town.

'You think it's those same fucks?' asked his brother Guido, behind the wheel.

'It most certainly sounds like it,' said Tomas.

'They were after Rossi too. That's why they spread out on that bridge.'

'You don't say.'

'Yeah. I'm pretty sure.' He glanced across at him. 'You think he'll give us to midnight, like you asked?'

'I don't think we should count on it.'

'Then what?'

'Let us start with some silence, oh my brother. I need to think.'

They passed through Moccono, reached the entrance to their drive. It wound through olive groves to a paved forecourt bordered by shrubberies and pines. It was one of their own properties, held through an offshore company that not even the Critelli brothers knew about.

Tomas got out. He went down the garage ramp to unlock and raise its door. There was a silver Range Rover parked inside. He reversed it out to make space for the SUV, where no one would find it unless things had already gone to shit. Guido parked it and came out again. He lowered and locked the garage door then joined him in the Range Rover. Tomas slid across to let him take the wheel. He always let Guido drive, if he could. It wasn't that he disliked driving as such. It was that it made it easier to think.

'Well?' asked Guido.

'We go back,' said Tomas. 'We watch the house for any sign of our good friends in blue uniforms.'

'And if they turn up?'

Tomas spread his hands. 'Then what choice will we have, oh my brother?'

IV

Cesco waited until he reached the open roads outside Cosenza before opening the Harley up. Its acceleration almost blew him off the back. He didn't much care for Dieter, but the man knew how to buy a bike. His mind raced as he sped along. He replayed his brief conversation with the man from the black SUV. He knew better than most the nature of such men. They'd weep salty tears about the importance of honour. Then they'd chop up puppies for their parts. So he didn't for one moment believe his midnight promise. Yet it had been so oddly specific that it didn't just offer Cesco a window, it offered him a *clue*.

The roads were so improved since he'd been here last that he barely recognised them. New housing developments had sprung up everywhere. He almost missed his turning. But the road up to the hilltop was unforgettable, scoring its way upwards in sharp zigzags. He took the last hairpin and there it was, the high perimeter wall exactly as he recalled, only recently whitewashed and fitted with new CCTV cameras. Men in khaki slacks and short-sleeved blue shirts stood on either side of a security booth, their Beretta sub-machine guns raised high enough to warn rather than threaten. He let gravity slow him to a halt some ten paces shy of them, then stood up the Harley and spread his hands wide.

One of the men gestured him off. He dismounted, slowly unstrapped and took off his helmet. He set it on the seat then took a couple of steps towards them with his arms still outstretched, despite the fearful throbbing from the shotgun pellets. 'I need to see your boss,' he said.

The man grunted. 'Sure you do.'

'Please. I'm begging you.'

'Not today. No chance. No visitors, not under any circumstances.'

'A life's at stake.'

'So go to the police. That's what they're for.'

'The police can't help. Not with this. Only Judge Mancuso.'

'Then come back tomorrow.'

'Tomorrow will be too late.'

'That's quite a problem then.'

'How about a message?' pleaded Cesco. 'Can you at least get him a message?'

The men glanced at one another. His obvious desperation was getting through. 'Saying what?' asked one.

Cesco gave himself a moment. He had one shot at this. Carmen's name *might* get Baldassare's attention. But there was another that was sure to. And fuck it, it was time. He stuck out his chest, he lifted his chin. For the first time in fifteen years, he felt a certain pride in himself. 'Tell him that Giovanni Carbone is here to see him,' he said. 'And that this is my home you bastards are all living in.'

Baldassare looked up irritably from his work when Sandro knocked and entered. 'What is it now?' he asked.

'There's a man here to see you, sir,' said Sandro.

'Didn't I make myself clear?' scowled Baldassare. 'No disturbances. No exceptions.'

'Yes, sir. But he's claiming... Forgive me, sir, but he's claiming to be Giovanni Carbone. You know. Federico's grandson.'

Baldassare stood up, electrified. 'Giovanni Carbone is dead. He was murdered fifteen years ago with his twin sister, then dumped at sea.'

'Yes, sir. I know. But that's what he's saying. And he's about the right age and they sent up a photograph from the gate, and I have to tell you...' He came over to the desk holding out his phone.

Baldassare saw instantly what Sandro meant: the man unquestionably had Federico's strong chin and bright blue eyes. There was something else too. He could have sworn he'd seen him recently, though he couldn't work out where. 'Have him brought up,' he said. They went together to the front door. Carbone arrived a minute later in the back of one of their Toyota Land Cruisers. The moment he stepped out, Baldassare knew it to be true. It was the proud way he held himself, despite his ruined shirt and the blood dripping down his arm. In a daze, he went down the steps to greet him. 'Your sister?' he asked.

Carbone shook his head. 'No.'

'I'm so sorry.'

He waved it aside for more urgent matters. 'The American woman Carmen Nero. The one you visited in hospital yesterday morning. The 'Ndrangheta have her.'

Baldassare stared at him. 'What do you mean, they have her?'

'They've taken her hostage,' he said. 'What do you think I mean?'

'Hostage? Are you sure?'

'Of course I'm fucking sure.' He gestured at the sleeve of his shirt, caked with blood. 'They'll kill her unless we can find her.'

'Tell me. Tell me everything.'

'I will. I swear. Once we're on our way.'

'Our way where?'

'To their base. We need to get there before they move her.'

Baldassare stared at him. His heart longed to believe but his head yelled caution. Carbone should be dead. Maybe he'd survived by vowing loyalty to the Critellis. Maybe this was some kind of elaborate trap. 'We're not going anywhere,' he said. 'Not until I understand. How do you even know this woman?'

'I was the one who found her.'

'You? Cesco Rossi? The archaeologist?'

'Yes. No.' His frustration was palpable. 'Rossi is the name I'm going by at the moment. I can hardly use my real one, can I? But no, I'm not an archaeologist.'

'Then what are you?'

'I'm a conman,' he said flatly. 'A conman and a thief.'

Baldassare stared at him. He'd taken countless confessions in his time. None quite like this. A sudden glimpse of a fourteen-year-old-boy who'd somehow survived the slaughter of his family, traumatised and alone. Who could blame him for doing whatever it took to survive? 'Tell me more.'

'I was down in Scilla,' said Cesco. 'I got rumbled. I had to get out fast. Giulia Surace had invited me to stay. I arrived to find her and her father already dead, but Carmen still alive. Then I learned that the Suraces had been closing in on Alaric's tomb. So I thought, why not? I went to the hospital to chat Carmen up, thinking she might know something. You and I actually passed in the corridor.'

Baldassare nodded. He had him now. 'You had long hair and a beard.'

'Yes. Anyway, I hooked up with her. She figured out what had got the Suraces so excited: some kind of feature revealed by Google's latest set of satellite photos. It looked so promising that Giulia took the first train down, bringing a drone camera with her. This made no sense to me. Why take more photographs? Why not go straight there with a metal detector and a spade? But Carmen worked out why. It was because they *couldn't*. It was because the feature in question is on a plot of land protected by high walls, thick hedges and CCTV. We parked right by it this morning.'

Baldassare pinched the bridge of his nose, the better to get it clear in his mind. 'Go on.'

'I'm guessing now, but I'm sure I'm right. The Suraces flew their drone over the site in question, in order to make sure that there really was something there. There was. So they moved on to the next stage, which was to run a ground-penetrating radar over it, to see exactly what they were dealing with before they started to dig. The Suraces saw themselves as amateur archaeologists rather than treasure hunters, you see. They wanted to do it properly. So Giulia invited Carmen to stay for the weekend as a pretext for having her bring down the GPR down. She invited me too, because she thought I knew how to use it. Then they went to see the landowners to ask permission to run the survey, explaining to them that they believed they'd found Alaric's tomb on their land. Unfortunately, the landowners were 'Ndrangheta. Now imagine telling the 'Ndrangheta that they've got a fabulous lost tomb buried on their land, and that only you know about it.'

'That's why they killed them? For Alaric's gold?'

'And why they burned their farmhouse too,' nodded Cesco. 'The drone still had their photographs on it, you see, so they needed to destroy it before anyone could find them and realise their significance. And yes, before you ask, I know for sure it was them who set the fire. I saw them at it.'

'You *what*?'

His face blazed with shame. 'I'll tell you everything, I swear. Every shitty detail. But on the way, okay? Every minute we waste is more time for them to get away.'

'One last question. Why me? Why not the police?'

'They vowed to kill her if I went to them. You know how those bastards leak. But they also told me they'd let her live if I kept quiet until midnight. Bullshit. She's seen their faces. But I asked myself, why midnight? What's happening before midnight that these guys might care about?'

'My press conference,' muttered Baldassare. He felt a terrible agitation of the heart. Perhaps God existed after all. Perhaps, despite everything, He even listened to the prayers of desperate men. Or maybe this was merely the Devil having fun. There was only one way to find out. He turned to Sandro. 'All our men, every last one. I want them out here now. Body armour, guns, crowbars, bolt cutters, whatever you need. We've got work to do.'

Chapter Eighteen

I

Baldassare had a helicopter at his disposal, but he rarely used it for raids. The noise it made too often gave their approach away to the very people they were after, giving them enough time to flee or hide. Even the option was denied him today, however, for his pilot Faustino had the weekend off, leaving them no choice but to take the three Land Cruisers instead.

His men suited up and came out one by one. Sandro brought with him a first aid kit, a clean white shirt and a tablet on which Cesco quickly found the farmhouse for them to punch its coordinates into their satnavs. Then they set off in convoy, the weight of the armoured vehicles making their tyres screech around the hairpins down to the main road. Baldassare was all-in now. He brought up Operation Trinity on his phone, intending to topple the first domino, but the way the car lurched around the bends made him feel quite sick, so he waited until they squealed out onto the road beneath before pressing send. The calls started coming in almost at once from the various chiefs – ostensibly to seek confirmation of the orders, but in truth to protest the lack of notice. He told them, with uncharacteristic brusqueness, to do as they were told. Then he turned to talk to the two men in the back seat. Sandro, like all his bodyguards, was trained in trauma management. He'd already stripped Cesco of his torn and bloodied shirt and now was plucking pellets from his arm and shoulder with a pair of tweezers. 'How is he?' he asked.

'I'm fine,' said Cesco.

'I wasn't talking to you.'

'He's fine,' said Sandro. 'None have gone too deep.'

'Good,' said Baldassare. He turned to Cesco. 'You said you'd tell me everything.' And, to his credit, Cesco did. Even as Sandro cleaned and dressed his wounds, he described how the 'Ndrangheta had kidnapped him and his sister fifteen years before, how he alone had escaped and fled to England before returning to Italy again. Baldassare barely even needed to prompt him. It all came flooding out, a confession as much as a statement, particularly once he reached the past three days, the time he'd spent with Carmen, his obvious pride at the breakthroughs she'd made, his shame at his betrayals. He was still talking when they reached Via Virgilio. He hurried through the end of his account then leaned forward between the seats, the better to direct Manfredo. 'Next right,' he said. 'That track there.'

Manfredo barely decelerated, screeching the Land Cruiser into the turn up a dusty farm track. Baldassare had to hang on to the door handle as they jolted over potholes. The five-bar steel gate at the top was closed and padlocked. Manfredo glanced at Baldassare. Baldassare turned to Cesco. 'How sure are you?' he asked.

'One hundred per cent,' said Cesco.

'Take it,' ordered Baldassare.

Manfredo nodded and kept his foot down. The bull bars and sheer weight of their Land Cruiser tore the gate from its hinges and knocked it flat. They rattled over it as a pair of Rottweilers away to their left barked furiously and hurled themselves impotently against their wire mesh cages. They pulled up in a line in the cobbled courtyard of a small white farmhouse with two outbuildings. No sign of anyone, nor any vehicles. 'Stay here,' Baldassare told Cesco. He and his men spilled out of their cars, guns at the ready. They bellowed exhortations to give each other courage and to unnerve anyone inside. Manfredo pounded on the front door. Aldo smashed it with a sledgehammer. They ran in, spread out. Baldassare vaguely noticed a strong smell of heating oil as he went into the kitchen. There was stale coffee in the percolator and the dishwasher door was open, half stacked with plates. But there were no photographs on the fridge or walls, no bills or postcards, no sign of family life.

'In here,' shouted Aldo.

Baldassare ran through. It was a kind of computer room with two monitors on the wall playing five-second clips of CCTV footage from different cameras while local police radio channels played in the background. Cesco was right. This was it, the missing cell he'd been hunting. But too late. The bastards had already fled. They hurried upstairs. Four beds were unmade, four wardrobes filled with clothes, four sets of toiletries in the bathrooms. He took out his phone to call in forensics to glean what information they could, to search for hidden chambers and the like. But it was a desperate hope and his heart turned to lead inside his chest.

Then, in the roof space above, the first bars of 'Ancora tu' began to play.

II

With three hours to kill at Rome Ciampino before her flight down to Lamezia Terme, Zara bought herself a slice of cake and an iced tea at a café, took them to an empty table. She opened up her laptop and began drafting an email to Carmen Nero, explaining who she was and how she'd been in Sorrento for a talk when the story of Alaric and his tomb had—

A man came to stand beside her. He coughed into his fist for her attention. 'Excuse me,' he said. 'Is this seat taken?'

She glanced up to gesture it was all his, then returned to her struggle with the email. As a child, her parents had instilled in her a loathing of false witness so fierce that it had ultimately rebounded on them all, causing her rift with them and her entire community too. She'd managed to overcome it to some extent in social situations, but it still made her profoundly uncomfortable. As a result, she couldn't get the tone right. She'd think she had it only to read it back again and be dissatisfied.

'Off anywhere interesting?' asked the man.

She looked up again. Sunshine turned the window behind him into a light box. All she could see was silhouette. Then he came into better focus. Late thirties, athletic build, a navy blazer over a white silk shirt open at the collar. He had short spiky black hair, two-day stubble and that cockiness that some men have, tricking you into thinking them handsome even when they're not. 'Lamezia,' she said.

'Huh.' He took a small swig from a bottle of beer, set it back down. 'On your own, then?'

'My husband's gone to arrange our hire car.'

He glanced down at her ring finger and grinned. 'Liar,' he said. 'If you don't want to talk to me, just say so.'

'I don't want to talk to you.'

'See. How hard was that?' He took another swig. 'So, work or pleasure?'

She sighed, slapped closed her laptop, returned it to its bag. She stood and walked away, pulling her suitcase behind her, its wheels bumping over the uneven flooring. But then, when she reached the café exit, she couldn't help but glance around. He grinned at her and raised his beer. She scowled and went in search of a screen on which to check her flight, even though her gate wouldn't be announced for another hour yet. She found an empty seat then resumed her efforts at the email, looking up every time a man walked towards her, worried that it was him. But he didn't reappear.

The longer she worked on the damned email, the less certain she became. In search of inspiration, she revisited the discussion board. Carmen had posted an update the night before, including photographs of some new friend she'd made and of the Busento river as taken from their balcony, watermarked with the name of a well-known booking website. She visited it now and searched Cosenza rentals until she found the apartment in question, along with its calendar and precise location.

And it was only a short walk from her hotel too.

III

Cesco had no weapon or body armour, and he was so sore from the shotgun pellets that it took him a good minute to pull on the clean white shirt Sandro had brought him. He went inside the farmhouse to find everyone already upstairs. He was on his way to join them when a mobile phone began to play. He recognised the tune instantly from last night, and for a moment he froze, recalling the whoomp that the device had made, the fireball that had erupted up the stairs.

'Bomb!' he yelled. 'Everybody out!'

They all turned to look blankly at him. He yelled again then turned and fled, hoping to communicate urgency with panic. It worked a treat. They came after him, scrambling out the front door even as it triggered. The whole roof seemed to lift up. Windows shattered and shards of glass flew everywhere. A torrent of flaming kerosene spilled down the stairs and splashed like molten lava out into the courtyard, driving them further and further back, threatening to engulf the Land Cruisers until they reversed them away. Then they stood in silent awe as the inferno consumed the house, destroying any evidence that they might have hoped to recover, and any secret chambers too.

The thought that Carmen might still have been hidden in there somewhere was unbearable to Cesco. In a daze, he followed the others as they checked the two outbuildings, if only to give himself something to do. The first was empty. The second contained a banged-up dump truck and a black van. Back outside, he wandered too close to the caged Rottweilers. They went crazy, hurling themselves at their wire mesh, trying to get at him with such savage fury that he lost his nerve and turned back. But then he stopped and took a second look.

The two cages were set either side of a gate into the field beyond, almost as if they'd been put there to intimidate. Except there was no 'as if'. That was *exactly* why they were there. A little dizzily, he walked between them to the gate, ignoring their wild rage. A meadow ran all the way down to the road. It was rocky and patchy in places, though covered elsewhere by tall grasses and bright wild flowers. Hardly prime land, yet not only had the owners grown tall thick hawthorn hedges all around it, they'd built a high wall at its far end too, fitted with a steel gate, barbed wire and CCTV cameras. All that and the Rottweilers too. And not to protect the tomb either, because they hadn't even known it was there.

Suddenly he was a fourteen-year-old boy again, waking groggy from chloroform to find himself and his twin sister Claudia lying bound and gagged in the back of a van. The rear doors opening abruptly. A glimpse of starry sky. Slung over the shoulder of a burly man who'd reeked of stale sweat – a smell that for years had triggered panic attacks whenever he'd caught a whiff of it from a passing stranger. Lugged across a rough and stony field, not unlike this one. A hatch lifting. Steps down into darkness. A dank dungeon with rusted bars and ancient graffiti scratched into its damp walls. The dirt floor and rotten mattresses. The squalor of that metal bucket. All relics of the 'Ndrangheta's kidnap era.

The 'Ndrangheta had moved on to more profitable activities. But the lairs were all still out there. Lairs that might still be in use, say for storing drugs or guns. Lairs that might show up on Google Earth, looking just how an ancient tomb might look. Numbly, he took his phone from his pocket, but its screen was too small for his purpose. What he needed was the tablet on which he'd located this farmhouse for the satnavs. He turned and raced back up to the courtyard, yelling as he went.

IV

Baldassare was mostly a peaceable man, but hatred consumed him as he gazed at the conflagration. It wasn't just the destruction of precious evidence, it was that someone had clearly been watching in order to trigger the firebomb at the precise moment it would cause maximum casualties.

Shouting behind. He turned to see Cesco running wildly into the courtyard yelling for the tablet. Sandro was using it to film the fire, but Cesco snatched it from him. Something in his urgency rekindled a flicker of hope in Baldassare's chest. 'Talk to me,' he said, hurrying across.

Cesco didn't even look up, too busy bringing up Google Earth, zooming in first on the farmhouse then on the field beneath. 'That feature the Suraces spotted on the satellite photographs, then again with their drone. The one Carmen found for herself this morning.'

'What about it?'

'It's not Alaric's tomb at all. It's something else altogether. *That's* why the Suraces had to die.'

It took Baldassare a moment to understand. Then his skin tingled. How could he, of all people, have been so blind? 'Can you find it?' he demanded.

'If you give me some fucking space.'

'Stand back,' ordered Baldassare. 'Give him room.' But he himself stayed at Cesco's shoulder, watching transfixed. The map loaded. There were the roofs of the farmhouse, its outbuildings and the farm track. A pulsing red dot appeared, courtesy of the tablet's GPS, to show their own precise location. But it was the meadow beneath that Cesco zoomed in on. He swept the screen this way and that, looking for the telltale feature he'd just spoken of. Suddenly he stopped. He zoomed in on a patch of earth then turned the screen to Baldassare for confirmation, but Baldassare couldn't see a thing. Cesco double-tapped the spot to place a turquoise marker pin in it, and now he saw it too: a rectangle of earth, a fraction paler than its surrounds, and with an extra dogleg at one end, as if for steps, and whose sides and ends were all too straight to be natural.

He grabbed the tablet from Cesco and set off running. The Rottweilers went berserk as he passed between them. He barely even noticed. The gate was bolted and padlocked. He vaulted it like a fifteen-year-old, then sprinted down the meadow slope, holding the tablet out in front of him so that he could watch the slow convergence of his own pulsing red dot and the turquoise pin that Cesco had just added, trusting to his feet not to let him down. He slowed and then stopped as the two finally came together, heaving for breath and his heart aching like a towel being wrung dry. His men now all arrived, and Cesco too. Maybe he'd already explained it to them somehow, because there was no need for orders; they all went straight down onto their hands and knees to search the ground.

'Here!' yelled Sandro. 'Over here!'

Baldassare ran across. A rusted iron ring lay hidden in the long grass. Sandro stood up and heaved at it and an almost perfectly camouflaged trapdoor reared up on well-oiled hinges. His men stood back in fear of gunfire, but Baldassare had no time for such caution. He barged his way between them, sprinted down the brick steps into the gloom. There was a landing halfway down. The steps turned at right angles. A thin young man in a black balaclava appeared on it, holding a gun in his wildly trembling hands. Baldassare slammed him into the wall with his shoulder then turned the corner and sprinted onwards even as a second man arrived at the foot, his face also concealed by a black balaclava, his left arm clamped around the neck of the American woman, a knife against her throat.

As a teenager, Baldassare had briefly joined his local boxing club. The coach there had at first expressed high hopes for him, thanks to his quick feet and eyes and hands; but after a fortnight he'd told him he'd never be any good so long as he remained squeamish about hitting people in the face. There was nothing remotely squeamish about the punch he threw now. It had every bit of his weight behind it and it connected with the man's nose and upper lip in a crunch of bone and flesh that smashed his head backwards and made the knife fly from his grasp. He didn't even slow to check on him or Carmen, but leaped over them into a chamber with a battery lamp on its floor, every detail of it familiar from the proof-of-life clips these monsters had been sending him each night for the past two months.

There was the table, the key upon it. He fumbled it in his haste to pick it up, but then he had it again, feeding it into the lock with both hands and turning it and hauling open the cage door even as his wife shrieked out his name again and again and his daughter burst into tears and then his arms were around them both, the warmth of them, the aliveness, the unbearable relief, the three of them howling in unison together, howling out their joy and fear and nausea and release as they fell to their knees in that cramped and noisome cell.

Chapter Nineteen

I

Cesco held back again as Baldassare and his men rushed down the steps into the site. They were professionals – armed, trained and equipped with body armour; he'd only get in their way. There was shouting now from below, but so confused that it was impossible to know what it meant. Then two of Baldassare's men emerged, hustling between them a handcuffed thin young man with blinking eyes. Two more bodyguards followed shortly afterwards, frogmarching a second youth with blood clotting into a red goatee around his mouth and chin. Then came Manfredo, his arm around Carmen's shoulders, and the relief so overwhelmed Cesco that he squatted down on the ground and bit the knuckle of his index finger.

They turned away from him, uphill towards the farmhouse. Carmen never once looked back. He considered going after her, to make sure she was okay. Except that wouldn't be the reason. It would be to let her know that, despite his numerous betrayals, he'd come through for her in the end. And that was too self-serving for his pride to bear.

More movement at the hatch. Baldassare himself now appeared, one arm around his wife, the other around his daughter, all three weeping helplessly. It was both too joyful and too painful for Cesco to bear. He'd structured his life never again to be vulnerable to such strong emotion. Yet now he felt only envy.

Sirens in the distance. A stream of police cars and fire engines began bumping up the track. To stay here would make for some difficult interviews. He'd have to go through his history again. Knowing the police, his identity was certain to leak. If he left right now, on the other hand, he could be back in Cosenza in half an hour. Hire a taxi out to the villa for the Harley then swing by the apartment for his things. From there he could head wherever he wished, and start over. As for his past coming out, Baldassare owed him big right now. An email asking him and his team to keep quiet about his involvement should do the trick.

He bowed his head, hunched his shoulders and hurried down to the bottom gate. He climbed it by its hinges, trod down the barbed wire on top, careful of his new shirt, then lowered himself on the other side. He waited until the road was clear then hurried across it into a fallow field at whose foot the Busento sedately ran, the sound of its burbling like gentle laughter at the downfall of yet another fool of Alaric.

II

The silver Range Rover was parked against a low stone wall on the hilltop directly across the Busento valley from the smouldering farmhouse.

'Well, that went well,' said Tomas.

'I spent hours setting up that fucking ceiling,' grumbled Guido. 'How did they get out in time?'

'Our good friend Cesco Rossi,' said Tomas.

'That little fuck,' said Guido. He popped the last of his salami and cheese sandwich into his mouth, only to realise he had something else to say. He chewed it down to manageable size then swallowed it away. 'I told you those brats wouldn't have the balls to off the bitches,' he said. 'Never work with virgins. That's what I say.'

Tomas shrugged. 'We used what we were given.'

'You think they'll talk?'

'They never have before. Why start now?'

'That American cunt will. *And* she's seen our faces now.'

Tomas looked sideways at his brother, searching for signs of reproach. It had been Tomas's decision to let Carmen Nero live that first day; his decision to go out bareheaded that same morning too, once it had become obvious that she and Rossi were on their way to the farmhouse. He'd hoped to intercept them before they got there, lest the GPS on their phones lead the police straight to them after they'd disappeared. He'd planned to drive their van on a few kilometres to set up a murder–suicide. And, even in Calabria, you could hardly drive around wearing balaclavas. 'What choice did we have, oh my brother?'

'I'm not saying we had a choice,' said Guido hurriedly.

'I'm glad to hear that.'

'Every decision you've made, it's been absolutely the right decision.' He smiled ingratiatingly at Tomas to make sure his apology had been accepted. Relieved, he crumpled up his sandwich's wrapping and tossed it out the window. 'We've just had shitty luck, that's all.'

'Yes,' agreed Tomas.

Ever since the Suraces had come to see them, asking to run a survey in their meadow, it had been one crisis after another. Tomas had done his best but the truth was they had failed. Their leverage over Judge Mancuso was gone. The Critelli brothers were almost certainly now facing long stretches – if indeed they ever left prison again. And they were not the kind of men to entertain arguments about bad luck, however justified. Nor to let failure go unpunished.

Tomas gestured at Guido to set off for home. He had some serious thinking to do.

III

Lamezia Terme was only a short hop south of Rome. Zara spent the flight marking essays on her laptop. On landing, she went directly to her car-rental booth. The clerk gave her keys, a map and her bay number, which she promptly forgot. She walked along the line of cars, pressing the key fob until a scarlet Renault hatchback gave a satisfying clunk and its lights flashed orange. She stowed her bag in the boot then took out her printed copy of her hotel reservation to punch its address into her phone's satnav. Then she heard footsteps approaching fast and she whirled around to see the man from the café striding towards her, a pair of bags slung over his shoulders.

'You,' she said.

'Me,' he agreed. He stopped a pace short of her, reached into his jacket pocket for his wallet, took out his identity card for her inspection. 'Dov Mandel at your service. The minister told you to expect me, yes?'

'You're Dov? But... what was that absurd pantomime at the café?'

'I needed to know if I could trust you.'

'Trust me?'

'Not to blab about what you're doing here to the first good-looking man who asked you. And you did okay. Not brilliantly, but okay.' He opened the Renault's rear door, tossed his bags onto the seats. He plucked the car key from her hand before she realised what he was doing then took her hotel booking form too. 'Nice,' he said. He opened the driver door, got in, pushed back the seat. 'Well?' he asked. 'Aren't you coming?'

'But... are we allowed to be seen together?'

'Allowed!' he laughed. 'It's just for the drive up. I need to brief you on some shit.'

'I'd better drive,' she said. 'You're not named on the—'

'Just get in, will you?'

She climbed in the passenger side, belted herself in. He reversed so sharply out of their parking spot that it flung her against her straps. He thrust the Renault into gear and roared away, hitting speed bumps like he was trying to use them to take off, screeching around a pair of roundabouts then out onto dual carriageway.

'Brief me on what, exactly?' she asked. 'I'm only here for a look around.'

'Is that what the minister told you?'

'Yes. Why?'

He gave a grunt. 'Fucking politicians,' he said.

'I don't understand. What's going on?'

'You need to get something in your head right now,' he told her. 'You're not here for a look around. At least, you are. But you can't think of it that way. You've been asked to do this by your government. That means you're here on a mission. And being here on a mission puts you in jeopardy, whether you like it or not.'

'A mission!' She laughed, a little uncertainly. 'You're being ridiculous.'

'No. I'm not. I'm really not.' He squinted at the road ahead until he saw a turning. He indicated and took it, driving along a residential street that ended in a development of unfinished houses that loomed around them like ghostly ruins. He bumped across deep ruts left by heavy machinery and came finally to a halt. He switched off the engine, released his seat belt from its buckle, then turned in his seat to face her. 'I need you to listen to me very carefully,' he told her. 'In our line of work, what you're *actually* doing in a place means nothing. What matters is what the locals *think* you're doing. Tell me this: how many years in jail do you think an Italian court would give you for plotting to steal the Menorah and the other temple treasures?'

'But… that's crazy,' she protested. 'That's not why I'm here.'

'*I* know that,' he said, with exasperation. 'And *you* know that. But why would *they* believe you? If they catch you sniffing around Alaric's tomb, they'll assume the worst. Because that's what people do. Even if you can convince the police, you can always count on some shit-stirring newspaper columnist or politician on the make to denounce you as an agent of the Jewish state. They'll make your presence here an affront to national pride. And then the government will have to act, even if they know it's bullshit, because nothing generates outrage like an affront to national pride. Besides, you'll be great leverage for them. They'll offer to exchange you for a spy of their own, or for concessions on some trade deal or other. And if our guys say no, if they disown you, the Italians will lock you up without a qualm until they reconsider.'

She stared at him, hoping that he was pulling her leg. But his face was stony. 'Lock *us* up without a qualm, you mean,' she said.

'Afraid not. My job gives me diplomatic immunity. Does yours?' He studied her closely, nodded with satisfaction when he saw dismay bloom in her eyes. His own expression immediately softened. 'I'm not telling you this to scare you,' he said. 'I'm telling you to make you listen. To make you careful. Nothing bad is going to happen. You know why not? Because you've got me looking out for you, and I'm the best there is at this, though I say so myself. I've run over two dozen missions now, and not one of them has ever gone even slightly wrong. That's because I'm trained, I have experience, I see problems early. You don't. You need to remember that. Understand?'

'I guess.'

He shifted closer to her in his seat. In the confined space, it made her uncomfortably aware how little she knew about this man, how far out in the middle of nowhere they were parked. 'You guess?' he said. 'You *guess*? What the fuck does *guess* mean?'

'I'm just saying Avram never said anything about—'

'You're Israeli, yes? How old? Forty?'

Her cheeks burned. 'Thirty-three.'

'So you've served in the army?'

'Of course.'

'Well consider yourself back in service. I'm a lieutenant colonel, which makes me your commanding officer. And I'm not going to have a blemish on my record because you refuse to take this seriously. Because you get careless, because you say something stupid, because you miss a cue I've given you.'

'I don't even—'

'I'm still talking.'

'But I—'

'*I said I'm still talking.*'

She instantly fell silent, her heart thumping, flooding her system with adrenaline that burnished everything around them with a peculiar sheen, his complexion and the gleam of his teeth and the whites of his eyes. She became exquisitely aware of his nearness, his breath upon her face, the mix of cologne and sweat. 'It may be that I need to make contact with you in public places,' he told her. 'If that happens, I may have to couch things like they're suggestions. They won't be suggestions. You need to remember that. They'll be orders. Orders from your commanding officer. So you'll obey them, even if you don't fully understand them, even if they make you uncomfortable. Do you understand?'

'I... Yes.'

'Yes what?'

She frowned in puzzlement. 'Yes, sir?'

'Don't fucking call me sir,' he said. 'Not ever. Not out loud. Think it in your head, yes. Think it all the time. But not out loud. You understand?'

'Yes... Yes.'

'Yes, what?'

'Yes, I understand.'

'That's better,' he said. He glared at her a few moments longer with a look of revulsion on his face, as if it disgusted him even to be in same car as her. She felt herself shrinking into her seat, ugly and small and useless. Then suddenly he broke into a smile, as if tossing a treat to a pet corgi – and to her shame she couldn't help herself, she smiled weakly back at him. He grinned and belted himself in once more. Then he turned the ignition back on and screeched into a violent U-turn, as if nothing at all had just happened.

Chapter Twenty

I

There was nothing the matter with Carmen. Nothing physical, at least. Nothing other than having spent a good chunk of her day in mortal terror. She refused all offers of medical help and insisted on being taken directly to Cosenza police station so that she could give her statement while her memory was fresh and her anger hot. The station was in chaos, however. Dozens of 'Ndrangheta suspects had been arrested that afternoon and were being processed. Her escorting officer parked her in reception while he went in search of someone with decent English. She never saw him again. An hour passed. She asked at the desk. A kindly young woman made her a cup of mint tea and tried valiantly to take her statement, but her English simply wasn't up to it, so Carmen volunteered to write it all down herself. Once she'd started, it all came out – not just what had happened that day, but the truth of the Surace murders too: how she'd in fact remained conscious throughout, witnessing the men in balaclavas as they'd murdered Vittorio and Giulia Surace, the grotesque conversation they'd had.

The office door opened abruptly. The *ispettore* walked in, holding her purse, which he returned to her with a show of gratitude and deference. They held an awkward conversation, translated as best as the woman officer could manage. Carmen asked about her phone and passport. Neither had been found, but he promised to send them on if they turned up. In the meantime, could he show her some mugshots for her two escaped abductors? She looked through several pages of photos, but saw neither. He asked whether she'd come back in the morning to work with a sketch artist. She agreed. He thanked her, then asked her not to talk to anyone yet about what had happened, as operations were ongoing and further arrests planned. She agreed to this too, then returned to her statement, finishing it – with a kind of bitter satisfaction – with an account of how Cesco had gone to the Suraces' farmhouse last night and burned it down.

Her bravado was by now wearing thin. She felt a reaction coming on. She signed her statement, took a copy for herself, then left. Night had fallen. It had turned cold and gusty. It began to spit with rain as she walked, then turned suddenly into such a deluge that she had to run the last fifty metres for the sanctuary of her lobby. She dripped freely on the stairs as she made her way to the apartment, only to hesitate on the landing.

What if Cesco was still here? What if he was inside?

The door was locked. She listened a moment at it then opened it quietly and poked in her head. The place was empty. Sometimes you just knew. She called out anyway. Then, leaving the door ajar just in case, she checked each room in turn. His clothes and bag were gone, his duvet flapped out neatly over his bed. His keys were on the bedside table, but not her phone. There was no note, no apology, no effort at explanation or excuse. She told herself she was glad that he hadn't tried to defend the indefensible. And yet, inside, she ached.

II

The road from Lamezia Terme to Cosenza ran north alongside the coast for much of the way, long dark strips of nothingness punctuated by quaint fishing villages with drab accretions of industrial estates and modern apartment blocks. Dov grew bored. He searched the radio for music to drum his fingers to. 'Your plan,' he said.

'My plan?' asked Zara.

'The minister told me your first step was to hook up with some American woman.'

'Yes. I was trying to write her an email at the airport. Only I kept being disturbed.'

'You haven't sent it, then? You need help?'

She shook her head. 'She posted a picture of her apartment on my message board. I was planning to bump into her in the morning.'

He slid her a look. 'Seriously? That's easier than an email?'

She flushed a little. 'I can always send one if this doesn't work.'

'You know what she looks like, then?'

'Everyone on our discussion board has a profile photograph. Anyway, I'm hoping that she recognises me. I'm fairly well known in our community.'

'A celeb, huh. Who'd have thought?'

The radio pipped the hour. An announcer read the news. There'd been great excitement in Cosenza that afternoon, it turned out. A dramatic hostage rescue and dozens of Mafia arrests. Dov scowled. It meant the police would be out in force. Sure enough, when they reached Cosenza, the night sky fluttered blue. But they made it to Zara's hotel without alarm. It was large and modern, with a car park to its rear and a restaurant on its ground floor open to anyone, not just guests. He found an empty bay in the shadows then reached into the back to unzip his bag and take out a burner phone and its charger. 'This is for contacting me,' he told Zara. 'My number's already programmed in. Don't use it for anything else, okay?'

'Okay.'

'Text me your room number the moment you're in.'

'Where will you be staying?'

'You don't need to know that. Now go on in. Don't talk to anyone you don't need to. Order room service then get an early night. Tomorrow's a big day. Understand?'

'I understand.'

'Good.' He watched her fetch her bags from the boot then go inside. She had a nice walk. He took a fresh shirt, underwear and toiletries from his overnight bag and packed them into his laptop case. Ten minutes passed. His phone pinged. Zara was in room 512. He pulled on a baseball cap and dark glasses, slung his laptop bag over his shoulder then went around the front to enter the restaurant that way. It was large, dimly lit and almost empty. He ordered a beer and a cheeseburger then sat in the darkest available booth.

On a mission this delicate, Dov couldn't afford to leave a trail. That made accommodation awkward. Hotels insisted on seeing a passport, booking websites required a credit card. Avram had given him 5,000 euros in cash for incidental expenses, but even that would mean having to meet someone to hand it over. And he could hardly sleep in the Renault, not with the police on high alert.

His burger arrived. He squeezed a couple of sachets of ketchup onto the chips then scoffed it all down. He grabbed his laptop bag again then found the stairs and walked briskly up to the fifth floor, keeping his head down from the cameras. There was a tray on the floor outside Zara's room, a half-eaten tagliatelle in a creamy sauce and the smears of chocolate dessert. He checked both ways to make sure the corridor was empty, then knocked. Footsteps padded on carpet. 'Who's there?' asked Zara.

'Me.'

She opened the door a little way. 'What is it?'

He put a finger to his lips then pushed his way inside and closed the door behind him. He made his way past a shiny white bathroom into a warmly lit room of powder blue, furnished with a desk, an armchair, a large-screen TV and a king-sized bed. He pressed down on the mattress. 'Nice,' he said. 'Just so you know, I sleep right side.'

'You *what*? Like hell!'

He turned to stare at her. 'Have you forgotten who's in charge here?'

'I don't care. You're not staying in my room.'

'I'm staying wherever the fuck I want,' he said, advancing on her. She backed away against the wall. He still came on, intruding into her space, their bodies almost touching, staring at her until she dropped her eyes. Women were like horses that way. You only needed to break them once. He nodded at her and walked off, leaving her still wilted.

A floor-length white net curtain covered a smoked-glass balcony door. He slid it open. The gust of fresh night air made the net billow as he stepped out. Pink and blue neon crosses adorned the roofs of nearby churches. He could see the flutter of police lights, the red stream of tail lights on a one-way road, the white span of an illuminated suspension bridge that swept like an angel's wing across the glossy black strip of a river. He leaned over the railing to look straight down five storeys to hard tarmac beneath.

Perfect.

He went back inside, closed the door behind him. Zara was still against the wall, forearms up like a boxer on a standing count. He winked at her then kicked off his shoes and stretched out on his side of the king-size. There was a remote control on the bedside table. He turned on the TV then started flipping channels in the hope of finding something halfway decent to watch. Then he smiled up at her and patted the bed beside him to invite her to come join him.

III

There were no provisions to speak of in the Moccono house, so Tomas and Guido stopped at a store on the way back from Cosenza. It began to pour as they set off with their purchases, misting up the glass even with the heating on, so that they had to buzz the windows down a hair, even though it meant being spattered by rain.

They parked right by the front door. The guttering was so clogged that the rainwater poured over its side like a bead curtain, splashing down the collar of Tomas's jacket as he wiggled the key in the stiff lock. It was cold inside. He tried the lights. Nothing happened. The grid around here was notoriously prone to failure in the rain, let alone in a storm like this – but at least they had a back-up generator. He found a torch in the kitchen then went down into the basement to start it.

The rain abruptly stopped, leaving everything slick and dark. Clear sky reappeared, even a little warmth. Neither felt like cooking, so Guido went back into town for pizza. They turned on the outside lights and went out onto the covered terrace where they tore the pizzas apart with their bare hands and washed them down with a good coarse red that made the throat burn. Rainwater dripped from the eaves and gutters, like percussionists on a soft jam. The soil of the olive groves fizzed with moisture, releasing a perfume so rich it was almost intoxicating. The cicadas began their joyful screech. They opened a second bottle. Despite the setbacks of the day, a bellyful of pizza and red wine gave Tomas as profound a sense of contentment as he could remember. 'I've been thinking,' he said.

'Uh-oh,' said Guido.

Tomas threw his brother an affectionate look. He loved him more than anyone in the world, even more than his two sons, who he barely saw these days anyway. He and Guido had been inseparable their whole lives, but especially since moving to Amsterdam in their teens after Luca Critelli had asked their father to set up a base there, from which to supply their larger Western European customers with cocaine. He'd made a tremendous success of it too, despite sporadic turf wars with the Albanians and Russians.

Liver cancer had taken their father four years before. As the elder son, Guido should by rights have succeeded him, but they'd both known that Tomas was the better choice. They'd agreed to call themselves partners, therefore, while letting Tomas make the decisions that mattered. Another man might have settled for carrying on as before. Not Tomas. He'd had an insatiable need to outdo his father, driven by the knowledge that he'd always held him in contempt, simply because he'd loved reading as a boy, and had wet his bed for a while after moving to Holland, and because he'd always been squeamish at the sight of blood.

The way his father had mocked him for this had given others licence to do the same. Tomas had said nothing while his father had still lived. But it had been the first thing he'd needed to address once the cancer had won. He and Guido had therefore taken a team to surprise the Albanians one night. They'd caught them in their own warehouse, taking them captive before they'd realised what was happening. He'd isolated their three bosses then made their foot soldiers watch as he himself had hacked off their heads one by one with a hunting knife. Guido had offered to do it for him – it was all just meat to him – but Tomas had insisted. He'd suffered nightmares for months afterwards, in which those three men had returned from the dead to do the same to him; but no one had ever again called him soft.

The surviving Albanians had fallen into line. The Russians too. The threat of decapitation had that effect on people. It terrified them far more than the thought of merely dying. Their turnover had quickly doubled, then had reached nine figures. Their profitability had been insane until a vast shipment of cocaine had been seized in Gioia Tauro and the Critellis had been arrested. Soon enough, they'd run out of product to sell. That was when the Critellis had ordered him and Guido to come down here personally to carry out the Mancuso kidnap. *Ordered* them, mind, not asked. Because that was the 'Ndrangheta for you. To the 'Ndrangheta, Amsterdam meant shit. Only Calabria mattered.

'You ever wonder about moving back?' he asked.

Guido looked curiously at him. 'I thought we'd decided.'

'We'd decided better to rule in Amsterdam than serve here. But we wouldn't be serving, would we?'

'You're suggesting we take over?'

'Someone's going to, oh my brother. Why not us?'

'We don't have the numbers.'

'No one has the numbers. Everyone's in jail. Yet someone will end up boss. Someone always does.'

'What about our oath?'

'We did our best by it.'

'The brothers won't see it that way.'

'No. But if we do this, they're first to go. Along with their families. It'll be how we announce ourselves.'

'Oh.'

Tomas reached out to touch his arm. 'You like their cousin Magdalena still, don't you?'

Guido shrugged. 'She's always been nice to me.'

'Fine. She can live, then. If she bends the knee.'

Silence fell. Tomas let it. Guido was not an imaginative man, but once an idea took root, you'd need a tractor to pull it out. He drained his glass, refilled it, then drained that one too. 'How would we go about it?' he asked finally.

Tomas was a strategist. He understood how power worked. Everything they needed to run Cosenza was already in place. Their South American suppliers, the ships' crews, customs officers, customers, drivers, pushers, politicians, judges and police. Such people had no loyalty to the Critellis, only to the envelope and the gun. But Guido, he knew, wasn't asking about that. He was a soldier. What interested him was blood. 'We call Amsterdam,' he said. 'We have Massimo put together a team. A dozen should be plenty. Good Calabrian stock. Loyal only to us. They'll need to bring their own guns, which means coming by road. Give them the order tonight, they can be here Wednesday. As for the brothers, there are plenty of good men inside with no reason to love them. Offer six figures a head, they'll be dead by nightfall. Then we'll set a new arse upon the throne.'

'Whose? Yours or mine?'

'Depends on whether people come to kiss it or kick it.'

'Fuck you,' laughed Guido.

'Well?' asked Tomas.

The sky had by now cleared completely. It was a perfect spill of stars. Amsterdam had its pleasures, especially while one was young, but they were neither of them that any more. They were Calabrian at heart, and nothing Holland had to offer could compare to a night like this. Guido's chin lifted as he looked up at it, at all those constellations named for warriors and gods. His chest swelled with mountain air. 'Why not?' he demanded. 'Why the fuck not?'

Tomas raised his glass. 'The brothers are dead,' he said.

'Long live the brothers,' replied Guido.

Chapter Twenty-One

I

Carmen poured herself a large glass of white wine then knocked half of it straight back. She felt so restless and alone that she turned on the local news purely for the company of voices. There was only one story, of course, though it had different strands. An inset screen showed a line of empty chairs behind a table covered by microphones waiting for Baldassare's announcement of charges against the Critelli brothers and their 'ndrine, while the rolling caption at the foot of the screen advised that it was running late because Baldassare was passing on the duty to a deputy, who needed to be briefed. In the meantime, a panel of studio guests breathlessly discussed the emerging details of the kidnapping and rescue of Baldassare's wife and daughter.

Carmen already knew much of the story. She'd heard it first-hand from Alessandra in snatched whispers whenever their guards had left them. How death threats had persuaded her and Bettina to move to Sweden until the Critellis affair was finished. How they'd all missed each other so much that they'd rented a villa on the coast for the weekend and flown home, only for masked men to burst in on them and inject them with some anaesthetic drug. The two of them had then awoken in that dreadful dungeon, the slow passage of days since marked only by meals and newspapers brought for proof-of-life videos.

It explained, of course, why Baldassare had pressed her so hard that morning in the hospital. He'd realised the deeper significance of the ketamine. The thought that he might despise her for her earlier silence was too uncomfortable to bear. She could hardly call him, not with everything going on, so she put her apology into an email instead, and attached a copy of her statement to the police.

A flurry of activity in the press conference hall. It went full screen. A blaze of camera flashes and an excited buzz of chatter announced Baldassare himself. He looked so rumpled and drained that it was no surprise that he began the press conference by announcing – as best Carmen could follow – that he'd be taking an indefinite break directly after this was over for himself and his family to recuperate from their ordeal, passing the case on to the able deputies on either side of him, whom he proceeded to introduce. Then he began reading out the charges. His delivery was so dry and matter of fact that the TV station spiced it up with footage of the Critellis and their acolytes at the moments of their arrest – a strangely interchangeable procession of paunchy middle-aged men in leather jackets and with the same contemptuous stares as they were bundled into the back of police cars – as if they all knew they were being filmed, and wanted to look their best.

The charges continued. She grew bored. She checked the fridge for food. Pasta, butter, eggs, pancetta, Parmesan and garlic. Plenty for a carbonara. She filled a large saucepan with water, added oil and salt, put it on a burner. She melted butter in a smaller pan then fried the pancetta and diced garlic to a golden brown. She grated a knob of Parmesan, whipped it with an egg, then stirred it into the garlic and pancetta, tossing the fusilli into the water as it came finally to the boil.

On TV, Baldassare finished reading out the charges and invited questions instead. The third one was from a BBC correspondent, asking in English how that day's hostage rescue had come about. Carmen hurried from the kitchen to turn the volume up. Operation Trinity had been in the works for months, Baldassare replied, also in English. From even before the kidnapping of his wife and daughter, key 'Ndrangheta suspects and properties had been under intensive surveillance. He hadn't known for sure where his wife and daughter were being held, so they'd waited until the last possible moment, both to gather maximum information and in the hope of a lucky break. But this afternoon, with his time up, he'd finally given the order to go.

At this, the last glowing ember of hope that Cesco might after all have had something to do with her rescue turned black inside Carmen's chest, and so died.

The smoke alarm began suddenly to shriek. She rushed back to the hob. Too late. Her carbonara was an omelette; her fusilli was mush. Too weary to start over, she stirred it all together in a cereal bowl and ate it with a spoon. 'Fuck you, Cesco,' she muttered.

She rinsed her plate and pans, refilled her glass, then undertook a task she'd been dreading since her return – running an internet search for Cesco Rossi PhD, archaeologist of Oxford. She did find a few traces of him, on message boards and the like, but nothing he couldn't easily have planted himself. While she was at it, however, she came across contact details for Karen Porter. She sent her an email, therefore, explaining who she was and how a man named Cesco Rossi had been claiming to have helped her on her Syracuse documentary, but that she had reason to be suspicious. The answer came back just five minutes later. Carmen held her hand up in front of the screen, to protect herself from the blow that she knew full well was coming. Sure enough, Karen had never heard of Cesco Rossi, and he'd certainly never helped her on any of her books or programmes. Who was he? Did she need to be concerned? Carmen wrote straight back, assuring her that everything was fine, the situation had been taken care of locally. Then she set about changing the passwords to all her social media and other accounts, in case Cesco – or whatever his real name was – had managed to hack into her phone. It left her feeling so dispirited that she went to bed early, then paid for it by lying there awake in the darkness. After all the turmoil and terror she'd been through that day, how come this was the thing that hurt?

'Fuck you, Cesco,' she said again.

And, finally, she slept.

II

Cesco spent the evening in the seaside town of Rosarno, two-thirds of the way between Cosenza and Scilla, distant enough from each that he'd be safe from being recognised. He took his day's allowance from an ATM then bought painkillers and fresh dressings for his back and shoulder from a pharmacy, as well as writing paper, envelopes and a pen from the general store next door.

He grew hungry. He took an outside table at a restaurant where he was waited on by a very Caesar-looking man, with an aristocratic nose and forward-curling sideburns. He ate grilled fish with a deliciously crisp and salted skin then sat back in his chair. His arm and shoulder began aching fiercely. He washed down a pair of painkillers with water. Lights on the harbour wall flickered like fireflies. A band a little way along the front played wine-bar music, only for the waves to keep shushing them. He finished his dinner, then over coffee wrote a letter of apology to his old landlady Donatella that he sealed into an envelope along with the cash from the ATM. It was a ruse he'd used before when breaking into a place, to give himself an excuse should he be caught. Yet this time, for some reason, the words actually resonated. He went for a walk. A corpulent man who'd been selling lottery tickets along the front climbed into a tiny three-wheeler that sank almost to the tarmac beneath his weight. He met Cesco's gaze with a poignant smile, trying to be amused rather than ashamed by his own absurdity. Utterly drained by now, Cesco wanted only to find a bed and sleep. But he didn't let himself. Church bells tolled midnight. He took a new day's allowance from the ATM, then climbed back on the Harley and set off south.

He reached Scilla a little after one. Its streets were empty and quiet save for the low mutter of his own engine. He parked a street away from his apartment building, checked that no one was around, then walked briskly but without haste to his front door. All the lights were out. He checked again that he was alone. His key still fit. Once inside he took off his shoes then went upstairs, tiptoeing past Donatella's front door. He reached his apartment, put his ear to the door. Silence. This lock hadn't been changed either. He slipped inside. Using his phone's torch, he padded through to the kitchen. There was a toolkit beneath the sink. He took a screwdriver from it then placed a chair against the wall, standing on it to unscrew the air vent panel. His envelope was still inside, covered with grit and dust. He wiped it with his sleeve. Its flap was tucked in rather than stuck down. He checked inside to make sure everything was still there, including his driving licence under his next name and bank cards for various savings accounts. He clamped it between his knees and screwed the panel back in. Then he climbed back down and replaced the chair by the table.

The envelope was too big for his pocket and he didn't want to fold it, so he tucked it into the waistband at the back of his trousers instead, hiding it beneath his jacket. Then he took out his note to Donatella. He'd only written it to give himself an excuse if he were caught. Or so he'd told himself. But now that he was here, the desire to make amends overcame him. He set it on the kitchen table and turned for the door before he could change his mind.

There was a scuffing noise in the passage. The lights flickered on and then Donatella herself appeared, dressed in fluffy slippers and a frilly pink dressing gown, and with a look of intense satisfaction on her face. And, for the second time that day, Cesco found himself staring at the wrong end of a double-barrelled shotgun, this one aimed directly at his face.

Chapter Twenty-Two

I

'I knew you'd be back,' gloated Donatella. 'All those pretty clothes. Men like you are too cheap to leave behind pretty clothes.'

'Men like me?' asked Cesco.

'Frauds. Conmen.' Holding her shotgun in one hand, she reached into the pocket of her dressing gown for her phone. 'Thieves.'

'Please don't.'

'Why shouldn't I?'

'You won't get the rest of your money if you do.'

'The rest!' she scoffed.

'It's on the table,' he said, blessing his sudden attack of conscience. Rarely if ever could scruples have been rewarded so quickly. 'It's not everything I owe but it's all I can afford right now.'

She squinted at him for several seconds, expecting him to back down. When he didn't, she gestured him aside then went across. Her shotgun barely wavered as she set down her phone to open the flap of the envelope and fan out the banknotes with her thumb. 'You stole from others too,' she said grudgingly.

'I'll get to them in time.'

'What happened?' she mocked. 'Did you meet a *girl*?'

'I'm sick of my life, that's all.'

'No one forced you to it. You chose it all by yourself.'

'Yes.'

Her lower lip trembled. 'Get out,' she said.

He nodded towards his bedroom. 'And my things?'

'I'll be keeping those,' she told him, 'until I get the rest.'

'But I—'

She picked up her phone again. 'Out,' she said. 'Before I change my mind.'

II

Dov woke early, as he always did on missions. He turned off his alarm before it could sound, then showered, shaved and groomed himself in the mirror, gelling his hair and spiking it just so. Then he stood beside the bed and gazed down at Zara. She'd put on a baggy sweatshirt and cheesecloth trousers before getting into bed with him last night, protecting her virtue with shapelessness. Then she'd turned onto her side to show him her back. Irritation flared. She should be so lucky. In fact, just for the hell of it, he decided there and then that he'd have her before the job was done. He took hold of the white duvet and tugged it back in a single sharp movement. She woke in confusion and grabbed it and pulled it back over herself. 'What?' she asked.

He held up his phone. 'Your login.'

'My *what*?'

'You can't go hunting this Nero woman yourself. She's too likely to spot you. Fuck that up and the mission will be over before it starts. So I'll find her, then I'll call you and direct you where to go. For that, I need to know where she's staying, what she looks like, what plans she makes. That means access to your discussion board.'

'I'll do it myself. I'll send you everything you need.'

'We're here for our country, Zara. That might not mean anything to you. It does to me. So change your fucking password later, if you must. But give it to me now.' She glared defiantly at him for several seconds, but then she gave in. He tapped in her details then nodded in satisfaction. 'I'll be off, then,' he said, pocketing the car keys. 'Wait here for my call.'

Carmen woke to the happy discovery that she no longer cared about Cesco. Unfortunately, that was largely because she was too worried about her upcoming appointment with the police sketch artist to have room for anything else. Yesterday's hot fury with the kidnappers had burned itself out, as she'd known it would, leaving behind only the chilling memory of Cemetery Teeth sawing through the throats of Vittorio and Giulia, and the perverse, soft-spoken civility of Famine Eyes as he'd crouched beside her to explain the deal he was offering, the consequences of breach. Giving the police their descriptions would mean breaching that deal in a major way.

Yet she meant to do it all the same.

She put coffee on to brew then went down to the cafe for croissants. A man with spiked black hair was leaving as she went in, coffee in one hand, a pastry in the other. She stood back and held the door open for him, but he didn't acknowledge her with so much as a glance, simply turned his back on her instead. A copy of the local paper was lying on the counter, its front page a huge splash of Baldassare, Alessandra and Bettina hugged tearfully together. She bought her croissants then went next door for a copy of the paper to browse over breakfast. Her spoken Italian might be wretched but she could read it well enough.

An article on an inside page caught her eye. A curator from a town called Ginosa had seen pictures of Vittorio's hoard on the news, and had recognised them instantly, for they'd all been stolen from his private museum five years before, after being bequeathed by a local farmer. Carmen gave a groan of laughter and dismay. After all that, Vittorio hadn't even found his key pieces here. He'd stolen them instead, presumably to convince his increasingly sceptical investors that Alaric truly was nearby. *That* was why he'd never tried to sell them, not even when desperate for cash. To have done so would have been to invite discovery. He'd been a fraud from the outset. Except that that wasn't quite fair. A true believer, rather, so convinced of his case that he'd fabricated the evidence to support it. Not the first to fall into that trap. Nor the last either.

She checked her watch. Time to leave. She was at the door when a thought struck her. She hurried back to check. Yes, it was as she'd thought. Ginosa was in Puglia, heel of the Italian boot. There was no record of Alaric ever visiting it. How, then, had his ring got there? How, then, those brooches? Another thing: the stolen artefacts had apparently been part of a larger bequest. Was it possible that that larger bequest contained other important pieces? Pieces that might say something new and interesting about the Visigoths in Italy, and which would give her thesis its missing punch?

She checked the time again. It was leave now or be late. But she needed to know. There were two museums in Ginosa, it transpired. The bequest had been left to the smaller of the two, a privately owned ethnographic affair with a useless website – a single page with a brief description of the town and its history, a photograph of its façade, a thumbnail map, hours of opening and contact details. Her Italian wasn't up to calling and asking. Besides, could she really trust some museum volunteer to decide for her what was Visigothic and what was not? No. She needed to pay it a visit. Her driving licence was back in Rome and a taxi would bust her budget, so she checked trains instead. The lack of connections meant that, even if she were to leave right now, she couldn't reach it before it shut. It was closed all day tomorrow too. Wednesday, then. If she left Cosenza on the 7.05, she could have a good two hours at the museum and still be back in Rome by nightfall.

Next door, church bells began to toll. She grabbed the paper and her purse then hurried for the door.

Chapter Twenty-Three

I

Cesco was through with Calabria. Through, indeed, with the entire Italian south. All he wanted right now was to point the Harley north and not stop until he found himself some obscure small town in which to rest awhile, bedding in his new identity while making plans for the future.

The coast road passed too close to Cosenza for comfort, so he cut across Calabria's mountainous spine at Catanzaro, passing through Crotone and Cariati to the Pollino National Park, where a lane closure for a bad accident so hampered his progress that by nine thirty he'd only just reached Campotenese. He was so saddle sore, hungry and weary by now that, when he needed to refuel, he chose a petrol station with a cafe attached, in which to shut his eyes for half an hour before jolting himself awake again with a large *espresso*.

There was a young Austrian family in the station shop when he went to pay for his fuel. The husband was at the till, holding back the years with an unconvincing comb-over and teenage jeans. But it was the wife who caught Cesco's eye, with her tousled short fair hair and freckled pale skin save for the reddened armbands where the sun had exploited the gap between sleeves and lotion. She was dressed in a loose peach halter top and lemon slacks of unusual cut, so that Cesco couldn't quite decide whether she was wearing her trousers short or her culottes long. She was looking after their two kids, a rascally boy and a giggly young girl who both kept pillaging sweets and toys from the shelves, while she pleaded with fond exasperation for them to stop, too helplessly in love with them both to be able quite to lose her temper, hard though she tried.

They left before him. He watched through the window as they climbed into a white people carrier and then set off. Bittersweet memories overwhelmed him as he went out to his bike, of his childhood here in Italy and then in England too, with Emilia and Richard, Arthur and Lizzie.

Family. That was what he was missing. A family of his own.

Carmen came to his mind then, the possibility of happiness he'd thrown away. He swore loudly. Then again, even louder. Self-conscious suddenly, he looked around. A bearded trucker in baggy blue jeans and an unzipped tan jacket was leaning against the side of his cab, watching with sympathetic amusement. Cesco nodded at him. Then he climbed back on his bike, started it up and roared away.

II

The sketch artist was a thinly bearded thirty-something called Pietro, of such extreme earnestness and eagerness to please that Carmen had to fight the urge to laugh. He'd studied in London, he told her, in fluent if accented English as he led her to an interview room, where they sat either side of a plain pine table with a jug of water already on it, two glasses, and a plate of sugared biscuits so stale that she took one nibble and then threw the rest in the bin. He was a cartoonist by profession. His work had been published in all the region's papers, and once or twice in the nationals. Police sketches were only a sideline, but an enjoyable and rewarding one. He'd helped capture at least a dozen suspects, including several very dangerous men. He knew how to get the best out of witnesses, too, so she was to trust him and follow his instructions as closely as she could. They had two portraits to draw, he understood, but for the moment he wanted her to concentrate on just one of them, whichever she preferred.

Carmen closed her eyes and thought back to yesterday morning, with Cesco speeding off down the road in his van and the black SUV screeching again to a halt beside her. Its window buzzing down as she stooped to talk, enabling her to recognise the two men in the front as Famine Eyes and Cemetery Teeth. Famine Eyes had been the boss, but it was Cemetery Teeth who'd had the more distinctive features. She brought him to her mind now, only to discover a kind of uncertainty principle at work; for as soon as she began trying to describe him, her mental portrait of him simply vanished. She kept her eyes closed and remained completely still, therefore, letting his image settle upon her mind like a butterfly upon her finger, not even looking directly at it lest she scare it away. She let herself absorb the details instead. His fat lower lip and open, hanging mouth. His teeth – spaced, pitted and grey. His nose, bulbous and misshapen, like a lump of putty shaped crudely by a thumb. His protruding small ears and receding hairline, his dull eyes beneath his hooded lids and prominent brow ridge, his dyed black hair revealed by the grey threads in his eyebrows and stubble, and his throat so deeply pitted by childhood pox that it looked to have been stippled with a matchstick.

She waited patiently until she had it all. Then she began to talk.

Chapter Twenty-Four

I

For the first time in months, the sun was up before Baldassare. The bedroom grew sticky from its warmth upon the heavy curtains. He checked the bedside clock and realised he'd slept almost twelve hours. They all had, after returning home from last night's duties to giant helpings of pasta before crashing early, all three of them in bed together in a tangle of arms and legs. Even so, he felt exhausted. Ever since the kidnapping, he'd been impelled by furious purpose. Now, with that purpose finally fulfilled, his sails hung slack for lack of wind.

He sat up wearily then dragged himself to the bathroom to wash and dress. He made a tour of the house, making sure to embrace and thank every one of his bodyguards yet again for all they'd done for him. He heaved an armchair outside the bedroom door, to keep watch while he worked, then opened up his laptop. He had nearly five hundred new emails from friends and colleagues, from journalists and others. He answered them one by one, thanking everyone for their sympathy and support with courteous expressions of gratitude that for some reason he didn't remotely feel.

One of his emails was from Carmen, appending a copy of her police statement. He read it through three times, then reopened Cesco's message from the afternoon before, in which he'd begged Baldassare to keep secret his true identity. He was toggling back and forth between the two of them when Alessandra came tiptoeing out of the bedroom in her white nightgown, a finger to her lips. He waited until she'd closed the door behind her. 'How is she?' he whispered.

'Still sleeping.'

'Good.' He shifted across to make space for her in the armchair. She snuggled in beside him, her thigh against his own. The warmth of her. How was it possible to miss something so simple so absurdly? 'I need your advice,' he said.

She put a fond arm around his shoulders. 'Of course you do.'

Last night, on their return home from the press conference, he'd tried to explain the truth behind their rescue, but Alessandra had been too tired to care. He told her now instead. She looked at him in growing astonishment. 'That poor Carbone boy?' she murmured. 'He survived? What about his sister?'

Baldassare shook his head. 'Apparently not. Which I think may be the problem.'

'Problem?'

'Read his email for yourself. He claims to be afraid that the 'Ndrangheta will learn his true identity and come after him. Yet no one that fearful of them could have done what he did yesterday.'

'Then…?'

'Imagine what would happen if he were to reappear. The Carbone boy not only still alive after all these years, but also instrumental in finding you and Bee and Carmen in what might plausibly be the same bunker in which he and his sister had once been held. There'd be a media frenzy. He'd be forced to explain what had happened. He'd have to *relive* it. Can you blame him for not wanting that?'

'Yet he told you.'

'Yes. Because he had to. It was his only way to save Carmen.'

'Ah,' she said. She was silent a few moments. 'And she? Does she feel the same way?'

'That's the thing. I never can read women. Not with confidence.' He brought up her police statement, directed her to its last few paragraphs. 'She's clearly furious with him,' he said. 'But is that because she hates him, or because she doesn't?'

Alessandra was silent as she read. 'I can't tell,' she said finally. 'Not from this. I don't know her well enough.'

'Me neither.'

'How long have they known each other?'

'Only a day or two. But it took me less time than that with you.'

She slid him a look. 'You want to go see her, don't you? To say cruel things about him, and watch how she reacts.'

'Would you mind so very much?'

She took his hand in hers. She raised it to her mouth. 'If he's the one who got us out of that hellhole, my love, I'd mind very much indeed if you didn't.'

II

For a man whose cartoons had been published in all the region's papers, Pietro proved surprisingly diffident about his work. He shielded his pad behind his forearm and wouldn't let Carmen look until he was satisfied. When finally he showed it to her, he made a face like a kicked puppy at her frown of dissatisfaction – even though it was herself she was dissatisfied with, her inability to remember and describe. But he soon pulled himself together. It was only a first draft, he assured her. A starting point, something to build on. They went through it feature by feature, starting with the line and colour of his hair, the height and width of his forehead, the spacing of his eyes. After each question, she'd close her eyes again and wait for the butterfly to settle. Whenever she got completely stuck, he'd prompt her with a catalogue of photofit examples he kept on his laptop, and she'd choose the closest. And finally, between them, they produced a likeness that, while far from photographic, was certainly evocative of the man – not just his looks but his character too – and which she couldn't work out how further to improve.

They broke for coffee before the second sketch. They stood at the machine and talked of Andalusia, where both had spent some time. She stretched her legs and went to the toilets to splash water on her face. Her brain was tired by now, however, and Famine Eyes proved more elusive – not least because what had affected her most about him had been his manner rather than his features; and how on earth was she to describe that? She did her best, however, and eventually they were done. They went together to give them to the *ispettore*. His assistant stopped them with the imperial manner of those who revel in their vicarious authority. He was busy on a *very* important phone call, she told them. They should leave the sketches with her.

Pietro agreed, and bid her farewell. Carmen did not, however, for she had unrelated questions she wanted answered. The very important phone call came finally to its end. She went in. The *ispettore* studied the sketches then thanked her for her help. She asked about her passport and phone. He shook his head but assured her in sign language and stilted English that he'd contact her if either turned up. She gave him Professor Bianchi's email address at Sapienza University, to deal direct with him about the return of the ground-penetrating radar. She asked if she was free to leave Cosenza. She was. She wished him well and took her leave, proud of herself for having seen a hard duty through, yet perversely deflated not to be needed any more. Church bells sounded midday as she reached reception. The sun was dazzling against the station's glass frontage. Her mouth was parched from all her talking. If anyone had ever earned themselves a bowl of ice cream, she'd earned it with her efforts that morning. And, if memory served, there was a *gelateria* directly across the road.

III

Two and a half hours had now passed since Zara had arrived at the *gelateria*, summoned by a text from Dov. She'd taken a pavement table in full view of the police station's front doors, so that Carmen would see her as she came out. Her sunshade kept rocking and creaking, as though it couldn't quite get comfortable. She knew exactly how it felt. Killing time didn't come easily to her. She'd already nursed two coffees like hospice patients, and nibbled her way through a mango sorbet with a long spoon. But still no sign of Carmen. To make matters worse, she'd so over-rehearsed her cover story that it had drained of meaning. An old university friend had married her Italian sweetheart in Sorrento the previous weekend. She'd decided to make the most of it by visiting Amalfi and Capri. Then news of Alaric had broken. With Cosenza only a short drive away…

She wanted to run it by Dov, but he was several tables away, his back turned to her. She sent him a text instead. He checked his phone and scowled back at her. Bells tolled midday. Carmen had been inside almost three hours. It didn't seem feasible. Zara got to her feet then walked along the road. A blonde woman in a shiny leather skirt and scarlet cork platforms came out of a side door at that moment, stooping to hold the hands of two young girls in school uniform. With a thrill of indignation, she turned on her heel and marched over to Dov's table. 'You idiot,' she hissed. 'There's another exit.'

'Sit down,' said Dov.

'What for? She left hours ago.'

'Sit the fuck down.'

There was something in his voice. She glanced around. A young woman was trotting down the police station steps and heading straight towards them. She saw Zara and stopped before she even reached their pavement, then gave a puzzled smile and hesitantly approached. 'Professor Gold,' she frowned. 'Is that you?'

Chapter Twenty-Five

I

It hadn't only been false witness that Zara's parents and their community had abhorred. They'd frowned with almost equal severity on the theatre, cinema and other such forms of make-believe. One of her cousins had once become an actor in Tel Aviv. He'd never been talked of again. But suddenly she found herself thrust on stage and, to her immense relief, her lines came naturally. 'Carmen Nero,' she smiled, holding out her hand to shake. 'What an extraordinary coincidence. I was just writing you an email.'

'An email?'

She glanced down at Dov. His face was stone. But it was too late now to pretend she didn't know him. 'This is my friend Dov,' she said. 'We were in Sorrento for a wedding. I've been telling him for weeks about how beautiful the Amalfi coast is, so we agreed to stay on a few days, to head up to Capri. Then you went and posted that photograph of those Alaric artefacts, and I've been transfixed ever since.'

'I didn't even realise you'd been following.'

'I know, I know. It's silly, but I felt ashamed. Every year, I give my new students the exact same introductory lecture. I'm sure you know the one. How archaeology isn't about the hunt for fabulous lost treasures any more. Then this happens and I can't look away. And Cosenza was only two hours away. It seemed almost like it was meant to be. So I'm afraid I bullied poor Dov into coming here instead.'

For a moment she feared Dov would refuse his cue. But then he got to his feet and smiled warmly. 'No bullying required,' he said. 'What can Capri offer, after all, that Cosenza can't?'

They laughed together, but then Carmen gave a grimace. 'I wish you'd sent that email,' she said. 'I could have saved you a drive.'

'Oh?'

'We found Alaric's tomb yesterday. At least, we found the thing we thought might be his tomb. It wasn't his tomb at all. It wasn't any kind of tomb. It was something else altogether.' She glanced over her shoulder at the police station, as though wondering how much to tell them. Then her expression cleared. She took a local newspaper from beneath her arm and flapped it to an inside page, struggling to hold it against the faint breeze. 'That photograph I posted. It turns out those pieces weren't even from around here.'

Zara took the paper and read the article. When she realised what it meant, she couldn't help but laugh. 'How about that?' she said, passing it on to Dov. 'All this way for nothing.' But then she frowned. 'Puglia?'

Carmen grinned. 'That's exactly what I was wondering. The gold solidus and the dolphin, sure. The brooches maybe. But that ring makes zero sense.' She turned to address Dov directly, to include him in the conversation. 'Alaric was in Italy for years. But he never went anywhere near Puglia, not as far as we know. Though our sources are so thin that tracking his movements is hellishly hard. Like trying to guess a jigsaw from seven surviving pieces.'

'And you think these artefacts might be piece number eight?' suggested Dov.

'Maybe. And maybe piece number nine is still in the museum.' Then she added, with just a hint of shame: 'I was actually planning to go visit it, except it's a nightmare without a car.'

Zara glanced at Dov. He shrugged and spread his hands. She considered for a moment. The chances of finding anything in Ginosa were vanishingly small. But their first flight home wasn't until tomorrow anyway, and the less time she spent alone with Dov, the happier she'd be. So she turned back to Carmen with a smile. 'Then it's just as well we have one, isn't it?'

II

It was on the Naples ring road when exhaustion finally got the better of Cesco. He woke from a micro-sleep to find himself veering into a container lorry. In his rush to save himself, he overcorrected and took the Harley fishtailing across two lanes, fighting to stay upright amid the screech of brakes and blare of horns.

He pulled into the next lay-by to give his heart a chance to settle. He needed to get some sleep. Yet he had too many enemies in Naples to make that an attractive option, while his near miss had given him enough adrenaline to make it a little further. He looped around the city to reach the coast at Pozzuoli, where he decided to call it quits. It was still low season. He had his pick of *pensiones*. He found one with rear parking then went inside. A kindly looking woman, all teeth and moles, was perched on a tall stool behind reception. She shook her head at him when he asked for a room, and gave an explanation he was too tired to take in. He thrust banknotes at her until she sighed in exasperation and led him upstairs. Now he understood. The room hadn't yet been made up. He shooed her to the door and told her he wasn't to be disturbed. Then he stripped off his jacket, shoes and jeans and dived head first onto the bed as if into a swimming pool, to be swallowed up by sleep even as hit the water.

III

Carmen looked from Zara to Dov and back again. There was a peculiar tension between the pair of them, as though she'd surprised them in the middle of a fight. The last thing she wanted, if so, was to exacerbate it with a futile six-hour round trip. 'Are you sure about this?' she asked doubtfully. 'Ginosa's quite a hike.'

'For you as well as us,' said Zara.

'Yes. But I've got a thesis at stake.'

'How far is it exactly?' asked Dov.

'Two hours, I'd guess,' said Carmen. 'Maybe three.'

'Two hours!' he scoffed, waving it away.

'Maybe three. Then the same again coming back.' She frowned at them. 'You will be coming back, yes?'

'Of course,' said Dov. 'I've already had to cancel one hotel room for tonight. Damned if I'll cancel a second.' His brow furrowed. 'Though, while we're vaguely on the subject, may I ask a favour?'

'Of course,' said Carmen. 'What?'

'The fact of the matter is, I'm technically a married man. Only for another few weeks, but still. I'd hate for my kids to find out about me and Zara before I'm ready to tell them. So if you could keep us to yourself...'

'I won't say a word,' promised Carmen.

'Great,' said Dov. He clapped his hands together. 'Then how about this: you didn't come over here to say hi. You came for ice cream. Don't even try to deny it, I saw it in your eyes. So you stay here with Zara and gorge yourself while I go fetch the car. It's not far. I'll be back before you know it.' He nodded cheerfully then headed off before they could argue, his leather jacket slung over his shoulder on the hook of his finger. Carmen stared after him. Something about the way he moved reminded her of that man in the cafe that morning. Except it couldn't be him, so she shrugged it off and went inside.

The neat rows of brightly coloured ice creams and sorbets beneath the impeccably polished glass made her mouth water. She ordered scoops of chocolate and lemon, then went outside to eat. She asked Zara about her Sorrento wedding, but Zara had no interest in discussing that. All she cared about was Alaric. Carmen answered cautiously at first, mindful that a police investigation was still in progress. But this was Professor Zara Gold. If she couldn't trust her, who could she trust? And it was such a relief to talk to someone uninvolved that soon it all came spilling out: Vittorio, Giulia and the GPR; her brief alliance with Cesco Rossi, and how he'd proved a fraud; how she'd fallen into the hands of the 'Ndrangheta before being rescued by Baldassare and his men. It was a treat to watch Zara, the way her mouth dropped, the perfect circles of her eyes. She was describing her morning with the sketch artist when Dov reappeared, tooting for their attention from a scarlet Renault. They hurried over. Carmen got in the back. A leaflet of some kind had slipped beneath the passenger seat. Thinking it might be important, she pinched it out between her fingertips only to find it was just a car-hire map of Calabria. She passed it forward all the same, for Zara to put away in the glove compartment.

'You *have* to hear what Carmen's been up to,' Zara told Dov.

'I never should have said anything,' wailed Carmen. She meant it too. Zara she trusted, but there something off-putting about Dov, particularly when he smiled. But it was too late now, so out it all came again. Dov kept glancing round at her, his disbelief apparent. 'What did I tell you?' said Zara when she was done. They pressed her with questions for a while. She answered as best she could. But even the best tales wind eventually to their end. Silence fell. Dov shook his head and let out a long breath as if to draw a line beneath it all, then turned on the radio and searched channels until he found some Bach.

The day was warm, the car stuffy. Their tyres made lullaby on the tarmac. Carmen's eyelids grew heavy. Every kilometre they put between themselves and Cosenza leached more tension out of her. Her head lolled against the window, startling her back awake. She shook herself and sat up. Her head lolled again. She found an angle of repose between the seat back and the window and gave herself permission to close her eyes just for a minute or two, vowing to herself that on no account was she to let herself fall asleep.

And, so vowing, she fell.

Chapter Twenty-Six

I

Dov adjusted his rear-view mirror so that he could keep an eye on Carmen in the back seat. Her eyes were closed, her mouth open, while the steady rasp of her breathing indicated that she was now fast asleep. He turned to Zara with a glare. 'What was I supposed to do?' she asked defensively. 'Pretend I didn't know you?'

'How about not coming to my table at all?' he said, switching to Hebrew, just in case. 'How many times do I have to tell you things?'

'The police station had a side door.'

'I know it had a fucking side door. I was watching it.'

'Bullshit. You couldn't even see it from your table.'

'There was a shoe shop across the street. I could see its reflection in the glass.'

'Oh,' said Zara.

'Oh,' said Dov. He checked on Carmen again. She was still out, a little saliva glistening at the corner of her mouth. He reached across to pop the glove compartment, take out the car-hire map. 'And this! Who the hell flies into Lamezia Terme for a wedding in Sorrento?'

'You were the one who fetched the car. You should have checked to—'

'Your map. Your mistake.' He buzzed down his window and tossed it out, watching in his wing mirror as it flapped after them like a wounded bird. Reception on the Bach began to go. He found some Rossini instead. They reached the Gulf of Taranto, the arch of the Italian boot. The sky was clear but hazy, the water still and pale. There were grey shapes in the distance, like a ghost armada. They drove

199

another forty minutes then turned inland and uphill towards Ginosa. Dov took a turn at the edge of town deliberately sharply, to lurch Carmen awake. She sat up and rubbed her eyes. He smiled warmly at her. 'Back with us?' he asked.

'I'm so sorry,' she said. 'The last few days, you've no idea.'

'No worries. The greatest compliment you can pay a driver – isn't that what they say?'

The streets were narrow; the houses whitewashed. They found the ethnographic museum near the top of town, a one-storey building in need of paint. It had five parking bays outside, four of which were empty. Dov reversed into the one closest to the entrance. 'You two go on in,' he said. 'I think I'll take a stroll.'

'Are you not coming?' asked Carmen.

'I'm not a museum guy, to be honest. Not on an afternoon like this. Give me a *centro storico* any day. A *centro storico* and a beer.'

'But that's terrible,' said Carmen. 'After driving us all this way.'

Dov smiled, touched by her concern. What a shame it was that, thanks to Zara's amateurish blundering, he was now almost certainly going to have to kill her too.

II

As a boy, Tomas Gentile had loved to watch his father doing his household chores. No job had been beyond him. There'd been nothing he couldn't fix. He'd already been rich by then, so it hadn't been a question of saving money. He'd done it because the ability to keep one's house and possessions in good working order had been an important part of what it meant to be a man.

There was a wooden ladder in the basement. Tomas carried it outside to unclog the gutters and downpipes of sodden handfuls of moss and pine needles. The pine trees themselves needed cutting down to size, but that would take a chainsaw, the noise of which might draw unwelcome attention. He oiled the hinges and locks on all the doors and windows, cleaning them while he was at it and making a note of which needed repair or replacement. He weeded and swept the paved forecourt then cut back the shrubberies with a pair of clippers.

A message came in on his phone. It had an attachment. He opened it and studied it for a while. He hadn't been lying to that American woman. They really did have sources in the Cosenza police who'd be happy to sell her out for a hundred euros. He went inside and found Guido at the stove, wearing a small pink apron with white trim as he cooked up a batch of red sauce. 'That smells good,' he told him.

'It's the rosemary.'

'I know it's the rosemary,' said Tomas. 'I'm just saying, it smells good.' He held out his tablet and said: 'The police have sketches.'

Guido scooped up sauce on his wooden spoon. He blew on it to cool it before taking a small taste, letting it sit on his tongue before swallowing it. 'That American bitch?' he asked.

'Yes.'

Guido wiped his hands on his apron before taking the phone. 'Would you look at the fucking teeth she's given me,' he said balefully. 'Mine don't look anything like that.'

'You could brush them more, you know, oh my brother.'

'Fuck you, brush them more. How would brushing make them straight?'

'Forget your teeth. What about the likenesses? Do you think we could be recognised from them?'

Guido looked at them again. 'Recognised, no. Suspected, sure.'

Tomas nodded. 'That's what I think too. I think if the police see us, they'll arrest us and take us in, just in case. Then they'll invite her to the station to look at us. She will say yes, that's them. And that will be that.'

Guido pinched sea salt between thumb and forefinger, crumbling it into his sauce. 'What are we gonna do?'

'According to her apartment listing, she's checking out on Wednesday morning. With everything that's happened, she might not even stay that long. And who can say where she'll go then?' He still had her passport so she wouldn't be heading back to America any time soon. But that was the best that could be said for the situation.

'We can't risk waiting for Massimo and the boys. Nor can we ask the Critellis. We'll have to take care of her ourselves.'

Guido looked unhappily down at his sauce. 'Now?'

'Not in daylight, no. Not with every policeman in Cosenza having those sketches. After it gets dark.'

Guido gave his pan another stir. 'Tonight, then.'

'Yes,' said Tomas. 'Tonight.'

III

A Japanese family of six was leaving the museum as Carmen and Zara arrived, identical expressions of polite bemusement on their faces, as if convinced there had to have been a real museum in there somewhere, they just hadn't been able to find it. They waited until they were all out then went on in. The small foyer had a reception desk at which a woman with toothpick arms and hair like blue candyfloss hurriedly closed a paperback with a lurid jacket and hid it on her knees beneath her desk. She gave them two tickets and a pair of introductory leaflets in exchange for the entrance fees that Carmen insisted on paying. There were six rooms in total. The first dealt with the region's Palaeolithic origins; the second, its Magna Graecia pomp. They ignored both of those and walked straight to the third, a special collection dedicated to the finds of a local farmer, Genaro 'Il Siciliano' Scopece, whose full-length, sepia-tinted photograph was on the wall by the door: bald-headed but with thick grey stubble, dressed in a checked shirt and heavy jacket, holding a long staff with a knobbly end, and a glint in his eye that said that if the photographer cared to come a fraction closer, he'd find out what the knobbly end was for.

There was a short biography inset into the photograph with his name and dates. His family had apparently owned and worked land around Ginosa for three hundred years. Too young himself for active service in the Second World War, he'd volunteered for the *Genio Guastatori* instead, helping to clear Italy's battlefields of unexploded munitions. It had given him a love for metal detection that had lasted his whole life. He'd been a common sight in the fields and valleys around Ginosa, particularly after his retirement, sweeping them for the artefacts here on display. Unfortunately, his passion for treasure hunting hadn't been matched by diligence at record keeping, so it was impossible to say precisely where each piece was found, but the collection as a whole gave a fascinating glimpse of the town and larger region's long and vibrant history.

There were glass-topped display cabinets against the walls, and more running down the centre, with the exhibits arranged thematically rather than by era. The first two had a military motif, with arrowheads, a shell casing, various military buttons, a pair of pitted knives and what was optimistically billed as the hilt of a Roman short sword. Then came jewellery, with rings, bracelets and other pieces — as well as colour photographs of Vittorio's ring and brooches, their absence explained by a faded photocopy of a newspaper article about the theft.

Farm implements. Cutlery through the ages. Coins of varying vintages and interest. The gold solidus had been the star of that particular show, its absence again marked and explained by the same photocopied clipping. But there were other interesting coins too, staters from Magna Graecia all the way up to rare lire from the Italian Republic, along with others in too poor condition to identify, artfully arranged to spill out of a pair of small wooden chests. None that Carmen could see could plausibly be attributed to Alaric or his Visigoths, however, so she glanced at Zara with an apologetic smile, hoping that she wouldn't hold this wasted trip against her, only to be startled by her flushed face and shining eyes. She asked the question with an eyebrow. Zara hesitated then pointed to the left of the two troves. 'The one with the cup.'

Carmen leaned closer. The glass lid was old and scratched, and the way the strip lighting reflected made it hard to be sure. But yes, one of the coins did indeed seem to be stamped with a cup. 'And?' she asked.

Again that hesitation. 'I'd need to see the other side.' She made her way back to reception. Carmen could hear her talking animatedly. Then she reappeared with the receptionist, who unlocked the glass lid and lifted it like a bonnet. Zara pointed to the coin. The receptionist pulled on a pair of loose white gloves then took it delicately between her fingers, turned it to its obverse. Carmen peered closely. Again, she could see a design, but it was almost impossible to make out what. 'A fleur-de-lis?' she hazarded.

'No,' said Zara. 'Three fruits hanging from a branch.'

'Oh. Yes.' She saw it now. 'Well?'

'A half-shekel. Year two of the Siege of Jerusalem.'

'A half-shekel?' frowned Carmen. 'But that makes no...' She stopped herself then gazed at Zara in astonishment. When Titus had led the Roman army to Israel to suppress the Great Revolt, thousands of rural Jews had fled to Jerusalem for sanctuary. They'd stayed there for the next three years, during which time they'd minted their own coins – including this one, apparently – until Titus had finally seized the city and torn down the temple, stripping both of their wealth and treasures to take back to Rome in triumph. And, realising that, Carmen realised something else too. It wasn't Alaric himself that had brought Zara here from Sorrento. It was the whiff of sacred treasures.

The larger mystery remained, however. What was this coin doing in Ginosa at all? The coin and the sealstone too? Carmen wandered back over to the photograph of Genaro Scopece, the man who'd found them both, whose family had lived here for three hundred years and who'd been a common sight in the fields and valleys around Ginosa, particularly after his retirement. The one they'd called...

A monstrous suspicion came suddenly to her. She marched back over to the cabinet. 'This man Genaro Scopece,' she demanded, folding her arms in anger. 'Why was he known as *Il Siciliano*?'

Chapter Twenty-Seven

I

The curator's pupils flickered like flies trapped beneath a shot glass. 'It was his nickname,' she said.

'I get that,' said Carmen drily. 'What I'm asking is *why* was it his nickname? His family had lived here three hundred years. So why call him the Sicilian? Unless he'd lived in Sicily, that is? Is that where he found this coin?'

'How could we possibly know that? I told you. He left no records.'

'But he *might* have found them there, yes? Or anywhere else he travelled, for that matter.'

It was Zara's turn to fold her arms. 'Where exactly on Sicily did he live?'

'He didn't,' said the woman. But her defiance wilted beneath their joint gazes. 'He did live for a while *in* Sicilì.'

'Sicilì?'

'It's a village,' she sighed. 'In the Cilento. His wife had a farm there. But then she died and he came home.'

'The Cilento?' asked Zara, tapping it into her phone.

'South of Sorrento,' said Carmen with a slight frown, for Zara and Dov must have driven through it on their drive down from Sorrento. She turned back to the curator. 'How long did he live there?'

'I don't know. We don't have dates.'

'Roughly, then. A year? Five? Ten?' The flush on the curator's face gave her away. Carmen stared at her in disbelief. 'Twenty? *Thirty?*'

'I'm sure it can't have been as much as thirty,' she said, shuffling her feet uncomfortably, like a shy teen at a dance.

An unfamiliar fury welled inside Carmen. 'This room is a fraud,' she said. 'This whole room.'

Zara tugged her sleeve. Carmen shook her off, thinking she was only seeking to calm her. Then she took her by her wrist and held out her phone. 'Look,' she said. Carmen took it irritably. A map of Sicilì was open on the screen. She was about to ask what she was supposed to be looking at when she noticed the river it was on. More particularly, she noticed its name.

For it was a river called the Bussento.

II

It was late afternoon when Cesco woke, aching in every joint. Standing up was a nightmare. He hobbled to the sink to splash cold water on his face, then washed down a pair of painkillers. The aching and the stiffness slowly eased. He zombie-walked down the hallway for a hot shower then sat on his bed to clean and dress his shotgun wounds as best he could. He struggled into fresh clothes then took his laptop out onto the Pozzuoli Lungomare.

There was a chill breeze, and only a few hardy swimmers and sunbathers were out. The sea broke half-heartedly against the rocks and shingle, before lazily withdrawing. Further out, a murmuration of starlings drew swirls, vortices and other astonishing patterns in the sky. No wonder the Romans had used them for augury. He took a beer at a cafe with Wi-Fi. Baldassare had replied to his email, thanking him earnestly for his part in saving his family, while chiding him for slipping away before he could say it in person. He gave him his word that he'd keep his identity secret as long as he wished. And he added that he had some momentous news – news too sensitive for email, but which he'd very much like to discuss in person.

The last thing Cesco wanted was a return to Cosenza. He replied suggesting a video chat instead. Baldassare responded almost at once, claiming reasons it needed to be face-to-face. But Cesco didn't have to come back if he didn't wish. Name a time and place within reason, and Baldassare would meet him there.

Cesco played piano on his laptop keyboard. He even began composing a reply asking tartly how he could be sure it wasn't some kind of trap, but he deleted it before sending. He'd helped Baldassare save his wife and daughter. The man would die rather than betray him. With a sigh, he decided to accept. He opened a map in his browser, with Pozzuoli at the top and Cosenza at the bottom, then looked for somewhere roughly halfway between. Polla would do nicely. He was still too sore and tired to face a long ride tomorrow, however, so he suggested they meet midday on Thursday, choosing a cafe at random and including his new phone number just in case.

Perfect, replied Baldassare. He'd see him there.

III

Carmen and Zara stepped out of the museum into late afternoon sunshine that provided almost too perfect a metaphor for their fumbling search for Alaric. Was it possible, was it truly possible, that after hundreds of years of failed efforts to find Alaric's tomb near Cosenza, it was actually in the Cilento instead? Zara was clearly thinking exactly the same. 'Do we know this river was even called the Bussento back then?'

Carmen nodded. She already knew the answer, though its significance had never occurred to her before. She took back the phone and on its map followed the river a few kilometres downstream to the coast – and yes, there it was, the small resort town of Policastro. 'This used to be a major Roman port,' she told Zara. 'Policastro Buxentum. Policastro on the Bussento.'

The piazza was signposted, and only a short walk. They set off towards it. Then Zara stopped dead and took Carmen's arm. 'Damn it,' she said. 'It doesn't work.'

'Why not?'

'Jordanes,' she said. 'I haven't read his history of the Goths in years. But doesn't he say that Alaric was buried beneath the Busento *near Cosenza*? I mean he actually specifies Cosenza, I'm sure of it.'

'Oh,' said Carmen. 'Yes. You're right.'

They walked on slowly, deflated by disappointment. They reached the piazza. Dov was sitting at an outside table drinking coffee. He saw them and came hurrying. 'You were quick,' he said. Then, looking from face to face, he said: 'You've found something, haven't you?'

'Not exactly,' said Zara. 'We thought we had, but it turns out not.' She explained about the half-shekel, the second Bussento and the Roman historian Jordanes. An overburdened moped drove by, the screech of its engine forcing them into silence until it passed. The interlude gave Carmen a chance for further thought – for the discovery of a second Bussento near which Visigothic artefacts might well have been found was too great a coincidence to give up so easily.

Then she saw it.

'Jordanes didn't witness Alaric's burial himself,' she told them. 'All he did was summarise the history of the Goths written by another historian called Cassiodorus, whose original has since been lost.'

'So?' asked Dov.

'Cassiodorus didn't witness the burial himself either. In fact, he wasn't even born for another seventy-odd years after Alaric's death. But he worked in the Gothic court where he had full access to their archives, and to the leading families too. And he seems to have been a reliable chronicler elsewhere, so his account has to be taken seriously.'

'Okay.'

'The thing is, both Cassiodorus and Jordanes had strong connections to Calabria. Cassiodorus wasn't just born and raised there, he retired there too, to a monastery he himself founded not that far from Cosenza. As for Jordanes, we're not one hundred per cent sure it was the same person, but there was a Bishop Jordanes of Crotone around the same time. And Crotone is close to Cosenza too.'

Dov frowned. 'But surely that just makes their testimony stronger?'

'No. Think about it. Imagine you're either of these two men. You read in your source material that Alaric was laid to rest beneath a river called the Bussento in southern Italy. That's great! You know the Busento well. You visited it as a child. It's only a day's ride away. It's just a few kilometres long, so while there's no mention of Cosenza in the text you read, you know by definition it must have been close to it. You add that detail in, therefore, in perfect good faith, and throw in a little local colour too. But in fact it wasn't the Cosenza Busento at all. It was this other one. And here's the thing: we have an independent report of Alaric's death from a guy called Philostorgius who was alive when it happened. He only records it as an aside, and doesn't mention the burial at all, which is why historians have always preferred Cassiodorus. But he states that Alaric died in Campania, not Calabria.'

Dov nodded. 'And this place Sicilì is in Campania?'

'Exactly.'

'And it makes sense, does it? Historically, I mean?'

Carmen glanced at Zara. Zara gestured for her to keep talking. 'Okay,' she said. 'The generally accepted narrative goes something like this: Alaric and his men grew sick of wandering around Italy. It's tough, living off the land, especially in the winter. What they longed for was a homeland of their own. That's why they besieged Rome in the first place, to pressure the emperor into giving them one. He refused. So they sacked Rome and took their loot south, planning to cross the Mediterranean to Carthage, which was fertile and weakly defended. But they lost so many men just trying to reach Sicily that they fell back to Cosenza, where Alaric died. But that last part makes no sense. It was two hundred kilometres back to Cosenza. That's not a falling back. It's a retreat. A retracing. The only way it makes sense is if Alaric had given up on Carthage altogether and had decided to head north to France or Spain instead – exactly as his brother-in-law Athaulf did after inheriting the crown. In which case, Policastro would have made *far* more sense than Cosenza as a place to pass the winter. It was warmer, more fertile and most of all it had a major port for bringing in supplies, to be paid for with their Roman gold. If you had a large army to see through till spring, which would you choose?'

Dov nodded. 'So what do we do now?' he asked.

'How about we go to Sicilì,' suggested Zara, 'and take a look?'

Chapter Twenty-Eight

I

Tomas Gentile knew the building that Carmen Nero was staying in from his prior monitoring of her phone. Her specific apartment became apparent when he and Guido arrived to scout it out, thanks to the balcony flowerpots that matched the website photograph. Its lights were out, however. Maybe she and Cesco Rossi had both left town. Certainly Rossi was likely gone, after fleeing them and crashing his van. But Nero had given those sketches to the police that same morning, which suggested she at least was still around. There were parking spaces outside the building, but in a kind of cul-de-sac that would leave them at risk of being trapped by a traffic snarl-up. He had Guido park on the bridge road instead, choosing a spot with views of the building's front door and Nero's apartment.

'Want me to do it?' asked Guido.

Tomas shook his head. Jobs like these required subtlety and quick thinking, not exactly Guido's strengths. If the nightmares came, so be it. After all, one didn't judge a man by how he felt but by what he did. 'Wait here,' he said. 'Keep the engine running.' He turned up his jacket collar, put on his dark glasses and baseball cap. He got out and stood against the car to tuck the hunting knife and automatic pistol into his waistband, hiding them beneath his jacket. Then he made his way down a flight of steps into the cul-de-sac and across to the building. It had a glass front door. He could see the brightly lit lobby inside with two rows of letterboxes and a CCTV camera. It had a keypad lock and intercom buzzers for each apartment.

There was a fir tree across the way. He loitered against it for ten minutes before a woman came out holding a furled umbrella and looking nervously upwards. He grabbed the door before it closed and slipped inside, head averted from the camera. He hurried light-footed up to the top floor. A TV was playing across the landing, but Nero's apartment was silent. It had a peephole but no doorbell. He took his gun in his hand then stood to one side and knocked. There was no response. He knocked louder. Still nothing. He hid his gun again then went back down and out to the car.

'No luck?' asked Guido sympathetically.

'She's not there.'

'What now, then?'

Tomas looked around. The evening *passeggiata* was underway, couples streaming arm in arm towards Corso Mazzini to greet with astonishment and delight the exact same people they'd greeted with astonishment and delight the night before. But they were away from the street lamps here, with a clear line of sight of Nero's apartment and the building's front door. They were highly unlikely to find anything better. 'We wait,' he said.

II

Lightning ripped open the sky as they approached Cosenza, letting the heavens fall. Rain swept in frenzied flurries across their windscreen. Huge puddles formed upon the motorway, so that each car sent up a great curtain of white spray to blind the one behind. Within a minute or two, traffic had seized up.

Zara took her phone back out. She'd been trying, on and off, to find a place to stay in Sicilì itself. But in vain. The town had no hotel, nor even an inn with rooms. It did have two apartments for rent, and a nearby *agriturismo*, but all were fully booked. And it was hard to judge the options further afield on her small screen with her battery already running low, so they'd agreed to leave it for the night then head up in the morning, taking whatever they could find. But now, idly searching for more information on Sicilì itself, she landed on a municipal website she hadn't seen before with helpful lists of local shops, businesses and properties for rent. Most were in the neighbouring town of Morigerati, but it also included the three Sicilì properties she'd already seen, and a fourth which she had not – a two-bedroom cottage on the lower fringes of the town, whose owner, Faustino – according to its brief blurb – had moved to Rome for work, and so rented it out for a little extra income. She described it to Dov and Carmen. They urged her to call the number. Faustino himself answered on the second ring. Background noises made it clear he was out with friends. They each had to shout to make themselves heard. He and his girlfriend would be visiting Sicilì the weekend after next, he told her, but it was free until then. It was fully furnished and they'd find the key beneath a brick outside the door, but they had to understand that it was not the Ritz. There was neither Wi-Fi nor signal for their mobiles, though they could find both up in Sicilì itself. As for the cottage, it was a thing of beauty in fine weather but cranky in the bad, suffering from draughts, damp and temperamental plumbing. Were they still interested?

Zara assured him that they were, and asked what it would cost. Faustino quoted an absurdly small sum per night, then asked her to leave it in cash on the kitchen table when they left. Or not, he joked, as she preferred. What was he going to do about it?

'So it's free tonight?' asked Dov, once she'd reported back.

'I guess,' she said.

'Then how about it?'

Zara squinted sideways at him. 'Seriously?'

'Why not? If we pack quickly, we can be there by midnight. I mean, be honest. Where would you rather wake tomorrow morning? Sicilì or Cosenza?'

Zara didn't answer at once. On the one hand, she didn't want Dov sharing her hotel room again that night. On the other, the cottage only had two bedrooms. But her silence only offered Carmen the chance to speak. 'I'd be glad to see the back of Cosenza,' she admitted.

'Excellent,' grinned Dov. 'Sicilì it is.'

III

A clap of thunder announced the storm. Soon it was tipping down. The windows of the silver Range Rover quickly misted up. Tomas had to rub the windscreen to keep watch. An evening service ended in the cul-de-sac church. Congregants came trickling out, huddled against the rain. In the tangle of traffic that ensued, he almost missed the scarlet Renault as it pulled up outside Nero's building. Its rear door opened and a woman scurried inside, her arm above her head. Thirty seconds later, Nero's apartment lights came on and then the woman herself walked by a window. 'She's back,' he said.

Guido nodded. 'You sure you want to do it yourself?'

'Just keep the engine on.'

He pulled his cap back on, turned up his collar then hurried down the steps to resume his post beneath the fir tree. It offered less shelter than he'd hoped, the wind sweeping sheets of rain against his legs, his shoes quickly becoming soaked. He was looking about for somewhere better when Nero appeared in the lobby carrying an overnight bag. She came to the door. He reached for his gun. She cupped her hands around her eyes to peer out through the glass at the dismal weather, then stepped back again, set down her bag and checked her watch. Perhaps she was waiting for the rain to abate before heading off. Or perhaps someone was coming to pick her up. He considered shooting her through the door. But she was far enough back that he couldn't be certain of even hitting her. If she got away, he might not get another chance.

The rain slowed and then stopped almost as abruptly as it had started. Still Nero stayed inside. Five more minutes passed. Then the scarlet Renault from before pulled up in a slosh of water. The driver tooted for her attention then got out and hurried around to open the hatchback for her overnight bag, even as she picked it up and came out.

It was his moment.

He tugged the brim of his cap down low then zipped his jacket up over his chin, leaving himself a viewing slit like a medieval helmet. He held his gun down by his side then walked briskly forward, timing his approach to reach Nero as she swung her bag into the boot, waiting until the very last moment so that he couldn't possibly miss.

IV

It was the slap of shoes on the flagstones that did it. There was something so purposeful about them that Dov instinctively glanced around. He took in all at once the man approaching, the deliberate way he'd hidden his face between baseball cap and collar, how his eyes were fixed on Carmen and the gun he was holding against his leg. Dov's bodyguard training instantly kicked in, those three dull years in the secret service. He stepped across the man even as he raised the gun. He grabbed his wrist in one hand and the barrel of the gun in the other, wresting it from his startled grip. Their gazes briefly locked. There was a strange moment of mutual recognition, each appreciating the other for what he was. Then the man tore himself free and hurried off into the night, glancing all around as if expecting the police to come swarming. Dov was too startled to stop him or go after him. He watched instead as he fled up a flight of steps onto the bridge road where he climbed into a silver Range Rover that sped straight off. Dov glanced around at Carmen, utterly unaware of what had so nearly befallen her. 'Get in,' he told her. 'I need something from my bag.' She nodded and climbed in.

That man had surely been 'Ndrangheta. His partner too. Possibly the very two Carmen had described to the sketch artist that morning, seeking to silence her before she could identify them in person. And now he had their gun, with their fingerprints still on it. He unzipped his suitcase for a T-shirt with which to wipe clean those parts of the gun that he himself had touched, then he zipped it away in an empty pouch. He closed the hatchback, got back in behind the wheel, pulled a three-point turn. He checked every which way as he joined the bridge road. There was no sign of the silver Range Rover, but maybe they'd have other ways of tracking her. And they knew about him now, so he needed to be alert. It wouldn't be easy. He'd seen too little of the

214

man's face to be confident of recognising him again – and he hadn't seen his partner at all. Ideally, he'd get hold of a copy of Carmen's sketches, except he could hardly ask for them. He glanced around at her, still oblivious of her close call. 'Forgive me,' he said, 'but there's something been bugging me all day.'

'Yes?' she asked.

'Those sketches you did this morning. This will make me sound like an idiot, but how does that even work? When I was at that bar in Ginosa, I gave it a shot myself, trying to see if I could describe my mother's face from memory. My own dear mother! And, honestly, it was hopeless.'

Carmen smiled. 'It's harder than you'd think, isn't it?'

'Damn right. So how did you do it? I mean, take those two men you described this morning, for example. What sort of things did you say?'

Chapter Twenty-Nine

I

Faustino proved perfectly correct. His cottage was not the Ritz.

They reached it a little before midnight, having stopped for provisions along the way. It lay at the foot of a short, steep drive so badly potholed that it made the Renault lumber like an arthritic bull. To Zara's consternation, there was neither brick nor key by the front door; to her relief, they found both outside the back door instead. It was chilly inside, and musty too. The kitchen walls were a sweaty yellow, as if they'd caught the flu, while the old cream refrigerator muttered and grumbled like an elderly concierge woken in the small hours. The bed linen had that clamminess to it, as if taken out of the drier too soon, and every time the loo was flushed, the plumbing made plaintive didgeridoo noises.

Yet the place had an undeniable charm even so, especially with the pellet heater lit and an improvised supper of bread, cheese, ham and red wine on the table. Zara waited until Dov had chosen his chair, then sat as far from him as she could. He promptly stood to top up their glasses then sat back down beside her, resting his arm on the back of her chair, stroking her nape with his thumb, impervious to the looks she slid him. They cleared the table, said good night, went to their rooms. The moment Dov closed the door, his smile vanished. 'The hell was that?' he hissed.

'The hell was what?'

'We're supposed to be lovers. What kind of lover flinches from their partner?'

'You shouldn't have touched me.'

'For fuck's sake! I'm playing a role. You should be too. You may already have put our mission into serious jeopardy.'

'Sure!'

'Are you blind?' he asked in exasperation. 'Carmen's not stupid. She's already worked out we're here for the temple treasure, thanks to that half-shekel. Now you've got her doubting our friendship too. How long before she realises the truth? How long before she tells someone?' He squinted at her. 'Or maybe that's what you want. Maybe you're trying to sabotage us.'

'Don't be absurd. I just don't like being touched, that's all.'

He glowered at her some more before finally relenting. 'Okay. Maybe we can still fix it.'

'How?'

He put a finger to his lips. Zara fell silent. They could hear the gamelan tinkle of clothes being put away on metal hangers next door. Dov nodded. 'She'll be able to hear everything we get up to,' he said.

She looked at him in alarm. 'What do you mean?' she asked.

'What do you think I mean?'

'You can't be serious.'

'Have you got a better way to convince her we're lovers?' He took her by her wrist. His grip was so fierce that when she tried to pull away she only burned her skin. He pulled her over to the bed then threw her down on her back. He leaned in over her, resting his weight upon his hands. His breath was hot upon her face, smelling of cheese and red wine. Her heart pounded madly. 'This is not a game,' he said. 'Our mission is at stake. The temple treasures. Your freedom. Are you really going to risk it all for some childish notion of virtue?' He put his hand on her waist and ran it up over her breast.

She knuckled him in his eye then rolled free and scrambled to her feet. 'Never, ever do that again,' she warned.

'Or what?'

'You'll find that out when you next wake.'

He laughed and shook his head. 'You're no fun,' he said. 'You're no fun at all.'

Baldassare couldn't sleep. He rose in the early hours and took up his post outside the bedroom door, checking his new messages. The *ispettore* had sent through a number of reports overnight, including transcripts and recordings of the statement Alessandra and Bettina had given together yesterday afternoon. He'd offered to sit with them, but Alessandra had asked him not to, for there were certain parts of their ordeal they'd find easier to recount without his feelings to consider. He jacked in a pair of earbuds and listened now. Within minutes, he was weeping freely both at what they'd suffered and the calm courage with which they described it. That ordeal completed, he listened to recordings of interviews with the two 'Ndrangheta thugs they'd arrested. They were young and fearful, but they'd been well coached to keep their mouths shut until their lawyers arrived. One of them might have been cracked by a skilful inquisitor, but to his frustration the questioning had been so confrontational that the opportunity had been missed.

A preliminary search of the dungeon had taken place. It seemed to date back at least as far as the 1970s, when kidnapping had been in vogue. The meadow had been thickly wooded back then, making it a perfect hide, but, after the authorities had clamped down hard, the trees had been logged for lumber, leaving the hatch exposed and making it risky to enter or leave by daylight. That, presumably, was why the proof-of-life clips they'd sent him had always arrived after dark.

Significant traces of cocaine and heroin had been found, suggesting it had been used since for storing drugs. And over two dozen graffiti had been found, of which photographs were appended, including one that consisted only of the letters DCGC scratched low down on the wall.

Carmen's sketches had also arrived. He stared at the two faces. He didn't recognise either, exactly, but he knew the type well. The first, with the wretched teeth, was middle-aged, lumpy, unprepossessing, a little stupid even, yet possessed of an awful power thanks to his unthinking capacity for violence and murder. But it was his companion who unnerved Baldassare, a rarer yet more dangerous breed. With his full lips and haunted eyes, he looked not only highly intelligent but imaginative and sensitive too. Baldassare had come across similar men twice before. They scared the life out of him. In ordinary families, their attributes would have been recognised, prized and nurtured. They'd have found rewarding careers in the arts or sciences. But both had grown up in Mafia families, and Mafia families were not like that. Sensitivity, intelligence and imagination were not gifts to such people. They were weaknesses to be mocked and despised. And, being sensitive and intelligent, those boys quickly understood this and so learned to use those same gifts to contort themselves into acceptability, creating a twisted parody of what they might otherwise have been. For lack of a better way of putting it, they became monsters. Only monsters of exceptional intelligence, imagination and sensitivity. And driven too. Driven to prove that they weren't the weaklings and cowards that others might think them. The two bloodiest and most unrelenting Mafia wars Baldassare had ever witnessed had both been started by such men.

He felt a draught on his neck. He turned to see Alessandra standing there. 'Are those them?' she asked, before he could close the laptop. 'The ones who got away?'

He pulled out his earbuds. 'We think maybe. Do they... look familiar?'

'Those teeth, yes. A bit. But they wore balaclavas. And anyway it was mostly the kids who dealt with us, the two you already caught.' Baldassare made room for her on the chair. She snuggled in beside him and took his arm. 'I got them talking once or twice. I thought it would make it harder for them, you know, when the time came. But then their shift would end and they'd be flint again when they returned. Angry with me too.'

He glanced curiously at her. She hadn't mentioned that before. 'You think they were being monitored?'

'It wouldn't surprise me. Everything they did, it felt... *considered*.'

'As if they'd done it before?'

'Maybe. Why?'

'No reason,' said Baldassare.

III

Dov was up early. He made coffee then scribbled a note to Zara and Carmen explaining that his office needed him on an important conference call. He'd therefore taken the car in search of Wi-Fi – he hoped they didn't mind. But, should they need him or the car, just send a text and he'd come straight back.

The sky was a pearl as he set off, a topaz by the time he reached Policastro. The railway station's ticket office wasn't yet open, but there were machines on either platform. He ducked his face from the CCTV and bought himself an open-ended single to Lamezia Terme Airport. He drove down to the seafront and the half-empty marina, then bumped his way north along the sandy track behind the beach to where the Bussento debouched into the sea. The track turned inland. So did he. He drove by a water sports club whose canoes were pulled up on the bank like basking crocodiles, and with slalom poles strung like wind chimes across the river. The track turned from rutted sand to rutted mud. The chalets grew shabby. He passed beneath road and railway bridges into a scrubby hinterland, too far from the sea to develop, too close to farm. He pulled on his handbrake and got out.

A wall of rushes tall as trees blocked him from the river. He pushed between them, taking care not to tread them down or leave footprints. The river ran fat and slow, and there was another thick wall of rushes on its far bank. Not a sign of human life anywhere. Only half an hour's walk from the railway station too. It could hardly have been better. He liked to be able to visualise things, so he made a pistol of his hand and imitated shooting both Zara and Carmen in the head with the gun he'd wrested from that 'Ndrangheta hit man, then tossing it into the rushes for the police to find. Yes, it would work. The only question was how to get them here. But they'd come for the Bussento, after all. It shouldn't be beyond him.

Satisfied with his morning's work, he returned to the Renault then drove off south along the coast, looking for somewhere charming to take breakfast.

Chapter Thirty

I

Carmen woke to the sound of the door closing and the car driving off, but tiredness persuaded her to doze on half an hour longer. She rose, dressed and went through, where she added a postscript to Dov's note to let Zara know she'd gone into town for breakfast. Then she shouldered her laptop and headed out.

It had been too dark last night to see much. This morning showed the cottage in serious need of work, with bricks placed strategically on its roof tiles to stop leaks, and black rainwater stains beneath its windowsills, like tearful mascara. But its garden was a quirky delight, sheltered from the road by a line of angel-wing cacti.

The hairpin road up into Sicilì was steep. She soon felt it in her calves. The town itself was small and picturesque, its terracotta rooftops all connected by cat's cradles of electrical wires. She reached a charming sloped piazza with a single cafe serving also as *gelateria*, restaurant, bar and pizzeria. Watermelon husks lay on the cobbles beside its door, like shelled green turtles. Men drinking coffee at the bar turned in unison to appraise her, making her Italian even more tortured than usual. She asked for a cappuccino, a pastry and the Wi-Fi password, then sat at an outside table to check her messages.

Baldassare had thanked her for her statement. Certain things she'd written had distressed him, however. He'd very much like the opportunity to discuss them with her in person, if possible. The last thing Carmen wanted was to return to Cosenza, so she wrote back that she'd come to the Cilento for a few days, and was planning to return directly to Rome. But she was happy to video chat any time he liked.

Her Sapienza professor Matteo Bianchi had also been in touch, thanking her for helping recover his ground-penetrating radar. So too the *ispettore*, with the welcome news that her passport and phone had been found, and asking what he should do with them. She was replying with her Rome address when a new email arrived from Baldassare. By happy coincidence, he'd be driving up to the Cilento for lunch tomorrow, and would gladly come and see her before or after. She sighed but wrote back with her Sicilì address and suggested he come at around three. Then, making a virtue of necessity, she asked if he'd collect her passport and phone from the *ispettore*, and bring them with him.

He assured her that he would.

Zara arrived in the piazza. Carmen waved her over. A waitress came out to take her order. Zara asked her about Genaro Scopece, the metal detectorist who'd left his finds to the Ginosa museum. She shook her head but went back inside for the proprietor, a cheerful, portly man whose bushy grey eyebrows danced like flirtatious caterpillars whenever he got lost in thought. 'Scopece?' he frowned. 'Genaro Scopece?'

'He came from Puglia,' suggested Zara. 'Then he went back.'

'Oh, *him*.' He looked perplexed that such a man could possibly be of interest. 'But he left here, what, twenty years ago now?'

Zara nodded. 'That sounds right. Do you know where he lived?'

'Of course. Of course. His wife Nunzia and her brother Anton co-owned the farm across the river. Your friend lived with them there. After she died, there was nothing left for him here. He packed up his truck and went.'

'This brother-in-law? Is he still around?'

'Anton? No. He died years ago. His widow too. And their daughter Maria lives in Milan now.' He looked downcast at this, as though he'd once been sweet on her. 'Why the interest?'

'He found some interesting pieces with his metal detector,' said Zara. 'He left them to a museum in Puglia. It's a nice story.'

'He was always out with that damned contraption. We used to laugh at him. Now people are writing stories about him!'

'What happened to the farm?'

'Maria sold it to the Russos. They added the land to their own then turned the house into an *agriturismo. Agriturismo* Russo. You want to see?'

'Please.'

He led them up an outside staircase onto a roof terrace with heavy wrought iron tables and umbrellas furled against the wind. He stood at a low parapet wall and pointed across the valley to where great swathes of woodland had been cleared for orchards. 'That land there,' he said. 'All those figs and olives. And that white building at the foot of that drive. That was their house.'

'The *agriturismo*,' suggested Zara.

'Exactly. Isabella Russo was your friend's neighbour growing up. She knew him as well as anyone, which isn't saying much. I'll call her for you, if you like, though the signal down there is wretched. But if they have guests in at the moment, that's for sure where you're going to find her.'

II

Cesco slept like the dead and woke late. His shoulder was stiff and throbbing, which so hampered his movements that by the time he'd washed and changed the dressing, they'd stopped serving breakfast. He took a stroll along the front. A motorcycle delivery man drove by with crates of bottled water clamped between his legs. An elderly woman lowered a wicker basket on a rope to the bakery beneath to collect the morning's takings. He stopped at a cafe where two men squabbled over dominoes with the forgiving anger of lifelong friends. He bought himself an apricot croissant and a bottle of sparkling water, then found a bench by the sea wall on which to eat.

A pair of young teenage girls sauntered past, thin white bathing robes flapping loose over the macaw swimsuits beneath. They walked ten paces by then swivelled on their heels like catwalk models to come back past him again, this time unable to stop themselves glancing at him as they passed. He winked at them and they ran off, hiding giggles behind their hands. It put him into an unexpectedly cheerful mood. Then his phone buzzed. A text from Baldassare. He assumed he wanted to cancel or postpone tomorrow's meeting. But he was wrong.

> **Forgive me, but a question about your poor sister, if I may. Did you always call her Claudia, or did you have a nickname for her? Specifically, a nickname beginning with the letter D? Baldassare**

Cesco froze a moment or two. Even after all these years, he found it difficult to think of Claudia.

> **We used to call her Didi. Why?**

> **We found some graffiti in that place. Including one that read DCGC.**

A heavy lump formed in the pit of Cesco's stomach. He wrote:

> **I wanted people to know what had happened to us.**

> **The men who took you – did you ever see their faces?**

For several years after being kidnapped, Cesco had suffered from sporadic panic attacks. They'd usually been triggered by the smell of brine and engine oil, or by the voices of tourists talking in a very distinctive European accent. The attacks had always started with the exact same shortness of breath and clamminess of skin that he was experiencing right now. Fear that the attacks might return unnerved him as much as the symptoms themselves. He allowed himself time for them to settle, therefore, before replying.

> **Not exactly. They always wore balaclavas. We only ever saw their eyes and teeth.**

> **Teeth? Why teeth?**

Cesco squinted at his phone.

> **They were wearing balaclavas. On balaclavas, that's where the holes are.**

> **Forgive me, but no. On balaclavas, the holes are for the eyes and mouth, not for the teeth.**

> **Are you on drugs?**

Several minutes passed without reply. Only when he began to relax again did he realise quite how tense he'd become. When enough time had elapsed, he gave himself permission to power down his phone. He had a peculiar sense of being watched. He looked up sharply to see those two young teenage girls from before standing a little way along the front. They'd bought themselves ice creams, which had started to melt in the sunshine, dribbling over their hands and dripping onto the paved promenade, similar looks of empathy and alarm on their faces; and suddenly Claudia was right there with him, more vividly than she'd been in years, and the old grief welled up inside him, and he jumped to his feet and ran off along the road, looking for somewhere private before anyone could see him cry.

III

The Bussento valley was so steeply sided that it looked almost as though they could loose an arrow from the cafe's terrace and hit the *agriturismo*'s roof. But walking there, as Zara and Carmen soon discovered, was another matter altogether. For one thing, the road was steep and growing tacky in the sunshine, so that their trainers gripped it a little too well, their feet chafing against the inners and soles with every jolting step, letting them feel tomorrow's blisters. For another, the nearest bridge was a full three kilometres away. Then it was the same again along a rural lane to the mouth of the *agriturismo*'s drive.

Isabella Russo was indeed there, making packed lunches for a party of tourist hikers. She was an angular woman with grizzled hair, kindly eyes and a lopsided face that made her look perpetually perplexed. She spent the entire conversation wiping her hands on her apron, as though she'd been cooking with paste. She remembered Scopece, of course she did. He'd been Sicili's bogeyman growing up. All the local children had followed him when he'd gone out with his machine, making up whispered stories about the people he'd murdered and buried on his land.

'You spied on him?' asked Zara. 'Where?'

'By the river, mostly,' she said. 'And up by the grotto.'

'The grotto?'

She waved vaguely back towards the bridge they'd crossed. 'The grotto.'

'And he found stuff?'

'I imagine, the amount he looked. Though he never shared it with anyone. His wife Nunzia, I suppose. They were very close. But no one else. He kept it all in an old outbuilding here that he locked with chains and padlocks. We dared each other to break in, but no one ever did. Honestly, we really believed there might be bodies.' She gave a little shiver. 'He was such a forbidding man. Sometimes you'd feel sorry for him, you'd smile or nod or even say good day. He'd glare at you and give you nightmares.' She glanced over her shoulder, anxious about the two saucepans on her stove. 'Oh. And you know why he left?'

'Because his wife died?'

'Yes. But there were rumours too. About what he'd done to his niece Maria. Anton and Elena were powerless while Nunzia was still alive. She owned half the farm and wouldn't hear a word against him. But the moment she was dead and buried, Anton confronted Genaro with a cheque in one hand and a shotgun in the other. He took the cheque.' The rattle of a saucepan lid made her look around. 'I'm sorry,' she said. 'I really must go.'

'Of course,' said Zara. 'And thanks.'

Chapter Thirty-One

I

It took Cesco half an hour after his exchange with Baldassare to compose himself enough to turn his phone back on. His anxiety came flooding back when he saw he had a new text waiting.

> **Forgive me for pursuing this, my friend. I know how traumatic it must be. But I can't stop thinking about the parallels between what happened to our two families. Yes, it's the 'Ndrangheta, kidnapping is in their blood. Yes, of course it made sense to use the same facilities that had served them well before. But what if there's more to it even than that?**

Cesco sat at the first bench he came to then took a long deep breath to steel himself.

> **More how?**

Your family was much loved. Your grandfather in particular was both respected and feared. Had the Critelli brothers used their own people to kidnap you and your sister, one of them might well have said something to tip him off. It would therefore have been prudent for the Critellis to bring in outsiders for the job. Most likely, members of one of their overseas operations. And, when it came to kidnapping my family, again they couldn't use locals. All their best people were in custody or under surveillance. Who would you turn to, if you were them? Someone new, or someone who'd handled a successful kidnapping for you before?

Cesco's heart seemed to falter inside his chest.

Are you saying these are the same men?

I'm saying we should at least consider the possibility. Hence my question about teeth. I need to know if they were memorable in some way. Take a look at the attached two sketches.

The signal was weak. The files downloaded with frustrating slowness. But finally two sketches appeared, the left-hand one of which showed a thug with discoloured and misshapen teeth. He stared at it, unnerved.

Who did these? Did Carmen do these?

I can't tell you that.

She's the only one who saw their faces.

His phone rang in his hand. 'Forget who did the damn sketches,' said Baldassare. 'What matters is the men. Is it them?'

Cesco hesitated. 'I told you. They wore balaclavas.'

'You must have some idea.'

'It wasn't like that. You weren't there. It was dark. They made us face the wall whenever they brought food or changed the bucket. And the only one who ever spoke to us was older than these two. Even back then, I mean, and that was years ago.'

'But...?'

'Who said anything about a but?'

'It was in your voice.'

Cesco took a deep breath. 'There were three of them. The older guy and a couple of younger ones who did what the older guy told them. We caught odd glimpses of them, and yes, one had bad teeth. Not as bad as these, but bad. Anyway, Carmen didn't draw these herself, right? She described them to an artist.'

'Exactly. Exactly.'

So it was you, thought Cesco in dismay. *You reckless fucking idiot.* 'There's something else,' he said. 'I thought it might be my imagination, but if you're right...'

'Yes?'

'The older man's voice. It haunted me for years. He was 'Ndrangheta, no doubt about it. He used the exact same vernacular they all did. But it had a quality to it. Not an accent exactly. An intonation. A cadence. As if he'd been living abroad. The guy I spoke with the other day, he was also Calabrian. And he had something similar, only even more pronounced.'

'Similar? Or the same?'

'I don't know. My ear's not good enough. But it gave me a jolt when I heard it, I'll tell you that much. And something else. On the boat that night...'

'The boat?' asked Baldassare.

'The night they, you know... It was...' He tried to bring it to his mind but, even after all these years, he couldn't do it, he flinched from it like a blade from a spinning whetstone. 'I can't,' he said. 'I'm sorry. Please don't ask me to—'

'It's okay,' said Baldassare soothingly. 'It's okay.' He waited a few moments before speaking again. 'We'll leave it there for now, shall we?'

'Yes. Yes. You'll let me know of any developments?'

'Of course. Of course.'

'Was this... was this what tomorrow was about?'

'No. That's something else altogether. Something I'm very much looking forward to. So don't you dare think of cancelling. And thank you for this. You've been a great help.'

'Good. Good.' He killed the call then set off again, trying to walk the agitation from his arms and legs, taking turns at random until he no longer had any idea of where he was or where he was headed. But it was no good. He came to an abrupt halt and took out his phone to study Carmen's sketches once more.

Was this them? Was this really *them*? And if so...

For all his years away, Cesco was Calabrian still. The notion of destiny was bred into his bones. For years now, he'd been telling himself that his return to Italy and his movements since had been forced on him by circumstance. But he'd always known the truth of it deep down. He'd been drawing ever closer to Cosenza because he had unfinished business there. He just hadn't been quite ready for it. Ready or not, however, the time had now come. For that was the thing about being Calabrian. That was the main thing. When it came to family, there was only one law, and it was the old one.

Eye for eye, tooth for tooth; blood for blood, life for life.

If this was them... If this was truly them...

People were going to die.

The Bussento footpath was narrow, forcing Carmen and Zara into single file. The river itself ran wide and deep, its bottom scattered with stones as smooth and large as flat brown loaves. Trees stooped branches to the water, tickling ripples with their leaves and catching plastic bags that swelled like windsocks in the breeze. The embankments on either side grew taller and steeper, until finally making the transition from valley into gorge, from whose sheer grey walls a few hardy shrubs clung like unnerved mountaineers.

The footpath split away from the river, taking them up through an overgrown orchard to a small parking area and a stone staircase that zigzagged back down to the valley floor, its trees covered by brilliant green moss that straggled from their branches like fur from the limbs of an orangutan. A designated nature reserve, so a sign informed them, where the Bussento emerged from the mountain it entered near the town of Caselle in Pittari, some six kilometres away. A young woman on a deckchair relieved them of five euros each and pointed them along another footpath. A rumbling noise grew louder as they walked, like a train approaching a station. They reached a wooden deck. A cliff face rose sheer in front of them, riven by a great cleft, as though some ancient god of war had struck it with his axe. They made their way inside, trading the bright sunshine for such cool darkness that, for a moment, it left them blind.

In Carmen's mind, grottos were little more than shallow scrapings in the rock. The Bussento grotto was not like that at all. It was vast. Overwhelming. A staircase had been hewn down through the limestone, emerging onto a wooden walkway fixed to its left-hand wall. This led to a slatted bridge that straddled the chasm above the river to reach a second passage hewn in the right-hand wall that led yet deeper into the grotto, but which had been roped off to tourists, turning the bridge into a viewing platform. Carmen gripped its rail and stared deeper into the cavern. It bent slowly around to her right before vanishing into the darkness. Huge stalactites hung from its high ceiling, while, far beneath her feet, the Bussento ran with seeming placidity until it reached the grotto mouth, where its waters were churned into a violent white froth as it squeezed out between a mess of tumbled boulders.

Many millions of years before, there'd have been a great lake on the far side of this mountain. Over the geological ages since, its waters had literally dissolved this karst limestone, eating its way through six full kilometres of it before finally making breach high above their heads, releasing the Bussento to flow down to the sea. And it had continued eroding the rock ever since, so that the same river now ran far beneath their feet instead, creating this vast cavern in the process. A natural phenomenon, then, yet with the same feel to it as a sacred site in an exotic land, a place of reverence and hush. Perhaps that was why neither she nor Zara said a word. Or perhaps because no word was truly needed. For such was the Gothic grandeur of the place that it was quite obvious to them both: if you had a king to bury, a man you loved and worshipped, and if you had no cathedral of your own, nor time to build one, *this* was the place you'd choose.

Chapter Thirty-Two

I

As Gioia Tauro was to cocaine, so Naples was to arms. A vast proportion of Europe's illicit weaponry flooded in daily through the city's ports. It was here that Islamist jihadis sourced guns and explosives for their city slaughters, here that separatist groups armed themselves for their struggles, here that organised crime tooled up for its gang wars. The Camorra didn't care who you were, just that you had cash and the right contacts – and Cesco was lucky enough to have both.

The only downside was that his contacts were the exact same people he'd fled Naples to get away from.

He had no number for Rosaria, so he headed for her apartment – a three-bed Vomero penthouse overlooking the Bay of Naples. The hill was so steep here that the block's back entrance was actually on its third floor, reached across a short stub of footbridge from the road as it doubled back behind. He parked the Harley, rang the bell. An asthmatic woman answered. Rosaria had moved on the year before, she told him between her gasps. But she'd left a forwarding address in Secondigliano. Did he want it? He did not. He knew it all too well already.

He wound back down the hairpin hill to Chiaia then cut through the noisy tight alleys of the Spanish quarter, weaving between tourists and the weary traders pushing carts of bling. He passed Università then cut east to Piazza Nolana, named for the pair of medieval turrets that squatted like a pair of buttocks either side of the arsehole street behind. He rumbled along it then down the familiar ramp of the private parking garage. He parked in his old spot then nodded to an open-mouthed Fernando in his glass booth and made his way back up onto the street. The hookers were out as ever. He walked towards them. One of the older ones put on a smile and came to meet him. She recognised him and stopped dead. Her eyes went wide with alarm; she made a shooing motion with her hand to warn him to get out. He shook his head. 'Call her,' he said. 'Tell her I'm back.' Then he turned and made his way between the turrets out onto the piazza.

His old bar was open for business, he saw, but he had no desire to explain himself to his old boss and colleagues, or indeed to bring trouble down upon their heads, so he found himself a cold stone bench instead, and settled down to wait.

II

Carmen gazed deep into the grotto, trying to penetrate its darkness with her old childhood imagination, to see it as might a Visigoth king whose pagan childhood had only partly been trammelled by Christian doctrine. Alaric had most likely died of malaria, the Roman fever. If so, his court physicians might well have had him brought here, both for its fresh clean water and for the sanctuary it offered from the hot afternoon sun. And it was all too easy for her to see him choosing it as his last resting place, both for its beauty and tranquillity. 'I think this is it,' she said softly. 'Heaven help me, but I do.'

'On what evidence?' asked Zara.

'Scopece's artefacts. Where else could they have come from?'

'We need more than that to go on. Anyway, the Visigoths diverted the river, didn't they? How on earth could anyone divert *this*?'

Carmen looked down again. 'You couldn't,' she admitted. 'Not once it was inside the mountain. But perhaps before. What was that place again? Caselle in Pittari? We need to go see it.'

Zara nodded. 'I'll call Dov.'

There was no signal inside or even outside the grotto. Instead, they found another rock staircase that zigzagged up the gorge to the town of Morigerati directly above. Zara texted Dov when they arrived. He replied that he was still tied up but that they should go have lunch. He'd come and collect them in an hour or so.

Morigerati was a little larger than Sicilì. But only a little. They wandered it for a while, looking for somewhere to eat. A cobbled alley was cordoned off as workmen laid a jigsaw of new stones, pounding them level in their wet cement with a sledgehammer and a wooden plank. They found a cafe with a pergola terrace where they lunched on chickpea and goat's cheese tagliatelle, bowls of pistachio ice cream and coffees that arrived even as Dov texted to say he was five minutes out.

They settled up and went to meet him. Zara told him of their morning's discoveries as they set off up a mountain pass to Caselle in Pittari. Carmen sat in the back and gazed out over forested hillsides down to the startling blue Tyrrhenian Sea. They were high enough here that the vineyards still wore their orange winter netting, the peaks their caps of ice. Low timber barriers protected the road from landslides, while from all sides came the growl and screech of chainsaws replenishing stocks of household fuel. They turned right at a junction along a road that lay across a narrow valley from Caselle in Pittari, a town of tall thin houses huddled tightly on a hilltop, like too many commuters crammed into a carriage. A sign alerted them to where the Bussento entered the mountain. They parked on the verge and took a moment to admire the view out over the countryside, including a lake shaped like the lid of a grand piano, penned behind a grey dam wall.

A rock staircase slashed the wooded hillside like a Zorro blade. The trees sang with wildlife as they set off down. An eagle perched on a bare branch squirted out an imperious jet of bright white shit in their direction. They crossed a footbridge over a deep sinkhole then emerged from the trees to be confronted by a toe-tingling wall of rock, as though a mountain had simply sheared in two to leave behind this vast and craggy cliff face, turned by the afternoon sunlight into a Cilento Rushmore.

Downwards they went, ever downwards. They heard rushing water ahead. A sign warned them of surges from the Lake Sabetta dam. Then they were beside the Bussento itself, gushing along the narrow valley floor before being swallowed by the ogreish mouth of a vast cavern, around which shrubs grew like misshapen teeth from every ledge and crevice. There were no helpful walkways here. They had to make their own way along the bank then across the river by leaping from boulder to boulder. They were almost there before Carmen realised Dov wasn't with them. She glanced around and saw him wandering off upstream instead. A last look up. The cliff rose so sheer above her that she almost toppled over backwards. Three tiny black specks circled high in the sky above them — birds of prey waiting patiently for lunch. They entered the cave. It lacked the Gothic splendour of the grotto, far wider but not so tall. It bent away from the afternoon sunlight too, swiftly leaving them in such darkness that Zara took out her phone for its torch. Declarations of young love had been scratched into the rock, with other graffiti so worn by damp and time that it was hard to make them out at all.

The way grew too difficult for Zara, but Carmen borrowed her phone and pressed on, shimmying along a wall, leaping athletically from boulder to boulder. She spotted what looked like markings in the ceiling, but it was impossible to make them out from the cavern floor. The limestone was gaunt with clefts and fissures. Though cold and slippery, the wall was an easier climb than the one in her university gym. Lack of light was the greater problem. She kept pausing to map out her next section. She anchored herself to the wall with one hand then reached out Zara's camera phone in the other, tapping out photographs with her finger, the flashes dazzling in the darkness.

'What have you found?' asked Zara.

'I'm not sure,' said Carmen. She flipped through the pictures she'd taken. It looked like a pair of outspread wings. 'Maybe a bird of some kind.'

Dov appeared at the cavern mouth. He cupped his hands around his eyes as he peered into the darkness. 'Hey!' he called out. 'Are you guys still in here?'

'Yes,' said Zara. 'Why?'

'I just got a text from the damned airline. A fuck-up with our flights. We need to deal with it right now. Just you, Zara. But out here, where there's a signal.'

Zara looked up at Carmen. 'Will you be okay?'

'I'll be fine,' Carmen assured her.

'Okay. I'll only be a moment.'

Carmen watched her pick her way back along the bank to the cavern mouth. Then she and Dov vanished out of sight. Such a clumsy lie about their flights. Yet Zara had played along. All Carmen's separate threads of doubt at once wove themselves into a single cloth. It *had* been Dov rather than some doppelgänger in the cafe that first morning, which surely meant that their later meeting at the *gelateria* had been planned, not chance. The way Zara had recoiled from Dov last night, implying they weren't even lovers. And the Calabrian car-hire map beneath the seat that meant they'd flown in to Lamezia, making a lie of their story about a Sorrento wedding.

No. They were here for a different reason. They were here for the temple treasures.

And she was helping them.

One thing to realise; another to respond. Making unsupported accusations against Zara would only invite indignant denials that might ruin her own career before it had even started. She had no friends to turn to, no reputation, no qualifications of note. No place to stay except the cottage, no transport except the car. She couldn't even speak the damned language. Baldassare was visiting tomorrow, yes, and would be disposed both to trust her and to help. But it was hardly his area and he was already carrying more than enough burdens for any one man.

For a moment, she resolved to put it from her mind, to pretend she hadn't noticed anything amiss. But then, perversely, she remembered Cesco sitting beside her hospital bed spouting his pious bullshit about the duty they owed archaeology. It had meant nothing to him, of course, but it had to her. And it was a duty she owed still.

She climbed carefully back down from her ledge and picked her way along the wall then headed for the cavern mouth, holding Zara's phone out in front of her, searching for a signal.

Chapter Thirty-Three

I

La Università di Napoli Federico II was only a short walk from Piazza Nolana, making Cesco's old bar-pizzeria a favoured haunt for students killing time between lectures. In fine weather, they'd sit out at the sunshade tables, smoking, drinking, eating ice creams and sharing pizzas. But one of the students had stood out from the rest. Older, solitary, diligent. She'd been an evening regular, ordering herself a light snack and a non-alcoholic drink then sitting alone at an inside table with a view of the Nolana turrets. Then she'd put in earbuds to review her day's lectures, jotting notes on a yellow pad and checking references in her textbooks.

Cesco had tried flirting lightly with her on her first couple of visits, as he'd flirted lightly with all of the single women who came in. But his efforts had only made her smile, and not in a good way, so he'd left her alone after that. Yet his pride had undeniably been stung.

She'd been thirty or so, a year or two older than himself. Short, plump and typically dressed in biker chic, with tight leather trousers and studded jackets, her fingers and throat glittering with gemstones in silver and platinum settings. Her best feature had been her gorgeous long black hair. She'd normally come in with it already hanging loose, but one night it had been raining outside, so she'd still been wearing her motorcycle helmet. She'd taken it off right in front of him, shaking out her hair so that it had tumbled in oiled black coils almost down to her waist. She hadn't meant it to be erotic, but it had been. She'd caught him staring open-mouthed at her, and had scowled indignantly, as though he'd taken an unforgivable liberty. He'd even feared she

240

might make a complaint. But she hadn't. And the next time she'd come in, she'd still been wearing her helmet, even though it had been dry out. And then she'd waited until he was watching before she'd taken it off too.

A couple of nights later, she'd ordered a rare second drink. She'd asked him about his accent when he'd brought it over. Then she'd left him a ten-euro tip with a phone number written on it. It was almost closing time so he'd asked permission to slip off early. He'd hurried after her, footsteps ringing on the piazza cobbles. She hadn't even looked around, vanishing instead into a private parking garage. He hadn't known what to do, worrying that he'd misread the situation, that the phone number had already been on the banknote. The whores had watched him dithering and had made such fun of him that he'd almost turned tail. But then Rosaria had come roaring up the exit ramp on a sumptuous cherry-and-cream Ducati and pulled up right beside him. 'Well?' she'd asked, as he stood there foolishly. 'Are you getting on or what?'

There'd been no rear bar for him to hold on to. He'd rested his hands primly on her waist instead. She'd accelerated away so fast it had almost blown him off the back. He'd grabbed on to her for dear life. He'd thought she was doing it to impress. But no. It was simply how she rode. How she'd been in bed too. In everything. When Rosaria wanted something, she took it. Within a week, he'd virtually moved in. She gave him keys to her apartment and a wardrobe for the clothes she bought him. Better still, because the commute from her place to the bar was such a nightmare on public transport, and because her term had ended for the summer, she'd lent him her Ducati and her pass to the private garage, slumming it herself in a powder-blue Mercedes soft top.

It had all seemed too good to be true.

Then three fearsome young men had turned up when he was alone at her apartment one afternoon, and he'd realised that it was.

Dov waited until he and Zara were clear of the cavern before speaking. 'Well? What have you found?'

'Some symbols in the roof,' said Zara.

'Gothic?'

'I haven't seen them yet. Is that really why you called me out?'

'I've something to show you.' He turned and led her along the bank, past the steps down which they'd arrived and then onwards upstream towards the hydroelectric dam. The way grew ever more tangled. They had to clamber over boulders and pick paths around thorn bushes. The gorge narrowed and its gradient steepened, so that the river turned for a while into a fierce cataract, towards the top of which a large number of unusually massive boulders had been deposited by a landslide. The trunk of a fallen tree was pinned by the press of water against two of these boulders, forming a crude barrier that had caught so much silt and other debris that it had formed a natural dam, forcing the entire Bussento through the narrow remaining channel, roaring and splashing furiously. But then they were above it and the gorge opened wide, turning the river into a surprisingly placid lake.

Dov spread his hands to indicate it all. 'You were asking how the Visigoths diverted the river,' he said. 'I give you the answer.'

She looked around in puzzlement. It was several seconds before she saw it. All those huge boulders they'd just passed weren't the product of some ancient landslide. No. They'd been dragged here deliberately as bulwarks for a dam built across the gorge's throat, to be completed with earthworks and timbers from these hillsides. With a slave army at their disposal, and such abundant raw materials to hand, it would have been simple for the Visigoths to pen the Bussento here for days at a time, especially before the autumn rains started in earnest. If they then fitted it with a crude sluice gate, they could even withdraw their slaves from the caves at set intervals in order to drain it themselves before damming it up again for another tranche of time.

'It's possible, then,' she murmured. 'He really could be in there.'

'Yes,' agreed Dov. 'I think he could be.'

'What now?'

'I report back to Avram. You downplay it with Carmen. Convince her there's nothing here. Put her on a train back to Rome, if you can. Then we'll set about exploring it properly.'

They fell silent on their return, the better to concentrate on their footing. Zara became aware of Carmen's voice ahead, chattering to someone. Only she couldn't hear whoever she was chattering to. They hurried forward and found her talking on Zara's phone.

'What the hell!' protested Zara.

'I'm so sorry,' said Carmen. She ended the call and came to meet them, her cheeks flushed with excitement or exertion. 'I couldn't find you anywhere. And I *had* to know. That symbol in the roof. I managed to catch it perfectly on one of my shots. It's an eagle holding a standard or a cross, something like that. Look for yourselves. I'd swear it's Visigothic. But what do I know, right? So I sent it to Professor Bianchi.'

'Professor Bianchi?' asked Dov.

'My Sapienza professor,' explained Carmen, nodding vigorously, as if to persuade them of the rightness of her action. 'One of the world's great experts.'

'And?' asked Zara. 'What did he say?'

She beamed happily at them both. 'He thinks they're the real thing too. He's promised to notify the Ministry of Culture for us. And he's coming down on Friday with an assistant, to see them for himself.'

Chapter Thirty-Four

I

Dov dropped Zara and Carmen back at the cottage then excused himself with an invented work commitment and headed straight off again. He drove safely out of earshot then clutched the wheel and yelled at his windscreen. Carmen had been lying through her teeth. She hadn't called her professor to ask his opinion of the symbols. She'd called him because she'd realised what they were up to, and wanted help. Yet alongside the dismay there was admiration too, and the perverse euphoria he always felt when he found himself in jeopardy.

His first task now was to find out what he was dealing with. He took the back road out of Sicilì to the small parking area above the grotto, then hurried down the stone staircase to its foot, where he paid his five euros to the pretty girl in the deckchair. He expected to find another cave like the one in Caselle in Pittari. But it wasn't that way at all. He stood upon the viewing platform bridge and drank it in. Zara and Carmen had been right. Caselle was a cavern. This was a cathedral.

The passage at the far end of the bridge was roped off to the public. Dov checked he was alone then ducked beneath it. It quickly grew dark. He turned on his phone's torch. The passage took him gently downwards, its ceiling so low that in places he had to stoop. Cobwebs caught in his face, while patches of dryish clay on the floor took and held his footprints. That his were the only ones there suggested that he was the first person down here in at least a week, probably much longer. The sound of rushing water diminished. Then it grew loud again. The tunnel opened up on his left and there was the Bussento right by his feet, frothing luminescent against the rocks. He squatted down. The way the cavern curved meant that he could only see the far end of the viewing platform he'd just crossed, silhouetted against the pale glow of the grotto's mouth. Upstream, by contrast, the total darkness made a mockery of his torch's beam. He cupped his hand in the icy water to judge its speed. Ten kilometres an hour or so. Certainly too swift to swim against. And the walls, though craggy, looked difficult to traverse at speed.

He retreated up the passage and back to his car. He had no signal for his phone so he drove until he found one. He searched online for outdoors sports stores nearby. There were plenty of small ones, for the Cilento was a hiker's paradise, but the nearest of any real size was in Potenza, an hour's drive away. He set off at once, to reach it before it closed, and called Avram on his way.

'So that's it,' he grumbled, once Dov had brought him up to speed. 'We have to hold off until this professor has been and gone.'

'And if he finds it? What then?'

'Do you have a better idea?'

'I do. But it means moving fast.' He explained what he had in mind, the implications for them both.

Avram grunted when he was done. 'Are you serious?' he asked.

'I'm the one taking the big risk,' pointed out Dov. 'All you stand to lose is a few pennies.'

'They're not your pennies.'

'Nor my election neither.'

'Fine,' said Avram. 'You do your part. I'll do mine. But call me the moment you get back out.'

II

It was ninety minutes before Rosaria turned up, riding a new Ducati, at the head of a small posse of young toughs on gleaming white Vespas. She stood up her bike a few paces from him and took off her helmet as she walked towards him. But there was no tumble of long black hair this time. She'd had it shaven into a crude black flat top, as though a landscape gardener had laid a sod of scorched turf upon her scalp. Gone too were the designer clothes, replaced by dirty baggy jeans and a weathered leather jacket with ripped-off sleeves, perhaps to show off her new ink. She wore black lipstick too, and studs through her nose and lower lip, as well as lines of silver rings in either ear, as if she intended to hang a pair of shower curtains from them.

'You haven't changed one bit,' he told her.

'Fuck you too. What are you doing here?'

'I need a favour.'

Rosaria snorted incredulously. 'You? A favour? From me?'

'Yes. Me. A favour. From you.'

'The only favour you're going to get is walking out of here alive.'

'We used to be friends.'

'We used to fuck. And you ran drugs for me. That's all.'

Quite true, this, though it had taken Cesco inexcusably long to realise. Specifically, it had taken until that afternoon when one of Rosaria's brothers and two of her cousins had turned up at her flat. They'd learned somehow that she'd found herself a new toy boy, and so – being the kind of people they were – they'd had him checked out to make sure he wasn't undercover. His lack of a past had thrown up red flags, so they'd forced him at gunpoint into an SUV with tinted windows and had driven him out to the notorious Horseshoe housing estate in Secondigliano, where they'd strapped him to a chair for a gunpoint interrogation. Terrified, he'd confessed to his life of petty fraud and thievery. They'd checked it out as he'd talked, finding traces of him under his various aliases. A humiliation for himself, a grand entertainment for them. But his venality had pleased them too.

It had made him one of them.

Any interrogation reveals a certain amount about the questioners. That was how Cesco had learned who these men were, that Rosaria was the niece of a Camorra boss. He'd found out, too, that – alongside her studies – she'd been running the gang's stable of whores and pushers off Piazza Nolana. That was why she'd come so often to his bar. More particularly, it was why she'd parked her Ducati in that garage every day: it had a hidden compartment beneath its seat, through which she'd delivered new product and taken out earnings. And it was why she'd picked him up too – because, with the summer holidays almost upon her, she'd needed a dupe to carry on muling for her.

'If that was all I was to you, why have your brother make me propose?'

Her eyes popped. 'Propose? You? To me?'

'Ask him if you don't believe me. It was that or end up in the bay.'

'That little bastard,' she muttered. But then she focused back on Cesco, more furious even than before. 'So that's why you ran, eh? So as not to marry me?'

'It wasn't you I ran from. It was your brother. Your family. I'm not that kind of man.'

'Yet here you are.'

'Like I said, I need a favour.'

'Go on.'

'A gun. A box of shells.'

'A gun!' she scoffed. 'You'd only shoot your own balls off.'

'You'd be surprised,' said Cesco. This too was true. His grandfather had put in an underground shooting range at his villa, for his guards to practise in. Cesco had so loved it that, for his twelfth birthday, his father had given him a Beretta U22 Neos of his own to keep down there, and he'd taught him how to use it too. He'd been a natural, as it had turned out – so much so that the Critelli brothers had started eyeing him up for jobs; because no one paid much attention to a fourteen-year-old kid on the back of a moped. It hadn't occurred to Cesco until much later, but he'd since come to believe that one of the factors in his grandfather turning *pentito* had been his horror at the thought of him becoming another Critelli hit man.

'What do you want it for?'

'What do you think?'

'You'll have to do better than that.'

'Okay, then. I used to have a sister.'

'A sister? But you told me...' She stared at him a while then shook her head. 'I never knew you at all, did I?'

'No.'

'Okay, then. It'll cost you one thousand.'

'I've only got six hundred. Six hundred is the rate.'

'Not from me, it isn't. From me it's one thousand.'

'Fine. When? Where?'

'Midday tomorrow. The Horseshoe. Ask anyone on duty. They'll tell you where to find me.' She gave him a final look of scorn and sorrow then returned to her bike. She pulled a tight turn and led her posse off. He watched them out of sight then texted Baldassare to push tomorrow's meeting back until later in the day. Then he headed back to the parking garage for his Harley to set off back to Pozzuoli.

III

The Potenza hiking superstore had everything Dov could have wished for. An inflatable black rubber dinghy with a wood-slat floor, a foot pump and a four-stroke outboard. A helmet and a strap-on lamp, two torches and plenty of spare batteries. Waterproof boots and gloves. A climbing harness, two coils of lightweight rope and a set of spring-loaded cams to fix to fissures in the rock. A neoprene suit to keep him warm and dry. A utility belt, a dozen energy bars and a waterproof camera with embedded light and an extensible selfie stick. Then he settled up with the cash Avram had given him for incidentals.

They was no way to fit it all in the back of the Renault, so he and the assistant stripped it of packaging, folded down the back seats and moved the front seats as far forward as they'd go. Even so, the hatchback wouldn't close until they strapped it in with rope and some orange mesh. Then he set off back to Sicilì, taking it nice and slow. It was dark by the time he arrived. The parking area was empty, as was the grotto. It took him four trips to lug all his equipment down the passages to the river's bank. He changed there into his neoprene suit, boots, gloves and safety helmet. He inflated the dinghy, attached the outboard, packed it with everything he needed. Then he climbed in and set off upstream, churning out a pale phosphorescence of wake.

Bats flickered in the gloom. Shadows moved at the periphery of his vision. He shone his torch this way and that, searching the walls for Gothic graffiti. He held his camera underwater on its selfie stick, checking the footage every few seconds. He found nothing. The river was fast yet mostly smooth, except in the few places where fallen rocks rippled or even breached the surface, where he slowed to a cautious speed. The noise of rushing water grew louder and louder, until the thunder of it drowned out even his outboard. A pale blur ahead resolved into a kind of cataract as the Bussento cascaded down a steep ramp of tumbled rocks. He secured the dinghy to a knob of rock with his mooring rope then shone his torch this way and that, looking for some way forward. But, even if he made it up the cataract, he'd only reach – as best as he could tell – the foot of a monstrous waterfall that lay beyond.

Any previous expedition would almost certainly have stopped here, as indeed Athaulf and his Visigoths would have too, had they even been here in the first place. Yet a mischievous voice whispered inside his head: *How could he know? How could he know for sure?* After all, he was not some amateur cave diver. He was a veteran of Israel's Sayeret Matkal, the greatest commando unit in the history of the world.

The familiar euphoria filled him, that godlike cocktail of recklessness and invulnerability that came from knowing you were the best at what you did. He pulled on his climbing harness and belt then loaded himself up with two coils of rope, his set of cams and a rock hammer. He strapped his helmet tight beneath his chin, turned on its lamp. He found solid holds on the wall then set off sideways, crabbing above the cataract as it raged beneath him like a maddened Cyclops, grabbing at his ankles with its spume. He fitted cams into the fissures that he found, threaded through a coil of rope. The overhang still strained his fingers and his biceps. He was out of practice, and unfit. But at last he reached the top of the cataract and the foot of the waterfall – a fat and ragged sinkhole some six or seven metres high, down which the entire Bussento thundered like down a drainpipe in a storm. He studied it in his torchlight, watching closely for paths and patterns. He ate a pair of energy bars, washing them down with water scooped up from the torrent. Then he set off, anchoring himself to the cracks in the wall.

The river roared by him like an underground train in a tight tunnel. One misstep and the weight of it would rip him from the wall and smash him against the rocks beneath. He'd be dead before he even knew it. The knowledge didn't frighten him, however. It simply made him concentrate all the more fiercely. And it filled him with an extraordinary exhilaration too.

He'd never felt quite so alive.

His progress was blocked several times. He didn't push his luck, but rather retreated until he found another path. The cold burned his cheeks and nose. It wormed its way inside his gloves, made sausages of his fingers. But finally he hauled himself up onto the sinkhole's topmost lip and stretched out on his back on a narrow strip of rock at the foot of a large new chamber, the beam of his helmet torch sweeping over the ceiling high above him as he stared upwards, first in puzzlement, but then in disbelief.

Chapter Thirty-Five

I

It was first light by the time Dov made it back to his embarkation point. He could see the faint grey of it around the grotto mouth. Lugging everything back to the Renault would take four trips, greatly increasing the chance of being seen. And he'd be wretchedly unlucky if anyone else came down here today. He changed back into his clothes, deflated the dinghy and stowed it and his other gear out of reach of the water. Then he hurried back up and out to the Renault. He disposed of the orange mesh and rope in the trees, replaced the seats as they'd been before, then set off looking for a signal for his phone with which to call Israel. 'I've found him,' he announced, when Avram answered. 'I've found Alaric.'

A beat of silence. 'You're sure?'

'I've found a large chamber at the top of a waterfall a kilometre inside the caves.' He wanted to sound matter-of-fact, as though it was the sort of thing he did every day, but he couldn't manage it, the triumph was too much. 'It has gemstones hammered into its ceiling and a huge block of white marble embedded in the floor beneath the river. If that's not Alaric's tomb, what the hell is it?'

'Do you have pictures?' asked Avram.

'And footage too. I'll encrypt it all and send it through when I get a chance.'

'This marble block? The one beneath the water. Can we get at it? Can we get at it to open it?'

'We?' asked Dov drily.

'Damn right, we. Do you think I'd miss an opportunity like this? Well? Can we get at it? Assuming it opens, that is. Without letting in the river.'

'You don't ask much, do you? It's been underwater sixteen hundred years. I think we can assume the river's already in.'

'Not with what's at stake. If we should damage it unnecessarily...'

'Fine,' said Dov. 'I'll go check something out and let you know. How about at your end? Is everything arranged?'

'I've booked flights, if that's what you mean. My usual charter from Tel Aviv to Corfu. Then a completely separate one from Corfu to Sorrento. We leave here before noon and will be with you around three p.m. Italian time.'

'Good. I'll have Yonatan get in touch direct. Sort out the details between yourselves. Me, I need to grab some sleep.'

He drove through Caselle in Pittari, then on a few minutes more before turning off the main road down a track of fresh black tarmac that wound through woods down to the shore of Lake Sabetta. There were two buildings on the far bank that – save for the bank of satellite dishes on their roof – looked more like Swiss mountain chalets than a hydroelectric plant; yet that was what they were, reachable only by the road that ran along the curved top of the dam wall, protected by a security gate, 'Keep Out' notices, barbed wire and CCTV.

He parked out of the camera's field of view to encrypt his footage and photographs and send them to Avram and his partner Yonatan. He got out. A lame piebald dog yapped at him. He feinted to kick it and it whimpered piteously and limped away, burrowing beneath a loose flap of wire fencing.

The morning was silent save for birdsong and the gush of a mountain spring he couldn't see, decanting both the recent rains and the spring thaw into the lake. It seemed very full to him, close to the top of the dam wall. A rowing boat was pulled up on the grassy bank. There were no lights on in any of the buildings, no vehicles in the car park. Small hydroelectric plants like this often ran unattended, he knew, being monitored and run from a command centre elsewhere.

His phone rang. It was Yonatan, the ex-Mossad agent with whom he'd founded Gordian Sword, a business intelligence outfit explicitly designed to solve the problems their competitors dared not touch, by the simple expedient of cutting straight through them. 'Is this footage for real?' he demanded.

'It's for real.'

'Shit. I can hardly believe it.'

'I know.'

'What do we do?'

'Get your arses over here, that's what. Avram's already arranged the flights. Deal with him directly. We'll need at least five men, apart from ourselves. And one of them should be Noah.'

'Noah?' He sounded doubtful. 'He's hardly mission material.'

'I'm aware of that,' said Dov. Their client list was almost exclusively made up of oligarchs and others who didn't much care about cost, only about effectiveness and discretion. So they'd made the decision from the outset to recruit only the very best, typically battle-hardened veterans of Mossad or Dov's own elite commando unit the Sayeret Matkal. But Noah Zuckman was an exception. He was elite in his own way, with a very particular skill set, yet he had no experience of jobs like this.

But they were going to need him tonight.

The reaction set in on his drive back to Sicilì. His adrenaline ebbed, letting the exhaustion in. His eyelids were barely slits as he rolled down the cottage drive. He made his way unsteadily through the kitchen door, then to the bedroom. Zara woke to the noise he made. She rolled onto her back and held the sheet up to her throat with puppy paws. 'Where have you been?' she asked.

'I told you. Briefing our lords and masters.' He put a hand to his mouth to hide a huge yawn that briefly cleared his head of tiredness. 'That meant Wi-Fi and privacy. So I took a room in Policastro.' He unbuttoned and stripped off his shirt as he talked, tossed it on a chair. 'You've no idea the hornet's nest we've kicked up. One crazy, crazy night.'

'How so?'

'Avram called the prime minister. I don't know what he told him, but now he seems to be convinced the Menorah is as good as found.'

'Oh hell. It's nothing like—'

'I know. I know. I tried to explain. But you know what men of destiny are like. They think everything's meant. Anyway, they've agreed a plan of sorts. The Italians are always short of money. So we're going to have one of our cultural fronts offer funding in exchange for certain rights over anything that's found. But we need an archaeologist of international standing to lead our side of it. The prime minister wants you.'

Her eyes went cartoon wide. 'Me?'

'Would that be a problem? I'd have thought it an honour.'

'It is. It is. It's just, I have a job, I have students.'

'The timetable is up for discussion. What matters is getting the Italians to sign on before Carmen's professor can mess it up. Our cultural attaché is flying down this afternoon. We're going to show him Caselle and the Grotto. Then we'll fly back to Rome with him tonight for a meeting at the Ministry of Culture first thing tomorrow.'

'When does he get here?' asked Zara.

'Three. Sorrento Airport.' He sat on the bed to take off his socks. 'That's a good ninety minutes from here, so we'll need to leave around one.'

'And Carmen?'

'Spin her a story. Tell her that, as nothing will be happening here until her professor arrives, we've decided to visit Amalfi after all, spend the night in Positano.'

'What if she wants to come?'

He laughed. 'On our romantic getaway? Get real. Anyway, doesn't she have some friend coming this afternoon?'

'Oh yes. I forgot.'

'Settled, then.' He pulled back the sheet, climbed in beside her. 'Now get the fuck out of here. And take Carmen with you. I don't care where, just so long as it's quiet out there. But make sure you're back by twelve thirty, ready to go.'

Breakfast in Cesco's *pensione* consisted of stale toast, cold coffee and a text from Baldassare agreeing to postpone his meeting until late afternoon, though asking in return that it be shifted further south, as he needed to be home in good time for the celebratory dinner his daughter planned to cook that night, an occasion he could hardly miss. How about five p.m. in Buonabitacolo? Cesco checked it out. It was only an extra half-hour's drive, so he replied that it would be fine.

His appointment with Rosaria wasn't until noon, but he meant to get there early. He packed up his belongings, settled his account and was out by nine. He stopped at an ATM for the extra cash he needed then set off south. The skies turned grey and then almost black. It began, suddenly, to pour. Traffic congealed. He passed beneath a series of high bridges from which fell frayed grey ropes of water, twisting and whipping in the wind, unthreading back into raindrops that pattered all around him. Sunlight finally returned, and some warmth. A roar engulfed him as he approached Secondigliano, the cool shadow of a passenger jet on its approach to Napoli International.

The Harley was too juicy a plum to leave on these streets, so he parked it in a private garage then bought himself a hoodie and a pair of ill-fitting jeans from a second-hand shop. He smeared his face and hands with water from a pavement puddle then set off, doing his best to mimic the shambling urgency of a junkie cashed up for their next score. A mechanical digger was tamping down fresh tarmac with the flat of its scoop, filling the air outside the Horseshoe with that fragrant stench. He climbed a thinly grassed embankment, glittery with discarded vials and broken syringes. Two young men were on duty by a barricade of mattresses and broken furniture. They barely gave him a second glance. There was only a short queue at the payment window. He handed over his grubby banknote and received his vial, took it to a boarded-up doorway in the alley between two blocks with a good view of the courtyard. He sat there slumped but watching.

Dealing with Rosaria was one thing. Dealing with her Camorra family was another. Her brother and two of her cousins had once promised to kill him and dump his body in the Bay of Naples if he didn't propose to Rosaria. Cesco needed to make quite sure they weren't planning to make good on their threat.

III

Carmen was startled to find Zara waiting in the kitchen with her bag over her shoulder and the Renault's keys in her hand. 'Fancy going out for breakfast?' she asked.

'Sure. Where to?'

'There's a place called Roccagloriosa. It has something you'll want to see.'

'What about Dov?'

'He got back late. He wouldn't enjoy this anyway. I say we be the ones to leave him stranded for a change.'

Roccagloriosa was thirty minutes' drive. They spent another twenty searching for the museum which housed the ostensible reason for their visit: a plaque memorialising a campaign by the Roman general Stilicho, adoptive father of Galla Placidia, subject of Carmen's thesis. She'd read every biography of the man, yet had never heard of this. Most likely, then, a conscription campaign. The Roman army had always been hungry for Italian recruits, but it had been a fate so dreaded that men had cut off their thumbs rather than serve, forcing generals like Stilicho to depend ever more heavily on barbarians. Yet the sheer number of barbarians had provoked a furious nativist backlash that had seen Stilicho himself murdered and the wives and children of his barbarian troops massacred. The bereaved soldiers had flocked to Alaric in the aftermath, giving him both the numbers and the will to sack Rome, where thankfully they'd shown more mercy to the Romans than the Romans had shown them.

From the museum, they headed up to the town's ruined castle, from which a single glance showed how perfect the plain beneath would be for seeing out a winter: lush, well watered, protected on one side by a ring of high hills, the other by the sea. They took coffee in the piazza, where Zara finally divulged the real reason for their excursion. She and Dov had decided to resurrect their Amalfi plan. They planned to spend tonight in Positano before returning tomorrow in good time for Professor Bianchi. She hoped Carmen didn't mind. Carmen didn't. Not one bit. She didn't believe Zara's Amalfi story, but nor could she see how they could get up to any serious mischief before tomorrow afternoon. She gave her her blessing, and they returned in good spirits to the cottage where they found Dov up and at the kitchen table, breakfasting on orange juice and a buttered roll. They set off barely twenty minutes later, Carmen walking up the drive to wave them off and to make sure they'd really gone. Then, buoyed up by a glorious sense of release, she headed back inside to make herself some lunch.

Chapter Thirty-Six

I

It began to rain again in Naples, a swirling thin mist that did little more than lay a burnish on the courtyard flagstones, but which was chill enough to draw a handful of junkies into the relatively sheltered area around Cesco. He felt a mix of disgust and pity for these people. *There but for the grace of God*, as the old piety had it. But it was a platitude he'd never actually believed. He'd taken drugs himself, and had suffered plenty of hard times, but he'd never let himself fall apart like this.

A young man in filthy rags and an unkempt beard unfurled a tattered green sleeping bag then lay upon it with his arms hugged around a scrawny yellow dog. He'd barely settled when Rosaria arrived at the head of her small posse. They stood up their bikes then came swaggering right by them, so close that the dog bared its teeth and growled. One of the posse snarled back for a joke, and feinted to kick it. It lunged for his ankles. He swore and kicked it in its ribs. There was a horrible thud as it went flying. The young man rose in protest only to get set upon by five of them. He lay on the ground covering his face with his forearms as they kicked him. Then they headed in good spirits up a stairwell and out of sight.

The yellow dog limped back to the young man. He clutched his arms around it and stroked it, and then began to sob. The dog licked his face in an effort to bring him comfort, but it did no good. The sobs grew louder and more wretched. Cesco had never witnessed such utter despair in a fellow creature, such bewilderment at what his life had come to.

Cesco had come here early because he'd feared an ambush. He'd seen no hint of one. Yet now he sensed a trap of a different sort. The casual cruelty of these people was the truth of the Camorra. They fed on human misery and degradation, just as the 'Ndrangheta did. Sell him a gun? Of course they would. Seven hundred euros profit for doing shit all. And not a thought for who might get killed as a result. With startling clarity, he realised that *There but for the grace of God* applied to him after all. Had his grandfather not stood up to the Critellis on his behalf, he'd likely have turned out just like Rosaria and her acolytes. To buy a gun from such people would be to say his sacrifice and the massacre of his family counted for nothing.

Vengeance, yes. But not like this.

He rose to his feet and slowly approached the young man. His dog bared its teeth at him, but half-heartedly. He knelt at a cautious distance. 'Hey,' he said. The young man opened his eyes, tearful, bloodshot, defeated. Cesco set down his wad of euros. The young man stared blankly at them and then at him. Almost certainly, he'd waste the lot on drugs and be back here in a week, feeling just as sorry for himself as before, unable to understand how he'd ended up this way. But you never knew. Not for sure.

'Get out of here,' he told him. 'If not for yourself, then for your dog. He deserves better. And you won't get another chance.' Then he tugged his hoodie down over his face and shambled back towards the road.

II

Baldassare arrived at the Sicilì cottage at a few minutes after three. He sprang almost exuberantly from his silver BMW, now that the weight of his wife's and daughter's abduction had been lifted from his shoulders. Carmen hugged him warmly and asked after them. He assured them they were well then gave her back her passport and phone. Its battery was stone dead so she put it on its charger, then offered him something to drink. He asked for tea, but all she could find in the cupboard was half a packet of mint, which Baldassare thanked her warmly for then set untouched on the floor beside his chair. He sat back and clasped his hands across his stomach and gazed fondly at her, as if waiting for her to speak.

'It was you who asked to see me,' she observed.

He nodded several times. 'You know I read your statement?'

'That's what I sent it for.' She frowned. 'You're not mad at me for claiming to be unconscious when the Suraces got—'

'No, no, no,' he said hurriedly. 'No. Nothing like that. Nothing bad. I don't think.'

'Then…?'

'I was worried by your tone in it. You seemed so angry.'

'Aren't I allowed to be? After what those bastards did?'

'You misunderstand. I'm not talking about your anger at *them*. Of course you're right to be angry at *them*. I'm talking about your anger at Cesco.'

'Oh.' She felt herself stiffening. 'He's every bit as bad as any of them. He lied to me and he betrayed me. He went to the Suraces' farmhouse to steal a drone that he thought would lead him to Alaric's tomb. Then he burned the whole place down to cover his tracks.'

'No.'

'I assure you, yes. He as good as confessed it.'

'To going there for the drone, yes. He told me as much himself, and well before you wrote your statement too. It was, as you rightly say, a profound betrayal of you, and one of which I believe he is heartily ashamed. But the burning of the house, that was not him. That was your 'Ndrangheta friends. They realised on their own account about the drone, that there might be photographs on it that could lead us to that awful dungeon. So they burned it down.'

'Is that what Cesco told you? You can't believe a word he says.'

'Maybe not. But that much is true. The accelerant they used, and the mobile phone trigger, were identical to those they used to destroy their own farmhouse. It was them. No question.'

'Oh.' Carmen lifted her chin. 'He still went there to steal.'

'Yes. Which is how he was there when they turned up. He saw them torch the place. In fact, he was almost caught himself by the flames. He had to jump out of a first-floor window to save himself.

It spooked him, as I'm sure you can appreciate. He returned to your apartment with every intention of leaving town. He concocted a story about a deathbed aunt, then went into your room to tell you only to realise that it would mean leaving you exposed to those same people, unaware of the danger you were in. So he chose to stay instead, to look out for you while he tried to find some way to tell you the truth. But those men arrived in their SUV before he could.'

She folded her arms. 'At which point he drove off without me.'

'Because he saw them coming. He was trying to lead them away from you. Except you ran out into the road and waved them down.'

'So it's my fault now, is it?'

'I'm just telling you what happened. Would you like me to stop?'

'No.'

'They chased him into Cosenza. He took a corner too fast and crashed his van. He fled on foot, bleeding badly from shotgun pellets he'd been hit with. Any ordinary conman would surely have fled Cosenza at that point, yes? They'd have caught the first bus or train out, never to return. You know what Cesco did? He stole a Harley from a gang of German bikers then drove it out to see me. My security team refused to let him in – I had other matters on my mind, as I'm sure you can appreciate – so he gave them a message to pass on. This message *severely* compromised him, but he gave it anyway because it was the only way he could be certain of my attention. Then he bullied us into our cars and out to that wretched farmhouse, telling me along the way all the shameful details of his life, including everything he'd been up to since finding you with the Suraces. After we arrived, it was he who realised what was truly going on. It was he who found the bunker.'

'But you said on the news—'

'I know what I said on the news. I gave him my word.'

'Your word? Why?'

'Because those men were 'Ndrangheta. What other reason does he need?'

'So he's a coward, then? Is that what you're telling me?'

'No more a coward than someone who feigns concussion from an accident.'

261

'They'd have killed me then and there,' she said furiously. 'I had no choice.'

'And Cesco did?'

'They cut his friends' throats in front of him, did they? They vowed to kill him if he ever breathed a word?'

'Not exactly, no.'

'Not exactly!'

He picked up his mint tea at last and took a tiny sip, but only to buy himself a little time to think. 'If I tell you something in the strictest possible confidence, will you swear to me that you'll never repeat it? Not to anyone. Not ever.'

She waved a hand. 'Fine. What?'

'No,' he said. 'For this, I need you actually to swear.'

It was his demeanour as much as his words that got to her. 'Very well,' she said. 'I swear to you I'll never repeat it.'

'Thank you. Then do you remember that story I told you that morning in the hospital? About the twin boy and girl taken hostage by the 'Ndrangheta, then murdered and dumped at sea?'

'Of course. Why?'

He set his teacup and saucer carefully back on the floor. Then he lifted his eyes to hers. 'It turns out the boy survived.'

III

Sorrento Airport was a modest affair, serving only a handful of charter flights from within the Schengen area as well as those plutocrats fortunate enough to own villas in Capri and along the Amalfi Coast. Zara and Dov parked outside the private jet terminal then presented themselves at the desk. A woman with crimson lipstick the exact same shade as her uniform had them wait for fifteen minutes then escorted them herself to a vast hangar even as a white Learjet taxied into its open mouth.

The front hatch opened. Steps were let down. A uniformed inspector went aboard for all of ninety seconds, and then returned. A burly man in a black suit appeared at the hatchway to beckon them aboard. The way he stood at the top of the steps meant Zara had to turn sideways to pass him without touching. At once, she began to feel uneasy. Then she arrived in the passenger cabin and saw Avram Bernstein sitting by the window in a bank of four white leather seats either side of a polished walnut table, with other men seated behind him and to his side, men with granite faces and eyes like polished black pebbles. 'What the hell?' she said.

Avram gestured to the empty seat across the table from him then waited for her to settle. 'Do you know where your friend Dov was last night?' he asked.

She glanced at him, sitting alongside her. 'In Policastro. Briefing you and...' Then she fell silent, her cheeks burning. 'Where, then?'

Avram picked up an iPad from the seat beside him, held it out to her. She took it uncertainly. A video clip was cued up. She tapped it to set it playing. The lighting in it was so poor that it took her a few moments to work out what she was looking at: a cavern ceiling that glittered with a galaxy of gemstones of every size and colour. A thrill ran through her; she glanced again at Dov. He smiled and reached across her to close the first clip and set a second playing. This one started with a second or two of dark flowing water before the camera submerged and went blurry. Then a shape emerged from the murk, a white marble plinth with an inscription on its lid, though too obscured by grit and algae for her to read. 'Dear lord,' she muttered. She looked around in horror at all the hard-faced men. 'What the hell have you got planned?'

'You know exactly what,' said Avram. 'We're going in tonight.'

'But you *can't*. It's crazy. How could the prime minister even think of...' She buried her face in her hands, humiliated by her own naivety. 'He doesn't even know, does he?'

'He will soon enough.'

'You'll never get away with it. I'll tell the world.'

'And destroy your own reputation? I hardly think so.'

'I won't destroy anything. I'm no part of this.'

'No part of it?' mocked Avram. 'You and Dov flew into Lamezia on the same flight. You drove up to Cosenza in the same car – a car you hired yourself. You spent a night there together in a hotel room you booked. You introduced him to Carmen Nero as your lover, and you've been lying to her ever since, including again this morning, telling her you were off together to the Amalfi coast. Dov has recordings of it all. We'll release them, if you force us.'

'You bastards.' She glared at them both. They only looked amused. 'It won't help you,' she told them. 'Even if *I* stay quiet, word will still get out. Carmen and her professor will find this place. They'll realise what you've done.'

Avram's smile didn't falter. 'I most certainly hope so.'

'*What?*'

'I'll deny it furiously, of course. I'll be shocked and righteously indignant that anyone could suggest such a thing. I'll point to our prison mosaic and the chamber beneath it, and insist I found the pieces there. But think about it. What could be better for my reputation back home than credible allegations that I not only financed *but also personally led* a mission to reclaim the temple treasures from foreign soil? Especially with them powerless to do anything about it. You said it yourself. I'll be the new Ben-Gurion.'

'So that's why you're here. You want your own Entebbe.'

'I want our treasures back. That's all.'

She shook her head. 'Why even tell me this? What do you want from me?'

'I want you to come with us,' said Avram, his tone suddenly both urgent and solicitous. 'We *need* you. We're here as liberators, not thieves. We want the temple treasures, every last one of them. But not one object more. Now look at us! We're soldiers, not archaeologists or conservators. Would you trust any of us to distinguish Jewish artefacts from Roman? To bring them safely through a kilometre of river cavern?'

'I don't care. I won't be part of it.'

'As you wish. But know this: we're going in either way. Any damage we do out of ignorance and ineptitude will be on your head. And there's more. If tonight goes well, I'll be prime minister soon. I'll have full powers of patronage. I give you my most solemn word, Zara, that you can have whatever you want. *Anything*. Any dig, any museum, any university. I'll even give you the Ministry of Culture, if you wish. And the budget to go with it.'

'I told you. I don't care.'

'But you do care, you see. I was with you when we broke into that chamber. I saw your face when we found that other menorah. The way your hands trembled as you reached out for it, the depth of your dismay when you realised it was fake. Nothing thrills you like discovery. Admit it to yourself. *Embrace* it. Come with us tonight and you'll be first inside the tomb. The first person in sixteen hundred years to see Alaric and all his grave goods. The first to see the true Menorah, to touch it, to hold it. You, Zara Gold, will be the one to bring the emblem of our nation safely home again after its too-long wandering.'

'This is madness,' she said, clutching her face between her hands. 'This is absolute madness.'

Avram turned to Dov with a glittery smile. 'See. I told you she'd say yes.'

Chapter Thirty-Seven

I

Baldassare checked his watch in the manner of a man wanting an excuse to leave, then raised his eyebrows as if in shock at what he saw. He pushed himself to his feet. Another appointment, he told Carmen with a slight twinkle in his eye. An appointment, as it happened, with young Signor Cesco Rossi himself. He already had one piece of good news to give him. Would she be so kind as to allow him to add a second, in the form of her phone number and the permission to use it? She stared at him, still dizzy from his revelation about who Cesco really was. But now that she knew that, and how he'd saved her from that pit, it would have been beyond churlish to refuse.

She waved him off then went back inside. Her phone had recharged a little. She walked it up into Sicilì until it acquired a signal, then found a bench beneath a pine tree with a gap between the splats of bird shit just wide enough for her to perch while she checked her messages and responded to those that needed it. A frisson passed suddenly through her. Cesco might call at any moment. She had no idea what to say to him, no idea even how to treat him. Was he the fourteen-year-old orphan fighting to stay alive? The skilled conman who'd talked so glibly of duty at her hospital bedside? The false lover who'd gazed deep into her eyes before betraying her by going to rob the Suraces? Or the frantic wreck Baldassare had told her of, who'd saved her life by bringing him and his men to the Mafia farmhouse. But the point proved moot because her phone's battery died before he called, forcing her to return it to the cottage and its charger.

She took her book out onto the terrace, but she couldn't settle. She kept being prodded by the thought that Cesco might be trying to call. She kept going to check her phone but it was taking forever to recharge. She decided to take a walk while she waited, sternly instructing herself that on no account was she to waste so sparkling an afternoon brooding about Cesco.

Then she set off across the fields, brooding about Cesco.

II

The olive groves around the house had been so long neglected that it would take more than a day or two of pruning to put them right. But that didn't mean they shouldn't do what they could. Tomas chivvied Guido away from watching DVDs and out to join him. They put on boots and work gloves then went from tree to tree with a handsaw and a pair of bolt cutters, lopping off the dead wood and cutting back the branches, which they stacked beneath a tarpaulin for winter wood.

The sun was bright. The work was hot. They could, of course, have afforded power tools, but then the exertion was half the point. The sporadic rains of the last two days had turned the soil into a clayey mud that clumped heavily and made Tomas feel his age. They broke for a light lunch and then went back out. The sky grew grey and chill. Mid-afternoon, it began to drizzle, and they agreed to call it a day. They scraped the mud off on the edge of the terrace then stamped muddy hieroglyphs all over it before taking off their boots and going inside.

Guido headed to his room to take a shower. Tomas went to the kitchen for a tall glass of pomegranate juice. His mobile had buzzed him with alerts while he'd been working. He just hadn't heard it over the noise of their sawing. He allowed himself a satisfied smile when he saw the reason why. Handing Carmen Nero's phone and passport into the police had been a long shot, but it had paid off.

He rang Massimo to find out where he and his men were, then went in search of Guido. His shower was still running so he pounded three times on the bathroom door. The shower stopped and then Guido appeared naked at the door, suds still in his hair and his shoulders a bright red from the hot spray. 'What the hell can't wait?' he demanded.

'Our friend the American woman,' Tomas told him. 'She's turned on her phone.'

'You got her location?'

'Yes. A place called Sicilì.'

Guido glowered at him. 'The fuck you mean, a place called Sicily? How stupid do you think I am, I don't know Sicily?'

'Not *that* Sicily, oh my brother. A different one. A village in the Cilento.'

'Oh.' Guido thought a few moments. 'Where are Massimo and the others?'

'Just passed south of Naples. I've already given them their orders. They'll be there in an hour or so. But we should join them there as soon as we can.'

Guido grinned. 'Then I'd better put some clothes on, hadn't I?'

III

Buonabitacolo was an old town of narrow, cobbled streets that made Cesco's Harley judder like a jackhammer. Already sore from his long drive, he parked it in the first empty bay he found then walked the rest of the way. Baldassare's cafe was a short stroll from the piazza. He looked through the front window and saw the great man at a corner table. Baldassare saw him almost at the same moment. He stood and waved then bounded across to the door to greet him. Cesco offered him his hand to shake, but Baldassare brushed it indignantly aside and engulfed him in a bear hug instead, then went up on tiptoes to kiss him on both cheeks. 'You wretched young man,' he said, wagging a finger at him. 'You left that day before I could thank you properly.'

Cesco shrugged himself free. 'How is everyone?'

'Good. Glad to be home, of course. But it will take time. You know how these things are.'

'Yes,' said Cesco. 'I know how these things are.'

They stared at each other a moment. Baldassare slapped him on his shoulder then led him across to his corner table, calling out for more pastries and a coffee for his good friend as he went. There was a plate already there, empty save for crumbs and smears of icing. 'My first time out in months without a two-car escort and the Critellis to worry about,' said Baldassare. 'I mean to make the most of it.'

'What about your daughter's dinner? Won't you spoil your appetite?'

'Appetite has never been my problem. It's hunger that's the curse.' He picked up a small tan leather folio case from the floor beside his chair then unzipped it on the table. He took out a salmon folder plump with documents. 'Your grandfather was a career criminal,' he said. 'He and his good friend Luca Critelli started with next to nothing but quickly made themselves wealthy by kidnapping for ransom the children of rich parents. To their credit, they released their hostages unharmed – including in at least one instance when no ransom was ever paid. But still. When kidnapping became more trouble than it was worth, they turned to extortion instead, demanding money from honest businesses with threats of violence and arson. They took over Cosenza's produce business. Then building and waste disposal. When drugs became big business, they began shipping in vast quantities of cocaine from Colombia and Brazil, selling it on throughout Europe. I never had enough evidence to bring charges in court, but your grandfather was most certainly implicated in numerous beatings and half a dozen murders. All of rival gangsters, true. But still. He had your father inducted into the 'Ndrangheta at the age of fourteen, so that everything *he* ever earned was the proceeds of some crime or other.'

Cesco gazed at him. 'You had me come all this way to insult my family?'

'I am not insulting them. I am telling you the plain truth about them, because I don't want you to romanticise them. After they both died, I – acting on behalf of the state – seized every bit of wealth I could from both their estates. Every bit of it. And rightly so. They ruined the lives of countless good people. Your mother and your grandmother, however, were *not* 'Ndrangheta. Or perhaps I should say they were never *proven* to be. They each came into their marriages with property of their own. I sequestered it all too – frankly, because I could. With your immediate family dead, none of your more distant cousins even tried to dispute this. No doubt they feared the scrutiny a claim would bring.' He opened the folder, drew out two stapled documents. 'This first one is an inventory of your mother's personal assets. Some jewellery, as you can see. Various minor artworks, pieces of furniture and curios, along with a modest portfolio of bonds and shares. This second one is your grandmother's. She owned a small property near Reggio and the land on which your grandfather built his villa, the one we've taken over ourselves. So, then. As their only surviving direct descendent, you have a claim to both these estates. In my opinion, a very strong claim indeed. And, as I am essentially the person in charge of the case, my opinion matters a great deal.'

Cesco frowned at him. 'Are you saying you owe me money?'

'I'm saying the state does.'

'How much?'

'These valuations are old and approximate. We'd need to make new ones. But I expect somewhere in the region of two and a half million euros, after taxes.'

'Two and one half... You can't be serious.'

'I am completely serious. There is, however, a catch.'

Cesco snorted. 'Of course there is.'

'The catch is this: the person with a right to this money is Giovanni Carbone. In the eyes of the law, Giovanni Carbone is dead. I declared him so myself, thirteen years ago, after an 'Ndrangheta hit man confessed to having been party to the murders of him and his twin sister some eighteen months before, along with a hideous catalogue of other such crimes. For me to be able to advance your claim, you would need to establish you truly are Carbone. Not to *my* satisfaction, you understand. I am satisfied already. But in the eyes of the law. This needn't be an ordeal. We have your family DNA on file. Give me a cheek swab and I will take care of the rest. Apart from that, it's simply a matter of filling out certain forms and having your photograph taken. I've brought a complete set of documents and a camera. If you agree, we can do it all right now. Then I can get you your old name back, if you wish. Or help you with a new one, if you prefer. Cesco suits you, if you want my opinion. We also run a witness protection scheme of sorts, for Mafia targets. Hopelessly underfunded, of course, but then you won't need funds, just a new passport and a social security number for your taxes.'

'My taxes!'

'Yes,' said Baldassare. 'Your taxes. So that you can contribute to the country in which you were born and which you now choose to live. And not just continue to take, like your father and grandfather before you.'

Cesco flushed. 'And if the Critelli brothers find out about me? If they decide to finish the job?'

Their order arrived on a tin tray. Baldassare licked his lips at the sight of the glazed pastries, then selected the two largest and more lavishly iced for himself. He waited until the waitress had left before speaking again. 'The Critelli brothers don't give a shit about you,' he said, holding a hand beneath his chin to catch the flakes. 'They haven't for at least a decade. You know this perfectly well.'

'If I know it perfectly well, why have I been living like this?'

'Penance,' said Baldassare. 'For being still alive while your sister is dead.'

'Fuck you.'

Baldassare dabbed the corners of his mouth with his napkin. 'Tell me: is this how you'd have wanted Claudia to live, had she been the one to survive? This shrunken, selfish mockery of a thing you call a life? Or would you have wanted good things for her? To fall in love, to marry, to have children of her own?'

Cesco rose trembling to his feet. 'You have no idea about my life.'

'Sit down,' said Baldassare. 'Eat your pastry. You're right. I know nothing about your life. But I do know something about conmen. I've prosecuted enough of them. The best ones are amazingly convincing. The way they do sincerity. Bewilderment. Haplessness. Friendship. Anything you like, to gain the slightest advantage. But there's one emotion I've never seen any of them mimic persuasively. Can you guess which?'

'Which?' asked Cesco reluctantly.

'Panic,' said Baldassare. 'Specifically, panic on behalf of someone else. It's so visceral. At the farmhouse, when we couldn't find Carmen, that look on your face: it was too exactly how I felt about Alessandra and Bettina.'

'I had a responsibility,' said Cesco. 'That was all. I discharged it and then I left.'

Baldassare smiled knowingly. 'As you like.' He took the forms in one hand, his pen in the other. 'Then let me discharge my own responsibilities, and I'll leave too.'

Chapter Thirty-Eight

I

A member of this shameful expedition Zara might now be. A trusted member, clearly not. She was hustled out of the private jet terminal into the back of one of a pair of large rental vans that had been hired for the mission. It had small rear windows and bench seats fitted along either side; she sat opposite the companion they gave her – the burly, black-suited man who'd waved her aboard the plane, whose name, it turned out, was Yani, and who – Dov assured her cheerfully – would answer any questions she might have. And so he did, after a fashion, but only with meaningless grunts.

The drivers of the two vans and the Renault were each given their own list of tasks to perform. They headed in separate directions out of the airport. Her own van stopped several times for supplies, so that the back soon filled up. Waterproof clothing, flotation bags, a large inflatable dinghy, a giant roll of bubble wrap, an extensible aluminium ladder. The sheer scale of preparations unnerved her, making it ever clearer how completely she'd misjudged Avram. He wasn't the genial if driven man she'd thought him, but someone infinitely darker. And the more this bore in on her, the more she remembered the message his son Isaac had left on her voicemail.

> Paul Shapiro thought he could fuck with us too. And look what happened to him.

Zara had always dismissed this claim out of hand, and not just because Isaac had been a braggart drunk, or even because of the technical

273

difficulty of arranging for Shapiro to crash into the car in front of him then have a lorry ride up over him and crush him to death. No. What had convinced her was her certainty that Avram hadn't been that kind of man. But what if he was? Suddenly the nature of the accident wasn't such a problem. Maybe the brake tampering had merely been meant as a warning. Or maybe the lorry driver had been in on it too. As interior minister, Avram had almost unlimited power over which investigations to pursue and which to ignore. And for sure it had swatted away a troublesome gadfly. Where had the Bernstein money come from, after all? Their house in Jerusalem's most exclusive quarter, their villas in Netanya and Corfu, the private schools for the kids and the lavish garden parties they threw at least twice a year for the Israeli elite. And if he was capable of ordering one murder to spare himself some grief, why not a second? What made Zara herself untouchable? If she were to go public with Isaac's voicemails, it would almost certainly trigger an investigation into Shapiro's death, an investigation over which Avram would have no control. So was it possible that he'd ordered her murdered too?

The thought cast a new and sinister light on everything about this Italian adventure. Sure, Avram's ideal outcome would always have been to find Alaric and the Menorah. But he could hardly have relied on it. So he'd put a fallback plan in place: for Dov to kill her while she was over here, in such a way that no Bernstein could possibly be suspected. *That* was why he'd commandeered both her hire car and her hotel room without letting himself be seen with her. It explained, too, that malevolent smile on his lips after he'd looked over her hotel balcony five storeys down to the car park beneath, a perfect set-up for an unhappy suicide. But he'd had to ditch that plan once Carmen had seen them talking together at the *gelateria*. No wonder he'd been so furious. But rather than give up, he'd sought an alternative instead, pressing Carmen for details of those 'Ndrangheta killers so that he could blame them for their murders, all while protecting Avram from the voicemails and freeing him up to present the replica Menorah as the real thing. The thought made her feel sick. But not quite so sick as the one that followed. For if they came up dry in Alaric's tomb tonight, there'd be nothing to stop Dov from following through.

It took forty minutes for Cesco to fill in and sign the forms Baldassare had brought. It was unreal, the thought of an inheritance. He'd denied his identity for so long that he felt like an imposter. He was even tempted to walk away from it with his head held high. He'd stood on his own two feet for fifteen years, after all. Except that he hadn't, of course. He'd preyed instead on the generosity of people who'd believed him to be their friend, and whom he'd repaid with betrayal. He'd always justified this to himself as being necessary, and maybe it had been. But no longer. How high could he hold his head if he refused to change course or make amends? And a seed planted itself in his mind at that moment: the idea of reparations.

He asked about the investigation, whether the men in the sketches had yet been identified or caught. Baldassare threw him a look. 'Stay out of it,' he warned. 'Leave it to the professionals.'

'The professionals!'

'Yes. The professionals.'

'Those men killed my sister,' he said, allowing just a fraction of his anger to show. 'Maybe my whole family too. Don't I have a right to know?'

'Of course. And I'll tell you everything, I promise. But leave the hunt to us, eh? It's what your taxes will be for.'

They went to pay, only for Baldassare to be told his money was no good there. Without their knowledge, a small crowd had gathered outside, bursting into cheers and applause as he emerged, making him flush with embarrassment. He said a few self-deprecating words then found a rictus grin as they lined up to take their selfies. Then they hurried off at the first opportunity in search of a whitewashed wall to serve as backdrop for his photos of Cesco, before returning together to Baldassare's BMW. He buckled himself in then muted his phone for the drive, tossed it face down on the passenger seat. There was a slip of paper already on it, tousled at one end from being ripped from a spiral-bound notepad. He picked it up and contemplated it a moment, as if debating with himself what to do with it. 'One last thing,' he said.

'What?'

'That other appointment I had earlier this afternoon. It was with your friend Carmen. She's staying just down the road from here, as it happens. I had certain matters to discuss with her, and her passport and phone to return.'

'So?' asked Cesco. But then, unwillingly: 'How is she?'

'Remarkably well, all things considered. She's already put the whole horrid business behind her. Except in one respect. She's still furious with you.' He chuckled to himself at the memory. 'That's some gift you have, to make so kind a woman quite so angry. Especially a woman whose life you saved.'

'She doesn't know about that.'

'She does now,' said Baldassare. 'I told her. I told her everything. Even your real identity.'

Cesco stared at him in disbelief. 'You did *what*? You had no right.'

'Of course I had the right,' said Baldassare, turning on his ignition. 'More than the right. I had the duty. I owed you that much, and far, far more.'

'You *owed* me? And this is how you repay me? By betraying my confidence?'

'Yes.'

Cesco glared at him. To his consternation, Baldassare looked amused rather than put out. 'You're a foolish, proud young man,' he said. 'Far too proud ever to have told her yourself. The way you feel about her, the way she feels about you, that would be a shame.' He passed the note to Cesco. 'This is the address of the cottage she's staying in, and her phone number,' he said. He checked over his shoulder that the road was clear before releasing his handbrake and slowly moving off. 'I told her you'd be giving her a call. I expect she'll be waiting for it now.'

III

Massimo had been raised in Altavilla, a mountain village a few kilometres outside Cosenza. He knew all too well what such places were like. A convoy of cars with foreign plates was certain to set tongues wagging, the last thing he needed while hunting for Carmen Nero and her friends – or indeed when the police later arrived to investigate their deaths.

There was a petrol station on the motorway some fifteen minutes shy of Sicilì. He had all three cars in his convoy stop to top up while they had the chance, and stock up on snacks and drinks too. They might well have a long night ahead. Then he and his crew drove in alone to scope out Sicilì while the other two cars waited in a lay-by.

The GPS coordinates Tomas had sent through took them to a wooden bench beneath a pine tree a short walk from the piazza. He parked and got out to stretch his legs. An old woman was watering plants on her balcony. A couple of kids were pulling wheelies down the road. Apart from them, he could see no one – nor any scarlet Renault neither. He checked his phone. The Cilento's hilly terrain made for patchy signals, but right here it was strong. Maybe that was why Nero had come here. If so, there was every chance she'd be back. He turfed out Orsino to keep watch then headed back out to rejoin the others.

He set his iPad on his bonnet, brought up a road map of Sicilì and its surrounds. It was the usual tangle of lanes and tracks and drives, but most of them led nowhere. In fact, he noted, there were only two roads in and out of town – the one he'd just used himself, and another on the far side that cut across hills to Morigerati and the coast. Everything else was local, meaning that if it came to it they could lock the entire place down with just two cars, while the third went hunting.

But not yet.

He searched online for local hotels and *pensiones*, divvied them up between the teams. He gave them each a sector to search, house by house, should that initial effort come up dry. 'Take lots of photos,' he told them. 'Any woman under forty. Any man under fifty. Any red cars. Any Renaults. In fact, fuck it. Just photograph everything you see. Send them to the boss whenever you get a signal, and he can sort it out. Questions?'

'Sure,' grunted Taddeo. 'What if we find the bitch?'

Massimo gave him a look. 'The fuck you think? Kill her, of course.'

IV

Still holding the note with Carmen's contact details, Cesco glared at Baldassare as he headed out of town. How dare he? How *dare* he? To betray his confidence like that! It was outrageous, it was beyond the pale, it was… A sudden hotness in his chest, as if he'd just chomped on a chilli. He took a long deep breath. Carmen knew. She knew about him. She knew it all and yet was waiting for his call. But what would he say to her? What would he even say? How to explain himself? Where to start?

He glanced at the note, as if for a prompt. It bore a phone number and an address in a place called Sicilì. He'd never heard of it so he brought it up on his phone. Her house was by a river, he noticed. A river called the Bussento. He frowned in bemusement until he noticed its second 's'. A different river, then. But surely the similarity of name couldn't be a coincidence. Which meant that Carmen was after Alaric still. He laughed delightedly, not least because it gave him a peg on which to hang his call. He dialled her number but was kicked straight into voicemail, and his tongue swelled so suddenly in his mouth that he couldn't think what to say, and he hurriedly rang off.

Then he frowned.

Baldassare had just returned her phone to her. That's what he'd said. But how was that possible? He himself had flung it out of his van into a hedgerow. The only people who could plausibly have found it there were the ones who'd infected it with their surveillance app. They could have used its GPS coordinates to retrieve it in order to hand it in along with her passport, so that the police would know it was hers and get it back to her. Then, the moment she turned it on again, it would flash her location like a beacon.

He looked down the road, but Baldassare was already gone. He'd muted his phone for the drive too. Cesco swore out loud then rang his number anyway, to leave him a message. Then he punched Carmen's address into his phone's satnav and sprinted for his bike.

Chapter Thirty-Nine

I

Carmen got lost in thought as she trekked along the woodland trail. Unfortunately, as she discovered on turning back, she got lost in reality too. She trudged up a path expecting to find Sicilì at the top, only to find it taunting her from the next hilltop along. She took its bearings as best she could, but the woods here were thick and old, and the footpaths kept dividing and then dwindling into nothing. The sun dipped behind the western hills and the sky grew strangely clouded, as if by the paw prints of a pack of celestial hounds. The bristle of the trees softened into a dark fur. She began to fear that night would fall before she found her way home, when, to her great relief, she heard church bells tolling ahead – and, with a reinvigorated stride, she found herself back in a familiar field, the cottage just a short walk away.

Baldassare would definitely have seen Cesco by now. He'd have given him her number and told him that she was expecting his call. For all she knew, he'd already left a message on her phone. Not that she cared, of course. It was gravity alone that hurried her down the slope to rejoin the road; gravity and a certain abstract curiosity about whether reconciliation with him would even be possible. If he were frank about his dishonesty and sincere in his contrition, she could certainly imagine *forgiving* him for the wrongs he'd done her. In truth, she already had. She could foresee meeting him again, even enjoying his company. Yet how was she supposed to *trust* him? That was the nub of it. To put it bluntly, he was too skilled at what he did. And, without trust, could there be friendship worth the name?

She clambered over a farm gate, took the hairpin turn, arrived at the head of the cottage drive. A beast of a black motorbike was parked at the foot. She remembered Baldassare telling her of the Harley Cesco had stolen from those German bikers. She began to walk down towards it with that same childhood dizziness as when stepping off a merry-go-round. Then the man himself appeared around the side of the cottage, phone in one hand, helmet in the other, a harrowed look on his face that dissolved on seeing her into such unmistakeable gladness and relief to find her and to find her safe that without a further thought she ran across the small gap that still separated them, and flung her arms around him.

II

A splitting headache, yes. An upset stomach, yes. Clammy skin, yes. Noah Zuckman had all the symptoms of the flu. Except it wasn't flu he was coming down with. What he was coming down with, instead, was an existential case of regret. He'd been coming down with it since precisely 7.13 that same morning, when his boss Yonatan had called him at home to order him to report to Ben Gurion Airport with his passport and overnight bag.

Noah Zuckman didn't do overseas missions. At least, as a former officer of Unit 8200 of the Israeli Intelligence Corps, all the overseas missions he'd ever been involved with had been done from the comfort and safety of a bombproof command centre ten metres beneath the Negev Desert, from which he'd hacked with perfect impunity into the digital networks of Israel's strategic targets, stealing their secrets, mapping out their infrastructure and planting viruses that – should the need arise – would cripple their militaries, their economies, their power grids and communications systems. Yet here he now was, sitting in the back of a scarlet Renault as it pulled into the car park of a DIY superstore in a mall an hour south of Sorrento.

Dov pulled on the handbrake and turned around to him. 'You stay here,' he said.

'Gladly,' said Noah.

A contemptuous glance passed between his two bosses. Noah folded his arms and watched sullenly as they went inside, resenting how at ease they both were. It was clear they didn't trust him. He'd gleaned some details of their mission from the general chatter, but they hadn't even had the courtesy to brief him on his specific role. He kept an eye on the dashboard clock, though it was actually three minutes slow. Fifty-four minutes passed before the two men came back out, pushing a shopping trolley packed with plastic bags. Noah got out to help them pack it all away in the boot. One of their purchases was a chainsaw. Another was a sledgehammer. He looked at them in alarm. 'What the hell are we here to do?' he asked.

Yonatan and Dov exchanged another glance, debating whether the time had come. Dov smiled reassuringly at him. 'Get back in,' he said. 'We'll tell you on the way.' They all retook their seats. Dov adjusted his rear-view mirror to look Noah in the eye as he pulled out of the car park. 'You know about hydroelectric dams, right? They're one of your areas of expertise?'

'I'm not sure I'd—'

'You told us in your interview that you'd written code that would cripple Syria's hydroelectric system.'

'Yes, but—'

'Good. Because we're about to visit a remotely operated hydro-electric dam on Lake Sabetta. It controls the flow of a river called the Bussento, and we need you to stop it running for the night.'

'But...' Noah spread his hands, bewildered. 'Why bring me here for that? I have everything I need back home.'

'Because you're not going to hack it. If you do, they'll know for sure it was people like us. We can't have that. So you're going to disable it for us without hacking it. That way, they won't have a clue.'

'But... who else would want to disable it?'

'The dam is owned by a company called Como Energy,' said Dov. 'They operate hydroelectric plants all across Italy. They're building a new one on the Ombrone river, as it happens, and it's got the environmentalists all riled up. You know the kind of shit. An area of outstanding beauty. The only habitat of some newt called the Arno goby.'

'A goby is a fish,' muttered Noah.

'I beg your pardon?'

'I'm just saying, gobies are fish, not newts.'

'Newts *are* fish,' said Dov.

'No, actually, they're salamanders.'

Yonatan laughed and punched Dov on the shoulder. 'He told you, mate,' he said. But Noah could tell from his manner that it was actually him he was laughing at, not Dov, as though familiarity with the natural kingdom was something to be ashamed of. He stared glumly out of the window. No wonder they'd delayed telling him as long as possible: to give him no real chance to back out. It seemed incredible to him now that he'd ever agreed to work for these people. But corporate intelligence was the hot new thing, and all the rest of his team were constantly being approached, so he'd been flattered enough to take the meeting when his own turn had finally come. He'd never expected anything to come of it, for he'd loved the army, its discipline and order, the pride of working for one's nation, of knowing secrets that all the people he was protecting would shit themselves over if they knew. But the size of the offer Gordian Sword had made him had eaten away at him. All that fun he could be having! Holidays, a plush apartment, a fast car, the kind of sharp clothes worn by the kind of men that pretty women always snubbed him for. So he'd approached his commander about a promotion only to be laughed at and ordered back to his desk.

They left the motorway for a main road, the main road for a lane, the lane for a woodland track up which they bumped to a small clearing above a large lake, its surface grey with twilight. 'That's our baby,' said Dov, redundantly. 'And those are the control buildings down there.'

Noah stared across the lake. There were two cars in the car park. 'I thought you said it was remotely operated.'

'Relax. They're Italians. They'll leave soon enough.'

'And if they don't?'

'You worry about your end of it. Let us worry about ours. Okay?'

They got out and stretched. Yonatan relieved himself against a tree, so Noah tried to too – except it proved to be nerves, so that barely a trickle came out. They each prepared a backpack with everything they'd need. Dov took a ziplock bag from a pouch of his overnight case. It had a handgun inside.

'What the hell!' protested Noah.

'It's only a replica,' Dov assured him. 'For crowd control only. Or would you prefer to get trapped in there if anyone turns up?'

Noah stared at him, but he and Yonatan simply carried on going about their business as if this was all perfectly normal. He didn't know what to say, and so the moment passed. Yonatan fuelled the chainsaw then tested it by taking down a few branches. Dov covered their licence plates with fake ones then slapped Greenpeace and WWF stickers all over the bodywork. Then he called the drivers of the two rental vans to see how they were getting on and to give them their current coordinates for the rendezvous.

The sun set. Night began to fall. Still the two cars remained. They sat in the Renault and watched through field glasses until finally a side door opened and a man and woman came out, joking and jostling with each other. They set the alarm and locked the door then climbed into their separate cars and drove out over the dam, the steel security gate closing again behind them. They reached the main road then flashed each other farewell and headed off in opposite directions.

'Okay,' said Dov, starting the ignition. 'We're on.'

III

It couldn't last, this glorious sensation of having Carmen in his arms, so Cesco savoured it while it did, her cheek warm against his own and the crush of her embrace and the astonishing fact that she appeared to have forgiven him, even before he'd managed to blurt out his incoherent apologies for everything he'd done. Then he realised that to hold her any longer would be another betrayal to add to his long list, so he let go of her, stepped back, put his hands on her shoulders and assumed his most solemn expression. 'Baldassare returned your phone to you, yes?' he said. 'The one I took from you that day?'

'Yes. Why?'

'Have you used it yet?'

'I went up the road to check my messages. Why? What's going on?'

'How far up the road?'

'Into Sicilì. The nearest place with a signal. Cesco, what's this about?'

'Okay. The thing is this: I think your Cosenza friends are on their way.'

'My Cosenza friends? You don't mean...?'

He nodded. 'I think they did it that first afternoon, after they'd knocked you out. They unlocked your phone with your thumb then downloaded a surveillance app onto it with which to monitor you and the investigation. That's how they learned about the drone, and that they needed to burn down the Suraces' farmhouse. It's how they found us on that road that morning. And now they've contrived to have it returned to you, because they want to find you again.'

'But why?'

'Those sketches you did. You're the one person in the world who can say for sure that they truly are of them.'

'Oh shit,' she said.

'Will they be able to find this place?' he asked. 'By searching for rentals on the internet, for example?'

'If they look hard enough.'

'Then we need to get out of here right now. Is it only you?'

'Yes. No. There are two others. But they're away until tomorrow.'

'You'll need to warn them anyway. Have you got their number?'

'In my bag.' She led him around to the kitchen door to let them in. Her purse was on the table. She slung it over her shoulder.

'Oh,' said Cesco. 'We should take your phone too.'

'Won't that just lead them straight to us?'

'We'll take its battery out first. Then we'll give it to Baldassare. He may be able to use it as a lure.' She looked a little sick at this, as though the full truth of their predicament was only now sinking in. He took her by her hands. 'We need to catch these bastards while we can,' he told her, 'or you'll never feel safe again. That's a horrible way to live, trust me.'

She met his gaze with perfect assurance. 'I do,' she said.

Chapter Forty

I

Carmen locked up the cottage then she and Cesco hurried together around to his bike. He handed her his helmet to put on. She gave him a look. 'Not for safety,' he told her. 'To hide your face. You're the one they'll be looking for.'

'Oh,' she said. 'Yes.' She strapped it as tightly beneath her chin as it would go, but it still kept slipping forward. She climbed on pillion, hugged her arms around him. The seat and casing were both still warm from his earlier drive. The bike shuddered when he started it. It wasn't quite dark yet, but it was gloomy enough for the headlight. He eased them up the drive, making a slalom of the potholes. A navy SUV prowled slowly by as they reached the top. It had Dutch licence plates even though the men inside looked Italian. One of them held up his phone to photograph them as they drove past. Then they reached the next hairpin up and vanished.

Cesco gave it a moment then turned the other way. She could feel his heart pounding beneath his shirt. They leaned together into the sharp bends until the road straightened out at the valley floor. They approached the Bussento bridge. A second SUV was parked on its far side, hazard lights flashing. A man was standing in the middle of the road as if about to wave passing traffic down for help. Cesco must have noticed him for he braked sharply then turned left up an old sealed track that she hadn't even seen.

The trees pressed close on either side. The track grew ever rougher, the ancient tarmac breaking up into a mosaic of crazy paving. They drove for perhaps two minutes before arriving outside a low industrial building in a small clearing, dark and closed for the night. Several narrow footpaths led into the woods, but none looked as if they'd take the Harley very far. Cesco stilled it and doused the light. He tried his phone but found no signal. They looked back down the track to see if they were being followed, but there was nothing but the normal chitter of night-time creatures.

'What now?' asked Carmen.

'I don't know,' said Cesco. 'Were those your friends from Cosenza?'

'No. But they're likely with them, though, aren't they? At least two cars of them.'

'I left Baldassare a message. He'll get it soon enough. He'll flood this whole area with police. I say we stay put until they arrive.'

'And if those men come up here first?'

'We'll hear them in plenty of time. They'll never find us in these trees. Not at night.'

'Okay.' Carmen gave a little shiver. 'Thank God you came for me.'

There was a bench outside the building with a good view of the track up which they'd just arrived. He sat on it. 'Of course I came. I gave you my word, didn't I?'

Carmen settled beside him. 'You did? When?'

'That first afternoon. When I found you with Giulia and Vittorio.' She sensed rather than saw him tensing. 'I thought they'd killed all three of you. Then you twitched your arm. I knelt beside you. You opened your eyes and asked if they were gone. You said: "Don't leave me."'

'I don't remember that at all.'

'I know. But you did. So I gave you my word that I wouldn't, and you fell asleep again. As if you trusted me.' He took a deep breath. 'The thing is...'

'Yes?'

Another deep breath, then a third. 'Baldassare told you about me, yes? About who I once was. That I had a twin sister?'

She took his arm. 'Yes.'

'It's not like anything else, being a twin. It's not just that you do everything together, though you do. It's that you're a part of a larger organism. Like marriage is supposed to be. Parenthood. It comes with responsibilities as well as joys. After we were kidnapped... They didn't beat us or starve us or even threaten us much, but it was horrible all the same, and it would have been a million times worse without her. We gave each other strength, not least by vowing to one another that, whatever happened, we'd see it through together. In a perverse kind of way, I was even a little glad. It was my chance to prove myself her protector until our grandfather came through for us. Because I was certain that he would. He was a god to me. Far more so even than my own father. I was terrified yet at the same time I never truly believed that he'd fail us – let alone that he would kill himself or that our family would be slaughtered like that.'

'Oh, Cesco.'

'The days passed. Even being a hostage becomes routine. One night they put something in our food. I woke feeling nauseous and woozy. It was pitch black. The floor was swaying. There were fumes and an engine. We were on a boat. Some kind of hold on a boat. And stripped naked too. My head was fuzzy but terror is like a slap. I could hear Didi beside me. I butted her shoulder with my head. She muttered groggily then fell asleep again.' He began weeping as he talked; in the moonlight, Carmen could see tears glittering on his cheek. 'My wrists and ankles were tied, but the floor was wet and the rope was slick enough that I managed to work my hands free. But before I... before I...' He couldn't manage any more, however. He sat forward and rested his weight upon his knees.

She squeezed his arm. 'You don't have to tell me this, Cesco.'

He took a deep breath and pulled himself together. He sat back up and wiped his eyes and cheeks with his hand. 'I do,' he said. 'I really do. At least, I have to tell someone, it's been eating away at me too long. And, if I have to tell someone, I'd like it to be you. If that's okay?'

'Of course. Of course. Go on.'

'Before I could untie Didi, the hatchway was unbolted and opened. Two men jumped down. I feigned unconsciousness and held the rope behind my back as if my wrists were still tied. They didn't notice. They heaved us up and laid us on the deck beside a pair of old car engines tied by lengths of chain to a pair of empty body bags. They were chatting about some football tournament, as if it were nothing. They started with Didi, zipping her up inside. They assumed we were both still out cold, so they turned their backs on me. I grabbed the rail and hauled myself overboard. The boat was cruising fast enough that they were twenty metres away before they could bring it around. They shone their lamps and torches every which way. But the sea is a bitch to search at night, they kept looking in the wrong places. I managed to untie the rope around my ankles. That was when the bigger of the two men lifted Claudia up by her hair. He had this huge knife that he put against her throat.'

'Oh Christ,' said Carmen.

'His companion came to the railing. The shorter, thinner one. He cupped his hands around his mouth. "Your sweet sister," he shouted out. "Your beautiful brave sweet sister. Please don't make us do this to her. Come back and we can talk. Just talk. You both can live, I give you my word as a man of honour." Claudia was wide awake by now. The pain of being picked up by her hair, I guess. She realised what was happening, she kicked and fought and screamed. She screamed out my name again and again and begged me not to leave her. "Don't leave me, Gio," she cried. "Please don't leave me. Not like this."'

Carmen wrapped her arms around him, held his head against her chest. 'My poor Cesco,' she murmured. Then, unable to stop herself, even though she already knew the answer, she asked: 'What did you do?'

'I left her,' he said.

II

Noah's heart pumped like overworked bellows as they turned onto the main road and then drove for five minutes or so around the periphery of the lake. He feared calamity around every corner. The bellows somehow began pumping even harder when Dov turned off the road down the private track to the dam, turning off his lights and pulling onto the grass verge out of the CCTV camera's field of view. But, even as he feared he couldn't bear it any longer, a peculiar sensation overcame him, his senses so overloaded that he entered a kind of out-of-body fugue state in which he observed rather than was himself, freeing him from fear.

They got out and quietly closed their doors. They opened the hatchback, pulled on ski masks and gloves, strapped on backpacks. Dov took the sledgehammer, Yonatan the chainsaw. They filed in silence to the fence. Dov lifted a loose flap of wire. They slithered beneath. There was moonlight enough to cross the dam without torches. Perhaps it was only his imagination, but Noah could feel the heady shiver of the massive turbines turning far beneath his feet. They reached the far bank, made directly for the larger of the two buildings. Its door was alarmed and locked, but Yonatan was ex-Mossad and they were inside within a minute.

Motion-sensitive lights flickered on. Yonatan turned them off again while Dov disabled the CCTV. They closed the window shutters then turned one light back on. 'Okay,' said Dov to Noah. 'Over to you.'

The room was arrayed like the bridge of a ship, with two rows of desks facing a wall of large screens, all off. A semicircular command console in pride of place was equipped with a confusion of buttons, dials and switches. Noah walked over to it. At once, his nausea returned. He was at home with schematics. He understood code. Give him software to tinker with, he could make it dance waltzes. But physical structures like these were alien to him. He looked desperately around at Dov and Yonatan, hoping to explain himself, but they were already engaged on their own task, spray-painting the walls with gleeful slogans.

Save the Arno goby!
Capitalism is death
Environment before profit
And when we've destroyed this planet,
what then?

Noah swallowed and focused on the console. He could do this. All he had to do was shut the sluice gates and stop the turbines. It would take time to complete, but the procedure itself was simple enough. There was even a helpful diagram on the console itself. On the other hand, the regional command centre might see it happening and try to override it. There was a pair of glass-fronted server closets against the right-hand wall. He studied their configuration then simply switched off both communications servers, hoping it would be attributed to a glitch of some kind. He turned on the wall screens. They showed live data and CCTV feed from the sluice gates and turbines far below. He returned to the central console and started the shutdown. Orange warning lights at once began pulsing on the walls. Dov came across to check his progress. 'All done?' he asked, tossing away an empty spray can.

'You can't be serious,' protested Noah. 'I've barely started.'

'What else needs doing, then?'

Noah looked from the console up at the screen. The sluice gates were already beginning to close. When they were done, the river would stop running. Yet somehow that seemed anticlimactic. He said: 'This whole building, it's like the dashboard in a car.' He pointed at the CCTV feed. 'If you want to make sure the river stays stopped, I'd need to get down there and—'

'No time,' said Dov. 'And we only need a few hours.'

'Okay. Fine. He took a deep breath. 'Then have at it.'

Dov grinned. He pulled on a pair of insulated gloves, grabbed his sledgehammer then set about smashing the server closets and every other piece of electronic equipment in sight, while Yonatan used the chainsaw to slice through all the cabling, sending sparks flying. In five minutes, the room was a scrapyard.

'Enough,' said Dov. 'We need to go.'

They jogged back across the dam, scrambled beneath the fence and up to the Renault. They stripped off their gloves and masks, tossed everything in the back. Then they set off back up the track, waiting until they were at the main road before turning on their headlights. They drove briskly but not too quickly back around the lake. They saw not a glimmer of the police anywhere. Now that they were safe, Noah hugged himself and rocked back and forth. It was all he could do not to laugh, but it kept leaking from him anyway in odd little snorts that made Yonatan glance around. 'You okay, mate?' he asked.

'I'm fine, yes,' said Noah. 'It's just, that was so fucking cool.'

'How about that?' grinned Yonatan. 'Our man likes a bit of the good stuff after all.'

Noah nodded, he didn't trust himself to speak. Start giggling now, it would ruin everything. But screw the army! This was the life.

This, right here, this was the life.

III

Tomas and Guido were still twenty minutes from Sicilì when the latest batch of photographs came through from Massimo and his crew. Night had now fallen, so that the pictures of old crones had largely been replaced by middle-aged men in checked shirts and heavy jackets. On autopilot, he flipped straight past a young couple on a motorbike. Then he went back again. The woman was wearing a helmet so that he couldn't see her face. But the man...

He showed it to Guido. 'That pig's arse,' he muttered. 'What's *he* doing there?'

'What are any of them doing there, oh my brother?' he replied. Yet the question was a good one, and it made him uneasy, like the creaking of lake ice at start of thaw. Something was going on, to bring all these people here. Something he didn't understand. Yet he was good at sensing traps, and this didn't have the feel of one, so he set it aside for the moment and called Massimo back to let him know his target and to give him his orders. Then he nodded for Guido to up his pace a bit, so that they could reach Sicilì themselves in time for the capture.

The capture and the kill.

Chapter Forty-One

I

There was nothing Carmen could say to Cesco that didn't sound trite and inadequate. What use to tell him that he'd only been fourteen at the time, or that he'd most certainly have been murdered too if he'd gone back? He knew all that already, and yet it didn't help. How could it? She held him instead, stroking his hair, offering him time in the darkness to compose himself. 'How did you get back to shore?' she asked gently, when she judged it right.

He was silent so long, she feared she'd pressed too soon. Then he began to talk. 'I always was a strong swimmer,' he said. 'It was summer, the water was warm. I could see a lighthouse on the shore. I aimed for it until the current swept me away. Then I picked out other lights instead. I swam for hours. It was almost dawn when I reached land. I was exhausted, I couldn't even stand. There were rocks. I remember cutting my hands and feet on them, how the saltwater burned. I reached a small beach with a few holiday homes behind it. I was completely naked, like I said. I found some clothes hanging out to dry on a line. I stole a T-shirt that fitted me like a ball gown, and a pair of shorts that I had to clutch with both hands to stop them from falling down. One of the back doors was open. I sneaked into the kitchen for some string to hold them up. There was a bowl of coins by the front door so I filled my pockets then went into town looking for a payphone. But I passed a newspaper kiosk before I found one. There were photos of my family splashed across all the front pages. Their bodies in the restaurant. My parents, my grandmother, my little cousin Romeo. That was how I found out.'

'Oh my poor Cesco.'

'I guess that was why they'd decided to get rid of me and Claudia. They didn't need us any more. But I was too terrified to care about reasons. I just wanted to get safe. But how? My friends were all 'Ndrangheta. Every policeman I'd ever met had been on the take. There was only one person I completely trusted. My mother's best friend from school, a woman called Emilia. Her father had moved to Oxford to help his brother run a restaurant there. She'd stayed on to become a teacher, then had married another teacher at her school called Richard Stone. They had two kids: Arthur, a year older than me and Didi; Lizzie, a year younger. Not twins, but about as close as you can get. They came out to stay several times. We all got on really well, and it was a cheap holiday for them. Anyway, I trusted Emilia absolutely. She was so obviously good. You know how it shines in some people?'

'Yes. I know.'

'So there I was, desperate for help. I called international enquiries and somehow got the number for her school. She was there, thank God. She was... I can't tell you. She got on a flight to Naples that same evening and drove down to pick me up. We flew back to England the next morning, with me on her son's passport. We had the same colouring, and who looks that closely at a boy travelling with his mother? She and Richard took me in. The whole family were incredibly kind. I mean *incredibly* kind.' Carmen could feel the tears welling again inside him. 'They wanted to adopt me officially but I had terrible nightmares about those men finding out and coming after me so we did it covertly instead. They confided in their head teacher. She helped us arrange it all. It worked fine for the next few years, until I left school. Then it became a problem. Applying to university or for any proper kind of job meant risking the truth coming out. That wouldn't be bad just for me. It could have been ruinous for everyone who'd helped me too. Plus, to be frank, I was homesick. I missed Italy. I missed the language. I missed the sun. So one day the whole family went to visit Emilia's parents. I feigned sickness and stayed behind. I wrote a thank-you note then borrowed Arthur's passport, packed a bag and flew out. I stayed up north, as far from Cosenza as I could get, and I got by doing odd jobs and conning people. But of course that meant having to move every so often. And with each move I came a little further south.'

'Emilia and her family? Did you keep in touch?'

'No.' He seemed set to justify himself but then thought better of it. 'I sent Arthur back his passport, and then a couple of postcards to let them know I was okay. But they were so straight and honourable that frankly I was ashamed. It's hard to be a disappointment to people who—' He broke off suddenly. He sat up straight, a hushing finger to his lips. Now she heard it too: an engine straining at a gradient. She looked down the track even as headlights swept like a lighthouse beam around one of the hairpins below.

They got to their feet without a word. Cesco hurried to the Harley then they pushed it along one of the narrow footpaths, jolting over ruts and roots. They'd barely left the clearing when a pair of SUVs arrived behind them, their headlights illuminating the woods. Doors opened and slammed. Torches flashed. But she and Cesco pushed onwards and soon were out of sight and sound.

The cloud was thickening; so too the canopy of trees. Only rare shafts of moonlight made it through, lighting the grass like silver tinsel. The footpath degraded into an animal track that then vanished altogether. It was the end of the line for the Harley. They laid it out of sight behind a thorn bush then pushed on, fighting through the undergrowth, picking brambles from their clothes. Cesco kept checking his phone, but still no signal. Brief flashes from its torch helped them pick their way. A murmur ahead grew slowly into a rumble. Carmen put a hand on his forearm. 'You hear that?' she whispered. 'It's the river.'

'You mean the Bussento?' said Cesco, with just a hint of dryness in his voice.

'I'll tell you all about it, I swear,' she promised. 'But the point is that it has a footpath on this side. It leads to a grotto and then up some cliff steps to the next town along, a place called Morigerati. I know for a fact we can get a signal there.'

'Okay,' he said. 'Let's do it.'

The way grew absurdly tangled. They had to fight between fat bushes of fierce thorns. Night-time creatures scurried all around them, startled by their clumsy progress. Between the cloud and the thick canopy, it was almost pitch black. Carmen took Cesco's arm to stay with him. A bird took off from beneath her feet, giving her such a fright that she slid her hand down to the comfort of his. He interlaced fingers with her, gave her a reassuring squeeze. They reached the top of an embankment populated by stumpy trees that in the darkness seemed almost to claw like hands up out of the moist soft earth. The river was running at its foot; she could see it by the glints of reflected moonlight. It was possible that the 'Ndrangheta had looped around to cut them off, so they crouched there for a minute or so, letting their eyes adjust, making sure it was safe.

Cesco went down first, lurching in short bursts from tree to tree. She followed close behind. The soil was so loose that her feet kept sliding from under her. But they made it safely to the bottom. Lights blazed orange on a nearby hilltop, like the campfires of an invading army. 'Morigerati,' she murmured. Then she took Cesco by the hand once more, and they set off together towards it.

II

The two rental vans had already arrived at the rendezvous point above the Lake Sabetta dam by the time Dov, Yonatan and Noah returned to it. Among their other supplies, they'd brought a pair of satellite phones. Dov found a flat piece of ground in the clearing on which to set up the first of the dishes. With the help of a hand-held compass, he locked it onto its geostationary satellite, then opened up its companion laptop to show Noah how to use it, so that he might provide them with an early warning should the dam be repaired despite their sabotage, and the Bussento released once more.

That done, he and Yonatan grabbed their things and climbed into the back of the second van. Zara was already sitting there, across from Yani, glaring the world's bluntest daggers. Dov grinned and sat beside her even as they set off. 'I've got something for you,' he told her, rummaging through his bag. He took out a video camera, switched it on and began filming her, moving it around as she tried to hide her face behind her hand.

'Stop that!' she protested.

'Little bit shy, are we?' He held it out to her. 'You'll need to get over that fast. It's your official role tonight. Mission chronicler. Documenting for posterity our heroic efforts to reclaim our nation's treasures.'

'You can't be serious.'

'Oh, but I am. You never know when it might come in useful. So make sure you capture everything, from the moment we arrive inside the grotto until we leave. Our equipment, our journey, the chamber, the plinth, whatever we find beneath. And turn it on yourself every so often, like in the documentaries. You know. Talk about all that shit you've been telling me about Alaric and the two Bussentos, the sack of Jerusalem. In English, mind. We might need a wide audience. Oh, and keep repeating what outstanding patriots we all are, risking our lives and freedom to bring the Menorah and the other treasures safely home again.'

'Aren't I compromised enough already for you?' she asked sourly.

'Not by a long shot, no.'

'And if I refuse? If I throw your camera in the river?'

Dov gave her a savage grin. 'Do you really want to put that to the test?' he asked.

III

'That was dee-licious,' declared Baldassare, pushing away his empty plate before leaning back in his chair and folding his hands over his bulging stomach. 'Truly exquisite. The finest meal I have eaten in many, many years.'

'There's more,' grinned Bettina.

'More? *More?* How could there possibly be more? We've already eaten all the food in Cosenza. How will our poor neighbours survive?'

'I made a cassata cake. For your birthday that we missed.'

'Oh,' he said. He kept his smile going as best he could, though he could feel it dying behind his eyes. His birthday had been perhaps his lowest point. He'd spent most of it in bed, curled up in a ball. For the first time that night, he couldn't help but think of those two 'Ndrangheta fugitives, and the bitterness and hatred he felt were like his insides being given an acid bath. He waited until Bettina had gone through to the kitchen then felt for his phone to check for news. But his phone wasn't even in his pocket. He must have left in the car.

Alessandra sensed him about to rise. She covered his hand with her own. 'No,' she said. 'Not tonight. Can't you see how happy Bettina is?'

Bettina reached in her hand at that moment, to dim the lights. Then she backed in through the door holding the cassata cake on a silver platter, her eyes down and her tongue bitten sideways between her teeth in her concentration not to drop it. The three toy candles she'd planted in it fluttered weakly until she set it down in front of him, then instantly they sprang up strong and bright again. She smiled at him in triumph and the love he felt for her pierced his side like a crucifixion lance. Then he closed his eyes and made his wish and blew the candles out.

IV

The footpath walked very differently in the darkness, what with Carmen's nerves already frayed by the knowledge that the 'Ndrangheta were out in numbers hunting for her and Cesco. Imagination was mostly a gift, but she could have done without it right now, the way it turned every tree into a lurking figure, every rustle into an ambush.

Yet nothing happened.

The hilltop lights of Morigerati remained their beacon. They slowly drew closer. The footpath diverged from the river, as she remembered, taking them up through that unruly orchard. They'd almost reached the grotto staircase when they heard an engine and then a vehicle pulled into the small parking area to their left, crunching to a halt a stone's throw away, its headlights dazzling her and Cesco and forcing them to throw themselves to the ground. The headlights were thankfully turned off, only for a second vehicle to arrive, pulling up alongside the first. Men got out and began conferring in low, furtive voices. She could only think that the 'Ndrangheta had consulted a map, seen their possible escape route and come to cut them off. In which case they'd got here just in time.

The second set of headlights finally turned off. At once, Carmen grabbed Cesco by the wrist and led him hurrying forward to the stone steps down to the valley floor where that girl in the deckchair had sold them their grotto tickets. Their night vision had been utterly degraded by the headlights, however, which made the staircase a nightmare to navigate at speed. The steps were scattered with fallen branches that rustled and snapped whenever they trod on them. Worse, they were of different lengths and drops too, so that they kept being jolted by landing too soon, or finding only air where they'd expected solid ground. And now she heard a noise behind and glanced around to see a flash of torchlight. She feared for a moment that they must have been seen, that they were coming after them – yet they showed no urgency. It made no sense to her, but she didn't have time to puzzle it out. It took all her concentration to keep her footing until they finally reached the valley floor.

The ticket girl had sited her deckchair by the place where the path divided, the left-hand fork leading to the cliff steps up to Morigerati, the right-hand fork leading to the grotto. Carmen peeled her eyes for the split but she must have missed it in the darkness for they found themselves arriving on the wooden deck directly outside the grotto mouth. She muttered an apology to Cesco and made to turn back only to discover that their pursuers were still close behind. And now they had nowhere left to flee except into the grotto itself.

They went in and climbed down a few steps and crouched there to watch. A trail of dark figures now arrived outside, setting down weighty loads then rubbing their sore palms against their trousers before heading back the way they'd come. Her spirits began to lift. If they all left again, they could sneak out while they were gone.

But two of them remained. To her bemusement, they set a miniature satellite dish on the ground and aimed it up at the sky with the help of a compass. Then they opened up a laptop beside it, by the light of whose screen she finally saw their faces.

And one of them was Dov.

Chapter Forty-Two

I

From his vantage point above the Sabetta dam, Noah Zuckman trained his field glasses on the two cars that had just arrived in the power station's small car park. His earlier euphoria had long since evaporated. Courage was easier in the company of men like Dov and Yonatan, who each carried around with them an aura of invincibility. Now it bore in on him exactly how much trouble he'd be in if he was caught, the shame of it, the years he'd be facing in an Italian jail.

As best he could tell, the two cars belonged to the man and the woman who'd been here earlier. But it was dark and they'd vanished inside the control room before he could make out their faces. They evidently set about tidying up the wreckage. Every so often, the door would open and out would come another black bag. But now three more vehicles arrived in rapid succession. First, a pair of police cars. Then, less than a minute later, a white van.

The white van drove straight over to the second building. Two men got out, one of them carrying what looked like a metal toolbox. The woman went to meet them. She unlocked the door of the second building and they all went inside. Lights flickered and then came on. A couple of minutes passed and then the gate over the goods entrance began to scroll upwards, unfurling a carpet of yellow light over the tarmac apron. The two men emerged a minute later, one of them hauling a wooden crate on a hydraulic jack, the other still holding his toolbox. They went over to the control building then heaved the crate inside. The woman meanwhile lowered the scroll gate from the inside then turned off the lights, came back out and locked it up again, and went to join them.

As Noah had tried to explain to Dov earlier, to do real damage to the dam, they'd have needed to attack the sluice gates or the turbines themselves. But they'd had neither the time nor the access. All the equipment that Dov and Yonatan had destroyed with such savage glee was essentially modular. They could in theory be unplugged and new ones put in. It just hadn't occurred to Noah that they'd be able to do so before morning. But time was money, of course. Stalled turbines meant lost revenue. Besides, the lake was already high and more water was arriving all the time from the spring rains and the thaw.

A low purring noise came from behind him. The satellite phone. Dov must have set up the second one outside the grotto and was now establishing contact. Noah felt sick. What the hell was he going to tell him?

II

The realisation that it was Dov rather than the 'Ndrangheta outside the grotto upended Carmen's understanding of the situation. It didn't do all that much to improve it, however. For one thing, the 'Ndrangheta were still out there somewhere. For another, the furtiveness of Dov and his companions made it quite clear that they were up to no good.

She touched Cesco on the hand to draw him further down the steps into the grotto, so that she could tell him what she knew without being overheard. It was hard going in this total darkness, having to feel out each next step with their feet. But they reached the foot of the staircase at last. The river roared beneath them, but still she put her mouth to Cesco's ear, for you could never trust the acoustics of such places. 'They're not 'Ndrangheta,' she told him.

'Then who?'

'That couple I've been staying with. The guy with the laptop, that was the man.'

'Then why are we hiding from them?'

'I don't trust him. Him and the woman, they're both Israeli. I think that's why they're here.'

'How has their being Israeli got anything…' But then he worked it out for himself. 'They think Alaric's buried in here somewhere. And he's got the Menorah with him?'

'I think so, yes.'

'But… why?'

'Because it's the Bussento, of course. And those pieces that Vittorio had in his money belt almost certainly came from around here. Plus we found some Visigoth symbols in the cavern roof where the river enters the mountain.'

'That hardly justifies all this.'

'I know. All I can think is, I got suspicious of them yesterday, so I called my professor to have him come down. When I told this guy Dov, he got angry. He tried to hide it but it was obvious. Then he headed off alone last night. I didn't hear him come back in again either. But he slept way in this morning.'

'He came here, then,' said Cesco. 'He came here and found something. And now he's back with all these others to raid it before your professor arrives.'

'I think so, yes.'

'You know the guy. What will he do if he finds us?'

'I don't know,' she said. But there'd always been something unsettling about Dov. If it hadn't been for Zara, she'd have run a mile from him. And, if they were right about what they were up to, he and these others were here to break into an ancient site in order to steal priceless artefacts. They were risking years in jail. And Dov hadn't seemed the kind of man to let that happen when he had alternatives. 'But I'd rather not find out.'

'So what do we do?'

'There's another passage across the bridge. It's roped off, so I don't know where it leads. But maybe we can hide there until they're gone.' She led him across the viewing platform bridge. They ducked beneath the rope then made their way down the second passage, stooping their heads from its low ceiling, hands against the walls. They were safe enough here from being seen, so Cesco turned on his phone's torch. The floor was muddy in places, and bore the marks of recent footprints. Her heart sank at the sight. The noise of the river hushed then grew loud again. They reached the end of the passage to find a small black dinghy lying deflated on the rocks, together with an outboard engine, waterproofs and other pieces of equipment. And the left-hand wall completely opened up too, revealing the Bussento river rushing by their feet.

She anchored herself to a cleft in the rock then leaned out and looked downstream. There was a flash of lamplight on the viewing platform bridge as Dov and his men laboured across it with their heavy gear. The stark truth bore in on her. They were on their way down here. Her hoped-for refuge was no refuge at all. And it would take a miracle now to spare them being caught.

III

The cassata cake was demolished. Coffee and spirits had been served and drunk. They cleared the table together. Baldassare caught Alessandra's eye and, when she nodded, he slipped downstairs to the basement garage. His phone was on his passenger seat. He grabbed it and turned it on even as he headed back upstairs, checking messages as he went. His very first was from Cesco. Listening to it sent chills right through him. He sped through the rest of the messages, but there was nothing else of significance, nothing else from Cesco or from Carmen either. He called both their numbers but got only voicemail. With any luck, it only signified that they'd found each other and were in bed right now making up for wasted time. But he dared not count on it.

He hurried to the front door. Manfredo was on duty. 'I need everyone up and ready,' he told him. 'Send me Sandro. And tell Faustino to prep the 'copter.' He hurried through to his office, turned on his desktop screen, brought Sicilì up on a browser. Sandro came in. He told him what was happening then jotted Cesco's and Carmen's mobile numbers on a slip of paper. 'I need these traced,' he told him. 'Current location, if possible. Last recorded location, if not.'

'Yes, sir. On it now.'

Baldassare pondered a moment. He needed to get some kind of police presence to the cottage as soon as possible. That meant cutting out the middlemen and going straight to the nearest station. Sicilì itself was too small to have one of its own. The closest of any size was in Sapri on the coast. It looked no distance on his screen, but the high hills there would make it at least a half-hour's drive. He found its number and called it. A chirpy young woman answered. He asked her to put him through to the station chief. He'd already gone home for the night, she told him, but if he explained what this was about she could find someone appropriate to—

Baldassare rarely used his judge's voice. It felt like an abuse of power. But it unquestionably came in handy sometimes. 'This is Magistrate Baldassare Mancuso speaking,' he told her icily. 'Get me your station chief *right now*.'

IV

A miracle Carmen asked for; a miracle she received. Even as she stood there wondering how she and Cesco might escape, the Bussento seemed to lose its roar, and retreat a little from her shoes too. She thought at first it was wishful thinking, but then it carried on until it was undeniable.

Cesco was equally bewildered. 'What the hell?' he said.

'There's a dam the other side of the mountain,' she murmured. 'They must have shut it down.'

'Christ. Who *are* these people?'

Torchlight flared along the passage. They needed out of here right now. The Bussento was receding all the time, revealing banks on either side, steeply sloped yet walkable. Downstream would put them in sight of the viewing platform bridge, so they headed upstream instead. It was hard going, crabbing sideways with their backs against the karst. The feeble light of Cesco's torch was a firefly in the darkness, precious little help with Carmen's footing. And there being no chance of a signal down here, she put the battery back in her own phone and turned on its torch too.

The Bussento retreated further. The footing grew easier. Their shoes grew sodden, however, squelching with every step in the icy water. And still there was nowhere to hide. The silenced river and the cavern's peculiar acoustics meant they could hear orders being shouted, the rumble of outboards. Yet the river was now little more than a series of shallow ponds. Dinghies wouldn't be much quicker than walking. They kept going until they reached a ramp of rocks down which splashed the river's modest remnants. An orange rope threaded through spring-loaded cams confirmed that Dov had indeed been here last night. They clambered over boulders to the top, found themselves at the foot of a chimney down which fell what was left of the Bussento, while a second orange rope zigzagged up and out of view. Carmen glanced at Cesco. He shook his head in disbelief. Whatever else one might say about Dov, no one could deny his courage. The outboards grew louder behind. Glints of light shimmered off the cavern walls. There was nowhere down here to hide. Their only chance was carrying on. Besides, Carmen realised, she *had* to know. She tucked her phone into her waistband and tugged the rope to make sure it was secure.

Then, with a nod at Cesco, she began to climb.

Chapter Forty-Three

I

For the best part of two hours now, Tomas and Guido had been helping Massimo and his men search the woods around the industrial building, as well as making broader sweeps of the whole Sicilì area. They'd found no trace at all of Nero, Rossi or their other friends. All they knew for sure was that neither the scarlet Renault nor the black Harley had left Sicilì on either of its main roads, which meant that they were still here somehow, probably lying low in these very woods, waiting for them to give up. But there was so much ground to cover, and the darkness was so absolute, that it felt a hopeless task.

'Enough,' sighed Massimo. 'Let's call it a night. Start fresh in the morning.'

'They could be anywhere by then.'

'And how will searching these trees again help? Come on, boss. The guys are beat. They got three hours last night. Push them now, they'll be useless tomorrow.'

Tomas stared at him. It wasn't the disrespect that rankled. It was his being right. 'Where?'

'There's a hotel in Policastro with spare rooms and a night desk.'

'Fine. But leave those two at the cottage, just in case. And a man watching each of the roads out. Oh, and keep your phone on.'

'Are you not coming?'

Tomas shook his head. Nero and Rossi were here somewhere, he could sniff it. Lurking in the darkness, just waiting for them to give up. 'No,' he said. 'I'm not.'

It was as bizarre a boat trip as Zara could ever have imagined. Dov, Avram, herself and five others divided between their two inflatable dinghies, laden with an extensible aluminium ladder and the other supplies they'd brought, including a sledgehammer and a spike for breaking open the tomb, and scuba gear in case they found it flooded. There was too much for the boats, so they packed the surplus into a string of buoyant yellow waterproof bags that they towed behind them like barges. To make it even crazier, the Bussento was barely a river any more, but rather a series of shallow locks from which jagged boulders jutted, forcing them out of the dinghies to lift them clear. At least they had neoprene suits and booties to keep them dry and warm, and safety helmets with fitted lamps to see with.

Every ten minutes, Dov called Noah on the satellite link to reassure himself that the dam was still closed. And whenever his signal started to weaken, he found a suitable ledge on the riverbank on which to set another relay to give it another boost. All the while, Zara kept filming and talking to camera, describing the destruction of Jerusalem and the theft of Jewish treasures, of Roman triumphs and the Temple of Peace, of Alaric, Athaulf and the rest.

At length they reached a hummock of rock beneath a sinkhole. They moored the boats and found footing for their ladder, anchoring it to the wall with the rope already there. Dov made to lead the way, but Zara appealed to Avram to keep his promise. He nodded. She held the rungs with one hand while filming her ascent, trying to find grand phrases to match the moment, but only managing to sound breathless and pompous instead.

A new chamber came slowly into view, the one from Dov's photographs. It was broader than the cathedral-like nave beneath, but not so tall; yet it was made glorious by the myriad gemstones hammered into its ceiling, twinkling like a night sky in her helmet lamp. She reached the top. Her beam skittered over the rippled water and threw hallucinogenic patterns onto the limestone walls, so that for a mad moment she could have sworn she saw something moving way upstream. Except she couldn't have.

The chamber was largely drained, yet still a lake of sorts remained, surrounded by sloped banks and a helpful ledge or two for their equipment bags. But that wasn't what she cared about right now. What she cared about was being first to the marble block. She waded out into the lake, arms spread wide for balance as she negotiated the stony floor. And there it was – a pale white rectangle glimmering just beneath the surface, like something from Arthurian legend. She swept away the covering of grit and algae with her forearm, turning the water opaque. But then it cleared again, revealing an inscription finished with gold leaf. An eagle, just like the one on the Caselle roof, its wings outspread and with a cross held slantwise in its talons. And, directly beneath, the legend:

ALARICVS MAGNUS
REIKS GOTHORVM

Tears pricked at the corners of Zara's eyes.

They'd found him.

III

Baldassare had been on hold so long that he feared he'd been cut off. He was on the point of hanging up and calling back when finally there was a click and a new voice came on.

'Judge Mancuso, is that really you?'

'Yes. Listen. I have a situation—'

'Such an honour! What you did for your family, for our nation, a true inspiration for all of us in law—'

'Not now,' said Baldassare. 'Thank you, but not now. I need you to listen.'

'Of course, Judge. Whatever you—'

'You know the town of Sicilì?'

'Do I know it? They hold the most wonderful festival there every summer that my wife—'

'There's a cottage beneath it.' He gave him its address, insisting that he wrote it down, if only to shut him up for a moment. 'The woman staying there is the one we rescued from that dungeon, along with my wife and daughter. She's to be a key witness against the 'Ndrangheta. We think they may be after her right now.'

'Oh shit,' said the station chief.

'What is it?' asked Baldassare.

'We had a report from Sicilì earlier tonight,' he said, dragging the words out of himself. 'Three or four cars with foreign plates taking photographs of people. I let it go. Taking photographs is hardly illegal. And I'd already sent my two nearest cars to deal with vandalism at the Lake Sabetta dam. But if what you say is true...'

'These foreign plates. What nationality?'

'Dutch. Why?'

Baldassare nodded to himself. There'd long been rumours that the Critellis had a powerful and lucrative Amsterdam operation. Yet if the 'Ndrangheta were out hunting, it implied that Cesco had got to Carmen in time and they'd gone to ground – presumably somewhere without a signal for their phones. 'How long to get a car there?'

'A car? Half an hour. But one of my top guys retired there last year. He has a vineyard that produces the—'

'Call him. Have him check the cottage and report straight back. Tell him to be very, very careful. These people may have found it and be waiting. In the meantime, put a team together. Your best people. The kind not to back down from a gunfight with the Mafia.'

'I'll lead them in myself,' he promised.

'Excellent,' said Baldassare. 'Then I'll see you there.'

Chapter Forty-Four

I

The tomb was still covered by a skim of water. Dov and his men gathered at the sinkhole to scoop it out with their hands, lowering the level enough to reveal the lid and then a hairline crack that ran around its perimeter, so fine that it was only visible in places, yet of such perfect straightness that it could only be the join between body and lid. They gathered around it and gripped it as best they could, despite the slick surface. Then they tried to lift it. It didn't budge. They tried again and then a third time, giving it everything.

Nothing.

Zara crouched to study the join more closely. There was no obvious trace of mortar or cement. It appeared to be sealed only by the tightness of its fit. She ran her thumbnail along it and found the answer, for the line of it changed course at its downstream end, like the lid of a domino box, to be slid rather than lifted. They gripped it once more but this time they heaved sideways. It gave a fraction, enough to encourage them. They heaved again and again, and then a fourth time, and finally its resistance broke and it came sliding sweetly, so that in their jubilation they might have taken it all the way had Zara not yelled at them to stop, lest they not be able to fit it back in.

She shone her torch into the exposed cavity, bracing herself to find it flooded. But the seal had done its work supremely well, the space beneath so dry that there was even dust on the steps beneath. They led down to a landing then turned sharp right out of view. Before anyone else could move, she hoisted herself up over the lip onto the top step, water spilling from her in dark pools. Her heart racing, she set off down the stairs, ducking her head beneath the rim of the marble lid, filming as she went, the walls inscribed with spirals, swirls, vortices and other patterns picked out in silver leaf.

Then she reached the landing below and turned to look.

Since first seeing Dov's short clip, Zara had entertained all kind of wild ideas of what they might find down here. None came even close. The staircase fanned out into a large chamber with rough-hewn walls and a massive pillar at its heart, carved from the limestone bedrock in the shape of an enormous tree, whose many spreading branches had been so cunningly shaped that they seemed actually to bow beneath the weight of the roof they were holding up, before being subsumed into it, and around whose trunk a giant snake was coiled.

A snake in a sacred tree was a key component of the Judaeo-Christian creation myth. Yet Gothic lore had had something very similar too. And it was clear to Zara at a glance that this was no Garden of Eden but rather Yggdrasil, the 'world tree' of Germanic myth – not least because its very name had been a corruption of Odin's horse, in turn a euphemism for the gallows from which the Goths had hanged their sacrificial victims. And so it was here. For dozens of nooses dangled from its branches, of rope so desiccated that the touch of a single finger would surely burst them into dust. And its crop of grisly fruit lay scattered beneath, the skeletal and part-mummified remains of at least fifty victims.

Until this moment, the slaves that Athaulf had put to death to keep the secret of this place had been mere abstracts to Zara, not men of flesh and bone. The horror of this sight changed all that. Yet she was a professional too, and this was an historic moment, so she filmed the chamber floor even as she made her way down to it. Then she picked her path towards that huge trunk, careful of the sculpted roots that slithered serpent-like across the floor to the walls, whose fractured limestone had been carved into hellish arrays of tormented faces and figures reaching up for succour or salvation.

Her pace was too slow for Dov and Avram. They pushed rudely past her on either side. Unwilling to cede priority, she went with them, rounding the vast trunk to see what lay beyond. A wide arched doorway led into a second, smaller chamber, much more as Zara would have expected. Hexagonal and with a vaulted, domed ceiling, its walls were gorgeously sculpted and painted with what appeared to be scenes from Alaric's life, its floor laid with black-and-white tiles in concentric circles around a granite plinth on which stood a sarcophagus of pink-veined marble, whose matching lid was lying on the floor beside it, and which contained a skeleton in ragged robes of white and purple. But that wasn't what struck them all most forcibly. What struck them all most forcibly was that the chamber was otherwise entirely empty.

'Robbed,' muttered Avram. Then louder and more angrily, as if it were he himself who'd been cheated. 'Robbed!'

Zara ignored him. It was still an astonishing find; she was still an archaeologist. She examined the skeleton first, noting the broken fingers, wrists and jawbone, no doubt snapped by robbers impatient for the precious jewellery in which Alaric had been laid out. Then she turned her attention to the five walls, starting to the right of the doorway, the bedrock sculpted in deep relief to create a rich and detailed scene that had then been finished with metallic leaf and paint of remarkable freshness, so that, despite its dusty coat, it glowed and shone in her torchlight – as did all the walls, indeed.

A boy – surely Alaric himself – holding a spear some twice his height, its butt pinned against a rock as a demon-faced warrior impaled itself upon its tip as it strained to reach him with its sword. A Hun, no doubt, thought by the Goths to be the progeny of witches and the wild spirits of the steppes – and so feared by them that it had sent them fleeing across the Danube into Roman territory.

Zara filmed every detail of it before moving to the second panel. A young general now, Alaric led a ragged horde through a wintry mountain pass, holding his horse by its bridle while two children rode on it, wrapped in what appeared to be his own fur coat. Directly opposite the doorway now, Alaric stood outside a city under siege – presumably Rome itself – magnified by a trick of perspective into looking taller than its walls, while a harvest moon hung low and red beside his head and the night sky glittered with gemstones in familiar constellations. She paused longest in front of this panel, for it offered the largest and clearest portrait of the man himself: handsome and battle-scarred, with a trim beard and long golden hair combed into ropes then arranged into a side knot. He wore the battered armour of a combat veteran rather than a general, his round shield pitted and its pointed boss stained with blood, as too was the long-bladed sword leaning against his hip. Only his imperious posture and the crested helmet he held casually down by his side spoke of his true rank.

The fourth panel shrunk him back to mortal size, gathered with his generals on what must have been the Calabrian shore, staring in frustration across at Sicily, their Carthage ambitions frustrated by those narrow yet impassable straits. And now the final scene, lying on his deathbed in a glade outside this very grotto, while grief-stricken family and troops filed past, much as they themselves were now filing from panel to panel in this ever more congested chamber. So congested did it grow, indeed, that Dov looked around at everybody gathered in that small space, and then remarked in a voice of quiet but unmistakeable fury: 'Which one of you idiots is supposed to be keeping watch?'

II

Hunkered down behind a rocky outcrop a short distance upstream of the tomb, Cesco watched the last of the Israelis vanish down into it. Immediately he turned on his torch and glanced at Carmen. She nodded unhesitatingly. They needed to get out of here now. They needed to reach Morigerati and call in help.

Their clothes were wet but they could still get wetter. They stripped them off and waded out into the water holding them bundled above their heads. 'If they spot us,' whispered Cesco, 'you make a run for it. I'll hold them back.'

'But I can't just leave you—'

'You must. Getting help is the best chance for us both. You know it is.'

The iciness of the water soon had them shuddering with cold, but the footing was so treacherous that they dared not rush. Any stumble would send a wave splashing over the tomb's lip. The marble glowed palely in his torchlight, enough to use it as a guidepost. They'd just passed it when, to Cesco's horror, he heard footsteps coming from inside the tomb. He glanced around as its mouth glowed bright. Then one of the Israelis climbed into view, muttering to himself. The beam of his helmet lamp picked them out instantly. There was a moment of frozen disbelief on both sides. Then everything seemed to happen at once.

The Israeli bellowed for help even as Cesco shouted at Carmen to run for it. Instantly, she started splashing through the water for the sinkhole. The Israeli dived in to stop her. Cesco threw himself on him to hold him back. They flailed and splashed in the water. More Israelis arrived. Carmen reached the sinkhole ladder. But that was the last Cesco saw, for a second Israeli put his arm around his throat at that moment and dragged him backwards underwater.

He thrashed and struggled as best he could, but only succeeded in lacerating his skin on the limestone and burning through the small reservoir of air already in his system. The need to breathe quickly grew urgent, but his face was still underwater and now there were knees pressed into his shoulders, into his legs and stomach, and his brain was throbbing madly with the need for air, throbbing with the knowledge that he wouldn't be able to hold out much longer; and then it happened, he couldn't fight it any more, he opened his mouth and drew the waters of the Bussento river deep into his lungs.

III

'Shut it,' said Tomas Gentile.

'I never said a word,' grumbled Guido.

'You were thinking it.'

'Come on. How many times are we gonna drive around this fucking town? They're not here.'

'They *are* here. I can sniff the bastards.'

They passed once more the cottage Rossi and Nero had left hours earlier on their motorbike. Its lights were still off, its driveway empty, but their headlights picked out his two men lurking in the bushes.

Some ambush that would be! He wanted to give them shit, except that there was no signal for his phone. And stopping to shout at them would only make it worse. Then they were past them anyway, taking hairpins down to the valley floor.

'A nice, soft mattress,' murmured Guido. 'A good breakfast. Some daylight to search in.'

'I said shut it,' said Tomas. He had a sudden hankering to listen to the night. The slope was steep enough here to freewheel so he gestured to Guido to cut the engine while he buzzed down his window. Silence fell, save for the whisper of their tyres on the tarmac and the distant yapping of a dog. The road flattened out as they reached the valley floor. They began to lose speed. Guido made to turn the engine back on but Tomas held up his finger. They reached the bridge, came almost to a complete halt on its hump, but still had just enough momentum to crest it and roll down the far side where they came finally to a halt. The dog fell quiet. So too their tyres. And now the silence was complete.

Too complete.

'Wait here,' said Tomas. He took his torch, got out, scrambled down the bank to the river itself. It was as he'd thought. The river that had been flowing so briskly on their arrival had now run almost dry. He dipped a fingertip into a puddle, held it up to the faint breeze. How could a river simply stop like this? What, if anything, did it mean? He was still brooding on these questions while he trudged back up to the car. That was when he saw the sign. He hadn't seen it earlier, because it was on this side of the river only, and they'd always approached it from the other direction.

Fiume Bussento, it read. The Bussento river.

Tomas had been just thirteen years old when he had moved with his family to Amsterdam. But he'd spent his childhood in Cosenza, enchanted like every other kid there by stories of Alaric and his fabulous tomb. The very same people who'd been searching Cosenza's Busento for it had now relocated here to this second Bussento. There was no way that could be coincidence. Nor surely could it be coincidence that it had stopped running tonight, so soon after Rossi and Nero had vanished into the woods just a short hike from it.

He couldn't yet see the detail of it, but the overview suddenly became crystal clear. Nero and her friends had found Alaric's tomb. They'd somehow stopped the river in order to loot it. Which put a completely different complexion on those two white vans he'd seen in that small parking area above that tourist grotto. He'd ignored them before, too focused on the scarlet Renault and the motorbike. But how much loot could one cart away in a Renault, after all? How much on a bike? A pair of rental vans was another matter altogether.

He felt euphoric as he climbed back in the car. 'We've got the bastards,' he told his brother.

'Are you sure?'

Tomas grinned. 'And maybe a billion in Roman gold too.'

IV

Gunfire cracked out even as Avram hurried up the steps to the tomb mouth. Two shots, the noise of them echoing in the chamber. He could only think that one of Dov's men had somehow gone crazy. Then he arrived at the top to see, in the crazily dancing torchlight, Dov at the sinkhole aiming down a gun, and some poor wretch struggling as he was held underwater by Yonatan and Ezra.

He jumped down into the water and waded over to them. 'Let him up!' he yelled, hauling them off. 'Let him up.'

Almost reluctantly, they lifted the man's head above the surface then turned him onto his side. Water gushed out of his mouth. He coughed and choked then gasped for air. They dragged him to the bank and threw him down even as Dov shepherded a second intruder – a woman – back up the ladder to the top. She raised her hands above her head and threw anguished looks at her companion.

Avram turned in bewilderment to Dov. 'What the hell?' he demanded. 'Do you know these people?'

'She's Carmen Nero,' said Dov. 'The American woman we hooked up with. But the man, no idea.'

'He's Cesco Rossi,' said Zara, from the tomb steps. 'Her friend from Cosenza.'

316

Avram frowned. 'I thought you said he was a conman.'

'Yes. But it's still him. She posted his photograph on my discussion board.'

Avram grunted. 'What the hell are they doing here?'

Dov glared at Zara. 'Ask *her*.'

'What's that supposed to mean?' retorted Zara.

'We were supposed to be lovers. She treated me like I was a disease. Of course Nero got suspicious. Of course she realised our Amalfi trip was bullshit. Her professor wasn't going to be here in time, so she asked this guy for help. They spotted the river had stopped and came to explore.'

Avram nodded. It explained their presence but didn't help him decide what to do. Release them, they'd go straight to the police. The whole story would spill out. Bringing the temple treasures back to Israel would be a triumph. But raiding an empty tomb would only make him look ridiculous. His so-called allies in the Knesset would line up behind him, the better to stab him in the back. There'd be inquiries into his life. The bribes would be discovered. The oil companies, the arms sales, the prison contracts. The investigation into that journalist's death would be reopened, his cover-up exposed. His career would end in disgrace, imprisonment. That couldn't be allowed. Yet the alternative dismayed him. It was one thing to order people killed from a distance; another when you were staring at their faces.

Dov gave his gun to Yani, along with instructions to watch Carmen and Cesco, then beckoned Avram out of earshot. 'We always knew it might end this way,' he said. 'That's why you sent me here, remember?'

'For Zara,' said Avram. 'Not these other two.'

'One. Three. What's the difference?'

Avram hesitated. To men like Dov, scruples were weakness. 'We had a narrative before,' he said. 'A lonely woman throwing herself from a hotel balcony. It made sense. As did an 'Ndrangheta hit on the prosecution's key witness and her companion. But how would that explain this Rossi guy? Especially half drowned and torn up by the limestone. And what if they told people where they were going? What if their phones could be traced? What if they were seen?'

Dov nodded. 'You're right,' he admitted. 'An 'Ndrangheta hit won't cut it any more. But look at what we have here. Three archaeologists hot on the trail of Alaric. They shut off the river then come exploring. They find his tomb. They open it and go inside. Unfortunately, the dam engineers reopen the sluice gates sooner than expected. The river starts flowing again. It catches all three of them still down there. They try to get out, but too late.'

'Will they repair the dam in time?'

Dov nodded. 'Noah thinks so.'

'I didn't hear him say that.'

'He didn't say it. I just know how to read the little shit. Think about it. Why have their team work through the night unless they believe they can get it done quickly? So I say we do this then get out of here. I'll have Noah drive Zara's Renault over. We'll leave it in the parking area for the investigators to find. They'll put two and two together. They'll shut the dam back down then come exploring. They'll find the tomb with the bodies still inside. Everything will speak for itself. Then you give it a month to settle down before announcing the discovery of your replica Menorah beneath your prison, and you ride it to your triumph.'

Avram digested this in silence. He looked around at Zara and the other two. 'We drown them, then? We drown all three of them then leave their bodies below?'

'If you want to be prime minister.'

He could taste the disgust in his mouth, like biting into an apple only to find it rotten. 'Very well,' he said, as though it were his own idea. 'Call your man at the dam. Make sure they're still working on the repairs. Have him come meet us here. Then do it.'

Chapter Forty-Five

I

Zara watched numbly as Avram conferred with Dov. She didn't know the specifics of their discussion, but she was certain of its import. They were discussing whether to kill her, Carmen and Cesco, or to let them live. The realisation prompted her to wade across to where the two of them were sitting, naked save for their underwear, shivering with cold, hugging each other for warmth and comfort.

Carmen had thrown her clothes down on a ledge. Zara fetched them now, draped her shirt over her shoulders. There was no shirt for Cesco, but she handed him Carmen's jeans for him to wipe himself dry with, which was something. She looked back across at Avram and Dov, still deep in conversation. Then they turned as one to look at her, identical expressions on their faces.

Just like that, she knew.

They didn't come straight over, but rather went first to the sinkhole where they talked on the radio to Noah at the dam. Whatever he told them seemed to satisfy them. They turned again with those same dead gazes then waded across. Zara's strength left her at the sight. Her limbs went weak. She backed away, losing balance and stumbling onto her backside. Her helmet slipped as she fell, its beam running across the gemstone ceiling like a searchlight above a city, making it twinkle like a night sky. She had a momentary yet transcendent glimpse of the smallness of her life set against the vastness of time and space; the smallness of this whole world and all that was in it too. But she saw something else as well. Something more urgent and infinitely more practical. 'Look!' she cried, pointing upwards. 'Look!'

Avram stopped to stare. 'At what?'

'Those stones,' she said. 'All those precious stones!'

'What about them?'

'Think about it,' she said, speaking English for Carmen and Cesco's benefit, for they were all in this together now, and needed each other's help to survive. 'Alaric's tomb was robbed, yes? That's what we all believe, yes? But what kind of tomb robber would leave all these stones behind, when they're just begging to be taken?'

Avram frowned. 'What are you saying?'

'I'm saying that it's not Alaric's tomb we've found. It can't be.'

'There must have been sixty bodies down there,' said Dov irritably. 'Who'd kill that many over a fake tomb?'

'I'm not saying it's fake,' replied Zara. 'But think about what building it here would have involved. Your first job would be damming the Bussento at Caselle, creating an artificial lake and making the river run dry. Everyone along this whole coast would have known what was going on. They'd hardly have needed slaves to tell them. And Athaulf was anxious to get moving. Maybe he left a detachment here to guard the place for a while. But they'd eventually have left too, leaving it wide open. Not easy to get back in, I grant you. Not without a slave army. But possible. Then they'd have come up here and found it, just as you did, from the gemstone ceiling and the marble tomb. So why then kill all those slaves? Athaulf wasn't a monster.'

'Go on,' said Avram. 'Tell us.'

'In order to keep a *different* secret. A secret known only to a very select few. A secret designed to keep Alaric safe from robbers even if robbers did eventually make their way in. The secret of a third chamber.'

Avram squinted at her. 'You're saying the one downstairs is a decoy? That that lid was left off that sarcophagus to fool anyone who made it in?'

'Except not only a decoy,' said Zara. 'A genuine antechamber that honours Alaric as a great king, but with his real tomb somewhere else. *That's* why Athaulf put the slaves to death – so that they couldn't reveal the true secret of this place: that they'd dug another burial chamber for Alaric somewhere beyond the two we've already found.'

'Then where the fuck is it?' demanded Dov.

'Let us look,' she pleaded. 'We'll find it for you.'

'We?'

She gestured across at Carmen and Cesco. 'They know archaeology,' she said. 'They know the Goths. They can help me read the walls.'

Avram's eyes bored into her. 'You'd better be right about this,' he said.

Or what? she thought. *You'll kill us anyway.* But all she said was: 'Watch.'

II

Tomas had little idea what to expect at the parking area. But he had to assume at least four antagonists: Nero, Rossi and the two from the scarlet Renault. He further had to assume that they had the gun that man had wrested from him back in Cosenza. And that was the very minimum. The two rental vans suggested there could well be more. If they'd truly found Alaric's tomb and were looting it, they'd likely be in Sicilì a while. Yet he could easily imagine them using the cottage as their base – to store their booty, say, or to grab some shut-eye. He therefore decided to leave his two men watching it and instead collected Orsino and Taddeo from their posts monitoring the roads out of town. Then they drove to the parking area.

The white vans were still there. They got out to inspect them. Their doors were locked and their bonnets cold. They each bore Napoli plates and stickers from the same Sorrento car-hire agency. One of them had rear windows. Tomas shone in his torch. Bench seating down either side and mounds of discarded packaging. He revised upwards their likely numbers. They got back in the Range Rover then drove up the road until he found a signal for his mobile. He gestured for Guido to pull in while he made the call.

'The fuck?' groaned Massimo, when finally he answered.

'I've found them,' Tomas told him.

Strange noises at the other end. Massimo sitting up in bed then slapping himself awake. 'The sweetest fucking dream,' he said.

'Not half as sweet as this,' Tomas assured him. 'You know that parking area with the two white rental vans? Meet us there as soon as you can.'

'All of us?'

'All of you. And tooled. We're going to war.'

'Okay,' he said. 'Half an hour.'

They sat in the darkness waiting. Twenty minutes passed. The road from Sicilì finally began to glow with headlights. They heard an engine. Tomas was about to get out to wave them down when suddenly a scarlet fucking Renault turned a corner and came into view. 'Down,' he said. They all ducked. Tomas risked a glance as it drove by. Only one person in it – a man he hadn't seen before, trying to hide his weak chin behind a wispy goatee. He drove by to the parking area, then stopped.

Tomas and the others got out quietly. They made their way after it on foot. The man was standing by the Renault, setting a miniature satellite dish up on its roof. He was so intent on his task that he had no idea they were there until Guido clamped a hand over his mouth. At once he began thrashing like a speared fish. But Guido pressed his knife into his throat and he fell still.

Tomas went to stand in front of him. His eyes were wet with panic and self-pity. This was going to be easy. 'Calm yourself, oh my good friend,' he said. 'We mean you no harm, I swear this on the grave of my poor dear mother. We live here, that is all. We worry for our children. All these strange vehicles. All this suspicious activity! We want to know what's going on. You can understand that, I'm sure. So answer a few questions for me and you'll be free. Do you understand?' He waited for the man to nod, then continued. 'And you won't call out if we let you speak?' A shake of his head this time, enough to send the tears spilling down his cheeks. 'Very good, my friend,' said Tomas. 'You see how painless this is going to be.' He gestured for Guido to loosen his grip over his mouth a little. 'Now, let's start with your name.'

'Noah,' sobbed the man. 'Noah Zuckman.'

'And where are you from, Noah Zuckman?'

'Israel.'

Tomas arched his eyebrows. Would tonight never stop delivering surprises? 'Israel?'

'I shouldn't even be here,' snivelled Zuckman, almost choking over the words. 'I don't do overseas jobs.'

'Is it just you from Israel, or your friends too?'

'All of us.'

'And you're here for Alaric, yes?'

'Yes. But they haven't found him. At least, they've found his tomb. But there's nothing inside. It's already been robbed.'

'Oh,' said Tomas. A disappointment, but it didn't affect his main purpose. 'Are they on their way back out, then?'

'Yes.'

'How many?'

His eyes slid to the side to make the count. 'Eight.'

'Armed?'

'No.' But there was a quaver in his voice.

'Thank you,' said Tomas. 'You've been most helpful.'

'Then I can go?'

'I gave you my word, didn't I? Though I need your word in return, not to contact your companions or go to our good friends in blue uniforms.'

'I swear it! I swear it on my life.'

'Good.' More headlights now, and engine noise. Massimo and the others had arrived. Zuckman stared in bewilderment as they pulled up in a row and his men got out, tucking handguns into their waistbands. He gave a low moan and his legs gave way beneath him. Tomas glanced at Guido. 'Not the knife,' he said. 'Too messy.'

Guido thought a moment. 'His neck?' he suggested.

'Yes,' said Tomas, looking away. 'His neck.'

It was Zara's tone more than her words that convinced Carmen they were in a fight for their lives. She glanced at Cesco, still pale and shivery from his near drowning, and he nodded to let her know he too understood. She took and pressed his hand. Dov gestured them to their feet and over to the tomb. The water was as cold as ever, yet Carmen was so exhausted that it had almost lost its power over her. Zara helped her and Cesco up onto the top step then they headed down in single file, followed by Dov and his men.

They reached a landing. Zara made the turn and carried on, but Carmen and Cesco stopped dead at the sight of what lay below – until Dov prodded them down to the chamber floor. A path of sorts had already been cleared through the gruesome windfall, allowing them no time to study it. They passed through an arched doorway into a burial chamber with fabulously sculpted walls and a sarcophagus of pink marble on a plinth.

The plinth was the obvious place to begin their search for any hidden chamber. The sarcophagus itself proved too heavy to lift, but they managed to twist it this way and that until they'd satisfied themselves that nothing lay beneath. Zara led Carmen and Cesco on a tour of the walls. They stopped by unspoken agreement before the largest and grandest of the tableaux – Alaric standing outside the gates of Rome, scene of his greatest triumph. His *only* triumph, in truth, for while he'd clearly been a charismatic and beloved leader, his battlefield record had been mixed at best. Even Rome hadn't been the victory he'd sought. He'd wanted a homeland, not plunder. Respect and fair treatment. Yet the emperor had sacrificed the Eternal City and all its treasure rather than give him that.

The gates had been set back a little way into the bedrock, Carmen noticed, then covered by a wood veneer that had curled up in places. She crouched down to peel off a fat strip of it. The stone beneath was paler than elsewhere, smoother to the touch. There was a gap, too, thin as a razor blade, between the gates and its posts. One of the Israelis saw her running her fingernail down it and excitedly shoved her aside. He and his comrades then tried to push the gates back into the wall, to lift them or slide them sideways. But in vain. Carmen glanced at Cesco then at the doorway behind them. They edged towards it. But their gunman guard Yani stepped across their path.

'We only want to look,' said Carmen. 'In case you guys missed something.'

'Such as?'

'How can we know until we've looked?'

Yani turned to Dov. Dov nodded. They went together out into the first chamber. Carmen borrowed a torch to light up the tree, then followed its roots as they slithered across the floor to the clusters of tortured figures hewn from the limestone. In Germanic lore, Yggdrasil had connected nine separate realms, one of which had indeed been called Hel. But the hell of their conception had been a dreary, ghostlike place, all wraiths and quiet misery. The hell of everlasting torment depicted here had been a very Christian concept. And Christianity had had only three realms to speak of. Hell, earth and heaven. Their hell had been a pit. It had existed *beneath* – just like the hell depicted here. Above that had come the earthly plain, the one in which they were standing right now, and which the sarcophagus chamber was in too. Then, above that, only heaven – which surely was where the Goths would have wanted Alaric.

She stared up at the ceiling. There surely wasn't enough space between it and the river above to accommodate a burial chamber. But Yggdrasil's branches spread out in all directions before being subsumed into the limestone. Unfortunately, she could see not a glimmer of heaven in the gaps between. Only one branch, indeed, made it as far as a wall at all, reaching it directly above the doorway into the sarcophagus chamber, perhaps implying that it was heaven after all, despite those worldly tableaux. Except that now she noticed that its ceiling was ribbed, as if to brace it. Yet it was hewn from the bedrock and therefore had no need of bracing. So perhaps that wasn't a rib at all. Perhaps it was, instead, the continuation of the branch, passing across the ceiling of the second chamber before finally ending in the night sky above the gates of Rome.

In the chamber upstairs, gemstones had been pressed at random into existing clefts and fissures. Down here, by contrast, they'd been set to recreate real constellations. There was Orion, for example. There Ursa Major. There Andromeda and Taurus. She was no astronomer herself, but the ancients most certainly had been. They'd known their stars so well that she'd have bet good money that these constellations were in proper relation to each other, perhaps even how the sky had looked on the night they'd taken Rome. And then there was the moon itself, by which the tip of the branch finally stopped, almost as if touching it in benediction.

She found herself staring at it, transfixed both by its size and colour too, finished not with the silver leaf one might have expected, but rather with bronze or even copper, to give it a faintly pitted look as well as a distinctly reddish hue, the one it sometimes took on when near the horizon. It happened because light from a low hanging moon had to pass through so much more of the earth's atmosphere to reach its surface that most photons of shorter wavelengths were deflected away by heavy molecules in the air, leaving the oranges and reds to arrive alone.

The ancients hadn't known the physics behind this, of course, but they'd certainly have known the *effect*. Even the Visigoths. Perhaps even *particularly* the Visigoths. There was a tantalising clue from a fourth-century evangelical bishop called Ulfilas, who'd been so determined to bring Christianity to the Goths that he'd devised a script for them just so that he could then translate the Bible into it. Ulfilas had been almost completely faithful to the original text. So faithful, indeed, that his rare divergences had intrigued historians ever since. Why had he left out entirely the Book of Kings, for example? Was it because it was so bellicose, and he'd considered the Goths quite violent enough already, thank you? More pertinently, he'd also completely fabricated an admonition against moon worship that appeared nowhere in the original – suggesting strongly that it was a practice of the Goths that he'd wanted desperately to stop.

Cultures and traditions didn't change overnight. The old ways always lingered – as evidenced by this tomb itself, with its mix of pagan and Christian iconography. Long after nominally converting to Christianity, Gothic generals like Alaric had consulted soothsayers who'd used lunar cycles to divine auspicious days for feasts, marriages and burials. He'd never have risked launching an assault on a city like Rome without assurances that the moon would smile upon the endeavour — the exact same moon that Carmen was gazing at right now. The way it bulged, the way it gleamed, and the colour of it too — for all the world like a great brass button hanging low over the city's walls, just begging to be pushed.

Chapter Forty-Six

I

The helicopter gave wide berth to Sicilì, lest the noise of its approach alert the 'Ndrangheta to their arrival. They set down instead in the empty car park of a pizzeria on the Caselle road, where four unmarked police cars were arranged as promised in a square, their headlights marking out their landing area. Baldassare was first out, running hunched beneath the blades to where Giuseppe, the Sapri station chief, was waiting with his retired policeman Zeno, a grizzled, short, broad-shouldered man with a piercing eye and a crunching handshake.

They squeezed together into the back seat of the lead car. Zeno repeated the story he'd told Baldassare once already, for it had been largely drowned out by the relentless roar of the helicopter cabin. How he'd thought it prudent to survey the cottage first, so had hidden behind a cactus hedge to watch while his wife drove by with her headlights on full beam before turning around at the bottom of the hill and driving back past again. 'There are at least two of them,' he said. 'One in the trees by the back door. The second on a bench by the pond. There may be more inside, but I didn't see them.'

'Outstanding work, officer. Truly outstanding. And you'll thank your wife for me, if I don't get the chance myself?'

Zeno flushed. 'Of course, Judge. She'll be honoured.'

The cottage lay the far side of Sicilì. They slowed as they approached, staggering their arrival to avoid the look of a convoy. The place was still and quiet, as befitted an Italian hill village in the small hours. Yet precisely because it was so still and quiet, their presence was likely to be spotted soon, however discreet they were.

If they were to take these people by surprise, they needed to go in now.

II

Zara stood back against the wall of the sarcophagus chamber, the better to film Dov and his men as they tried in vain to storm the Roman gates. She had no appetite for her assignment any more, yet she carried on with it all the same out of some vague hope that if she pretended that everything was normal, Avram and Dov would let her live. Perhaps. But, if not, it was just about possible that this footage might one day provide the evidence that locked them all up for life.

Brute force failed to budge the gates. No surprise there. They'd by now stripped them of their veneer, revealing the massive slab of granite behind. Yonatan and three others hurried off upstairs to fetch down the tools they'd brought to open the marble tomb. But that had been a completely different proposition to this. And once they'd emptied all their bags onto the floor, the only tools even worth trying were the sledgehammer and the spike – a brute to wield in the confined space, barely even chipping the granite. They needed some kind of jackhammer, that was the truth of it. A jackhammer and several hours. But they had neither.

Avram started checking his watch at regular intervals. As if he'd set himself a deadline, and they were almost at it. Hope began to desert Zara. Dread took its place. She looked around for Carmen and Cesco and saw them at the doorway. There was a brightness in Carmen's eye as she gazed, not at the gates of Rome themselves, nor at the men attacking it, but at the skyscape above their heads. Zara turned to look at it herself, curious as to what Carmen had seen. And suddenly she had it too. She cried out so loudly in her excitement and relief that everyone turned to look. And now they all saw it too.

The moon was set too high in the wall for them to apply pressure from the chamber floor. They gathered around the sarcophagus instead, working it back and forth until they slid it from its plinth and over to the wall. It took all of them to lift its lid back on, to give themselves a platform on which to stand. Then they clambered up upon it and pressed the head of the sledgehammer against the moon's pitted surface. They all took hold of its long handle and pushed together. And pushed. And pushed. A faint grating noise spurred them on. It ceded with painful slowness until it stopped and would go no further.

They looked around at each other, wondering what now. A faint scratching noise came from deep inside the wall, followed by the ghostly groan of wind in a ruined building. A moment of silence, then an eerie clanking of chains, as some antique system of counter-weights was waking from its long slumber. A low thud made the whole chamber tremble, showering them with grit and dust and prompting them to jump down from the sarcophagus. Then the gates of Rome gave a little shiver and began, with painful slowness, to rise like a portcullis up into the ceiling.

Too much had happened for Avram to keep his promise of priority. But Zara meant to be first anyway. She went down onto her stomach and wriggled beneath its base, careless of her back and buttocks scraping against its crushing weight. Then she was through and standing up on the other side, at the foot of a dusty white marble staircase plenty tall enough to keep whatever lay at its head safe from the Bussento should the antechambers flood. Others now came crawling in behind her. Carmen and Cesco, Yani with his gun, Dov and Yonatan and Avram too, each pausing a moment to absorb what they saw.

The staircase was wide enough for two, but Zara had no intention of sharing this moment, not if she could avoid it, so she stuck resolutely to the middle, claiming priority for her camera. Her legs trembled as she ascended; her heart beat in wild and unfamiliar rhythms, hungry to discover what lay ahead, yet fearful of disappointment too, and what would follow.

Matching oyster-shell niches had been cut into the walls either side. Oil lamps of exquisite craftsmanship alternated with ivory statuettes of beautiful young women at daily tasks: with alabaster vases painted with scenes of love and hunting and war; with bowls of wrought silver filled with precious and semi-precious stones; with golden caskets of ancient coins, of brooches and belt buckles. And these were just the stairs! She heard something being unzipped behind her and glanced around to see Yonatan opening a pouch on his neoprene suit in order to tip a bowl of gemstones into it.

'That's not what we're here for,' Avram told him angrily.

'It's not what *you're* here for,' retorted Yonatan. And it was like a starting gun for Dov's men, who now grabbed whatever came to hand. Only Yani kept his discipline, covering the three of them with his gun.

They reached the top step, followed closely by Avram carrying four of the yellow waterproof bags over his shoulder for his own sacred spoils. A short landing led to a wide arched doorway covered by a curtain of thick purple velvet so ancient that, when Zara tried to ease it gently to one side, it fell in a crumpled heap at her feet, throwing up a thick cloud of dust like a magician's squib, making them all blink and cough before it cleared again to reveal the chamber behind in the confusion of beams from their torches and helmet lamps.

Zara stood there a moment to drink it in. Never in her most fevered dreams had she imagined such a place. Its ceiling first – tall and domed and gleaming like a Byzantine chapel with gold and turquoise, with ruby and with emerald. The walls next, decorated with extraordinary mosaics of pastoral beauty, of gentle woodland whose boughs were bent by ripened fruit, of docile wildlife and a cascading river by which a pair of golden-haired young women in bright white gowns stooped to fill golden amphorae. As for the floor, it was laid with tiles of black and white – though in truth she couldn't see much of it from where she stood, so crowded was it with grave goods of astonishing richness and variety. But the heart of the chamber was different again, taken up as it was by a raised oval platform on which was arrayed the armour from the sculpture downstairs along with the skeletal remains of a pair of hunting dogs and a warhorse in ceremonial tack, arranged around a tall stepped plinth of pink marble upon which rested a golden anthropoid coffin of a size and grandeur to make Tutankhamun weep.

A nudge from behind. The others were pressing in. Zara had that numb, disembodied feeling as she walked, as if on a mattress of thick foam. Everywhere she turned her camera lay treasures more spectacular than the last. A long table to the right of the doorway was covered by a golden cloth laden with platters of desiccated meat, with crusted goblets and bowls of finely wrought silver containing the shrivelled husks of ancient fruit, with stoppered amphorae and jewelled caskets whose once exotic delights had long since been reduced to dust. Beyond that, a miser's attic of wooden chests stacked one upon the other, packed to overflowing with gold and silver coins, with jewellery and precious stones that had overspilled their vessels and fallen to the floor where they lay like iridescent gravel. A giant silver font on a porphyry stand contained a basin with a tall golden candleholder and a golden lamb from whose mouth holy water would once have poured. A half-dozen painted marble statues of the apostles clustered together, as if in conference. A majestic silver throne, its back and arms inlaid with amber, corals and other stones. A piece whose purpose she couldn't grasp, but seemingly made from solid gold, and decorated with enamelled bees and leaping dolphins with sapphires for their eyes.

Yet, despite all these and other wonders, she still hadn't seen what they'd come here for. She continued her circuit of the chamber, therefore, picking her way between the pieces, and suddenly her hopes were lifted by the sight of a sturdy long table on which six silver trumpets stood upon their bells next to a tall wide object covered by a thick embroidered white cloth. She drew closer. The trumpets were inscribed with antique Hebrew script. Her heart hammered like a woodpecker at a tree. Her left hand trembled wildly as she held her camera out to one side to capture the moment as she pulled the cloth off with her right. And there it was at last, glorious and unmistakeable, a massive, seven-branched candelabra that gleamed every bit as brightly as her dreams of it. She gave a low moan at the sight. She set down the camera on the table, angling it to catch what she was about to do next. She paused for a moment out of respect then took its stem and one of its branches in her hands, braced her legs and tried to lift. But it was too heavy for her. Far too heavy. She couldn't even tip it towards her. There was no question of this one being anything other than gold. She began to laugh at the realisation of everything this meant, and her laughter had a manic tinge to it, and it spread like a hot fever amongst Avram, Dov and their men, who all now began laughing too, laughing drunkenly at this extraordinary triumph and their sudden obscene wealth, so that it seemed that nothing could taint the moment.

But life has a way of punishing hubris. There was a panicked scamper of footsteps from the stairs at that moment, and they all looked around to see Ezra arriving in the doorway, breathing hard and with a hand to his side. 'The river,' he panted, even as he gazed in awe around the chamber. 'It's started running.'

Chapter Forty-Seven

I

It had felt a little like sacrilege to Cesco, picking up the curtain of purple velvet from where it had fallen in a heap on the floor, then wrapping it around his shoulders like a ragged robe. But for the first time in half an hour or so, he was now able to think of something other than how cold he was – able, indeed, to appreciate the dusty treasures that lay everywhere he looked: the stacks of golden plates, the chests of gem-encrusted cutlery and goblets; an inscribed stone casket containing what appeared to be several scroll holders of carved ivory, with the tantalising promise of lost texts; a large basket in which crucifixes of all styles and materials had been crammed higgledy-piggledy.

Zara began to laugh. All the others joined in. Then came news that the Bussento was running again and the mood flipped like a switch. Dov and his men were veterans, however, trained to respond to adversity with discipline and cool heads. They headed calmly but briskly for the staircase. But Avram had no intention of leaving without his trophy. 'Here!' he shouted.

'The river's running,' said Dov curtly. 'We need out of here.'

'It's *started* running,' retorted Avram. 'Or has the Sayeret Matkal taken to recruiting cowards?'

'Fuck you,' said Dov. But the taunt did the trick. He and his men went grudgingly to help. They heaved the Menorah above their heads, staggering beneath its weight. Avram meanwhile packed pairs of the silver trumpets into three waterproof bags that he then handed to Cesco, Zara and Carmen. They hurried downstairs. Serpents of foamy water slithered towards them across the Yggdrasil chamber floor, more spilling in at every moment, dragging at their ankles as they climbed the steps to the tomb mouth. They jumped down into the river, flowing strongly enough now that they had to lean into it like a slope. Cesco lost hold of his curtain robe and it was swept off down the sinkhole. Zara called for help closing the tomb lid to spare the tomb from further flooding. It took all their effort. The renewed cold made Cesco shudder. He looked around for something warm, saw only Carmen's trousers lying on the bank. He stuffed them in his trumpet bag for her to put on later.

They gathered at the sinkhole. The Israelis had tied a rope around the Menorah and were lowering it while the Bussento banged it against the walls then ripped it entirely from their grasp. A frantic scramble for the ladder ensued. Carmen, Zara and Cesco were pushed ever further back. Cesco waited till last of all, taking the full force of the Bussento on his head and shoulders. It was all he could do to cling on. Then, with a fearful screech of metal, the ladder simply buckled and collapsed. He fell on top of Carmen even as she turned onto her side and clutched her bag against her stomach to protect the trumpets within. He rolled off her as quickly as he could, tried to help her after him. But her ankle had got trapped between two rungs, and now the river was smashing down upon her. He grabbed her beneath her arms and dragged her out of the torrent, the ladder still caught around her foot like some toothless mantrap.

Most of the others had by now reached the inflatables, tugged tight against their mooring ropes by the reinvigorated river. They loaded the Menorah into the larger of the two, Avram and Dov sitting either side of it as its self-appointed stewards. But that was as much as it would take, forcing the other Israelis into the water to cling to its sides as they released it from its mooring. That left Zara with Yani and another Israeli in the second dinghy. Cesco yelled at them to wait, but they cast off anyway. He turned back to Carmen. She was bleeding and hobbling badly. The river had turned the ramp into a terrifying deluge. The only way down was on the rope Dov had left in the ceiling. He took Carmen's trumpet bag then hoisted her up by her waist. She gripped the rope with both hands, looped her good foot around it too. He watched anxiously as she worked her way down to the bottom, where she lowered herself gingerly, crying out when she dropped down and her ankle took the jolt.

He tossed down the two trumpet bags then grabbed the rope and quickly followed. He dropped down beside her. The bags were watertight. He unzipped them each a little way then blew air into them before sealing them tight again, making them as buoyant as he could. Their only light was from the lamps on the two dinghies ahead, being swept downriver so rapidly they had no need for their outboards. No time for further thought. They launched themselves into the river on their bags and instantly were whirled about like coracles in a storm. Cesco fed his arm through the straps of Carmen's bag to keep them together. Their ankles and knees kept banging and scraping rocks they couldn't see. They choked on unexpected mouthfuls of water. The cold was corrosive and exhausting. But eventually the turbulence began to slacken. It grew calmer. The glow of lamps was still in view ahead. Cesco kicked with his legs to keep pace, while they both steered and paddled with their free arms. Before they knew it, they heard the outboard of the Menorah dinghy going into reverse to slow it down as it neared the landing spot. Its occupants dragged it ashore then reached inside for their great treasure.

It was at that moment that they heard a shout, and then a deafening blast of gunfire erupted from up the passage, tearing into everything in its path.

II

Dov wasn't sure exactly what it was he heard: maybe the scuff of a boot or the creak of new leather; maybe a whispered command or a round being chambered. But his heart began pumping and his mind came to maximum alert even before the first shot was fired. He knew instantly what was going on. Those 'Ndrangheta killers from Cosenza had somehow tracked them down. And now they were in mortal peril.

He yelled warning to the others then ducked low and charged up the passage even as gunfire burst out above his head, muzzle flashes exploding in bright yellow bursts ahead of him and on either side. The dazzle of it after the darkness left him blinded. But the gunmen would be blinded too, and now he had their positions. He flung his fist at the nearest man, hit him in the gut with satisfying force. He grunted and went down, knocking into the man behind. Dov grabbed his right arm as he fell. He slid his hands down to his wrist then twisted his handgun from him. Exultation filled him as he brought it up to bear, the same exultation as when he'd faced the waterfall the night before. These Mafiosi fucks had no idea who they were dealing with. He was invincible, untouchable, a veteran of the Sayeret Matkal, the greatest fighting unit in the history of—

Something punched him in the ribcage. Then it punched him again, this time with such obscene force that it threw him onto his back. Above his head, the gunfire rattled on until a man shouted stop. Dov lay there bewildered. He didn't understand what was going on. He tried to sit up but there was a great weight upon his chest. It was all he could do to lift his chin. Several Mafiosi hurried past him down the passage to the landing point, but two of them sauntered over to him with insulting calm, shone torches down at his face. 'You,' grunted the smaller of them in amusement. He held up his gun for Dov to look at. 'Gonna take this one off me too?' he said.

'I'll kill you,' vowed Dov, his voice barely a whisper. 'I'll kill you both.'

'Sure you will,' said his companion. He stooped to press the hot muzzle of his handgun against the bridge of Dov's nose. 'Night, night,' he said.

III

Three of the Israelis were lying sprawled on the rocks at the landing place by the time Tomas reached them. A quick glance assured him that none of them was a threat. The only one showing any signs of life was keening with pain and exertion as he dragged himself with

337

his one good arm into the water, while Umberto and Salvatore stood either side of him, cracking tasteless jokes at his expense.

'Enough,' said Tomas irritably. 'Finish him.'

'Fine,' grumbled Salvatore. There came a volley of gunfire and he fell still.

Tomas turned to the others, lighting up their faces in turn, turning away as Guido finished them off. The last of them was an old bastard, lying half in and out of the water, hands clasped over his gut in a futile attempt to staunch the dark red slick. Tomas aimed down at his face. 'The American woman and her friend. Where?'

'Go to hell,' said the man.

Tomas didn't mean to pull the trigger. It was pure irritation. A fleck of bone and hair went flying from the man's forehead. Blood bubbled weakly out. He stepped back to avoid getting it on his shoes.

'Boss,' muttered Manfredo. 'Look at this.'

He turned to see him and Aldo standing either side of the deflated dinghy, their torches spotlighting a huge seven-branched candelabra inside. It looked like gold, except it surely couldn't be. Then they tried to lift it, and failed. He felt a sudden fluttering in his chest, like all the bats they'd disturbed in this great cavern. So Alaric's tomb hadn't been empty after all. Its riches were his for the taking. 'Up to the cars with it,' he ordered. 'Then come straight back.'

He watched Guido and the others heave it above their heads. They set off up the passage. But his mind was already elsewhere. There'd been eight people in the grotto, according to Noah Zuckman – though he'd lied about the tomb being empty so maybe he'd lied about that too. But if he were right, it would leave three unaccounted for. He stepped up to the water's edge, shone his torch this way and that. To his profound astonishment, a small black inflatable was even at that moment drifting by him on the current, three neoprene-clad figures hunkered down in it, a woman and two men, one of whom was lying prone on its floor and aiming a handgun directly at him – his own damned handgun, it had to be, the one taken from him in Cosenza. He dived for the floor even as the man fired, bullets hitting the rocks behind him, ricochets buzzing like angry hornets. He scurried for the passage then took stock. If he stayed here, the fight would be on equal terms. But if he could make the bridge...

He sprinted back up the passage, pushing past his men with the Menorah, yelling at Guido and a couple of others to follow. His footsteps and breathing echoed unnervingly in the confined space. He burst out onto the viewing platform, shone his torch both ways. Nothing. He leaned over the railing and there was the dinghy directly beneath, the gunman already stretched out on his back to aim straight up at him. He snapped off two more quick shots that made Tomas jump backwards. The bullets pinged off the grotto's ceiling.

Guido, Massimo and Umberto arrived on the bridge. He raised a hand to warn them then pointed beneath his feet. He counted down from three with his fingers then they all leaned over the railing and fired together. The gunman snapped off two more shots before they got him. Their bullets made his body dance. The second man in the dinghy grabbed for the dropped gun but they shot him too before he could turn it on them. But by then the woman had thrown herself overboard and vanished into the dark water.

The inflatable, meanwhile, was swept at increasing pace towards the grotto mouth, where an ancient rockfall forced the entire river through a narrow channel. It hit the first boulder so hard that it lifted clear up out of the water before slapping back down again, twisting onto its side and wedging fast. They turned their torches this way and that in an effort to find the woman. Instead, they found a man and woman clinging to a pair of buoyant bags. They turned to look up at the bridge when caught by the beams. Tomas's heart leaped as he recognised them.

Rossi and Nero at last!

He emptied most of his clip at them, but only sent up useless tufts of water. And then they were out of range. A moment later the river slammed them into the inflatable, buffering them from the rocks while dislodging it too, so that they all funnelled together through the channel and out of view.

'With me,' yelled Tomas. Then he set off running for the staircase and the grotto mouth.

Chapter Forty-Eight

I

The Bussento exited the grotto like the world's most brutal water slide. Zara was tossed this way and that as it churned between huge boulders. Her right leg caught in the cleft between two rocks and was twisted so sharply by her own momentum that her tibia snapped instantly and she felt splinters of bone rip through her skin. She opened her mouth to scream only for water to gush on in. She was certain she was about to drown when suddenly she was thrown backwards down a sharp drop into a narrow, deep lake, where the river seemed to take a breather after its violent emergence from the mountain.

She retched water from her lungs, composed herself a little. Her recent companion Yani was lying face down and motionless in shallows by the bank. She hardened her heart and swam right by him in a lopsided slow crawl, reaching the place where the river picked up again, sweeping her along with it, allowing her to concentrate on keeping her broken leg clear of its stony bed. Part of the right-hand bank ahead had collapsed into the river, creating a small inlet of still water covered by reeds and grasses and a skim of algae. She dragged herself over to it, turned onto her back. The pain from her leg was unbelievable. Only terror stopped her from crying out.

She glimpsed movement on the river. She held her breath. But it was only one of the waterproof bags floating by. The riverbank here was a mix of writhing pale roots and loamy soil. She dug her fingers into it to smear across her face for camouflage. She sank as low in the water as she could, stretched her legs out in front of her, tipped back her head to leave only her mouth, nose and eyes exposed. A rustling noise on the far bank. She caught and held her breath. Through the thin veil of reeds, she saw Cesco fighting his way through thorns then holding them aside for Carmen, limping badly and with blood dripping down her flank. She felt relief that they'd made it out this far, and longed to cry out to them, that they might share this ordeal together; but she knew too that she would only slow them down and give those bastard gunmen an easy quarry, so somehow she bit her tongue.

And then they were gone.

Silence fell. Half a minute passed. Cold and shock made her shiver, despite her neoprene. Her shivers turned to shudders. More rustling. Men's voices. Pain hammered at her leg like a miner at a coalface. She bit her hand to stop herself crying out. She had a sudden yearning for her parents, to see them once more before she died. What a fool she'd been, to let the estrangement persist. What a proud and stupid fool. She vowed to herself that it would be the first thing she'd put right if by some miracle she got out of this and made it home again. Then she shut her eyes and, for the first time in over a decade, she began to pray.

II

Tomas led Guido and four others out of the grotto into the grey morning murk. The river roared below them and to their left. He fought through trees and undergrowth then scrambled down a steep embankment to the edge of a lake. One of the Israelis was lying face down by the bank. He kicked him onto his back. A bullet hole in his neoprene suit had snagged on the rocks, tearing a zippered pouch wide open, allowing gemstones of astonishing size and colour to spill into the shallow, reddened water around him. At once, Massimo and the others lunged for them like piglets for a tit, stirring up sediment to obscure what they were after.

'Leave it,' yelled Tomas. But it was useless. Greed had them in its grip. He looked around, spied smears of blood on rocks on the far bank. He grabbed Guido by his arm as he scrabbled for gems with the others. 'Forget the damned stones,' he said. 'We need Rossi and the girl.'

Guido held up a ruby with childish awe. 'But look at the size of it!'

'Forget it,' snapped Tomas. 'If we get Rossi and the girl, it's *all* ours. The whole tomb. We'll be the richest men in Italy.'

Guido blinked and came back to his senses. 'Where are they?' he asked, lumbering to his feet.

Tomas pointed across the lake. They waded out into the water, swam with their guns above their heads. They climbed out the far bank, brushed themselves down. A thin animal track beside the river was marked by telltale wet footprints and spatters of blood.

'Ready, oh my brother?' asked Tomas.

Guido nodded. 'Let's do it,' he said.

III

Baldassare was not a man to send others into danger while he himself held back. Yet he, Giuseppe and Zeno were older and less capable than the others here, and liable only to get in the way.

Besides, they had a different contribution to make.

It was Baldassare himself who took the wheel, leading the way down the hairpin road towards the cottage. He drove slowly and with his headlights on full beam, both to dazzle the two 'Ndrangheta men while making it as easy as possible for the cars behind to follow, even with their own engines and headlights off. He passed by the cottage and carried on along the road while they peeled off one by one, freewheeling down the drive to the cottage forecourt. They pulled up in a row and piled yelling from their cars, overwhelming the two men without a shot being fired, then going through the cottage room by room to make sure it was clear.

It was all over before Baldassare joined them. The two thugs were already cuffed and sitting on hard chairs in separate rooms. But it took him only a single look into their eyes to reveal that the first shock of their capture had already passed, to be replaced by a familiar surly defiance. Give him a day or two and he might break them. But he didn't have a day or two. He had no time at all.

'Go outside,' murmured Aldo. 'I'll get them talking.'

Baldassare shook his head. He loathed these men more than words could say, and the lives of Cesco and Carmen were very much at stake. Yet he'd dedicated his life to the rule of law. And it wasn't in him to change that now, not even for this. But where did that leave him? What options did he have? He was still dithering when the kitchen door banged open and Sandro rushed in, his two-way radio crackling in his hand. 'Your woman,' he said. 'Your American woman.'

'What about her?' asked Baldassare.

'They've got a signal from her phone at last,' he said. 'And it seems she's on the move.'

Chapter Forty-Nine

I

The shock of being shot at then swept out of the grotto through the rocks had flooded Carmen's system with so much adrenaline that it was only now that she and Cesco were fleeing along this narrow track that her injuries began to announce themselves. Her twisted left ankle had swollen up and turned ugly colours, making her flinch every time she put weight on it. Her right knee was wrenched and there was a bad gash beneath her shoulder blade that had already stained her shirt red, with more blood spilling in watery streams down her legs to leave telltale marks with every step. She ripped off her sleeve and folded it into a wad with which to staunch it, yet it was hard to apply pressure while on the move.

Cesco kept hurrying ahead to find their path and clear the way before coming back to help her. He put his arm around her waist to take her weight as best he could. 'What now?' she asked, shivering with cold and fear.

'We find a place to cross the river,' he said. 'We follow the footpath down to the Sicilì road. We wave down a car.'

They pressed on in this way, taking paths of least resistance – wading through shallows, scrambling over rocks, fighting through thickets, always looking for a place to cross. It wasn't the river that was the main problem, fast-flowing though it was. It was that its far bank was rocky, steep and so thick with thorn bushes that there was no hope of climbing out. The sound of pursuit grew ever closer. At least two men. She could hear them shouting exhortations at one another, as though it were a hunt and they were having fun.

She felt increasingly light-headed. Perhaps it was mere loss of blood, but she couldn't get past the fact that she was slowing Cesco down and making pursuit so easy. Then it got abruptly worse, for their onward progress was blocked by a great wall of thorn bushes that ran from the foot of the gorge wall to their left all the way down the steep embankment to the river on their right, which looked every bit as hard to cross here as elsewhere – its far bank rising sharply from the water which then cascaded over a natural weir down to a craggy bed of rocks. Here the smaller of the two dinghies – completely deflated by now – had been caught, and the last Israeli was so tangled in its mooring rope that it was holding his head beneath the water. Their only option seemed to be to climb the embankment to the gorge wall, but its face was so sheer that Carmen would have hesitated to climb it even in prime condition and with the right equipment. Besides, the embankment soil was so soft that they'd leave a trail a child could follow.

It was Cesco who spotted their possible salvation – a thread of a gap beneath two of the thorn bushes burrowed by some small mammal. 'You first,' she told him. 'I'll be right behind.' He got down onto his front to worm and fight his way through, thorns raking long scratches on his bare back and legs. He stood up on the far side, beckoned for her to follow. But his passage had broken numerous branches and so churned up the earth that the men behind would find it easily, and they'd both be at their mercy once again. 'Go get help,' she urged him softly, rearranging the branches and brushing the earth to conceal his tracks. 'It's the best chance for us both. You know it is.' Then, refusing to look at his aghast expression, she set off up the embankment, digging her feet into the soft soil and smearing blood over the trunks of the saplings she used to help herself climb, deliberately leaving traces that the men behind couldn't possibly miss.

II

The watery footprints had long since stopped and the blood spatters were fewer and further between. Guido had started panting for breath and was constantly getting tangled in the bushes. And they dared not rush, for this terrain could have been designed for ambush. So Tomas needed all his concentration for the pursuit. Yet his mind kept wandering even so. He kept finding himself back inside the grotto, being taunted by that old man into pulling the trigger.

That fragment of bone and hair. That bubble of bright blood.

The nightmares would be bad tonight.

They reached a wall of thorns. The river looked impassable too. Not that it mattered, for there was a trail of blood and footsteps up the embankment that even Guido could have read. He waited for him to catch up then they set off together, guns held out ahead of them, ready for anything. They reached the foot of the gorge wall and caught a flash of colour a little way ahead. And then they were upon her – Carmen Nero hobbling along on an ankle swollen up like a melon and the colour of dusky plums – but no sign anywhere of Rossi. Nero turned to face them, her forearms crossed in front of her chest, her face pale yet resolute. Tomas aimed his gun at her face. 'Your friend,' he said. 'Where is he?'

'The police are on their way,' she told him. 'Run while you can. It's your only hope.' There was defiance in her eye, and vindication too. As though her own life was a price worth paying for Rossi's escape. And that could surely only mean one thing. It could surely only mean love. And what if he loved her too? What then?

'Get her,' Tomas told Guido.

Guido grabbed her by her wrist. He twisted it savagely up behind her back until she cried out. 'What now?' he asked.

'With me,' said Tomas. He led the way back to the wall of thorns. The embankment opened up again beneath them. 'The knife,' he told Guido. Guido took it from its sheath and pressed its tip beneath Nero's chin, forcing her up onto tiptoes. Tomas cupped his hands around his mouth. 'We have your friend,' he called out, his words echoing off the cliffs behind. 'Your beautiful brave friend, she who sacrificed herself that you might live.' The nobility of it touched his heart. His eyes moistened. 'Are you really the kind of man to leave such a woman to her fate? I beg you, come back and talk. That's all. Just talk. We can still sort something out, I promise. A way we all can live. You have my word.' His words died away. Their echoes too. The seconds passed and nothing happened. His heart sank. So much for honour. So much for love. He turned with genuine regret to Guido, to give him the command. But, to his surprise and gratification, he heard a rustling noise at the embankment's foot, and a moment later Rossi crawled out into view. Then he stood up tall and spread wide his arms. 'Very well, then,' he said. 'Let's talk.'

Chapter Fifty

I

Two separate phone masts on opposite sides of the valley had now picked up signals from Carmen's mobile, enabling them to place it in a strip of woodland either side of the local river. That still left an area several hundred metres long a good hike from the nearest road, so Baldassare ordered the helicopter to Sicilì's piazza then set off with Sandro, Andre and Giuseppe to meet it, taking Zeno with him too for his local knowledge.

Faustino touched down just long enough for them to board. They sprang back up into the sky and lurched violently forward. The night was in fast retreat, the terrain disaggregating into shades of grey then taking on colour too. They descended the valley to the river then flew upstream until they neared their search area. They overflew it twice but saw nothing, so Faustino found a glade to set them down.

Baldassare led the way down to the river, shouting out for Carmen and Cesco. The woods were thick and old and tangled. It was a fight to reach the bank. He could see no sign of anyone anywhere. But then he caught a flash of colour a little way downstream. The carrying strap of a yellow inflatable bag had been snagged by an overhanging branch. He plunged straight out into the water, indifferent to the cold, alternately wading and swimming. He untangled the bag from its branch, unzipped it as he waded back across. To his astonishment, it contained two antique silver trumpets as well as a pair of jeans. He felt through the pockets and found Carmen's mobile.

'What the hell?' asked Sandro, helping him up out of the water.

Baldassare turned to Zeno. 'What's upstream of here?' he asked.

348

'Nothing but woods and river,' shrugged Zeno. 'All the way to the Bussento grotto.'

'The *Bussento* grotto?' said Baldassare numbly. 'Are you telling me... Is this river called the Bussento?'

'Yes. Why?'

He turned to Giuseppe. 'That dam that was sabotaged last night. It's on this river, yes? It would have stopped it flowing?'

'How did you know?'

'Call your men,' he said. 'Send them to that grotto.' Then, despite the aching of his heart, he set off running back up through the trees for the 'copter.

II

Carmen's heart plunged when Cesco appeared below, distraught that he'd give himself up like this despite her efforts to save him. Yet, perversely and impossibly, it soared at the same time, because it put beyond question that he was the man she'd wanted him to be.

Tomas beckoned him upwards, to get him so close he couldn't miss. Cesco began a deliberate, slow ascent, his eyes flickering between the two men, not even looking down to check his footing. Carmen braced herself to yell at him to run, only for Guido to jab his knife up so hard that it pierced the skin under her chin, releasing a vampire trickle of blood to dribble down her throat. She tried to warn Cesco with her eyes instead, but he didn't once look her way; and, besides, there was no fear in his gaze, only purpose. That was when she realised why Tomas's challenge had sounded so familiar. It had sounded so familiar because it had been almost identical to the one Cesco had told her about in that other lifetime at the start of this crazy night, the one shouted out by the men holding his twin sister captive on that boat before they killed her right before his eyes.

She noticed something else then, something she'd unaccountably missed before. Cesco was wearing one of the neoprene bodysuits. He must have stripped it from that dead Israeli. It took her aback for a moment that he'd spend time on that with so much else going on.

349

But then she realised. He hadn't done it to stave off the cold, as she'd first assumed.

No. He'd done it to send her a message.

Chapter Fifty-One

I

The gemstone hunt was a game of rapidly diminishing returns. Massimo hadn't found a new one for a minute now. Then he had an epiphany. If *this* guy's pouch was stuffed so full of treasures, how about all those others they'd left back in the grotto? He got to his feet and raced off – only for his very urgency to tip off Umberto and Salvatore to his plan and come chasing after.

He had no torch. The passages were tight and dark. He had to feel them out with his hands. The bodies were as they'd left them, a grotesque tableau still lit by their own helmet lamps. He went down on his knees by the nearest, unzipped his backpack. An unimaginable wealth of rings and brooches spilled out. He laughed triumphantly as he stuffed everything back in the pack then slung it over his shoulder. He and the others went from body to body until they'd looted the lot, then they hurried back out of the grotto and to the stone staircase up to the parking area.

His legs were tiring badly by now. But a short burst of distant siren put some juice back into them. They came across the rest of their men, labouring under the weight of the Menorah, managing only a few steps at a time before setting it down again to rest. Massimo gazed at it in awe, its size and lustre and majesty, its sturdy stem and elegant long thin arms. They went to help, hoisting it above their heads like they were parading a championship trophy through the streets, and hurried as best they could up the remaining steps to the car park.

The Menorah wouldn't fit even in their roomiest SUV – not until they'd put down the back seats and shifted the front ones as far forward as they'd go. Even then, its base protruded from the back, so they hid it beneath a travel blanket then tied the back down with rope. Massimo went to the head of the staircase to yell for Tomas and Guido. But his words came echoing back without reply. Fuck them. They were grown-ups. They had their own Range Rover to get away in. It was every man for himself once the sirens started.

He took the wheel of the Menorah car himself, leading their small convoy along the single-track lane back towards Sicilì. The surface was wretched. Every time he jolted over a pothole, treasures would spill from his pockets onto his seat and the floor beneath. He glared warning at Taddeo in the passenger seat not to try to—

A black Explorer came hurtling around the corner ahead. They were both going so fast they had no time to brake. He wrenched the steering wheel around instead, taking them up a grassy bank, yet still clipping the other car, crunching up his front left wing and triggering his airbags. A hawthorn hedge raked their bodywork like a harpy's claw. Stones clattered into their undercarriage. They tipped so steeply that they had to lean sideways to keep themselves upright. But then they were past and thumping back down onto the tarmac.

A glance in the mirror. Orsino in the second SUV had screeched violently to a halt, nose-to-nose with the Explorer, only for Rafaele in the third car to slam into his rear and shunt him into the Explorer. Doors flew open. Men piled out. He heard the crackle of gunfire as—

'Car!' yelled Taddeo.

Massimo slammed on his brakes. Too late. They smashed head-on into a second black Explorer, bonnets crumpling. He was thrown forward against his seat belt and already deployed airbag, so that for the flicker of a moment he thought he was going to be okay. But then inertia from their too-sudden stop hurled the Menorah forward into the back of his seat, one of its arms spearing through the soft fabric and smashing into his spine even as he was pinned against the airbag.

The Menorah fell back again, releasing him to flop sideways in his seat. The remaining treasures from his pockets spilled all around his feet. A golden signet ring rolled to a stop directly beneath his left hand. It had a design inscribed into it, he now saw. It was the portrait of a kingly man, the kind of man he'd always dreamed himself to be. *Reach out for it*, he urged himself. *Reach out and take it and all can still be well*. But his hand refused to obey him, and then his eyes began to fail him too, his ears, his heart, his mind.

II

Carmen stared at Cesco as he climbed up the embankment, his feet slipping backwards a little with each step, precipitating tiny landslides of loose earth. She wanted to let him know she understood what he was up to, but she dared not signal it in any way, lest her captors see. Not that he once looked at her. His gaze flickered back and forth exclusively between the two men, Tomas with his handgun down against his side to tease him onwards, Guido with his knife jammed up beneath Carmen's chin.

On Cesco climbed, ever more slowly now, bringing himself slowly into easy range. Tempting them. Tempting them. Any moment now. Any moment. Her senses heightened. The world became apparent to her in the most microscopic detail. The twitter of the morning birds, the grey geckos frozen watchful on the tree trunks all around. Guido's almost lustful breathing, the faint rustle of leaf litter as Tomas shifted weight to raise his gun. It was her signal. She feinted left to push back Guido's knife-hand then hurled herself sideways at Tomas, grabbing at his arm even as he brought his gun up to bear, hauling it down again so that he wasted his first two shots in the soft earth.

Guido recovered almost instantly. He grabbed her by her hair and dragged her back. But too late. Cesco had already reached behind him for the gun he'd retrieved from the dinghy along with the neoprene suit. He fired three times at Guido, who grunted in shock, dropped his knife and staggered back against a tree. He still had Carmen by the hair, however. He dragged her down with him then clamped his free hand around her throat and began to throttle her. More shots cracked out, then the clunk of empty chambers. Carmen fumbled blindly on the ground and found a rock. She lifted it above her head and crunched it into Guido's face, finding that place where the cheekbone meets the eye. Blood spurted. He bellowed in pain and outrage. She tore herself free and scrambled away on her backside. He lunged after her, only for Cesco's bullets to go about their grisly work inside him. A fit of coughing overcame him, he sprayed red droplets all over her face then slumped back against the tree, staring at her in bemusement as realisation dawned that she'd be the one to see him off on this last grim journey. And now the dread arrived, waves of it at what might be waiting for him on the other side, all those souls he'd sent on ahead of him, waiting patiently for their vengeance. He looked beseechingly at her, as though it was in her power somehow to forgive. He opened his mouth to speak, but all that came out was blood. Then his head tipped backwards and he went still.

She rose unsteadily to her feet. A clattering noise grew loud as a helicopter thundered by, flying so low above the Bussento that its downdraught stirred ripples from the water. Baldassare himself was at its open hatch, looking every which way except up at where they were, wildly though she yelled and waved her arms. Then it was gone again. She turned to Cesco, locked with Tomas on the ground, churning up the soil as they rolled this way and that. Tomas momentarily freed his hand. He grabbed Guido's dropped knife and slashed it at Cesco's face. Cesco caught him by his wrist, the tip of its blade almost touching his eye. Carmen was still holding her rock. She hobbled across and slammed it down with all her strength on the back of Tomas's head. There was a sickening crunch. He collapsed and dropped the knife. Cesco pushed him onto his back while he was still dazed, pinned his shoulders beneath his knees. He picked up the knife himself then slapped Tomas across his cheek to bring him to his senses. The moment he saw the knife, he tried to buck Cesco off him, but Cesco was too heavy and strong and resolute. And finally he gave up. 'I'll kill you for this,' he said, furious at his own impotence. 'I'll have you killed.'

'No, you won't,' Cesco told him coldly. 'You missed your chance at that.'

'In Cosenza, yes,' said Tomas, grabbing at the lifeline. 'I could have killed you then, but no, I let you live. Now you owe me.'

'I'm not talking about Cosenza. I'm talking about that night on the boat fifteen years ago. When you and your brother tied old engines to body bags for me and my sister.'

'You?' said Tomas, turning pale. 'The Carbone boy?'

'Me,' said Cesco. 'The Carbone boy. And do your remember what you did to her when I didn't come back?' He played the knife this way and that in front of Tomas's eyes, catching sunrise on its blade. 'Because *I* do. I see it in my dreams every fucking night, the way you cut off her head.'

'That wasn't me,' cried Tomas, thrashing helplessly. 'It was Guido. It was Guido. Guido did that.'

'On your orders.'

'Please God, no,' he said, blanching white at what was coming. 'Not that. I beg you. Anything but that.'

The helicopter roar grew loud again. Carmen looked around to see it returning into view, slower and lower this time, hovering by the bank. She waved her arms again and this time Baldassare saw her. He and three other men jumped down, weapons half raised as they laboured up the steep embankment. Cesco realised he needed to hurry. He grabbed Tomas by a hank of hair and tugged his head to one side to expose the soft tissue of his throat. 'Look away,' he told Carmen. 'You're not to see this. No one should ever have to see this.'

'Then don't do it.'

'I have to. For Claudia. For my family. This is what revenge looks like.'

But Carmen refused to look away. She knelt instead on the roiled earth beside him. She hugged her arms around him then turned his face towards her so that she might kiss him once lovingly on the lips. 'No,' she told him. '*This* is what revenge looks like.'

Epilogue

Four weeks later
Morning

Zara's right leg was still in its cast, as it would be for several weeks yet. She boarded early, therefore, taking the front window seat so that she could stretch it and her single crutch out in front of her without tripping up the crew and other passengers. General boarding began. A surly looking man stuffed his bag into the overhead locker. He recognised her instantly; she could tell from the sour twitching of his lips. Yet the thrill of celebrity evidently overcame his dislike, for she could see him thinking up something witty to say as he took the seat beside her. She closed her eyes before he could succeed, and rested her head against the window.

The Italians had at last released her – and without charge too. Her willingness to tell all had played a part, but in truth Carmen's relentless lobbying of Baldassare Mancuso had been far more important – that and pressure from the Israeli government, eager to put the whole Menorah affair behind them. Not that that would be happening anytime soon. As far as Zara could make out, it was all anyone back home was talking about. And everyone seemed to have different views, except for on one point.

They all of them hated her.

The liberals hated her because clips of the footage she'd recorded during their grotto incursion had been leaked, making it seem like she'd originally been an enthusiastic participant in the heist. The hard-liners hated her because Avram, Dov and the others were their new martyrs, and she'd betrayed them. Everyone else hated her because the Bernstein family had been feeding all kinds of vile smears to their pet journalists, so that the whole country now believed her to be an arrogant, disloyal, alcoholic slut who thought herself too good for her childhood friends and her parents. Her university was no better. Its governors had summoned her to a crisis meeting in such blunt terms that she knew her job was already lost. Even Professor Kaufman had denounced her in a bid to save his own skin.

Yet she couldn't bring herself to care.

The flight was bumpy enough that the man in the seat beside her turned sickly pale and clutched his armrests. She ordered a glass of Pinot Noir and stared out the window. On landing, she was made to wait while everyone else disembarked. Her leg began to itch furiously beneath its cast. She rubbed it as best she could with the heel of her hand. A kindly stewardess came to warn of the hostile reception awaiting her. Yet it astonished her even so, stepping out into Ben Gurion's arrival hall to find herself confronted first by a barrage of TV cameras and flashbulbs, of shouted questions and thrust microphones, then by a crowd of hundreds of protesters held back by barriers and police. She steeled herself to walk this gauntlet, doing her best to remain dignified and impervious, but it was hard with her crutch and wheeled suitcase to manage, and with spittle-flecked people yelling at her and waving placards in her face. She couldn't believe how worked up they all were. But then outrage and hatred were the only way some people—

Out of the corner of her eye, she glimpsed a grey-haired woman dressed all in black standing behind the wheelchair of a stiffly upright old man with a tartan blanket over his knees. Instantly, she lost her rhythm. Her foot tangled with her crutch and she went sprawling. Flashbulbs popped. The crowd hooted and jeered and filmed it delightedly on their camera phones.

She stayed on hands and knees for a moment or two, blinking away the tears, gathering her breath, testing her hands and wrists to make sure she hadn't broken anything else. She was about to reach for her dropped crutch when the grey-haired woman dressed all in black appeared beside her. She stooped to pick up the crutch herself then she offered Zara a hand to help her to her feet.

'What are you doing here?' Zara asked her.

'You're our daughter,' replied her mother. 'You're in trouble. Where else would we be?'

Four weeks later
Stuttgart, Afternoon

Knöchel's instant diagnosis had proved correct. Dieter's anterior cruciate ligament had ripped almost clean through, leaving no option but surgery. Three weeks he'd had to wait for the swelling to go down. But eight days ago now, a tendon taken from some poor dead bastard's knee had finally been grafted into his own. He hadn't given a moment's thought to the donor beforehand. Why would he? But now, every time he unstrapped his cryo cuff to trade it for a freshly chilled one, he'd see the scarring from the screws holding his new tendon in place, and wonder. He'd even asked his surgeon about it. She'd assured him that his donor had been of good German stock, but with a little smirk on her lips that had set him brooding.

His knee was still only up to range-of-motion exercises, but his physio Gunnar still pushed him until his eyes watered, like he was punishing him because he hated fags. Dieter welcomed this. He wanted it to hurt. Pain meant it was doing good. And it reminded him of who'd done this to him too, and what he owed him in return.

Six months, everyone kept telling him. Six months before he could properly trust his knee again.

But fuck that.

Every evening, he'd scour the net for fresh news of Cesco Rossi. Turned out it wasn't even the bastard's real name. Turned out that he was actually 'Ndrangheta royalty. It made Dieter feel a little better about his own humiliation. But it didn't make him one whit more inclined to forgive or let it go.

Four months. That was as long as he was prepared to wait.

Four months and then he was off back to Italy with a new and larger crew, whatever nick his knee was in.

Four months and then Cesco Fucking Rossi PhD would come to know what humiliation, hurt and loss truly were.

Four months and the man was dead.

Four weeks later
Rome, Evening

Six o'clock already. Carmen could scarcely believe it. The days were simply whizzing by. It had felt like a crazy risk to throw aside most of her thesis and start over. But it had proved the right decision, for she was springing light-hearted out of bed every morning, her next few paragraphs already cued up in her fingertips – not because she knew more about Alaric than about Galla Placidia, or even half so much, but because her knowledge was hers alone, because she'd earned the right to speak it.

And there was more to come too.

The Italian Ministry of Culture had announced a first season of excavations at Morigerati later that year, once the rains had stopped for the summer. It was to be a joint venture between Napoli's famed Archaeological Museum – which had already taken charge of the Menorah, the silver trumpets and all the other recovered treasures – and Sapienza University, whose team was to be led by her own professor Matteo Bianchi, who'd not only invited her to be his assistant, but who'd also agreed to add Cesco to their roster of photographers.

That familiar creak upon the stairs. That warning knock. She jumped to her feet and hurried to let him in; she couldn't help herself. Cesco was spending so much time travelling to his old haunts, making amends to those he'd once cheated, that she was constantly hungry for the zing of his touch, the sparkle in his eyes and the way he'd swallow when he watched her undress. Such headiness couldn't last, she knew. All the more reason to savour it while it did.

'How was it?' she asked.

'Good,' he said. 'Good. Really good.'

'They didn't chide you, then? Or fly over all this way only to cut you dead?'

'Fine. Okay. You were right.'

'Of course I was.' He'd been panicking about the reunion ever since finally making contact with his English family, fearful that they'd still resent him for having vanished so abruptly from their lives. Sure. That was why – on learning not just of his reappearance but also of his difficulties with obtaining a new ID card and passport – they'd grabbed the first flight out that all of them could make. He gave her a final squeeze then let go. He wandered to her desk to check her word count, turned and raised an admiring eyebrow. 'They're looking forward to meeting you,' he told her. 'I'm afraid I've set an impossibly high bar.'

She laughed. 'Then I'll just have to scooch down beneath it. What time?'

'I booked the table for eight. But I've ordered the car a little early. There's something I need your help with first.'

'Yes?'

'Humour me. We'll do it on the way.'

She checked her watch. 'I'd best get ready, then.'

She saved and closed her thesis then took her new red dress to the shared bathroom to wash and get ready. Cesco gazed so hungrily at her on her return that only the timely arrival of their taxi stopped him from undoing all her good work. He took her hand as they made their way downstairs. The simplest of contacts, yet the most eloquent too. It made it absolutely clear to her that she didn't want him as her bedfellow or her boyfriend. She wanted him as her partner or even as her husband. She wanted to have children with him, a family of their own. But she hadn't found the courage yet to ask if he wanted this too, lest she bring their idyll crashing prematurely to a close.

He hurried ahead to open the taxi's rear door for her, slid in alongside. 'Via Siracusa,' he told their driver.

'Via Siracusa?' she frowned.

'You'll see.'

Her phone rang. Baldassare, with the latest news on the Cosenza 'Ndrangheta. She told him she had Cesco with her and put it on speaker. He had a lot to cover, as it turned out. The Critelli brothers had found out about the coup Tomas Gentile had been planning against them, and so had tried to have him killed. They'd failed. He'd been in solitary ever since, his nights tormented by demons, his days confessing eagerly to his hideous catalogue of crime. Seeing the writing on the wall, several key Critelli lieutenants had turned *pentiti* too. As a result, Baldassare and his team now had enough testimony not only to imprison them all for decades, but to arrest and charge numerous corrupt politicians, civil servants, customs officials and police officers too. The Amsterdam operation had been rolled up, along with similar cells in Munich, Rio and Sydney. And there'd been significant drug seizures in South America as well.

By the time Baldassare rang off, they'd reached the residential street that ran south of the Villa Torlonia. *Via Siracusa*. Of course! Carmen had walked through the villa's gardens a hundred times on her way to and from the university library, and she'd often told Cesco how much she loved them too. She slid him a curious look but his expression gave nothing away. He asked their driver to wait then led her up the front steps of a tall mid-terrace whose front door he opened with a set of estate agency keys. They went together up to the top floor. He led her into an unfurnished apartment, small enough that she could see most of it from the hallway.

'Well?' he asked.

'I don't... are you thinking of taking it?'

'Your place is too small for two. And your landlady hates me.'

'She hates everyone,' she said. 'It's how she is.'

He led her into the second bedroom, whose sash windows looked out over the Torlonia gardens. A Vespa buzzed by beneath. A doting mother leaned forward to arrange the bedding in her pram. 'I thought this could be your office,' he said.

She looked uncertainly at him. 'My office? Are you... Are you asking me to move in?'

'Of course,' he smiled. 'What did you think? But only if you like it. I can always carry on looking. But this is so quiet, and so close to your lovely gardens and the university.'

'But I could never afford my share of—'

'Stop it,' he said. 'For any other reason, yes. But not for that.'

She looked back out the window. It was what she'd been praying for – who was she trying to kid? To start a new life with Cesco in a place like this, a place all to themselves. Yet, now that it was upon her, she couldn't help recall that day in Cosenza Hospital, the way he'd sat beside her bed spouting pious bullshit in his effort to convince her to come join him in a different apartment. He must have read it on her face, for he took her hand again and pressed it between both of his. 'I'm not that person any more,' he said. 'Everything we've been through together, it's changed me completely. No. It's not even that. It's that it's freed me to become the person I'd otherwise have been all along. You must see that.'

'And you promise you'll never lie to me again?'

The question took him by surprise. He gave a little grimace. The silence stretched on so long she felt something painful about to break inside her chest. 'I'm sorry,' he said at last. 'I don't see how I can.'

'Oh,' she said, making to pull her hand from his. 'Thank you for being honest, at least.'

'I mean, think about it,' he said, refusing to let her go. 'What if one of the kids were to break your favourite piece of china, and they were so terrified of your temper that they begged me – I mean *begged* me – to tell you it was I who broke it?'

'*My* temper?' she protested. '*My* temper?'

'Yes. Exactly. Your temper. What then?'

'Very well,' she said, and her heart so swelled with happiness that it seemed a miracle to her that she didn't lift right up off the floor and float away. 'In *those* circumstances, and *only* those, then you may lie to me.'

Author's Note

I love the ancient world and I write stories about fabulous lost tombs for a living, so I'm a little ashamed to admit that I knew nothing about the death and burial of Alaric, the Visigoth king who famously sacked Rome in CE 410, until I visited the south of Italy on a family holiday. It's a remarkable and fascinating tale, one that still attracts treasure hunters from across the world, so I only hope I've done it justice.

Acknowledgements

My thanks – as ever – to my agent Luigi Bonomi, as well as to Michael Bhaskar and Kit Nevile at Canelo, and to my copy editor Seán Costello, who each helped make this book much better than it otherwise would have been. I'm also deeply indebted to all those who so kindly shared their knowledge with me during my various research trips – most particularly Maria Rosaria Di Mauro, who gave very generously of her time showing me around Morigerati, Caselle in Pittari and other parts of the Cilento. I'd also like to thank Demetria, Caterina and Felicia from the Bussento Grotto nature reserve for helping me to understand the river and the local cave system. I've deliberately changed some details for dramatic effect, and no doubt I've made a fair number of unwitting mistakes too. As always, these belong to me and me alone.